THE CASE OF THE
MOCHE ROLEX

Books and stories by T. Lee Harris

Twenty-Seven Cents of Luck (Short)
Cat in the Middle (Short)
Sweet Water From the Rock (Short)
Muddy Waters (Short)
Winter Wonderland (Novella)

In the Miller and Peale Series

Chicago Blues
New York Nights

In the Josh Katzen Series

Hanukkah Gelt (Short)
The Pecan Pie Affair (Short)
The Case of the Moche Rolex

In the Sitehuti and Nefer-Djenou Bastet series

To Be a Scribe (Short)
The Scribe Vanishes (Short)
Wanting the Fish (Short)
3 Tales of the Cat (Collection)

THE CASE OF THE
MOCHE ROLEX

T. LEE HARRIS

The Case of the Moche Rolex

Published by Hydra Publications, Goshen, KY 40026

Cover art and design: T. Lee Harris

ISBN 978-1-942212-71-3

THE CASE OF THE
MOCHE ROLEX

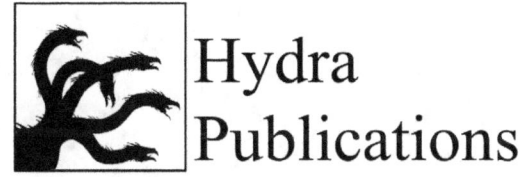

Hydra
Publications

CHAPTER 1

A drop of sweat spattered onto the Moche lord's upraised mace. Josh Katzen swore, gently blotted the splat, then mopped his own face with less care. Dammit. The heat in the small room was intense. It seemed that he was spending more time drying off than doing any actual drawing. Well, that was why he didn't use watercolor pencils in these sweatboxes.

Finger-combing long, sandy hair back from his face, he once again considered a haircut, and once again, decided against it. Best to leave it alone; long hair wasn't something anyone associated with the military man he used to be. Besides, when he wore it loose, it made his face look longer, thinner and even less like an Air Force officer. That was good. Re-twisting his ponytail, he held it against the back of his head and skewered it with a paintbrush into what friends called his Warrior's Knot. Looked weird, but it kept the hair off his neck and, in the heat of the windowless chamber, that was *very* good.

He tweaked the reflector's angle, then sat back, sipped water and studied the results. One more tap and it was exactly right. It had to be. Too much direct light on the delicate pigments he was copying would fade the ancient murals and nothing could bring them back. That would be a disaster. They'd been recorded the previous season; photographs — and he and Avi Rosenberg had used a new technique to make digital copies — still, nothing really beat an artist's rendering to get the true feel of a work. Good thing Doc Rosenberg agreed, or he wouldn't even be a part of this excavation, and though the beginnings were anything but auspicious, this was one dig he wouldn't have missed for the world.

When the crew had stepped down from the trucks that first season and he'd gotten a good look at the place, his heart had taken a nosedive. *Huaquero* pits were everywhere. There were so many holes and trenches, the place looked like it had been carpet bombed. Worse: none of the holes were recent. If even Peru's hardcore tomb looters had given up, the place *had* to be stripped bare. Everyone thought so. Well — everyone but Avi Rosenberg. Avi had piled out of the beat-up Mercedes bus and cheerfully instructed staff and students where to set up the base camp. They all complied, but they were simply going through the motions.

That changed a week into the dig when a student doing GPS mapping suddenly yelped and slid out of sight. Josh and Avi were closest and rushed over to peer into the hole to find the boy shaken, but unhurt, sitting on the littered floor of an ancient room. The room was lined with exquisite stirrup pots and votive offerings of copper, gold and jade not to mention five of the most magnificent pre-Columbian wall paintings to be discovered in decades. The room had quickly been named the War Room because of the many depictions of Moche warrior-priests in battle. Those were the paintings Josh now copied.

For the rest of that season, it seemed the more they cleared, the more they found, including several caches and the remains of a tantalizing, collapsed ceremonial platform. It hadn't slowed too much in the intervening seasons, either.

A small sound from the entrance spun him around. The intruder was a sinewy black and white cat, rubbing against the exposed adobe of the door frame. Katzen relaxed and laughed at himself. "Way to go, Twitchy. Old habits don't die, they have to be dragged out into the sunlight and staked."

Taking eye contact for an invitation, the cat hopped into Josh's lap and, purring loudly, rammed his head against Katzen's chest. It was pure coincidence that the pocket he rubbed against with the most enthusiasm contained a packet of beef jerky. Moments later, two more lithe shadows twined around his ankles, hopeful tails aloft.

"Cats," he laughed. The sound echoed oddly off the ancient walls. "How do you guys always manage to find me? Do I take a neon Kitty Sucker sign with me everywhere I go?"

In lieu of an answer, the original tuxedo cat pawed at the jerky and meowed. Sighing, Josh extracted the packet, tore up the beef and tossed it on the ground just outside the door. "Enjoy. Too hot to eat in here, anyway."

The hungry cats abandoned him for the food.

Amused, he watched them devour the beef. It was strange. Cats liked him and would unerringly seek him out wherever he was. It happened so consistently that people in the closest town, Piedras Rojas, had dubbed him Gatito, Little Cat, early on. Ironic, really. For decades, his working codename had been The Cat — for very different reasons, though. He suspected that his handlers had probably been having a private joke when they'd given him his new name. That was okay. He liked Katzen.

Pulling a bottle of sports drink from his cooler pack, he twisted the lid off and drained half of it. The drink was a bit sweeter than he liked, but the electrolytes helped against the Peruvian heat. He'd really burned through them since he'd started copying. He'd have to ask someone back home in Chicago to ship a few more down before he ran out completely.

He smiled slightly. It felt good to have friends — *real* friends. It had been a long time since people liked him for who he was, not what he could do for them. Sitting up straighter, he cautioned himself, *Don't go there. Get back to work. You owe Doc Rosenberg a lot and the least you can do is make decent copies of these murals for him.*

He picked up his pencils and lost himself again in the ancient masterpieces.

~*~

The sun had slipped behind the mountains and spicy smells wafted from the cooking tent by the time Katzen made his way back to base camp. A strange sense of homecoming washed over him as he veered toward the familiar hulk of the battered corrugated tin building that served as office, storage room and workshop. He shifted his bag on his shoulder and unconsciously picked up his pace. Why was it that the damned bag seemed heavier coming back than it did when he'd set out in the morning? Maybe a couple of the stray cats had stowed away. Yeah. He could see himself explaining that to Rosenberg and the grad students who shared the workshop with him.

A shout came from behind. "Josh! Hold up!"

Turning, he saw Dr. Harper Armand, the expedition's resident physician, loping across the commons with her characteristic slim-hipped grace. The rays of the dying sun sparked red glints in her shoulder-length blond hair. It would have been a truly enjoyable sight if not for the look of grim determination on her face. He'd never been so unhappy to be approached by a beautiful woman in his life — at least he couldn't dredge up an occasion.

He mustered a grin. "Hey, Harper. What did I do now?"

"More like what you didn't do. You skipped lunch again."

"Uhhhh. Yeah. I sort of got sidetracked." Unlocking the office door, he crossed to the worktable where his laptop and digital imaging equipment lived, and swung his pack and portfolio under it. Harper leaned against the door frame, a willowy, but effective roadblock.

She crossed her arms and tilted her head with a small smile. "Don't you mean sort of got sidetracked *as usual*. I hate to nag, but you push yourself way too hard."

"We all push hard."

"Yes, but the rest of us don't go off by ourselves into secluded places. Not to mention that you forget where you are and how long you've been there when you get working. Did you at least have water with you?"

"Absolutely! Wouldn't want to contaminate the sacred precincts with my corpse, would I?" He opened his cooler pack to reveal the empty bottles inside. He plucked one out and held it up, flashing his characteristic cocky grin. "See? Even some of the enhanced ones: fructose, electrolytes and all kinds of good stuff."

Frown morphing into a laugh, she stepped back from the door. "Okay, this round to you. The dragoness will slink back into her den— But!" She shook a finger at him. "Don't be surprised if I start sending people to check on you. I'm not going to let one of the best archaeological illustrators in the business kill himself on *my* watch. Get on over to the cook tent. I can lock up here."

He snapped a salute and headed for the dinner tent, feeling her intense gray eyes on him all the way. He barely managed to not break into a run.

The term "cook tent" was somewhat of a misnomer. The camp kitchen was in a tin-roofed pole structure outfitted with wooden tables, canvas chairs and a propane fueled stove. It was small and somewhat primitive, but functional. The cook, Manuel Conde — Manny — had put his own personal stamp on it. Strings of chiles and garlic hung from the wooden rafters and stacks of colorful terra cotta pots and dishes occupied the counters. He'd even built his own traditional brick and adobe oven just outside.

The oven was in use and the aroma of roasting chicken and potatoes wafted from it as he passed. It smelled great, but he needed to cool off before tackling anything solid. As he entered, the *cocina* was almost deserted except for Manny puttering in the galley and Avi Rosenberg and Victor Pale tucking into chicken and tortillas at one of the middle tables. Just beyond them, however, he beheld a wondrous sight: someone had procured ice. It glistened in the open cooler like diamonds. Diamonds studded with water bottles. He extracted a well-chilled one, pressed it to the back of his neck, then wandered over to join his friends.

For two men who were so alike in so many ways, Avi Rosenberg and Victor Pale couldn't have been more different physically. Both were tall, but Rosenberg was technically considered a giant at just shy of eight feet. Rosenberg was also muscular and deeply bronzed by years of working in the sun. His strength and build, combined with his wavy black hair had earned him the unwanted nickname of the Belzoni of American Archaeology. By contrast, Pale was slender and fair almost to the point of albinism, a look that stood him well in his younger days while fronting for the famous hard rock group, the Wolf Pack as the Pale Rider — even though he was once compared to a grain of rice who could play for the NBA. Neither man appreciated the comparisons and it was courting danger to mention it to either of them. Katzen slid into a vacant camp chair and rested the cold bottle against his throat.

Rosenberg elbowed Pale. "Look, Vic. A boiled shrimp. I didn't see that on the menu."

"Stuff you, Rosenberg." Katzen rolled the sweating bottle over his temples. It felt wonderful, he could almost feel his core temperature dropping.

"Nah. Not boiled," Vic said. "Sounds more steamed to me."

Josh sneered and re-applied the bottle to the back of his neck. "Enough about me, let's talk about *you* for a change. Anything interesting turn up while you were playing in the dirt, Avi? Maybe some dead thing for the Great White Wonder to practice on?"

Vic snorted and dipped a tortilla into the *salsa verde*. "Not so much as a pinky bone. The Jolly Jewish Giant, here, is falling down on the job."

"For shame!" Josh sat up straighter, opened the water and took a deep drink, then said, "Seriously, when I get back from the War Room, the excavation is always tarped over, so I can't see anything but this big orange thing rippling in the breeze. What's the progress on reconstructing the platform?

"Progress?" The archaeologist sat back in his chair with a sigh. "In a word: slowly." He shrugged. "But that's the way it needs to be. Digs always go slowly, but it's especially slow here. The overall structure is even more unstable than it looked at first. We have to take our time unless we want it to collapse again. It's already had enough help along those lines, anyway."

Vic looked up, "Yeah? Like how?"

Avi spooned salsa over his chicken, then said, "It's probably nothing."

"Bullshit. I've known you too long to buy that. There's something you don't like."

Josh sat forward, resting his elbows on the plank table. It was true that Avi had been unusually quiet the past few days, but there'd been no obvious reason. Maybe there was now.

Rosenberg dropped the spoon back into the bowl and glared into the sauce as if it were a scrying pool refusing him an answer. Finally he folded his arms onto the table and sat forward, unconsciously mirroring Katzen's move. "The collapse wasn't natural. From the look of things, the platform was deliberately collapsed sometime in recent history."

Pale's silver-white brows pulled together and he lowered his voice, asking, "How recent?"

"I can't give you a pinpoint answer, but the marks on the stucco and underlying adobe brick sure as hell look like a backhoe or something similar. The overgrowth we removed to get to that layer was pretty thick — more than a few season's growth. I'd say more than ten years. Maybe closer to twenty from the size of some of the trees."

"Which would put it in line with the age of the *huaquero* pits we found when first we got here," Katzen observed.

Rosenberg nodded. "Might be *huaqueros*. I've seen them do some destructive things in the past. Could be they thought the platform was all played out and knocked it over just for the hell of it."

"But you don't believe that," Vic said. It was a statement, not a question.

"That the site is bare of artifacts?" Rosenberg shook his head. "No, there's still something in there. I'm sure of that." He shrugged again. "Still, the objects that I find most useful are rarely the ones the *huaqueros* are after. Sure, the shiny stuff gets all the attention—"

" —and helps land the grants," Victor added.

"That, too," Avi agreed. "Still, you can't learn as much from a chunk of gold as you can from a pot that held a food offering. While I'd much rather find an undisturbed site, I'll gladly take the stuff the looters missed or passed by."

Harper entered and picked up a plate from the counter. She gave the empty space on the table in front of Josh a hard look that slid up and over him. He ignored her.

Pale caught the non-exchange and twitched a smile. "Don't let Harper bug you," he said. "Her intentions are good, but she can be annoying as hell. She's always following me around with a gallon bottle of sunscreen."

Avi shot his pigmentally challenged friend a glance. "Wonder why?"

"Perhaps it is because she knows how upsetting it would be if either our Pale Rider or our Little Cat should succumb to *Inti*." Diego Ruiz, the police chief of the nearby town of Piedras Rojas, said beside them. Ruiz was *Criollo*, but the Spanish blood had trumped the Indian. Tall and thin, the chief towered over most of the other residents of the town — not to mention Katzen, himself. Josh hadn't even noticed the man come in.

Vic flapped a dismissive hand. "Don't worry about me, Diego. I doubt even a sun god could get through that blocker Harper makes me use. Must be SPF sixty million at least."

Ruiz slid an earthenware cup of white corn soup onto the table in front of Josh, then dropped into the chair next to him, cradling a cup of coffee. Nodding toward the soup, he said, "Manny insists you eat that. It would be wise to do so. He is insulted that you did not come back for lunch and now you take nothing for dinner but cold water."

Josh glanced into the kitchen where the cook was pressing tortillas with undue violence. Unlike the chief, Manuel Conde was pure indio and at that moment, every line of his wiry frame vibrated with fury. Even his salt and pepper mustache bristled.

"Hmmmm. Yes," Josh said. He took a cautious sip. It stayed down, so he took a bigger swallow. It was up to Manny's usual standards, creamy and flavorful with just a hint of chili heat.

"Good. Something other than enhanced water and beef jerky," Harper Armand said, sliding her plate onto the table. A spoon clattered down beside Katzen's mug. "You'll need that, too. No one can actually drink one of Manny's corn chowders."

Josh regarded the remains of the soup in the bottom of the cup and picked up the spoon. "Yet another good point there, Doc."

"I swear," she said, a hint of Montana creeping into her voice. "Chasing after this bunch of supposedly intelligent academics makes me long for the good old days when I was simply running a surgical center and raising a son with learning disabilities."

Before she could pull out a chair, Diego Ruiz was on his feet, holding one out for her. She treated him to a warm smile as she sat.

Rosenberg put on a confused look. "Is she insulting us?"

"Must be insulting you," Vic said. "I'm a musician. Josh is an artist. You're the only academic I see here."

"Musician, huh?" Avi grinned. "Acid flashback or denying that you're a certified Medical Examiner?"

"I'm on vacation and a helluva long way from Cook County, Illinois. I can deny being a Medical Examiner all I want."

Avi turned his attention to the police chief. "So, is this a social call, Diego, or has someone disturbed the peace of Piedras Rojas?"

"It is both, yet not precisely either, Avi. I have need of Gatito's discerning eye." Ruiz shot a questioning look at Katzen. "If I may impose. . . ."

"No imposition, *Jefe*," Josh said. "Anything I can do to help."

Ruiz held up a finger. "*Momentito, por favor*." He motioned to Manny, who lugged a large wooden box out from behind his counter. He brought it to the table, then stood back. Ruiz unsnapped the latches, removed the lid and said, "Yesterday, my people intercepted a sale of looted artifacts by some local men.

Two are known *huaqueros*, but. . . ." He spread his hands. "I fear there may be more to the story."

Josh peered in. The cushioned compartments of the box held three gold objects, three stirrup pots and two jade carvings. "Ooooo. Pretty."

He lifted the pieces out one by one, finally setting aside one jade carving and all the ceramics. "Those are fakes. Good ones, but still fakes."

The chief tapped the box. "And these?"

"Are the real McCoy."

"Hah! I have felt something was wrong with their story from the start. Perhaps now we can get the truth from them. I can always count on my Little Cat. Some day I will steal you away from Dr. Rosenberg and draft you into my *huaquero* squad."

Josh gave a slight, noncommittal smile.

"Have to fight me for him, Diego. No way am I going to let anyone break up my Dream Team."

"Dream Team, huh?" Amused, Dr. Armand regarded her table companions. "Odd Squad might be more accurate."

Rosenberg grinned. "Watch out, Harper. You're part of the team, too." Pulling the box closer, he studied the artifacts within. After a moment he said, "Let me know if they tell you where these came from, okay, Diego? They're similar to what we're finding, but they certainly didn't come from this dig. A couple of them look older than ours, too."

The chief nodded. "We suspect they have stumbled upon a cache. Small pieces have been finding their way onto the market for several weeks." He paused and lifted one of the stirrup pots. "Along with a number of forgeries, it seems. Maybe now we will make some progress. This is the first time we have captured the artifacts still in the sellers' hands."

"If these guys have found a cache, I'd truly love to know where. A cache usually points to something larger close by."

Ruiz hummed agreement around a sip of coffee, then added with the air of a man casually tossing a lit match into a fireworks shed, "We also suspect they may be working with our old friend, el Mago."

Avi groaned. "Oh, not *that* schmuck again."

"Schmuck is too tame a word," Katzen said through gritted teeth. "I have a few others that might fit better."

Even Harper reacted, her face flushed with anger. "After what happened at the end of last year's season, I can understand how you both feel. I'm glad the students and I were well on our way home when it all happened."

"Ah ha! Do I finally get to hear what happened?" A grin split Pale's long, thin face. "Please go on, *Jefe*, these two blow me off whenever I ask for details. All I know is that this Mago guy tried to rip off some artifacts from the camp."

"Feh." Rosenberg waved it away. "It doesn't deserve being talked about. Some people like this Mago idiot understand nothing but violence."

"See? That's what I get." He jerked his thumb at Katzen. "That one just growls."

Josh didn't actually growl, but any comment he might have made was preempted by the cook removing the soup and slamming a plate of hot food onto the table in front of him. Manny jabbed a fork into the chunks of chicken and stood with arms folded like the embodiment of a Toltec warrior. Katzen considered it the better part of valor to start filling a tortilla.

"Ah, yes," Ruiz said. "I have heard so much about you that I forget you were not here in past years, Victor. You missed our excitement."

"Excitement," the archaeologist spat. "Is *that* what it's called?"

"Oh, *sí*!" Manny Conde's scowl became a wide grin. "It was most exciting! It was like an American movie. The masked bandits were defeated and ran away in fear of the heroes."

"Manny, you're over-dramatizing," Rosenberg snapped. "We stopped an attempted robbery. Period."

"I am afraid Manny's version is more correct," Ruiz said,"—regardless of how much Dr. Rosenberg wishes otherwise. I, myself, am not sorry it happened as it did."

He snagged a warm tortilla and continued, "This man who calls himself el Mago has been a thorn in the side of the police in this area for many years. He is accustomed to doing as he pleases. It was good to see him denied what he sought to take. I think he did not realize that Dr. Rosenberg and our Gatito are not the usual scholars."

Dr. Pale was amused. "Is he that arrogant or just uninformed?"

"Perhaps a little of both," the chief said. "It was the end of the season. Almost everyone had gone home. Dr. Rosenberg and Gatito were in the workshop packing artifacts for the *Museo* in Lima when Mago's men drove up in a truck. The men jumped out shouting, waving machetes and stormed the office. They are used to people fleeing before them and did not expect resistance. When the first one came through the door, Dr. Avi grabbed him and tossed him back into his friends like a child playing with rag dolls."

Rosenberg warned, "Diego. . . ."

"Did it not happen, my friend?" Ruiz paused, eyebrows raised. "Are my facts incorrect?"

The big archaeologist's only answer was to rip a tortilla in half and jam it into the salsa.

"This did not make the leader happy," Chief Ruiz continued. "He pulled a pistol on our Little Cat, not realizing that cats have claws. El Gatito brought the edge of his drawing board down onto the man's gun wrist, then against his head."

Katzen muttered, "Split a perfectly good drawing board, too."

"It ended that quickly. The raiders grabbed their injured leader and fled in the truck. I wish I could have seen it myself."

"Sounds like you did," Avi said.

"I have eyes and ears in many places," Ruiz indicated Manny, who was back in his kitchen happily clattering pans.

"Hope they had to nurse their injuries for a long time." Victor's silver-gray eyes went hard. "One reason I became a Medical Examiner was to make sure the guilty got their due punishment. Irks me to no end when they get away with it."

"The guy is smoke." This time, Katzen did growl.

"Doesn't Mago mean something like magician?" Pale asked.

Ruiz nodded. "It does, but he is also a human being. He is a man named Alberto Vargas, but few people remember that these days. Someday, though, el Mago will overstep himself and it is my hope that I will be there to catch him." He repacked the artifacts and placed them on the floor. "So, Joshua, I hear you have been making more beautiful drawings?"

"He certainly has," Harper said. "Attempting to give himself heatstroke was just an incidental."

"Oh, but this must not happen," the chief said. "You must take care, Gatito. How will I ever fill the empty spots on my office walls if you do not live to make more prints?"

"You're in luck, *Jefe*. Barring fire, flood or famine, there'll be plenty of prints by the end of this season." Katzen gave a lopsided smile. "Sheesh. I've only been doing this professionally for a few years. You folks make it sound like I'm some kind of master."

"Sssssshhhhhh," Avi broke in, grateful for the change in subject. "Don't tell him the truth or I'll have to pay him more." Becoming serious, he asked, "Josh, I've been as out of touch with your progress as you've been with mine. Where are you on the copying in the War Room?"

"I'm close to finished. I've got the main mural and the one from the south wall finished. I started the north fresco today. That leaves the two paintings flanking the door."

"The War Room? That is the small room at the peak of the hill that the student discoverd by accident?" Ruiz asked.

"That's the one," said Rosenberg. "The name seemed to fit since all the paintings depicted ceremonial fighting."

"It is amazing." Diego sat back. "So many beautiful things from a place everyone thought had nothing left. The sun god hides his treasures well. One wonders what *Inti* has been guarding in that ruined platform."

"We'll know soon enough. The students and I finished

removing the collapsed superstructure and shoring up what remains of the walls this afternoon. The main excavation starts in the morning."

Amelia Peters, Rosenberg's teaching assistant, peeked around the door, her freckle-sprinkled face a mask of uncertainty. Avi spotted her and motioned her over. "Hey 'Melia, what do you need?"

"Actually, I need Josh." Turning to Katzen, she said, "Could you take a look at the database laptop? It gave us that Blue Screen of Death again."

Katzen asked, "Same 0E error?"

The girl shoved an escaped wisp of red gold hair from her face and grinned ruefully. "Hard to tell with the mile long string of numbers and letters, but it looks like it."

Dropping his napkin, he pushed his chair back. "Okay, I think I know what the problem is—"

Harper cleared her throat.

Josh eyed the doctor, then sat back down. "And I'll fix it as soon as I finish dinner."

Amelia laughed. "Thanks, Josh. Don't rush. It'll wait and we have plenty of other things to do." With that, she hurried out.

"Computers," Dr. Armand said, shaking her head. "Josh had to take the one in the infirmary apart and replace some card or something just the other day."

"It wasn't anything big," Josh said. "It was just overheating. All it really needed was cleaning out. Dust gets into everything around here."

"All this and a painter, too," Harper said with an amused shake of her head.

"What?" Avi grinned at the doctor. "You thought I only wanted him on the team because he's a good artist?"

CHAPTER 2

Questing fingertips brushed an empty tray. The kneadable eraser was gone again. The thief hadn't run far and rolled over begging for a good scratch as soon as Katzen reached to reclaim his property. Sighing, he knelt and absently petted the marmalade bandit. It had been a frustrating day. The latest in a series of frustrating days. Between the cat stealing his materials and the parade of well-meaning students charged with keeping tabs on him, he'd accomplished little.

The soft rubber yielded under his fingers, toothmarks disappearing, as he stared at the mural, trying to reclaim the mood. Choosing a pencil, he drew the edge of it over a warrior's feather leaving just a hint of — hurried footsteps crunched up the trail outside. He dropped the pencil and hung his head in exasperation. Harper and the students meant well, but he was going to have to talk with the good doctor about this. Steeling himself for another onslaught of cheerful concern, he was mildly surprised when Amelia Peters peeked in, face flushed from the climb.

"Josh, I'm so sorry to interrupt, but Avi wants you back at the main dig as soon as possible."

"Okay. . . ." He set the drawing board aside. "What's up?"

"Oh, there isn't a problem—" She chewed her lip thoughtfully. "At least I don't *think* there is. They've cleared the area at the front of the platform and uncovered a burial. Well, bones and some jewelry, anyway."

He stood and worked the kinks out of his legs. "You don't sound real sure."

"I'm not. It's in an odd place for a formal burial. It might be more of a cache, but those don't usually contain a burial. Avi wants you to photograph it."

"I thought Cody Meredith was shooting the actual dig. Won't he be pissed if I horn in?"

She chuckled and rescued a pencil from the cat. "Not Cody. He's already rubbing his hands in anticipation of working with you. He's determined to learn your technique."

At the camp, Amelia veered off toward the excavation while Josh made for the workshop. Inside, he stowed his drawing things, grabbed the camera bag and hurried to join the others.

He was amazed at how much had been cleared. Where there had previously been a tumbled mass of of mud brick and scrub growth, now stood battered, but largely intact, adobe walls. The result was an area open to the sky, yet still partially enclosed. A tarp, stretched across an arrangement of poles as a sunshade, rippled in the faint breeze.

Avi Rosenberg loomed over the ongoing work like a sunburned colossus. Katzen could tell at a glance something was bugging him. A burial should have him smiling, instead, he looked grim. He'd been like that since discovering the backhoe marks on the collapsed mudbrick. Amelia Peters and Vic Pale stood beside him, faces shaded by broad-brimmed straw hats. Amelia busied herself recording grid measurements on a battered wooden clipboard, but Vic kept shooting glances at his old friend as if also puzzled by the mood. Josh came over to stand with them.

"You got here fast. I appreciate it," Avi said. "You have the camera?"

Josh patted the bag slung over his shoulder. "Fresh memory sticks, too."

"Great, let's get started. I want this recorded as we go."

Excavation progressed slowly as the team carefully removed rubble, stopping whenever they uncovered an artifact. There were a *lot* of artifacts. It was a crazy mixture that included delicately flaked obsidian pieces and turquoise-studded nose and ear plugs tangled with the remains of several classic Moche peanut necklaces.

Coming forward to watch Josh photograph three more gold peanuts that had been almost crushed flat by falling adobe, Rosenberg crouched beside him and murmured, "*You* see what's bugging me, don't you?"

"Yeah," Josh answered. "There's stuff from all over the place — it looks like some Hollywood set designer's idea of a treasure trove. All we lack is an iron-bound chest full of Spanish coins."

Dusting his hands, Rosenberg stood and told the students, "This is wrong, folks. We're dealing with a disturbed deposit and I don't just mean the collapse. We'll need to go even slower on this." At the collective groan from the sweat-soaked diggers, he said, "I know, I *know*! We're already slowed to glacier-speed. It's just there's something. . . ." He waved his hands ineffectually and finished weakly, ". . . wrong."

Amelia looked up from her clipboard. "Could *huaqueros* have dragged a body up here to strip it in better light?"

"Maybe," Rosenberg said. "But I'm seeing artifacts from pretty diverse eras. It's all Moche . . . ." He shrugged. "Okay, people, all we've got right now is a part of a hand and a couple ribs. Let's get this guy dug out and maybe we'll see what we're dealing with. Vic? You're our human remains expert, would you do the honors?"

Grinning, Dr. Pale took his trowel and brush and picked his way across the still-littered floor to crouch beside the exposed bones. Carefully brushing the soil away he said, "Oookay. Anterior of the left hand . . . from the angle of the metacarpals, the wrist and arm should be . . . can we lift this chunk of brick?"

As two students came over to lift the chunk of sun-baked mud, Josh took up a position beside the crouched Medical Examiner, ready to snap a picture as the area was cleared. Vic's slender hands moved like an orchestra conductor's as he guided the young men's actions. "Good . . . good . . . now straight up!"

Josh had just depressed the shutter button when Vic straightened so violently, he smacked into the wall behind him.

"Stop! Don't move another thing." Rubbing the back of his head, he asked, "Josh?"

Katzen, eyes locked on the camera's viewscreen, said slowly, "I see it, Doc."

Rosenberg dived into the pit. "What?"

Victor's silver-gray eyes slid toward the archaeologist. "The Moche lords were rich beyond belief, but I have never before heard of one wearing a Rolex watch."

"Shit." Avi pulled off his wire-rimmed glasses and massaged the bridge of his nose. "Okay, someone get Diego Ruiz up here. Looks like our dig just became a crime scene."

~*~

"There." Katzen leaned over Lt. Regina Quijano's shoulder, pointing to a place in the photo that filled the large LCD screen. "That's a good shot of the marks. They look like they were made by a backhoe blade. See? They're real regular. Nothing natural about them."

Regina tilted her head slightly and frowned. "*Sí.* I am no expert, but that is how it looks to me, as well. This is bad, Gatito. It has — *como se dice* — the rotten smell?"

"Too right, Gina. It struck Avi as wrong even before we found the skeleton. That's why he had Cody take so many photos of the marks and the way the walls were tumbled."

"I will be sure to show them to the *Jefe* as soon as we get back to the station house. We will ask around, too. Piedras Rojas is not that big. Surely someone must remember a thing like this — even after so many years."

"They might remember, but will they admit it? *Huaqueros* are a tight-lipped bunch and they get pretty nasty with those whose lips aren't so tight." The laptop beeped, and with a couple mouse clicks, Katzen ejected the portable hard drive. "That's the last file copied. You still have a little room on the drive, too. That's amazing considering how many images there are."

Regina put the small device in her shoulder pouch and gave him a smile. "There will be much to search through. *Muchas gracias* for making the copies."

"*De nada.* Anything to get this cleared up and the dig back on track."

He followed the lieutenant out of the workshop into the bright afternoon sun, pausing just long enough to let his eyes adjust from the dimmer light of the workshop. The normally noisy camp was hushed and people clustered in small, scattered groups. It looked like the aftermath of a funeral. Quijano thanked him again for the photos and headed toward where Chief Ruiz stood a distance removed talking on the police Land Rover's radio, gesturing forcefully. If anything, the Chief looked more unhappy than he had an hour before when he first arrived on the scene.

After a moment, Josh wandered over to where Amelia, Harper and Vic sat in the dubious shade of a scrubby tree. Just beyond the small group, Avi Rosenberg paced and fidgeted, periodically shooting anxious glances toward Ruiz.

Josh lowered himself to the ground next to Amelia. "Diego is still on the radio? This can't be good."

"More like on the radio *again*," Amelia said.

"He's trying to locate a coroner," Vic added. "He doesn't seem to be having a lot of luck."

Rosenberg stopped pacing and said, "He's been talking to a lot of people for a long time and the longer it goes, the unhappier he gets." He dropped to the ground behind Peters and Katzen. "I know how he feels."

Ruiz shut off the unit and stood for a moment staring at the ground. At length, he approached, arms spread wide in a gesture of helplessness. "I am sorry, my friends. It seems a tour bus overturned near the *Parque Nacional Huascarán* this morning."

There was a collective gasp. Suddenly, a skeleton at the dig site didn't seem so urgent. Harper Armand was on her feet in an instant. "How many casualties and what can we do to help?"

"I'm available, too." Dr. Pale stood up, brushing dirt off his khakis. "I've been in the middle of one of these before, back in Chicago. They'll need every hand they can get."

"Sí, Dr. Pale, Dr. Armand," Ruiz said. "Everyone is either there or on the way. I think, though, we are a bit too far north to be of any real service."

Harper Armand's brow furrowed, thinking hard. Finally she sighed and said, "As much as I hate to admit it, Diego, you're right. By the time we got there, it would be over. It looks like a short distance on the map, but most of it is straight up and straight down."

Diego nodded. "The mountains are both a blessing and a curse."

"We'll just have to bide our time until the crisis is over," Avi said quietly. "We can go on hiatus for a few days. . . ."

"I am afraid there is more," the Chief said. "We have only bones and bones lack priority. Even after the emergency is over, we will have to wait our turn. With the current workload, Dr. Ochoa estimates three more weeks at best."

"Three weeks?" Avi yelped, then sat down again — hard. "There goes the season."

Ruiz' gaze shifted into the distance. "Perhaps not. . . ," he began, then turned abruptly and hurried back toward the police Rover, saying only, "*Momentito, mis amigos.*"

The silence was oppressive and almost complete. The only sound was the low buzz of Diego Ruiz back at the Rover's radio. It was as if the surrounding birds and insects were experiencing the same desolation the excavation team felt. Katzen wondered if there would be enough time to finish the drawings of the warrior murals before they had to pack up and head home.

"We could move over to the west side of the site," Amelia said almost to herself. Louder, she added, "I know that was slated for next year, but I bet it would be fairly easy to switch."

Avi looked at the girl with raised eyebrows. "That could work. I was just sitting here being bummed out and not even considering alternatives." A huge grin split his tanned face. "That *will* work! Great idea, 'Melia. I don't know what I'd do without you."

Just then, the hills rang with "¡*EXITO!*"

Diego Ruiz dropped the microphone onto its hook and strode back to them, radiating triumph. "I have a solution to our problem, but it relies on our own Pale Rider."

"Me?" Vic looked up in confusion, then amended, "But, of course I'll do whatever I can."

"You have quite a fan in our Coroner, Doctor Ochoa, Victor," Ruiz continued. "He has the boxed sets of all your *Casebook: Beyond the Pale* television shows. He is more than willing to turn this case over to you."

Vic was wordless for a moment. "But I can't possibly work a crime scene! I'm a Medical Examiner, not a crime scene technician. In spite of what you see on television, crime scene investigation is far removed from pathology."

"But you know the procedures, yes? Dr. Ochoa says *Beyond the Pale* is often used in classrooms."

"Well . . . yes, but. . . ."

Avi leaned in. "Three weeks, Vic."

Pale groaned. "Why do I feel like I just got drafted?"

Ruiz clapped his hands in satisfaction. "It is settled. I will summon my people and you can instruct them." He hurried off.

Vic sighed. "I'm not certified for this. Nothing I do will stand in a court of law."

Avi said, "We're in the middle of the Peruvian mountains. Things work differently here." He clapped his friend on the back. Turning to the rest of the group he said, "Come on folks, we still need to change dig sites to accommodate the investigation. Let's get that rolling."

Josh turned to follow, but was hauled back as his arm was grabbed from behind.

"Oh, no you don't," Vic said. "I need a photog and you just got drafted with me."

CHAPTER 3

"That should be the last one," Katzen said stepping carefully away from the crumbling ancient walls. "I got the skeleton — well what we can see of the skeleton, anyway — from several angles. We're covered for before pics."

"Good," Pale said, stifling a yawn. "Man. I need more coffee."

Josh stowed the digital camera in its bag. "That's usually my line."

"Sorry. I didn't get much sleep last night. I don't mind admitting that I'm dreading today. With the adobe walls trying to fall in, this is a dicey recovery. Having a bunch of people learning forensic anthropology as they go is going to make it that much harder."

"Oh, come on. You'll be great and you know it. I've sat in on some of your seminars and you've handled way tougher crowds than the Piedras Rojas police department. I'll take a few grumpy cops over a roomful of Chicago freshmen any day."

They started across the camp toward the *cocina*. Delicious smells and the comforting clangs and bangs of Manny preparing breakfast grew stronger as they neared.

"It's all performance, Josh. I'll be fine once the curtain goes up. Until then, I have the 'What If' jitters." Vic stifled another yawn. "Speaking of what ifs: any idea how many officers we'll have up here?"

Josh chuckled. "Knowing Diego, as many as he can. He'd normally have to pay hard cash for this kind of training. He'll take full advantage. . . ." His voice trailed off and he stopped in his tracks, then he said, "Uhhhhhh. I think we *both* need more coffee. Lots of it."

Two of the three official police vehicles pulled into the camp. The dust the Rovers had raised made it hard to see who the passengers were, but Josh could tell one thing: both vehicles were full.

Vic groaned. "But . . . there are only twelve members in the entire department."

"Including part-timers," Josh added.

"Yeah. Including part-timers."

Manny Conde emerged from the *cocina* holding a steaming mug in each hand. "Gatito! Dr. Victor, is this what you. . . ." His words trailed off and his smile faded seeing the crowd exiting the the Land Rovers. He stared for a moment, spat something in Quechua, handed Vic and Josh their coffee, then disappeared back into the kitchen.

"For once, I'm glad I don't speak Quechua," Katzen muttered.

"I don't speak it either, but I think I agree with him," Vic said, then put on a smile and headed for the milling group. "Good morning, *Jefe*! Is there anyone left in town?"

"Good morning! It has been slow since we intercepted el Mago's people with the forged artifacts, so most of my officers are free to benefit from your teaching. All but Ortiz. He is close to retirement and has no need for special training. He can handle things at the station house until I return."

"Oh, you aren't staying?" Vic asked. Josh thought he detected a little relief in the ME's voice, but none of it showed outwardly.

"No, I regret that I cannot. Lt. Quijano will be in charge in my absence."

A small gasoline engine revved behind the cook tent and a few moments later, Manny's son, Luis, astride his motor scooter, zipped around and pelted toward town with break-neck speed. Josh considered the milling mass of officers, then regarded the plume of dust disappearing down the track. All-in-all, he thought, Luis had the best idea.

~*~

As soon as the dig became a crime scene, all of the artifacts became evidence. All finds were left in situ within the grid and tagged with cards Katzen printed up according to Dr. Pale's specifications. Later, they were photographed then logged into an evidence database Josh had set up.

Throughout the day, Josh found himself bopping between the police dig, the new archaeological site and the workshop; tagging evidence, coordinating the photography and keeping the team's computers up and running. He was busier than ever and *still* not getting the work done he was actually hired to do. It was hard to stay on track. Even harder with constant interruptions from students coming for help with the 3-D program. It was harder still not to snap when he'd heard the same question three or four times. Since Rosenberg frowned on murder, he wrote out a quick step-by-step guide that he handed out to the repeat questioners instead.

Cody Meredith, Katzen's photographic assistant, was an altogether different problem — if problem was the right word. The boy was the youngest student on the dig and he was enthusiastic. No. Not quite enough. Make that *ENTHUSIASTIC!!* He wasn't much on standing still, either.

"Wow! Just . . . *wow!*" Cody said, completing what had to be his fifth orbit of the tiny workshop. "This is just so great! I had no clue how precise crime scene photography had to be. No. *Clue!*"

The memory card checked out. Josh ejected it, slipped it into its vinyl sleeve and inserted another into the laptop's card reader. "There's an element of precision to any good photography, Code."

The boy dropped into a camp chair — finally. "Yeah, I know, but Dr. Pale is so exacting. Even pickier than *you* are. You shoulda heard my Mom on Skype last night. She's over the moon that I'm working with *the* Pale Rider." He was up and on the move again. "She has all the Wolfpack's records and all his solo stuff, too. I don't think she ever missed an episode of *Beyond the Pale* on TV, either."

The fifth card also checked out. Sliding it into the sleeve below the other, he said, "Victor is a professional at whatever he decides to do. You're lucky he's taking time with you. You should pay attention to what he tells you."

"You bet I will! Besides, Mom'd kill me if I didn't."

A shadow blocked the rectangle of light from the open door. "Ah ha! I thought I might find our missing photog in here." Amelia Peters brushed errant strands of strawberry blond hair back under her hairband. It fell right back into her face. "You better get your butt over to the crime scene, Kiddo. Dr. Pale is waiting on you."

Panic-stricken, Cody wheeled toward Katzen. "Oh geez I was supposed to get—

"Memory cards." Katzen zipped the carrying case and handed it to him. "There you go. All checked out and ready to rock-n-roll. Enough to last you into tomorrow."

"You're a lifesaver, Josh. Thanks!" Tucking the cards into his camera bag, the boy took off at a run.

"Annnnd he's off," Peters said looking after the retreating figure.

Katzen stood, suppressing a groan. "And so am I. I have to get *my* butt over to the new dig site to help Robert set up the 3-D grid."

"Noooo." Amelia folded tanned arms across her chest and her usually warm brown eyes grew hard. "No, you don't. I told Robert to stop bothering you. He's here to learn how to use that program *himself*, not how to whine for the technical adviser any time some real work needs to be done. He's going to follow that sheet of instructions you gave him. Or. Else."

Josh laughed. "I bet he didn't dare ask what the or else was."

"Damn straight!" A wide grin split her freckle-sprinkled face, then she lifted a finger and said, "Just a sec."

She darted out and returned a few moments later carrying a tray draped with one of Manny's colorful cotton towels. Putting it down on the workbench, she whipped the cloth off revealing two melon *aquas frescas* and two plates of pulled chicken, tortillas and roasted potatoes with various small bowls of sauces. "Taaaa daaa! Lunch."

"Is this some sort of Harper Armand pre-emptive strike?"

"I'm mutli-tasking." Amelia busied herself setting things out on the table. "I needed to come over here to find Cody, anyway, and the cook tent is close — *and* it's almost lunchtime. I can grab lunch, spell you while you eat, then go back and spell Avi while *he* eats."

"You're not a multi-tasker, you're a whirlwind."

Peters sneered at him and sat, piling chicken into a tortilla. "Let's dig in. I'm starved."

"You're always starved."

Amelia took a big bite of chicken and chewed happily at him, but hadn't even swallowed before one of the female students from Victor's dig rushed in. Breathlessly, the girl said, "Dr. Pale needs more of those little number cards."

Mutely, Katzen pointed to a stack of papers beside the laser printer. The student grabbed the stack and zoomed out.

Immediately after that, a grad student from the new site poked his head in. "Hey, Josh, what was that key combo to insert a photo link into the database?"

That was the beginning. During lunch there was a steady a steady parade of students and staff through the workshop. After a while, Amelia laid down her fork. "Is it *always* like this?"

"Pretty much," Katzen said with a shrug. "You should see it when Avi, Vic or Harper is here. Place really jumps then."

The girl munched in silence for a while, then nodded. "Right. I'll have a chat with Regina before I head back. Finish your lunch."

~*~

Things grew particularly mutinous after lunch. Few of the officers actually wanted to be there — with the exception of

Lt. Regina Quijano. The lieutenant seemed to have found her niche and peppered Victor with questions, transcribing his answers in her notebook. The rest were angry. Angry at their boss for conscripting them into the dig, but mostly they were angry with Dr. Pale who was being slow and meticulous. They were especially unhappy about the tedious chore of sifting the removed dirt through multiple screens.

The tension was infectious and even spread to the new archaeological site where they'd had to reset and start from the beginning. This left many students standing around with little to do. Never a good thing. As a result, Dr. Armand's on-site infirmary was standing room only with the consequences of people rushing across the camp at top speed as well as a couple punched noses.

Things were looking bad until Amelia Peters had enough. Rounding up some of the most vocal grad students, she marched them over to the crime scene and paired the experienced diggers and sifters up with the novice police officers. It didn't exactly stop the grumbling, but it did bring a measure of peace.

The whole day was insane. Finally, it was over and after dinner, the officers went home and exhausted students and staff collected in small groups for muted conversation or wandered off to their bunks. Josh let himself into the workshop and opened his laptop. He stopped and listened. Nothing. He was alone for the first time since daybreak. It was glorious!

~*~

It felt like a punch. Then he was falling, body curled around the ornate hilt of a knife protruding just under his ribs. Katzen awoke as he and the camp chair hit the floor. Gasping, he rolled to his knees grabbing for the dagger. It wasn't there. It hadn't been for several years. Shakily, he righted the chair and sat, glad as hell that canvas chairs didn't make a lot of noise when they hit rubber floormats. Did he scream? No, he didn't think so. Good.

Dammit dammit dammit. He hadn't had that flashback for a long time. Why now? What the hell triggered it *now*? Okay, finding a relatively new skeleton in an archaeological dig turned a routine excavation into a clusterfuck. Still, it was nowhere near the clusterfuck that last mission was — after all, no one on the expedition was trying to kill him. His eyes slid toward the pile of hand-written notes still waiting to be transcribed. Well, not deliberately, anyway.

Ooookay. Heart rate's through the roof. What did the shrink tell me. . . ? Yeah. Concentrate on good memories.

Taking deep, measured breaths, he pulled up better memories to drown out the bad ones. It was no surprise that the best of those featured the people he was currently with on the expedition. The last few years had been the happiest of his life. His heart slowed and his muscles unclenched. Eventually, he pulled the stack of scribbled notes over and resolutely resumed typing, not looking at the clock on the laptop's taskbar. He didn't even *want* to know what time it was. The panic attack and its aftermath had taken a big chunk, though, because the solar powered lamp was giving out. So was he.

"Why are you still working?" Vic Pale leaned into the room giving him a look that hovered somewhere between amusement and disgust. "Most of the camp is already in bed. Close it down for the night."

"Can't," Katzen half-yawned-half-groaned, working his shoulders. "The photos and notes from the crime scene are all entered and transcribed, but I'm not finished with the notes on relocating the excavation. Avi will have a conniption if they aren't available by the time they start tomorrow."

"No he won't," Avi said from the darkness behind Victor. Edging past into the light, he plunked a stack of plastic cups onto the table. "Told you he'd be here."

Pale followed him in. "Don't you get tired of being right all the time?"

"Not at all. It merely cements my reputation of an all-knowing, all-seeing bastard of a teacher."

"Yah?" Vic raised an eyebrow, then slid silver eyes toward Josh.

"Just humor him and nod. He gets cranky when anyone disagrees with him."

Rosenberg looked up from unfolding a canvas chair. "Pour already."

The ex-rocker placed a fresh bottle of whiskey and a container of ice next to the cups. Chuckling, he took three off the stack and doled glistening chunks between them. "I raided the ice chest. This is all she wrote until Manny brings more in the morning — which isn't all that far away," he added, pouring amber liquid over the ice.

Katzen accepted a cup and took a tentative sip. Bourbon. Not what he preferred, but it would do.

Rosenberg and Pale pulled chairs up to the table. Avi pointed at the laptop. "Off. Close it. It was a crazy day and it's officially over. This is unwind time, got it?"

Josh snapped out of his seat to full attention. "Yes, sir! As you say, SIR!"

"Oh, shut up," the archaeologist said as he topped off Katzen's cup. "You were always crappy at the spit and polish stuff, anyway."

Smirking, Josh sat, taking another sip of bourbon. Maybe he could get used to it if he worked at it. Maybe.

"I didn't know you back then, but I can't imagine you ever doing that without an edge of sarcasm," Vic said leaning back and stretching his legs out. "Oh man, it was a *helluva* day. My legs are screaming from all the kneeling and standing. It felt like I was on some sort of Catholic Mass drill team."

"Naaah, it's your body getting payback for all those times you gyrated around a stage beating amplifiers to death with guitars," Avi said.

"I never intentionally destroyed either a guitar or an amp," the rocker turned Medical Examiner said primly. "That was Hurricane Hattie."

"Yeah, yeah, shift the blame," Rosenberg said. "You gyrated, though. I personally saw you gyrate."

Josh let the bourbon work its way through his nervous system and enjoyed the brother-like banter between his friends. For men unrelated by blood, they were closer than Josh had ever been to his own brother. Come to think of it, matches and dynamite had a better relationship than he and his brother — or should that be that matches and dynamite had a *similar* relationship?

Suddenly, Avi dropped the banter. "Seriously, I want to apologize — to both of you. When Diego proposed that Vic take over the crime scene, all I was thinking of was getting my own season back on track. I had no idea he'd send the *entire* department all at once." He paused, then a smile tugged the corners of his mouth. "Although it is kinda funny how fast he jumped on it."

"Not hard to understand, though, " Katzen said. "Most small police forces are under-funded and under-staffed. Where else is he going to get this caliber of training for his people?"

Vic dredged a couple chunks of ice from the bowl. "His officers are not *quite* as thrilled as their chief. This afternoon bore a family resemblance to the French Revolution." He topped off his cup and took a big swig. "Still, while we're in credit/apology mode, I want to thank *you* for stepping up to the plate, Josh. I'd be pulling my hair out if it weren't for you — *and* Amelia. That girl's worth more than gold."

"That she is," Josh said. "She saved my toochis several times today, too. Her organizational skills verge on a super power."

The door opened quietly and the lady herself looked in. The dimming lamplight made her freckles stand out starkly so she looked even younger than her years. "I saw a light in here, so I thought I'd better check it out. I should have known it was you guys."

"Amelia! Were your ears burning?" Vic asked sitting up a little straighter. "Josh and I were just talking about how you saved our butts today. I'd probably have been headed for the guillotine in a rickety oxcart if you hadn't arrived with that army of grad students."

"Four is not an army, Dr. Pale," Amelia said with a laugh.

Vic tilted his head. "Are you sure about that? I've watched four roadies break down a full stage set, pack it into trucks and be half-way to the next gig in seconds flat. That's an army I wouldn't want to get in the way of."

She spotted the bottle and cups on the table. "Oh! Is that bourbon or Scotch?"

"Bourbon, but I'll live through it," Josh said.

"May I have some?" Catching Rosenberg and Pale's doubtful looks, she said, "Come on! I'm twenty-four years old. I *have* had alcohol before."

Ignoring his companions, Josh took the bottle, poured her a shot over ice and presented it to her with an exaggerated bow. "Your booze, M'Lady. After today, you've more than earned it."

She took the cup with a curtsy and a giggle. "Thank you, Sir Ka-niggit," then sat, sipped and sighed. "I never understood why my parents always ended the day with a cocktail. I think I do now."

Victor glanced at the door. "Now all we need is Harper and we can call this a staff meeting."

Amelia shook her head and took another sip. "She's already asleep. She has this technique where she clears her mind and POW, she's in Dreamland. Says she developed it in her early days as a resident doctor."

"Wish she'd teach it to me," Vic murmured. "There are all sorts of things I'd like to put out of my head."

I'd take a big dollop of that, too, thought Katzen. Quirking a smile, he said aloud, "Here's to the Dreamland Express."

Four plastic cups were raised in the failing lamplight.

CHAPTER 4

"I don't believe you," Rosenberg said, shaking his head. "As hot as it already is, you're gulping steaming coffee."

"Give me a break. Yesterday was long and the night wasn't much better." Josh took another deep pull at the mug. Truthfully, it could have been worse. The PTSD panic attacks could have returned. They hadn't and he was grateful.

The archaeologist made a doubtful noise deep in his throat, turned, then stopped abruptly. "I thought all the officers working the crime scene were already here," he said, frowning at a dusty PRPD Land Rover bumping up the road into camp.

"They are. Vic's briefing them over at the workshop as we speak," Josh said. "That's Diego."

The Rover parked in front of the infirmary. It seemed the chief's arrival wasn't completely unexpected because Amelia and Dr. Armand hurried out to meet him.

Avi closed his eyes and groaned. "Oooooh, shit. What's screwed up now?" Without another word, he strode across the commons.

Katzen hurried to catch up. Ahead, Ruiz opened the Rover's hatch and handed a small, black boxy thing to Amelia. The girl bounced happily in place, then wrapped him in a bear-hug. "These are perfect!"

"I am glad to be able to help." Chuckling, Ruiz disengaged himself from the hug, noticed the new arrivals and waved. "Good morning, my friends!"

"Morning, Diego," Rosenberg said cautiously. "I'll reserve judgment on the good part for the time being. Is there a problem?"

"Not any more," Amelia said, handing Rosenberg a battered walkie-talkie. "We *solved* one."

"Amelia got the idea yesterday while having lunch with Josh," Harper said.

The girl rolled her eyes. "More like I had lunch while he *tried* to eat. That workshop needs a revolving door. There was this steady stream of people with problems and questions — it was crazy! Then I remembered seeing Regina Quijano using a walkie-talkie."

"I have brought eight," Ruiz said pulling out two more units. "They are not exactly new and some work better than others, but they should do."

Avi turned the device around in his hands, then beamed. "Great idea, Kiddo!"

Amelia flushed, fidgeted a little, then went to help Ruiz unload the rest of the radios.

~*~

At first he'd been skeptical of the radios, but by the middle of the day, the slightly tinny crackle of conversation had become a pleasant background noise. He regarded the battered workshop door. It hadn't opened in at least fifteen minutes. That alone was worth it.

The radios even slowed Cody down. Thankfully. It wasn't that he didn't like the kid or wasn't glad to have an assistant; he did and he was. Only . . . he'd always had the sneaking suspicion that, at times, the temptation to just let Lex Luthor keep Jimmy Olsen must have trickled through Superman's mind. He now knew that *had* to be true.

Reaching for another page of hand-written notes, he found only bare table. He looked around for escaped sheets. There were none. He was *done*! Thank you, walkie-talkies! He'd never been able to finish the job that fast before. It had even helped streamline the crime scene dig, allowing Vic and his Piedras Rojas team to concentrate on recovering remains and evidence rather than running all over camp for anything they needed. If this kept up, he might even make it back to the War Room to finish copying the last frescoes. Now, *that* he'd enjoy.

Still smiling, he lifted his coffee cup — only to find it empty. Ah well, there couldn't always be sunshine. Avi wanted to show him something over at the new dig site, anyway. He'd hit the *cocina* for more coffee on the way.

As he stepped into the commons, he was surprised to see La Antigua Taberna's delivery van pulling into camp. Seeing the vehicle itself wasn't all that unusual. La Taberna was a cantina owned by Manuel Conde's family, and run by Manny's brother, Teodoro. When Manny was first hired as cook, it had been decided that the camp's provisions would be bought in conjunction with the cantina's. It was a cost-saving arrangement beneficial to both parties — but the week's supplies had already been delivered. Josh knew this because he'd helped unload them.

The truck pulled into the usual place beside the cook tent, but when the driver swung down, it wasn't Teodoro Conde. It was Teo's eldest daughter, Aida. Now that *was* a surprise. He'd rarely seen the young woman outside the Taberna where she waited tables and helped her mother in the kitchen of an evening.

He quickened his pace and called out, "*¡Hola, Aida!* What are you doing so far from home base?"

The beautiful young woman turned and a smile broke across her face like sunrise. "*¡Gatito!*" she exclaimed, and ran to greet him with a big kiss.

Laughing, Josh pulled away. "Whoa! Careful! Your father and uncle will skin me alive."

Aida sniffed and tossed her hair carelessly, then towed him back to the truck. Opening the back doors, she said, "With so many of the policia from town working up here, Uncle Manuel and cousin Luis needed extra supplies and help, so Papi sent me."

"Yeah, it *has* gotten a little more crowded since we uncovered our unexpected guest."

At the mention of the bones, her face clouded and she crossed herself. "Oh, Gatito, this is so terrible."

Surprised by the depth of her reaction, he asked, "Why?"

"Who but a *huaquero* would be buried in such a way and forgotten? Surely evil must follow such a one."

"Worried about ghosts?"

She laughed suddenly, her dark mood vanishing. "Of course not! My concern is with the living — the hungry living." She swatted him playfully and tugged at a big box. "Come, you will help me carry the food into the *cocina, sí?*"

"Foolish girl! Gatito has enough to do without doing our work, too," Manny Conde said, emerging from the cook tent. "Luis will help you. Quickly, now, today I will teach you how to roast *pollo y papas* in the clay oven and it takes time to heat."

"Seriously?" Josh said. "Oh man, I wish I could hang around for that. You're right, though, I gotta get over to the new site — right after my no coffee situation is rectified." He held his empty mug out. "*¿Por favor?*"

~*~

Katzen brushed loose soil away from the tiny green bead. Straightening, he rolled the vibrant artifact in the palm of his hand. "Yep," he said at last. "It's definitely a new pit; a few days old at most. My guess is they found a cache."

"My thoughts, too—" Suddenly angry, Rosenberg hurled a clump of clay against a boulder. "*Dammit!* I'd hoped they were done and had moved on from this place."

"It was only a matter of time," Katzen said. He dropped the lonely bead into an envelope, wrote the GPS co-ordinates on it and buttoned it into his shirt pocket. "El Mago and his goons have been circling for quite a while, anyway. Once we started pulling new finds out of the ground, we became an inevitable target."

"Tell me about it. I suppose we should count ourselves lucky that they've held off this long — especially after that dustup at the end of last season." He paused as a realization struck him. "That's why you've been so buggy about getting those murals copied, isn't it? You're afraid Mago's crew will come in with chainsaws and we'll wake up to rough-cut blank walls some morning."

"Busted. I didn't want to say it out loud. You know: if you don't say it, it won't happen?"

"I wish it worked that way."

"Ah ha! There you are!"

Startled, they turned to find Amelia Peters pushing through the tangled growth. "Robert said you two wandered off this way, but we couldn't raise you on the radio."

Josh looked down at the walkie-talkie clipped to his belt and togged the off-on switch a few times. Nothing. "Oops. Looks like my battery died. I'll have to head back to the workshop for a replacement." He grinned. "Some problems remain unchanged."

Rosenberg, looking concerned, held back a bramble to allow her to pass. "Is there a problem?"

"We found a—" she said, then broke off as she looked just beyond Katzen. "Oh. You found one, too. I bet there are lots more we haven't seen yet."

"I'm afraid you'll win that bet, 'Melia." The archaeologist shook his head. "Our nearest neighbor, Piedras Rojas is a fairly prosperous little town. It tends to make us forget that there are other towns and villages close by that are not."

Josh tapped the pocket containing the bead. "*Huaquero* invasion or no, I still have a stray bead and a dead battery on my hands. I'll head back to camp to catalog one and put the other in the charger."

Amelia chewed her lip. "Maybe I better come with you and get a fresh battery for my radio, too. Sounds kind of wussy, but with the *huaqueros* nosing around the dig again, I want to keep this guy in working order more than ever."

~*~

The cool, dim interior of the workshop was welcome after the trek through the dusty hills under the mid-day sun. Threatened heat-stroke and peril of robbers notwithstanding, Amelia had regained her characteristic good humor.

"I really need to hurry," she said, popping the old battery out and slotting it into the recharger. "They're about to start the actual *digging*."

"You'll be back on line in a jiffy," Josh said. The box of fresh power packs was right at the front of the supply cabinet. He broke the seal and tossed her one. "It's an archaeological excavation. There'll be plenty of digging to go around. Trust me. I've been to a few."

"I know it's silly, but this is the part I love most — the first day. The *promise* of discovery. Not that the actual discovery itself isn't exciting, but the mystery of what we'll find. . . ." Snapping the back on her radio, she tested it then said, "Well, that's me recharged. I better get this thing back before the parade starts marching through that door again."

The workshop door opened and Avi Rosenberg stepped through carrying three condensation-bedewed water bottles.

"Right on cue," Josh said.

Amelia burst out laughing.

Rosenberg's eyes narrowed. There was definitely a joke, but he wasn't sure what it was. "Ahhhh. Yeah. I brought you guys some water. The sun's brutal out there today."

Amelia took the offered bottle and hurried out. "Thanks! See you back at the site in a few!"

Chuckling, Josh watched the door swing shut, then said, "You need to marry that girl."

Rosenberg's eyes widened. "*WHAT?*" Glancing at the flimsy corrugated metal walls of the workshop, he lowered his voice. "What do you mean by that?"

"Whoa! Down, Big Fella." Josh said. "That was a joke."

Avi collapsed onto a stool and scrubbed his palms over his face. After a moment he managed, "Sorry, man. I know it was, it's just. . . ."

"Just that you can't be involved with a student in any way?"

"Exactly."

"She finishes her doctorate next year. She won't *be* a student then."

The big man jumped up and jabbed a finger in his friend's direction. "Dammit, Josh, she's a child."

"No, she's a young woman."

Avi said nothing, but was as close to blind fury as Josh had ever seen him. Josh leaned against the workbench and said quietly, "Look, I'm serious this time. Sure, it's hilarious to see the two of you going around pretending you hardly see each other—" he held up a hand to cut off Rosenberg's incipient tirade "—for the first day or so. After that it just gets to be painful."

"She looks on me as a teacher. A mentor. Period."

"Right." He paused. "Well in for a penny. . . . Man, you can't grieve forever. You have to move on."

Katzen braced himself for an explosion, but his friend's anger drained away as quickly as it had built. "Josh—" Rosenberg's voice caught. He swallowed hard. "You *know* the pain of losing someone close to you. You've been through it more than once. That suicide bomber took more than my wife and daughter that day in Tel-Aviv. It was like a part of my soul died with Revkah and Yasmin."

"You're right. I do know that pain. That's why I also know that you have to move on — or at least try to."

Avi laughed bitterly. "You and Vic. Do you have the same scriptwriter or something?"

Before Josh could respond, Rosenberg continued. "I've tried, man, I have. Since Revkah died I haven't been able to sustain a relationship with a woman my own age. How could I even consider one with a girl—" at Josh's look he corrected "—OKAY — *young woman* who is only slightly older than my own daughter would have been had she lived? I know a woman's age has never made a lot of difference to you, but it does to me." He took a deep breath. "Can we talk about something else? *Please?*"

"Hey! You make me sound like a cradle-robber or something!" Josh said in mock indignation.

"You know what I mean. Can we drop it now?"

Raising both hands in surrender, Josh said, "Okay. Subject officially changed: how is the new site coming along?"

"Good. It looks promising. We already had to move the location of the equipment table because, when we cleared the overgrowth, we discovered it was sitting in the middle of a paved courtyard."

"Wow. Another temple?"

"I don't think so—"

The walkie-talkie in the middle of the workbench crackled and Amelia's voice came through slightly distorted by the tiny speaker. "Dr. Rosenberg?"

They both stared at the device. It crackled again, "Dr. Rosenberg? We need you at the new dig site. No emergency, but we need to know where to start the first test pits."

Avi pressed the send button, "Be right there, 'Melia."

"Okay," she said and the radio went quiet.

Avi grinned at Josh. "Well, so much for resting for a few."

Josh tossed a bottle of water to him. "Don't forget this. It's not quite as good as sitting in the shade, but it beats desiccation by a damn sight."

~*~

It took longer than normal to set up in the War Room again. The days spent working the crime scene had broken his routine and it was harder to get back into the groove than he expected. The cats that had been hanging around in the hills had gone. Probably moved on to better hunting grounds when their easy food supply dried up.

Ingrates, Katzen thought with a chuckle. At least he wouldn't have to rescue his kneadable eraser every few minutes. He missed the furry thieves, though. Stroking them had often helped him break through when he was having trouble. He settled back, studying the flow of line and color in the ancient scenes, then picked up his pencils and lost himself in the artwork, tapping the reflectors from time to time to keep the light constant.

It seemed like no time had passed when, no matter how he tapped or readjusted the reflectors, it did no good. With a start, he realized that it was because the sun was setting and there simply wasn't enough light to reflect. Bummer. Still, he'd gotten a lot done. Tomorrow he'd finish the current drawing and get a start on the last mural. He'd have to rely on the solar lantern to pack his materials. Harper was going to hang him out to dry for losing track of time again. He was surprised that no one—

The radio crackled. "Josh . . . you do know it's getting dark, don't you?"

Sometimes he just plain hated being right. He lifted the radio. "Oh, is *that* why I can't see any more?"

Harper's answering laugh sounded odd through the small speaker. "That would probably be it, yes."

He started to reply, then stopped at the sound of small rocks sliding on the path outside. His good humor evaporated. "Okay, okay, I'm coming in now, you didn't have to send an escort."

"Escort?" Harper sounded confused. "I didn't send anyone."

Dread replaced irritation. "Ah. Just a sec."

Muting the walkie-talkie, he crept to the entrance and peeked out. Five men slid down the rockface on the other side of the small courtyard. They were coming from the opposite direction of camp and the waning sunlight glinted off of the two large chainsaws they carried.

Ducking back, he doused the lantern and keyed the radio. "Harper, get Avi and Regina ASAP. There's a group of *huaqueros* approaching the War Room from the north."

"Oh my god! Get out of there, Josh. NOW!"

"Can't. They have me boxed in." The scraping got louder. "Going silent. Hurry."

Turning off the radio, he put it down within arm's reach and used what natural light still bled into the chamber to search for a weapon. All he saw was his drawing board. *Deju vu all over again.* He snatched it up and took up a position beside the doorway. They were close enough now, he could hear them talking among themselves, voices low, their Spanish held the local accent.

"It will be fine." Said one. "Everyone is down in the camp or on the way back to town by now."

"Are you sure?"

"Of course. Look around. Do you see anyone?"

One was nervous. His words fairly quivered with it. "There are *policia* all over the camp, though. Maybe we should wait—"

"Shut up, Tomas," said another so close that Josh could probably have reached around and touched him. "El Mago wants these paintings, so we will get them for him."

The first man spoke again. He had to be right in the passage. "*Silencio*, Antonio, no one said we would not do the job, but there is no need to make it a picnic, either. Cut the things free so we can get out of here, get paid and go home."

The doorway and the short entry passage were narrow; a natural choke-point. Katzen knew the only way they could enter was single file with the bulky saws held out in front of them. That would be in his favor even if numbers weren't. Eyes now adjusted to the semi-darkness of the chamber, he waited until the long, flat blade of a chainsaw poked into the room. A moment later, the hands holding it came into view and he brought the board down edge first.

The man's scream resounded in the small space and the saw bounced across the floor flinging bits of packed earth in its wake.

Confusion broke out behind the howling *huaquero*. Josh took advantage of it and brought the board around again, slamming it into the injured man's forehead. The blow stunned him. A roundhouse kick added backward velocity and sent the dazed would-be thief stumbling into his compatriots. Katzen had hoped for a domino effect, but only partially got it. Numbers two and three went down according to plan. However, number four, a short, wiry young man, dove into the room over the struggling mass of arms, legs and equipment packs. The tomb robber rolled to his feet, brandishing a knife, but his eyes weren't used to the interior gloom and he couldn't see his opponent.

Josh didn't give him time to adjust and launched a kick. It missed, but made the man take a step back. Dropping the board, he grabbed the man's knife-hand and pulled hard, slamming the arm against the edge of the ancient adobe doorway. The bone snapped audibly, the knife clattered to the packed-earth floor and the man dropped to his knees clutching the injured arm. The dim light fell across the *huaquero's* face as he crabbed away to get out of Katzen's reach. Josh recoiled in surprise. It was a boy barely into his teens.

He paid for the lapse in concentration. He was seized from behind and thrown hard against the entryway. Head ringing, he stumbled through and fell into the twilight amid a storm of kicks and punches. The onslaught stopped as abruptly as it began as shouting and the pounding of many feet grew nearer. The three *huaqueros* that could, tried to run, but Katzen was too angry to let that happen. He tangled his foot in one's legs, causing him to pitch headlong and slide several feet. Avi Rosenberg was on the thief in a second, lifting the boy off the ground as casually as he would a kitten.

Lt. Regina Quijano and two other officers pelted past them on the trail of the runners.

Chief Ruiz and Harper Armand ran to Josh, who was trying to pull himself up. "Glad to see you, *Jefe*. Didn't know you were on site."

"I had just arrived when the alarm was raised," Diego said, pushing him back firmly. "Stay where you are, Gatito. The situation is in my hands now."

Grim-faced, Harper put her medical bag down and shined her flashlight into his eyes. "You have blood on your forehead. Is your vision blurry in any way?"

"I'm okay. They never really landed anything solid."

"*¡Dios!*" Diego's exclamation startled them both. They looked up to find him staring toward the young man Avi Rosenberg had hold of.

Harper looked first confused, then intensely sad. "Oh no. That's

Emilio Placido, isn't it?"

Josh frowned. "Placido? As in Officer Hernan Placido?"

"His son," Diego said quietly.

After a moment, Josh said, "There's two more inside. One's another kid. The kid's got a broken arm and the other guy probably has a helluva concussion."

Uncertain, Harper looked at Katzen, then past him through the dark square of the door. Soft sobbing came from inside the chamber.

"There's a solar lantern just to the right of the door — there's also a knife and a chainsaw somewhere in there, so be careful."

The police chief nodded, then headed into the chamber. Taking her medical bag, the doctor followed.

There were a few bad moments when Lt. Quijano and officers Reyes and Placido returned from their fruitless chase. It only took a second for Hernan Placido to notice his son looking small beside Dr. Rosenberg. The emotions that flashed across his square face were heartbreaking.

Avi relinquished the boy into his father's custody and came over to where Josh sat with his back against the rockface. "You okay?"

"More or less. Dammit. They're just kids."

"Sometimes age *is* irrelevant," the big man said. His eyes slid to where the police officer was glaring at his son in silence, torn between anger and tears. He looked away, staring up into the canopy of stars for a while before he said, "Well, I guess we know how they found their way to this particular site now."

Josh nodded mutely. He'd lied earlier. The *huaqueros* had landed a number of solid blows before the cavalry arrived. He could tell there'd been no serious damage, but there were going to be some uncomfortable days in his immediate future.

CHAPTER 5

It was a small room, most of it taken up by a stainless steel examination table that was worn to a satin finish by innumerable scrubbings. The battered wooden cabinets and counters usually held nothing more than cotton balls, alcohol and a few first-aid items; today, they were stacked with white pasteboard boxes and plastic Ziploc evidence bags. Josh Katzen edged past Regina Quijano to slide two more boxes onto the stack, they were long to accommodate leg bones and hung over the edge a little.

"That's the last of them," he said. "Now what?"

Victor Pale looked up from his checklist. "Now Regina and I put Humpty Dumpty back together again and you take photos of the process."

Avi Rosenberg still stood partway out in the hall to avoid adding his bulk to the already crowded room. He shook his head and said, "I dunno, guys. I've been watching you dig all this stuff out and it doesn't look like you have a helluva lot to go on. Even the artifacts you found with the bones don't say a lot. Yeah, they're all local, but from a wide range of cultures and eras. That tells us the guy was probably involved in looting, but not much else."

Victor's long face split in a grin. "You amaze me. You of all people should know how much can be learned from skeletal remains. For instance. . . ." He opened one of the long boxes and carefully removed a bone. "Left femur. Robust so most likely belonging to a male. From the length of the bone, we can estimate his height at around six feet. Fairly large muscle attachments, so I'd guess he walked a lot. Maybe hiked."

Rosenberg shrugged. "Safe assumption considering the area in which he was found and that we suspect he was a looter. This still doesn't tell us much."

Pale replaced the long bone in the box and opened another square one and carefully lifted the skull from it. "We can now add that our guy was Caucasian. Late forties, early fifties. COD single GSW—"

Lt. Quijano looked confused. "Excuse me, Dr. Pale. This COD I know: it is a postal fee, but GSW I do not know."

"In this case, COD stands for cause of death and GSW is shorthand for gunshot wound, 'Gina. Sorry about that. I tend to lapse into Medical Examinerese from time to time. Just jab me with an elbow if I get too cryptic." He placed the skull on the stainless steel examination table, and pointed to a round hole at the back of it. "Here's our cause of death: single gunshot wound to the back of the head. From the shattering, close range — execution style. Not a huge hole, not a small one . . . Probably something like a .32. No exit wound. The fragments are still in the skull."

"Avi's got a point," Josh said. "That describes the guy, but but doesn't tell us *who* he was."

"Ah! We have hope that this will do that for us." Regina dug in an evidence box and pulled out the bag holding the shattered gold wristwatch. "Chief Ruiz and Dr. Pale remembered a case where a murder victim was identified by the registration of his Rolex watch."

"I think I remember that," Josh said. "Back in the Eighties, right?"

Vic nodded. "A guy — or what was left of him — was pulled out of the English Channel in a fishing net. The only thing still identifiable was his watch. The Rolex folks keep very good records of their pieces."

"And. . . ," Regina said, lifting another bag, "he had many coins in his pockets. None newer than 1986."

"And, he's probably American," Vic added. "Most of the coins are US currency and his clothes seem to be American manufacture, too. Good quality. They stood up to a couple decades of burial pretty well."

"The *Jefe* isn't too happy about the man being *Americano*," Regina said frowning. "He says international things can get very messy."

"He's got that right," Katzen muttered, then looked around. "Pretty good room! A little small, but it's not a big clinic. Did Harper swing this?"

Rosenberg shifted in the doorway. "Yeah, she did. Truth to tell, though, the doctor was more than willing. The skeleton in the platform has become a hot topic around the square and in the *cantinas*."

Katzen laughed, "Yeah, I've been hearing some of that. Some of the theories are waaaaay out there."

"Well, let's try to produce some facts to go with the fantasy," Pale said, setting the now-empty skull box aside. He turned to Katzen. "I seem to keep apologizing to you in this thing. It's going to take you away from your copying for a few more days. I'm especially sorry given the *huaquero* incident last night."

Josh waved it away. "The way I look at it, the sooner this is done and in the hands of the proper authorities, the sooner we're *all* back to what we're here to do. Besides, this will get me out of Harper's sight. Every time she sees me, she reaches for the antiseptic and antibiotic cream."

Pale looked him over critically. "Well, you do look sorta like you fell over a cliff into a cactus patch."

Quijano nodded.

"Yeeeah. Ya sorta do," Rosenberg said.

"Ah," Katzen sneered. "It'll clear up in no time. Let's get to work."

~*~

The black Chevy Suburban's motor ran so quietly that the first Katzen knew of its approach was when he saw it stop in the middle of camp through the open door of the workshop. It couldn't have said "Official Vehicle" any clearer if it had signs painted on the doors. Through the heavily tinted windows, he could see two people, but that was the extent of it until the driver's door opened and a man stepped out onto the dusty commons. He wore a tailored linen suit and sunglasses; his short-cropped hair was shot through with gray. If the SUV said "Official", the man *screamed* "cop". Abruptly, he leaned back into the car, then straightened again.

From inside, a woman demanded, "Give that back!"

"Nope," the man said, pocketing a flat, square object. "You been messing with your damned puzzles since we left Trujillo. I'm tired of listening to myself talk."

The woman stepped out of the passenger side. She was pretty, younger than the man and dressed in a more feminine version of the linen suit. Her long dark hair was pulled into a twist at the back of her head and secured with a pair of silver combs. She was not a happy camper. "Stop treating me like a twelve-year-old."

The man pulled his sunglasses part-way down his nose and regarded her over them. "Then, stop acting like a twelve-year-old. We're here on official business, Tessa. There are plenty of other places I'd like to be, too. How 'bout you pretend you're a DSS agent for a little while? The sooner we pick up this report from this Pale guy, the sooner we can get our asses back to Trujillo and on the jet to Lima."

She slammed the car door and said, "Yeah. Crime scene data and a medical report on a pile of bones of some ex-pat thief who got himself killed. What moron let a has-been rock star who's watched too much CSI process a crime scene, anyway?"

The older man pointedly slid his sunglasses back into place using his middle finger, then strode toward the workshop.

Josh busied himself at his laptop, giving no indication he'd heard any of the exchange outside. He even managed a somewhat surprised look when the man rapped sharply on the wooden doorframe.

"Afternoon! Special Agent Reid Bramwell of the Diplomatic Security Service," he said, holding up a case containing a photo ID and a badge. "This is my partner Special Agent Theresa Caballero. We're here to see a Dr. Victor Pale? Police chief in Piedras Rojas said he was up here today."

Katzen plastered on a smile and came around the desk with his hand extended. "Hi! Josh Katzen, staff artist, photographer and general dogsbody. I bet you're here about our skeleton in the collapsed pyramid. I didn't know anyone had contacted the U.S. authorities yet."

"You'd win your bet, Mr. Katzen." Bramwell shook the proffered hand; his grip was firm and no-nonsense. "Actually, the *Policia Nacional* flagged us when your Chief Ruiz informed them the remains might be those of an American. Can you point us to Dr. Pale? We're here to collect copies of the forensic reports for the embassy in Lima."

"I can do better than that, just a sec." He lifted the walkie talkie. "Hey, Vic, you there?"

After a moment, Victor came back, "Ya, Josh, what do you need?"

"Special Agents Bramwell and Caballero from the Diplomatic Security Service are here to see you. About the guy in the platform."

"Ah. The omnipresent paperwork, bane of my existence even down here. I'm over at the new dig site, I can be there in a few."

"There we go. Sorta kinda modern technology making life easier in the Peruvian mountains." Katzen clipped the radio back onto his belt. "Would you guys like to wait in the *cocina*? We have hot coffee or cold water *or* if we're lucky, our cook, Manny, might have whipped up one of his *aguas frescas*. Those are not to be missed, I assure you."

Twenty minutes later, when Victor Pale entered, the three of them were at a table in the *cocina*, savoring cold glasses of Manny's melon *agua frescas*. He slid into a chair and handed each agent a stapled sheaf of paper. "Here it is, folks. Still warm from the printer."

Special Agent Caballero set aside her glass and began reading. Special Agent Bramwell looked at his copy and raised an eyebrow. "Cook County?"

"I'm an ME with Cook County, Illinois, back in the states. I already had all the forms on my laptop, so I used them as an expedient."

"Works for me," the agent said leafing through. He looked up again."Hey, weren't you some kinda rockgod or something?"

"I don't know about the deification," Pale said with a laugh, "but I *was* the lead singer and guitarist for the Wolfpack. That was a long time ago in another life, though." Not allowing a space for response, he slid on a pair of frameless reading glasses and launched into a preliminary analysis. "Our skeleton appears to be a six-foot tall Caucasian male, mid-forties to mid-fifties . . . that's the straight-forward stuff. The really interesting part is a bit of a chicken and egg thing. Death from the head wound was probably instantly fatal. The bullet was still in the cranial cavity — well, what was left of the bullet, anyway. The thing fragmented pretty badly, the weight was consistent with something like a .32 and the shrapnel probably scrambled things real good. Still, the collapse happened very close to the time of death. The bone of the skull was green enough when it happened that it compressed rather than crushed. That makes it kind of hard to say if if the actual bottom line was death by lead pellet or mudbrick." He leafed back a few pages. "Our guy was in pretty good shape. Not much dental work — couple cavities filled with silver amalgam, so there might still be a few records floating around if we can ever put a name to him."

Caballero looked up from her perusal of the printout. From her expression, Katzen wondered if Vic's professionalism had made her rethink her earlier comment about a has-been rock star who'd watched too many forensic TV shows. She wouldn't be the first to have to shift that mental gear.

The agent asked, "His clothes were American?"

Victor nodded. "The ones that had labels were. He was wearing something called a Photojournalist's Vest from the Banana Republic stores. I gather they're no longer made. That and the US coins in his pockets point to a date of death sometime in the mid-eighties."

"Whoa," Bramwell said. "That's almost ancient history. What else we got?"

"All-in-all, it was a pretty clean scene. No brass or other trace. Makes me wonder if the shooter cleaned up before toppling the structure onto the victim."

Katzen had been unobtrusively watching Caballero as they talked. There was a dichotomy about her that he found attractive: her almost masculine suit contrasting with the very feminine blouse, the severity of her hairstyle against the ornateness of what looked to be antique silver combs. She startled him a little by leaning forward and tapping a well-shaped lacquered nail against a page of the report.

"What about all this other stuff? These artifacts?" she asked.

"Now, *that* was a mess," Pale said. "They were all small objects. Mostly gold with a few silver and jade items thrown in. Best way to reconstruct is that the victim fell onto a cloth bag full of artifacts. This ripped a seam, spilling the objects onto the floor and the collapse of the structure further scattered them."

"The killer or killers just walked away from all that? Probably not an argument among thieves, then," she said.

"Good call," Josh agreed. "No thief is going to voluntarily leave loot lying there *then* drop a few tons of adobe on top of it."

Bramwell gave him an assessing look. "Pretty good observation, Mr. Katzen. Do you know much about law enforcement?"

Josh shook his head. "Nah. I've just had a few too many up close and personal experiences with *huaqueros* and would-be treasure hunters."

"Oh yeah." Bramwell said. "We're forever having to deal with some moron who comes down here thinking they can dig up a couple souvenirs for the office shelf back home. Now I think of it, didn't Chief Ruiz say you guys had an incident not too long ago?"

"We did," Josh said. "Ours was a pure home-grown problem, though. Some local boys hoping to score some stuff for our resident crimelord, el Mago."

"We've heard plenty about *him*, too," Caballero said, then flipped to another page in the stack in front of her. "This is amazingly thorough, Dr. Pale. How'd you get so much from a few dry bones? Magic?"

"You'd be amazed what dry bones can tell you if you know the right questions to ask," Vic answered with a smile. "Would you folks like to see the crime scene itself? It's not too far from here."

They stopped in the commons for the agents to put the paperwork into the SUV and for Bramwell to retrieve a battered digital camera from under the seat.

"Might as well snap a few pics of the site while we're there," he said checking the capacity of the memory card. "Nothing seems to make the brass smile like a couple blurry snapshots."

Katzen said, "If you need photos, I can dupe the memory cards of the ones I took during the excavation."

"That'd be great!" Bramwell said. "Much appreciated."

Caballero shaded her eyes and looked around. "Nice camp. Looks kind of permanent, though. More like a small community than a camp."

"You're not far wrong," Josh said. "We've been working this site for five years and there are probably that many more before we finish. Doesn't look like much on first glance, but there's a lot here."

Caballero's sudden smile lit her face, changing pretty to downright lovely. "This is an awful thing to say — especially coming from a law enforcement officer, but I can see where the treasure hunters are coming from. There's something sort of magical about the idea of unearthing some precious, ancient thing that no one has laid eyes on in thousands of years."

Bramwell snorted. "As long as she's been stationed here in Peru, you'd think she'd stop painting archaeological expeditions as something out of an Indiana Jones movie."

Caballero started to retort, then stopped, staring at a point beyond Katzen's shoulder. Finally she said. "Yeah? Well, I might have a point from time to time."

Josh didn't have to turn to know what the DSS agent was looking at. He turned, anyway. Yep. There was Dr. Avi Rosenberg striding across the compound, broad-brimmed straw hat jammed over the bandanna tied to corral his dark, wavy hair; his loose-fitting cotton shirt did little to conceal his physique. Josh hid a smile — he'd heard enough of the same comments before. If Rosenberg wasn't so damned impressive, he might be jealous. All *he* usually got were comments about James Cagney or bantam roosters.

Aloud, he said, "Enter Doc Rosenberg, stage right. Don't worry, he doesn't mind Indiana Jones so much, just don't call him Belzoni if you value life and limb."

Caballero looked confused. She whispered to her partner, "Who's Belzoni?"

Reid whispered back, "No clue. We'll Google it later."

As the big man neared, he called out, "Ah, Agents Bramwell and Caballero! I was hoping I could catch you before you left. I heard Josh announce you over the walkie-talkie earlier, but couldn't get away before now."

Reid Bramwell stepped forward, hand extended. "Dr. Rosenberg, I presume. I hope we haven't interrupted your work too much."

Bramwell tried not to look amazed as the archaeologist's bronzed hand engulfed his own. "You haven't interrupted my work anywhere near as much as the jerk who got my ceremonial platform dropped on him or the other jerks who dropped it on him. So, have you folks got everything you need? I'm anxious to get this behind us so we can get back on schedule."

"We think so, Doc," Caballero said, extending her own hand. "Once we sign for the physical evidence from Chief Ruiz on our way out of town, we should be set."

"He's boxing it up for us right now. All except one piece that I understand he sent on to a lab in Lima?"

"That would be the Rolex," Rosenberg said.

"That was it," Caballero nodded. "When we phoned him this morning, he said something about trying to get a name with it."

"That's what they tell me. Apparently, Rolex keeps very good records and this one was the real deal. Me? I wouldn't know. It's too new for my area of expertise."

"Just as long as no one pockets the evidence before it reaches its destination. Those things are valuable," Caballero said.

Josh laughed. "Not much worry there. The thing's in pretty bad shape after having a few tons of mud brick dropped on it. It has more value as evidence than as a watch at this point."

"Very true," Pale said. "It looked like someone whacked it with a sledge a few times." He jerked a thumb over his shoulder. "We were heading over to the platform. Want to come with?"

"Sure," Rosenberg said. "Let's move."

~*~

The light from the workshop doorway was blotted out as Avi Rosenberg leaned in. "Hey, they need Vic and me back at the dig. I'm gonna have to leave our friendly Feds in your hands. You okay with that?"

It never ceased to amaze Josh how much trouble his friend had with authority figures, especially those connected with the government. Josh laughed. "Yeah, I'll be fine. This is the last bunch of photos, so they'll be out of your hair soon."

The archaeologist nodded gravely, then turned to wave once at the agents and was gone. Through the now unblocked doorway, Katzen could see the two Special Agents waiting by the car for the photos he was duplicating. As he watched,

Caballero held out her hand and wiggled her fingers at her partner.

Bramwell shook his head, dug into his pocket and slapped the flat, square thing into her waiting palm. "There. You and these damned puzzles."

She sneered at him, leaned against the side of the SUV and started messing with the thing using her thumbs, her expression contented.

Her partner didn't look anywhere near as happy. He jerked the car door open and perched on the driver's seat, his long legs crossed on the SUV's rocker panel. He shot his cuff and glanced at his watch. "We made good time today. Providing we don't get held up in Piedras Rojas or anything like that, we'll be back in Trujillo in time to catch lunch before the flight to Lima."

"What time does the One Gopher Express take off?"

"Around three."

"Yeah?" Caballero perked up. "I might skip lunch, then. I have some errands I could run."

"Errands? In Trujillo? What the hell do you have to do in Trujillo?"

"Oh . . . shopping . . . shit like that," she said vaguely. "Nothing *you'll* want to do."

Her partner gave her a sharp look, but apparently decided against replying. At that same moment, Katzen's laptop chirped at him, and a pop up window announced that the duplication process had completed. Ejecting the card, he placed it into a manila envelope with the others.

"Good to go!" He called through the door.

Bramwell's gaze swiveled from his partner to Katzen. He slid out of the SUV to meet the artist halfway. "Thanks, these will make the brass very happy campers — they may never *look* at them, but they'll be happy."

"I understand. Bureaucracy is the same everywhere." He cocked his head for a better look at the plastic square in Caballero's hands. It was the kind of puzzle where the user unscrambled a picture by moving tiles around. "Hey! That's kind of cool. I've never seen one of those with an actual photograph on it."

"Don't try to touch it," Bramwell said, leaning forward with mock seriousness. "She may bite your hand off."

"My sister has these made for me," she said, pointedly ignoring her partner. " It's more fun than just getting plain family pictures. This one is from my parent's last anniversary party. I was stationed down here and couldn't make it back."

"Cool idea!" Katzen said.

"Aw, don't encourage her. She's addicted to the things." Bramwell waved it away. "Anyway, we're outta here. Thanks for all your help, Mr. Katzen."

CHAPTER 6

The Piedras Rojas police station had been built in the 1960s in that seemingly ubiquitous style that could have just as easily been an elementary school or municipal offices. That morning, it was full almost to overflowing. The town's police force wasn't all that large, but it seemed that every member was present. Add in the staff members of the dig site and it made for quite a crowd.

Avi Rosenberg, who distrusted the also ubiquitous molded plastic chairs, leaned against the wall beside Diego Ruiz' desk. "So the guys at Rolex *do* think they can get a name for you?"

"Oh, they are positive of this," Ruiz said. "What they were uncertain of is exactly when they could get the information to me. They have promised it sometime before their close of business today." The police chief shrugged."They are seven hours ahead of us, so that makes it interesting."

"Interesting is one way to describe it," Harper Armand said. "It's probably old hat to most of you guys, but it's pretty exciting from my point of view. This collection of bones was once a living, breathing human being and we're about to find out who he was."

"I can't speak for anyone else, but it never gets old for me, Harper," Vic Pale said. "I always get a buzz when my work pays off like this. Every time. Being able to speak for the dead is one of the main reasons I chose this career."

Yeah, Josh Katzen mused inwardly. He could certainly see how a thirteen-year-old who came home to discover his parents and sister brutally murdered could elicit that response. It would certainly have made *him* think hard about forensics. Then again, given his relationship with his family, he would have probably been the prime suspect had his parents and brother been found murdered. Movement caught his attention. He slid his eyes toward it to find Manny Conde slipping in the front door of the station. He smiled and pointed to an empty chair beside the desk.

After a moment of seeming indecision, Manny shook his head and sank resolutely into a chair beside the door with the air of a man on a mission.

Josh regarded the cook with speculation. There were a lot of bets riding on the identity of the dead man and Teo Conde was known to hold the book on a lot of them. He wondered if Manny had been tapped to be his brother's ears in the station. Shrugging, he turned his attention back to Ruiz. Just in time, it seemed, as the chief's computer chimed, announcing the arrival of an email.

"Ah! We have our response. . . ." Ruiz said, then grew silent as he read. His frown deepened.

Rosenberg pushed away from the wall. "So?"

The police chief hesitated. "We will need to request a comparison of dental records from the American consulate."

"We have a name, though?" Pale interjected.

"*Sí*. We have a name," Ruiz said sitting back. He looked very tired. "The watch was registered to a Herbert O. Deustch III, with home addresses in New York, Rome, London, Mexico City and Lima."

"Whoa, whoa, whoa!" Katzen said. "Deustch? *Herb* Deustch?"

Rosenberg groaned. "Oh man, this just keeps better and better."

"At least he's *dead*," Katzen muttered. "Better than if he should be alive and show up at the site with a shovel and swag bag."

Dr. Armand looked from stunned face to stunned face. At length she said, "Am I the only person here who doesn't know this name? Can someone enlighten me?"

"You aren't missing much, Harper," Pale said. "When I was still in the music scene, I moved in some of the same circles as his family — you know, the department store folks? This guy was the black sheep to put it mildly."

"He was a bad one. Prone to violence," Diego agreed.

"He was also one of the most infamous looters of antiquities of the last century. He was noted as much for his shady business dealings as his violent temper," Katzen said.

"The man is *still* infamous in archaeological circles," Rosenberg said. "Deustch and his ring of pals systematically looted sites all over the world and funneled the stolen artifacts through legitimate auction houses."

Amelia Peters, who had been listening quietly, looked puzzled. "I've heard about that and I always wondered how they managed it."

Josh answered without thinking. "There are a number of ways to do that, but Deustch mostly used the fake provenance gambit. He was from a well-connected family and they had a lot of friends who collected antiquities. He had a partner. An Italian national — also from a prominent family — who ran a chain of galleries in the US and Europe. Whenever they needed a history for a hot piece, all they had to do was create a false provenance from some friend's well-established collection and voila: instant legitimate artifact. Kickback for the friend and a big chunk of cash for Ol' Herb and his partner. Hard to say how many objects are sitting in museums around the world by virtue of a forged receipt."

The girl was wide-eyed. "Wow, Josh, you know a lot about that stuff."

"Not really, 'Melia. It's just that art and antiquities tend to overlap and what happened after Deustch vanished was pretty memorable."

"I remember that, too," said Vic. "Didn't a lot of his associates suddenly find themselves neck deep in legal trouble? Seems to me a couple others wound up dead."

"Yep," Josh said. "That was it. No one seemed to know what actually happened to the guy."

"What happened is pretty horrible," Amelia said. "Sure he was a bad guy, but who would have done something like this?"

"A bad man such as this one makes many enemies. The list of who would have wanted him dead would have been very long," Ruiz said quietly.

~*~

The expedition staff were still subdued as they left the police station. Given the circumstances of the man's death and the items found with him, they had expected their skeleton would belong to a looter. No one had expected to find it belonged to one of the most infamous looters of the past century.

They also weren't expecting a welcoming committee.

Standing between them and the camp's beat-up Mercedes van was what, at first glance, appeared to be half the town. On a closer look, it was merely the Conde family. There were times Josh wondered if the descriptions were mutually exclusive. Still, the family presence validated his earlier suspicion that Manny had been appointed official listener.

Teodoro Conde was older than Manuel by several years and was acting head of the Conde family, so it was no surprise when he stepped forward as spokesman. The man looked worried, almost frightened and his expression was mirrored in the faces of the group behind him.

"Dr. Avi," the *cantina* owner began respectfully. "We know that you do not believe in our rituals, but we would like to beg a favor of you. This man, the one who died in the pyramid. Some of us remember him. He was a very evil man."

"I certainly won't argue on that point, Teo. What's the favor?"

"Such evil does not go quietly, Dr. Avi. We would like for our shaman, Javier Guerrero, to perform a ceremony in the ruins to settle this troublesome spirit and send him on to the next world."

Rosenberg started to reply, then stopped and looked thoughtful.

Finally, he said, "Y'know what, Teo? Ordinarily, you'd be right about me and rituals — rituals of any kind, not just yours — but there's been something deeply wrong at the camp all this season. Tell Javier to come on up and bring his biggest guns with him."

A murmur of approval and relief swept through the crowd.

CHAPTER 7

The next morning, La Antigua Taberna's van pulled up with Manny at the wheel and people piling out of the back like a parade clown car. The man sitting in the passenger seat had to be the shaman, but he wasn't anything like Josh expected. His mental central casting department had automatically assigned an old man with a heavily lined face wearing richly embroidered alpaca wool Andean clothing. Perhaps Javier Guerrero would eventually look like that, but right then, he was a surprisingly young man with a face straight from a Moche portrait pot, dressed incongruously in faded blue jeans and a red plaid shirt.

Guerrero swung nimbly down from the truck and shook hands with everyone, then he squinted at the sky. "We have a little while before I can begin the ceremony. We must wait for the sun to reach its peak to honor Inti since we will be cleansing a place sacred to him."

With that, he moved a short distance away, and opening a pouch slung over his shoulder, withdrew a leather band with feathers stitched to it and a knife knapped from obsidian. He chanted briefly, holding the items out and up, then put the leather band around his forehead and strode into the tangle of trees that surrounded the camp. Chanting softly as he walked, he stopped periodically, head cocked to listen.

Manny leaned over and whispered, "He is letting the plants speak to him, to tell him which will be most important for this place."

Before long, the shaman had disappeared from sight into the woods.

~*~

When the sun reached its zenith, the members of the excavation team were sitting on the ground in a semi-circle along with Diego Ruiz and Regina Quijano. Directly in front of them, Javier Guerrero knelt over a three-legged incense burner, chanting in Quechua and wafting fragrant smoke from a lump of copal over the assemblage with a fan of condor feathers. Behind the shaman, several other townspeople accompanied the chant with rattles, pipes and drums. It was a heady mix. When Josh closed his eyes, he easily imagined how it must have looked when the ancient town was alive, and the ruins were new and fresh with bright paint. It became so vivid, it was a jolt to open his eyes to brown and tumbled adobe rather than the vibrant scene his mind had painted.

Javier had moved. He no longer knelt by the incense burner, but was filling a bowl with water from a large earthenware pitcher. He lifted the bowl and a bundle of fragrant, freshly cut flowers and herbs heavenward. Dipping the herbs into the water, the shaman moved toward the platform, half walking, half dancing, circling the ancient sacred grounds, sprinkling the water with the herbs like a cleansing rain. Setting the bowl aside, he took a mouthful of liquid from a bottle and sprayed it into the air over the tumbled platform. Dancing over to where the archaeology team sat, he sprayed another mouthful into the air over them. The fine mist smelled of pungent herbs and tingled slightly where it landed on Josh's exposed flesh. The shaman repeated the spray with a fresh bowl of water from the jug, then lifted the incense burner and fanned copal smoke over them, as well. On this third pass, he paused in front of Katzen, started to move on, then stopped and dropped to his knees.

Staring deeply into the artist's face, the shaman said, "Gatito, the spirits of this place swirl around you. The evil of this man, Deustch, has put you in more danger than the rest. You are in need of protection — beyond any that I can give, but you must remember that your greatest strength comes from who you are." With that he bowed his head into the incense and, fanning with the condor feathers, caused smoke to billow up around them both.

~*~

As the other participants of the ceremony got into the van to return to town, each one stopped to give Katzen a hug, kiss, shoulder squeeze or gift. In the end, he had two rosaries, several saint cards and a small jade amulet in the shape of a snarling jaguar in his pockets or around his neck.

Moses! He thought. *I feel like it was ME they found in the ruins.*

Someone gave him another shoulder squeeze from behind. It was Vic. Avi stood right behind him and both looked like someone had waltzed over their graves.

"Damn, Josh," Vic all but whispered."That was spooky!"

"Tell me about it," Katzen said. "I was just sitting there waffling between 'this is way cool' and 'ow my butt's going numb' when he comes out of left field with this Zoltar Speaks bit."

"But you didn't even know this guy, right? This Deustch?" Avi asked.

"Nope, not even in passing. He was a big deal in the antiquities market back then and I'd heard of him, but never met him. He disappeared real soon after I came onto the scene."

As the three walked back toward the cook tent, Rosenberg said, "Man! You guys know just how unspiritual I am, but right now *I'm* waffling between being glad I let them come up here and wondering what sort of can of worms I opened up."

His friends meant well, but Katzen had taken about as much sympathy as he could when he spotted Diego Ruiz companionably chatting up Harper Armand. Making a snap decision, he said, "Y'know. I'm sort of bugged, too. I think I want to kick back a little."

"Yeah?" Rosenberg said doubtfully. "I dunno. . . ."

"Avi, shut the fuck up," Pale said waving a warning finger in his friend's face. "Josh, I think that's an excellent idea! What did you have in mind?"

"I thought maybe I'd cadge a ride into town with the *Jefe*. Maybe grab a drink at la Antigua Taberna and stay over at the inn. A little scotch, a hot shower and a sleep-in day might go a long way to calm the heebie jeebies."

CHAPTER 8

Bumming a ride with Ruiz and Quijano was easy, but it didn't take long for him to question the decision. They had hardly left the camp when:

"*Por la cruz*, Josh!" Regina said. "I have seen Javier perform ceremonies before, but never has he done anything like this! Are you okay?"

"Of course he is, Lieutenant," said Ruiz. "Our Little Cat did not even know this evil man. Is this not true, Joshua?"

The echo of Avi's question gave him pause. "Like I said before, I knew *of* him. Very few people in my field don't. He's sort of like the big bad wolf that mommy and daddy archaeologists scare baby archaeologists with."

Both his companions laughed, but before he could take a relieved breath, Ruiz remarked, "I liked what Guerrero said at the last, though. That your strength comes from who you are."

Puzzled, Katzen glanced at Ruiz. "I don't get it. . . ."

"You are — how do they say this in the *Estados Unidos*? A fixer!"

"A fixer? Oh yeah, Diego. You've been watching too much American television."

"Really, *mi amigo*? How about what you did the first year you were here?" He leaned slightly back to address the lieutenant. "You remember, Regina? The time when Eduardo Tovar locked the key to the hotel safe *in* the safe?"

"Oh yes!" Regina said sitting forward with a huge grin. "I remember that. He came to the police station in hysterics because there was only one key and no one knew the combination since his grandfather died."

She reached over the seat back and poked Josh with her finger. "And you simply walked over to it and twirled the dial and it was open."

"Well, I had to do something, my laptop was in it."

Ruiz was laughing harder. "Oh. Of course that is all there was to it!"

"Come on, guys! It's a very old safe and wasn't hard to open. Eduardo could have opened it himself if he'd stopped wailing long enough."

"You have the fine touch of a thief about you, Gatito," Ruiz said as he guided the Rover to a stop in front of the busy cantina. "Was it after the second or third time you made Eduardo write the numbers down?"

"Fourth," Josh said as he slid out and leaned against the top of the door. "But who's counting?"

"Four times? The touch of a thief and the heart of a saint," Diego said.

"Uh huh. Me and Simon Templar." Josh straightened and closed the door. "Hey, why don't you guys come in, too? I'll buy you a couple drinks and you can sit and assassinate my character in relative comfort?"

Regina said, "I will take what you call a storm check? I have not been home all day. My family will be wondering what happened to me."

"Rain check, Gina, but I understand," Josh said. "How about you, *Jefe*?"

Ruiz shook his head. "Sadly I, too, must decline. I have had no word from a shaman, but I firmly believe this Herb Deutsch was evil incarnate. Even dead, he has generated more paperwork for this poor policeman than would a visit from the Pope himself."

Josh laughed and waved as they drove off, but his smile dimmed as they turned the corner out of sight. Stupid. He hadn't even thought about what he was doing with that damned safe of Tovar's, but apparently, Piedras Rojas never forgot it. What he'd said to Ruiz was the simple truth. He'd needed to get his laptop. Opening the safe himself had just been a natural response at the time. Thinking back, he winced at how often he must have tipped his hand and shown who and what he'd been. He was damned lucky to have landed in a place where they accepted that his intentions were good and himself at face value.

Entering la Antigua Taberna, he was met by the familiar smell of old wood, spilled beer and spicy food. To one side of the door, a group of men who worked part time at the excavation greeted him and across the room, Teodoro Conde, Manny's brother and owner of the cantina broke into a huge grin and waved him over. First glance wouldn't have told anyone they were brothers. Where Manny was small and wiry, Teo was built like a fireplug, short and solid.

Making a show of looking around, Teodoro said, "Gatito, I have procured something very special for you." From the mysterious recesses of the counter, he lifted a bottle so Katzen could just see the label.

Josh stared, then breathed, "The Glenlivet? Who do I have to kill?"

Teo's grin lit the room and he poured a double over ice. Pushing the glass over to Katzen, he said, "It is, as you *Norte Americanos* say, on the house."

Josh paused for a moment wondering if the news of the shaman's warning had preceded him into town. Maybe so, but, the *Norte Americanos* also had another saying. One about not looking a gift horse in the mouth. He lifted the glass in salute and said, *"Gracias, mi amigo!"*

Taking his drink, Katzen navigated the smoky barroom and took possession of the most remote booth he could find. He slid into the shadows, settled against the aged cushion and took a sip of the scotch. He exhaled appreciatively. It was the real thing for once.

Someone at his elbow said, "Good evening, Major."

He glanced up into the slightly sunburned face of an obviously Anglo tourist-type standing by the table. Clean-cut. A little too clean-cut. Katzen said, "Sorry, man, you've got the wrong guy."

"I don't think so." The man slid onto the seat opposite and Josh frowned. The man grinned. "Yep. You're the Major, all right. A little thinner and scruffier than Fuller's pics, but I'd know that scowl anywhere."

Something flat and solid landed in Josh's lap under the table. He knew before he looked what he'd see. He tossed it back a little harder than necessary and was gratified by a wince from his uninvited tablemate. "A full bird colonel. Should I be impressed? You people were supposed to leave me alone. That was part of the deal."

"That was before one of your old pals turned up dead in an archaeological dig."

"Herb Deutsch wasn't a friend of mine. I never even met the man. He disappeared from the antiquities scene a long time ago."

"And now we know where he went, don't we?"

"Why does the Pentagon care?" Katzen sat back and took another sip of whiskey. "More to the point, why should *I* care why the Pentagon cares? I'm retired."

"Come on, Durand. People like you never retire."

"Katzen."

"Huh?"

"The name is Joshua Katzen. Please use it."

"Oh. Sorry. Katzen."

"Look, DeVries — is that what you're using down here?"

DeVries laughed. "Sure. Vaughn DeVries, Pentagon desk pilot on a trip to exotic climes to check out the fishing and unwind from the bureaucratic hassle."

The waitress arrived and scootched in beside Katzen, hip-bumping him farther into the booth and giving him a proprietary peck on the cheek. Brushing thick, black hair away from her face, she said, "Gatito! I didn't know you come into town today. Here you come in and sit down and don't even say *hola* or introduce your friend to any of us."

He treated her to a smile, "Please accept my humble apologies, Aida. It was truly a last minute decision, and this is—"

DeVries partly stood and extended his hand across the table. "DeVries, Vaughn DeVries. I'm a friend of Josh's uncle and I promised I'd stop by to pay my regards." Aida took the offered hand as if she were afraid of being burned. He plunked back down into the seat, beaming at Josh. "And here I was all worried that I'd get lost finding my way out to that archaeology dig. Imagine how glad I was to see Josh, here, coming into this place right across from my hotel."

Josh shrugged and tried a reassuring smile on her.

Aida didn't look too reassured. Her dark, liquid eyes kept shooting nervous glances between Katzen and DeVries. Assuming the armor of competency, she said, "I am pleased to meet you, *señor* DeVries. What may I bring you, tonight? The special is *lomo saltado.*"

"Beef sauteed with onions and peppers," Katzen said. "It's very good."

"Sounds like it, but I think I'll just have what Josh is having and spring for another for him."

Aida treated them to a bright smile, but Josh could tell she left to fill the order reluctantly. DeVries watched her lithe form thread back toward the bar and asked, "Girlfriend?"

"No, just a friend. She's Teodoro's daughter — he owns this place. I've been working this dig for five years now." His nod took in the rest of the crowded tavern room. "Quite a few of these people are friends."

"And I'm not?"

Katzen threw back his head in a genuine laugh. "You scream

authority, Colonel. To a lot of these folks, that means nothing but trouble."

"You included, I guess." DeVries chuckled. "I'm the Man, huh?"

"Yep."

Teodoro brought the drinks himself and shot Katzen a searching look. Josh gave him a smile and said, "*Gracias,* Teo, it's been a long day and the scotch was just what I needed."

"*De nada,* Gatito," Teodoro looked hard at the lanky American, then back at Josh. "If you need anything else, you know where I am." With that, he returned to the bar.

"Shoo! Thought I was gonna get decked for a minute there," DeVries said.

Katzen's smile disappeared and he took a sip of his fresh drink. "The night is young, you still might."

"What's this Gatito stuff? That means cat, right?"

"Technically Little Cat. It's a play on my last name — that and the fact that cats like me. My second season here, there was a woman down from Mexico City with a pet jaguar. The cat took one look, came over, sat on me and started purring. From that point on, it was Big Cat and Little Cat. Little Cat stuck."

"Ah!" DeVries said with a look of understanding. "Fuller mentioned that if there was a cat around, it would make right for you. Guess he wasn't joking." He set his glass down and added, "For a minute there, I thought maybe you'd taken up the old business again. Cat burglar named Katzen would be pretty rich. Kinda like your old codename"

"Don't go there."

The man across the table became deadly serious. "Look, I don't mean to keep pissing you off. That's not why I'm here—"

"I don't give a tinker's damn why you're here, Colonel. You came, you saw me, I said fuck off."

"You're the best at what you do. Deustch stole—"

"No. Just no. I can get that in several other languages if it would help."

DeVries opened his mouth again, then his gaze shifted to something over Katzen's shoulder. "Talk about the Man, a guy in uniform is heading our way."

Josh glanced back and grinned. "Aida and Teo must really not like your smell. That's Diego Ruiz, the police chief." He waved and called, "*Hola, Jefe!*"

"Another friend?"

"You betcha."

Ruiz brightened and strode through the crowd toward the booth. "Gatito, I am glad to find you still here. I had feared you would have already gone to the hotel and — as you say — crashed."

"Very close, *Jefe*. Crash time looms and this beautiful scotch Teodoro provided has pushed the clock up, but I ran into a friend of the family here and got delayed."

Once again, DeVries half-stood and extended his hand. "Vaughn DeVries. Pleased to make your acquaintance, Chief Ruiz."

"*Mucho gusto en conocerte, señor* DeVries. What brings you to Piedras Rojas?"

"Well, I can't lie. I came here to look Josh up as a favor to his uncle Len. When he heard I was coming down here to do a little sightseeing and fishing, he told me where Josh was working and asked me to stop by to see how he's doing."

Josh scooted over in the booth and said, "Have a seat, Diego."

Ruiz had been listening to DeVries and weighing up his words. Josh could almost hear the gears whirring from where he sat. Suddenly, the chief straightened and said, "Oh, no thank you, Joshua. I must be getting back to the office. To be truthful, I actually came looking for you with ulterior motives. I wanted to steal you away for a technical problem at the police station. But if you are too busy. . . ."

"No, I'm about done here," Josh said. Draining his glass, he stood and said to DeVries, "It was good meeting you. Be sure to pass on my regards to Len when you see him."

He followed Ruiz out and was surprised at how much tension

flowed out of him as the door closed between himself and the Pentagon's messenger.

Ruiz said, "So, Gatito, Aida and Teodoro did not think you were too happy to meet this man, DeVries. Is he not who he says he is?"

Not waiting for an answer, the chief strolled toward the police station. Katzen fell in beside him. "They were on the money that I wasn't too happy to have DeVries join me — although he is who he says he is. Len did ask him to come down here and find me."

"This Len, it is him you are not happy with?"

"No, Len isn't the problem. As a matter of fact, I'm probably closer to Len than I am to my own father. It's just. . . ." He trailed off thoughtfully. Diego let the silence rest easily between them. Finally, Josh said, "Len and I haven't spoken for a while. As much as I care for him and as much as he's done for me, I thought I'd put that part of my life behind me. Surprised the hell out of me for DeVries to pop up like that."

They walked in silence again. Suddenly Ruiz said, "Did I ever tell you that my family were *huaqueros*?"

Surprised by the abrupt turn Josh said, "No, you didn't."

Ruiz nodded in the half-light of the street lamps. "My father, brothers, uncles . . . all of us. Even me when I was younger."

Josh was amazed, but he said nothing. He couldn't think of anything to say, anyway.

Ruiz continued, "One by one, I saw my brothers and uncles claimed by the violence. I thought nothing of it. It was the way of life. But then . . . one night, my youngest brother and I were digging into a ruin. We had found a cache of pottery. Beautiful things. I could almost feel the history when I touched them. We were turning to go home with our prizes when el Mago and his gang appeared out of the darkness."

Surprise stopped Josh in his tracks. "El Mago?"

"*Sí*. The same. He was an up and coming *huaquero* then, not the boss he is today. Still he and his crew had automatic rifles. My brother and I had only our digging tools. Mago demanded our prizes. My brother refused. Before my eyes, el Mago turned the rifle on my brother. As Ramon fell, he broke the pots and I realized in that moment the lie of my life. I knew we were not only killing ourselves, but our own history. Before they could turn their guns on me, I ran and I kept on running. I left town that night and went to Lima, determined to get a legitimate job, put myself through school and return to fight the thievery I had once been a part of."

"Wow. Not that I'm not flattered that you trust me enough to tell me all this, Diego, but I get the feeling this was to make a particular point."

"That it was, *mi amigo*. When I decided to change my life, my family turned their backs on me. It has cost me dearly, in many ways."

Sick realization washed over Josh. "Your wife. She was killed by el Mago, wasn't she?"

Diego nodded mutely. "She was. This beast thought that by hurting her, he could convince me that it wasn't worth pursuing him and his gang. He was wrong. The decisions I have made were the right ones. They make me who I am and I stand by them."

"Yeah, I've lost a lot that way, too. I think I see where you're going, though. The shaman said that my greatest strength comes from who I am."

Ruiz grinned and tapped the side of his nose with his forefinger, then said, "Ah! Here we are at the station. If you have time, we really do have a technical problem."

"There really is a sick computer?"

"There is — if you want to look at it tonight." Ruiz opened the door and let Josh precede him into the small office. He added, "You might want to put it off, though. I think it will be a long, hard job." He pointed to a desk in the corner.

Katzen followed his point and grimaced. "Oh geez. You really need to revoke Placido's internet privileges."

~*~

That night, the soft beds of the Posada de Piedras Rojas might as well have been red hot iron for all the rest Katzen got. Every time he dropped off to sleep, he was plagued with disjointed dreams in which he scaled a mountain toward a beautiful garden that he could just see at the top. Warm breezes carried hints of exotic fragrances down the slopes. Just as his fingers brushed the edge of the lush green turf, a demonic, distorted version of Uncle Sam jerked on a tether he hadn't noticed before, pulling him backwards. He scrabbled frantically at the turf, but it ripped away sending him plummeting down the mountain into a deep rift where the sounds of war sat him bolt upright, gasping, drenched in his own sweat.

CHAPTER 9

Morning found him groggy and irritable. Deciding he didn't really want to stay in proximity to the Pentagon wonk, he hitched a ride back to the dig on the truck bearing the weekly grocery delivery. Manny took one look at him, tsked and shoved a mug of coffee into his hands. It helped a little.

Force of habit propelled him toward the workshop. When he realized where he was going, he decided it wasn't such a bad idea. He had a day where there was nothing slated for him. A perfect time to get more work done in the War Room. With luck, he might actually finish the drawing.

It was not to be. No matter what he did, nothing worked quite the way it should. The illustration board kept catching on the edge of the portfolio, and the top popped off the pencil box when he tried to stow it in his pack. Pencils, erasers and rulers flew in every direction, bouncing and rolling with wild abandon. Swearing, he dropped to his knees and started to gather them up. It was a mark of both how upset he was and how badly his day was going that he didn't hear when Avi Rosenberg came in.

"Wow," Rosenberg said from behind him. "You're in a mood."

Katzen startled and came up hard against the edge of the worktable, knocking over his coffee which cascaded onto the floor in a fragrant waterfall. He swore with more conviction.

The archaeologist tossed him a roll of paper towels, then watched for a moment. "'Melia said you got back way early on the delivery truck and Manny said you looked like you'd been *dragged* by the truck."

No response but more muffled swearing.

He tried again, "Ummmm. I thought you were going to spend the night at the hotel and take the day off. Did something go wrong?"

"You could say that." Josh sat back on his heels, glared at the wad of sodden towels then tossed it at the trashcan. It missed. He hung his head for a moment, then looked up at Rosenberg. "Do me a favor. The next time Tonto heads into town, yell 'Don't go into town, man! They always beat you up!'"

Rosenberg frowned and closed the door firmly behind him. That was as close to a do not disturb sign as they had in the open camp. "This is bad. First swearing and now you're referencing comedy routines. What the hell happened?"

Katzen busied himself checking the half-finished drawing of the warrior mural for coffee splatters, then stowed it in his portfolio. The silence was broken only by the closing whisper of the nylon zipper. Finally, he said, "They're trying to call me back in."

"They?" Avi looked blank for a few beats, then realization widened his eyes. "But . . . they can't *do* that. They agreed to leave you alone."

Katzen quirked a bitter smile. "Avi, they can do whatever they damn well please. I hope you never have to discover that the same way I did."

It took a lot to render Avi Rosenberg speechless. This had done it. That suited Josh fine. He didn't feel much like talking, anyway. He pulled himself to his feet and set the now empty coffee mug upright. The stunned silence was broken by a light tap at the door.

Amelia Peters opened the door a crack and peeked in nervously. "Sorry to disturb you guys — I uhhh. . . . I know I should have used the radio, but . . . well, I heard all the crashes and swearing."

"Sorry, 'Melia," Katzen said, holding up a fistful of brown-stained paper towels. Coffee dripped onto the tabletop. "I'm not having a really good day."

"I see." Stepping farther into the room, she said uncertainly, "I hope this will make it better. You have a visitor."

Rosenberg and Katzen exchanged worried glances and Amelia got more uncomfortable. She ventured, "He says his name is DeVries and. . . ."

Suddenly a shadow filled the doorway behind the girl. She eeped in surprise as a lanky, sunburnt blond man bulled past her into the workshop.

The man grinned and said, "Heyas, Josh. Your policeman buddy hauled you off before we finished talking last night. Figured I'd just mosey on out here and get a look at what you do." He turned to Avi and extended his hand. "You gotta be Dr. Rosenberg. Len — that's Josh's uncle — he's all the time talking about what a favor you done for Josh to bring him in on your work. DeVries. Vaughn DeVries. Real pleased to meet you."

Avi shook the proffered hand. He didn't look quite so pleased.

Josh met Amelia's stricken gaze. The poor girl looked about to burst into tears. "I'm sorry," Amelia told him softly. "I thought he was waiting at the cook tent."

"Don't worry about it," Katzen said just as softly and shot her a bright grin. Swinging his kit onto his shoulder, he turned to DeVries and said in a more normal tone, "You almost missed me. I was just heading out to do a little drawing."

DeVries returned the grin. "Mind if I tag along?"

"Suit yourself, but remember, you asked for it."

Despite DeVries' best efforts to start a conversation, Katzen remained stubbornly silent until they got out of sight and earshot of the camp. At that point he suddenly dropped his kit and wheeled on his companion, face contorted with fury. "You mother-fucking bastard! Why did you come here? Do you think that if you screw everything up for me, I'll be forced to do what you want?"

Taken aback, DeVries raised both hands in a gesture of surrender. "Cool your jets, Durand. I'm only the messenger."

"Fuck that messenger shit—" The little artist closed the gap and jabbed a finger in the taller man's face. "—and it's Katzen. KAT. ZEN. Got it?"

The Air Force liked their fighter pilots to be compact and aggressive. Whatever Durand was calling himself these days, he was still up to spec. DeVries took a step back. "Okay. Katzen. I'm sorry. Look, we're not getting anywhere like this. I was sent here to talk to you not piss you off. Truce?"

Katzen's fist clenched, then dropped to his side. He turned away, saying, "Talk all you want. I gave you my answer last night. I'm not going back."

"You didn't even hear what I was asking."

"I don't need to. The person you came to talk to is dead. Go buy a Ouija board or find another patsy." Katzen swung his kit onto his shoulder and started back up the hill, fury propelling him in long strides.

DeVries scrambled after him. "Would it help if I told you that General Fuller has been fighting this for weeks?"

"No."

"Look, this is more important than you can imagine. A lot has gone into just getting me down here to see you."

Katzen made no reply, just kept moving. DeVries was struggling, but he managed to keep up. "He even went so far as insist they promote me to a full bird colonel because he knew you'd never listen to anyone who didn't outrank you."

Katzen stopped so suddenly, DeVries plowed into him. "Len did what?"

"Uh . . . yeah. He argued for a couple days. . . ."

To DeVries' amazement, Katzen dissolved into laughter. He laughed until his legs wouldn't hold him and he sat in the path, head on his knees, shoulders shaking. "Oh. Oh, man."

Amazement flashed over into anger. DeVries demanded, "Just what is so funny about me being promoted?"

Katzen coughed a few times and pulled himself to his feet, wiping tears from his eyes. After a few aborted tries at words, he managed, "Len must like you."

"Huh?"

"Len must like you and no one else must have bothered to look at my record. If they had, they would have seen how many times I'd been called on the carpet for insubordination."

Shrugging, DeVries looked blank.

"Rank," Katzen explained patiently. "It means bupkes to me."

Realization dawned. "Then. . . ."

"Yep. Len just wanted to bump your pay grade for landing you in a shit mission." Dusting himself off, he re-shouldered his kit and started back up the path, saying, "C'mon, *Colonel*. We still have a way to go."

It wasn't an incredibly long slog, but the path was rocky and a lot of it was uphill. *Very* uphill. At the end DeVries was limping and sweating like a pig. "Damn!" He said as he stopped to mop his face. "You do this every day?"

"Pretty much," Katzen replied with a shrug.

"The general said you were nuts."

At the top of the rise, there was a ruined mud brick building and a cleared plaza. At the edges of the clearing, several cats peeked out from the undergrowth, uncertain of the newcomer. Katzen rooted in his kit for a moment, then produced a pack of cat treats and a bottle of lemonade sports drink. He tossed the treats on the ground and the bottle to DeVries.

"Drink that slowly. I don't have many left," he said before ducking through an ancient doorway into the ruin.

The cool drink tasted like liquid gold to DeVries after the hard climb and he savored it for a moment before cautiously following Katzen. If the walk to the ruin had been that rough, who the hell knew what was on the other side of that door? Cautiously poking head and shoulders through and letting his eyes adjust to the gloom, DeVries stopped in open-mouthed amazement. Stepping slowly in, he did a 360 turn gawping at the ancient painted panels that adorned each wall.

"Stop me if you've heard this before, but WOW!"

In the center of the room, where a swath of light from the door fell, Katzen looked up from turning a jumble of metal sticks into an easel. "Yeah, I think I heard that one," he said with the first real smile DeVries had seen. "Wait. I think *I* said it."

A set of collapsible reflectors followed the easel and DeVries quickly stepped farther into the room, out of the light without being asked. Next thing out of the pack was an impossibly tiny bundle that magically became a camp stool. Katzen said, "Sorry. I don't usually have company when I'm copying, so I only have one chair."

Still dumbstruck by the ancient images, DeVries barely reacted — until a half-finished drawing was set on the easel.

"Ohhhhh," he breathed. "That's gonna be nice. If you do a print, I guarantee, the general will have this one in record time."

Katzen looked up again, his expression hard to read in the gloom. "Len buys my prints?"

"You didn't know? Hell, he has them all over his house. Keeps the one of that jug with the face on it behind the desk in his office." Closing up the water bottle, DeVries looked around. "Is this a safe place to talk?"

"Did you see anyone on our way up?" Katzen asked as he bent down and selected a pencil from the case open beside him.

"Guess not," DeVries said and sat on the floor being careful not to brush against anything. "Will you at least let me tell you why I'm here? Stomp on me all you want after. I just want to be able to report that you heard me out."

Katzen glanced over his shoulder, then quirked a grin. "Sure. Fire away. I don't mind a little background noise while I work."

"Shoo!" The lanky blond man released a relieved breath. "Thanks. I was afraid I was really gonna get my ass chewed when I went back to DC." He laughed and shook his head. "Don't even know where to start now."

"How about with whatever the hell it was Herb Deustch nicked."

"Oh yeah. That. That's a doozy. Somehow the guy managed to walk away with five kilograms of plutonium."

The pencil stopped moving. "Say again?"

"You heard right." DeVries took a pull at the lemonade. "Plutonium. About the same amount of material used in the Fat Man back in the forties."

"Five kilograms! That would be a big whack of bad day somewhere." He twisted around in the chair. "How did Deustch swing that? He was an art thief — an antiquities looter — the last time I looked. It takes a completely different skill set to score something like that."

"You'd know, wouldn't you?" DeVries treated him to a dopey grin. "General Fuller gave me your file to read before they sent me down. Shoooo! Even redacted . . . did you really enter Tehran wearing—"

Katzen impatiently waved it away, "Beside the point. *Seriously* beside the point. The point is that Herb Deustch never gave any indication of having been involved in anything like that before. How did a guy more familiar with breaking into Etruscan tombs manage to crack a military facility?"

"The short version is: he didn't. He stole it from someone who did."

"Ahhh. That makes more sense. I could see him not even trying to resist walking away with something valuable that wasn't bolted to the floor."

DeVries took another swig of lemonade, nodding as he swallowed. "Yep. The plutonium was stolen back in the 80s along with a lot of other military material — mostly experimental stuff and equipment in development from some lab they tell me I don't need to know where the hell it is. When we caught up with the crew who boosted it, everything was there but the plutonium. It was a major red-face moment for the military."

"So they covered it up," Katzen said with a smirk.

"Well, they kept it as quiet as they could."

"Suck up," Katzen scoffed.

DeVries ignored him and continued, "Several members of the crew had dealings with Deustch and pointed the finger at him for the plutonium growing legs. Washington looked at him hard, but nothing could be made to stick. After all was said and done, no one could prove anything more than he was visiting family in the States for a while, then he's back home in Peru."

"Doesn't surprise me. Even with the required shielding, that amount of material wouldn't take up much room. Heavy, yes, big no. Deustch would have had a shitload of channels to move something that size out of the country quickly and quietly."

"That's exactly what the intel guys figured. Then somebody, probably Deustch or one of his agents started making noises on the weapons black market that he had something unique to sell."

"Ouch. Not a real smart move. They not only hadn't let enough time pass, but there are ripples whenever something as hot as that goes missing. The Wall hadn't come down, yet, either. Making that much noise could have attracted some very unwanted attention."

"Very true. The way General Fuller tells it, the upper echelons of the Pentagon were quietly going batshit."

"I've seen that a few times. It ain't pretty. I'm assuming what happened next was nothing. That Deustch and the plutonium just dropped off the face of the earth."

"Exactly." DeVries was encouraged that Katzen was paying attention. "When more time passed, they wrote it off — well, as much as you can write something like that off. More like it went onto the back burner waiting for something to happen."

"Fade to close-up image of a calendar," Katzen said. "Pages being ripped off by the wind. Years pass. Cue the Piedras Rojas excavations and the discovery of the sensational Moche Rolex."

"Funny, but close enough. When Deustch turned up in your dig, it sent a whole bunch of people into a tizzy".

"Then someone noticed who the excavation's resident photographer was."

"Right again. They went into tizzy overdrive. Panic shot right to the top, I can tell you. They dragged Len in and told him to get his pet thief to find the stolen plutonium."

"Yeah, well, Fuller's Pet Thief thinks the Washington brass are fucking nuts." He made a disgusted noise. "I hate when they call me that."

"Well, it sort of made sense, didn't it? I mean you're already on the scene. You know the area."

"What? Just because I've been working a dig in Peru for a few years, this makes me the Daniel Boone of the Andes? Moses! What is it with you people?"

"Hey! Deustch's remains were found pretty close to the area he normally worked in. According to intel he was focusing on an area just north of Lima."

"That's five hundred miles to the south of here!"

"True."

"In the mountains."

"Well, yeah."

"I hate to break it to you, man, but while that area *might* be close to a major city, it's still wild and mostly unexplored — that is if you don't count the *huaqueros* — the looters. You know, the criminals with guns?" He mimed shooting.

DeVries lifted the lemonade bottle again, but discovered it was empty. He recapped it and said, "Do you think the looters might have found it? It's been out there a while."

Josh shook his head. "Nah. If they had, it would have resurfaced by now somehow — even if it was just rumors of *huaqueros* dropping dead from radiation poisoning."

"So where does that leave us?"

"Flapping in the wind, seems to me." Katzen turned back to his drawing. "From what you say, we have no map, no clue, no idea at all where Deustch might have hidden an item roughly the size of a large backpack other than it's probably in Peru?"

DeVries went quiet then said, "What if I told you that we might have a map or something?"

"I'm listening."

He was. DeVries stifled a grin and said, "Deustch was a compulsive record keeper. He encrypted everything, yeah, but the records we found helped Interpol bring down his whole antiquities network."

Katzen sat back. "Really. I wondered how that went to pieces so quickly. I mean, Deustch was the lynchpin, but it was a pretty extensive and self-sustaining operation."

"It probably would have just ticked over without him, but, shortly after the watchers realized Deustch had vanished in a puff of smoke, they pushed through a seizure order. We — jointly with the government of Peru, of course — impounded all of Deustch's property we could locate. Most of it is in a warehouse complex in Lima."

Then it happened. Katzen cocked his head in the move General Fuller called his Cat at the Mouse Hole look. Fuller said if he got this, they had him. DeVries stifled a whoop and asked as calmly as he could manage, "So how about it? Do you want to come back with me to look over what we have?"

Katzen stared straight ahead, but he didn't see the Moche Lord about to bring his mace down on the captive's head. The pictures that flashed through his head were far uglier and nothing that he ever wanted to commit to paper. The fact that there was such a big chunk of plutonium in the wind worried him. It would have been dangerous back in the 80s, but it was worse news now.

At length, he said, "Yeah. I'll go. Tell Len he wins this round."

CHAPTER 10

Rosenberg looked unhappier than Katzen had ever seen him. He sank onto a folding stool, running fingers through his hair. "Wow, this blows," he said at last.

"Hey, I'm sorry," Josh said. "I really hate to leave you in the lurch — especially with the load of shit finding Deustch's body has dropped on everyone."

Avi looked up angrily. "Shut it, Josh. I'm not upset with you." The big man stood so suddenly, the light camp chair was knocked aside. He loomed over DeVries who lost his smug smile. "It's this asshole who's pissing me off.

"Just who the hell do you think you are?" he demanded, punctuating his words with finger jabs to the slighter man's chest. "I know what all happened before. I was there for some of it. I've been here for what's happened after, too. Now, there's you showing up and ruining everything Josh has worked so hard to build."

"Just you wait a minute, Doc," DeVries said, taking a couple steps back. "That's not so. No one wants to do that. We just need Josh to help us, nothing has to change at all."

Rosenberg straightened and folded his arms across his chest. It made him look like an angry, bronze genie; DeVries wasn't too sure this was an improvement.

"Oh, I see," Rosenberg said slowly. "Disrupting my camp, distracting my students, intimidating my teaching assistant and dragging my staff photographer away for who knows how long in the middle of a dig is all perfectly normal. Nope, nope. Nothing there to make people look twice."

DeVries and Rosenberg squared off. Katzen was amazed. He'd seen Avi in mother hen mode with students before, but this was more grizzly bear than hen. Thinking quickly, he stepped between them. "Maybe not," he said.

Both men took a step back and looked down at him, a bantam rooster between the Sequoias. "Really," he continued. "There's a reason for me to go to Lima right now. A good reason."

"Yeah?" Rosenberg asked doubtfully.

"Yeah. The same reason we used when that camera crew came through to shoot the documentary last season."

"Right," Avi nodded uncertainly. "You went to the *Museo Nacional* to deliver pieces for conservation, but. . . ."

"But this time, I'll be returning the stolen artifacts we found with Deustch's remains to the *Museo* as per the request of *la Policia Nacional*." He grinned and spread his hands. "Ta da!"

Both DeVries and Rosenberg stared at him, then DeVries asked Rosenberg, "That makes sense in an insane sort of way. Is he always like this?"

"Yep," Avi said. "You get used to it after a while." He sighed deeply. "Well, *sort* of used to it."

~*~

The last carefully packed crate slid into place in the back of the battered green Land Rover. Avi ratcheted the tie-down into place and quietly asked Josh, "Are you sure you're okay with this?"

A barked laugh, and Josh said, "No. Not really, but what else can I do?"

"Try saying 'no'?" the archaeologist suggested with a cocked eyebrow.

"I've *been* saying no. It hasn't worked." Katzen leaned against the side of the Rover. He looked tired, then brightened a little. "Look at it this way. The stolen items recovered from the crime scene have to be delivered to the authorities in Lima, anyway. If I go and look at the stuff Colonel Obvious wants me to examine, I'm showing good faith."

"Do you really expect to find anything in this stuff that other folks haven't in all this time?"

"Nope." Josh grinned. "And the faster I can get to Lima to tell them that, the faster I'll be back."

Across the compound, DeVries came out of the cook tent carrying a parcel that, no doubt, contained a food offering from Manny's *cocina*. Avi frowned watching the man make his way over to where they stood. "I wish I was as certain as you are. I just don't trust this guy."

Josh swung into the driver's seat with a grin. "He's button-down military, you're a tie-dyed in the wool hippie. Who's surprised?"

~*~

"Man! You sure had those lab rats eating out of your hand," Devries said as he ushered Katzen into his Lima hotel room. "Now, those National Police? They didn't much like your smell, but those museum geeks? Shooo!"

Tossing his suitcase on the bed, Josh Katzen sighed. "You seem to have a lot of trouble with academics. Was it some sort of kindergarten trauma?"

"It's just when those guys were showing you those little pieces of cloth and going on—"

"Textiles."

"Come again?"

"Those were thousand-year-old textiles that our team unearthed last season, and I *was* excited about them. Those guys did a great job conserving them." Leaving DeVries standing looking dumbfounded, Katzen closed the door and examined the room, checking closets, opening drawers and glancing out the window. "If you want to work with me, DeVries, there's one thing you need to remember: It's not an act. I really do care about the artifacts."

Setting the laptop up on the desk, he said, "Who booked this place?"

"Uhh, I did," DeVries answered uncertainly.

"Good choice."

"Thanks — I think."

"No worries. It *is* a compliment," Katzen grinned. "I always dread when the Pentagon wonks book one for me. It's either one of the high profile luxury places with solid gold faucets and jacuzzis in every room or a fleabag dive where bedbugs go to die. This is a nice, solid middle of the road place."

"Well, anyway, I'm right down the hall in 423," DeVries said, then looked like he'd been struck by a bolt. "Oh, yeah!" He dropped his suitcase and dug into his jacket pocket. Pulling out a cell phone, he tossed it to Katzen. "I'm supposed to give this to you."

Katzen looked it over. "Ah. Clean burner, I assume."

DeVries grinned and handed him a slip of paper. "Yep. Here's my number. I think you know the drill."

"Sure," Katzen said, absently folding the paper into a pocket."I'll write it in every bar in downtown Lima."

DeVries tried to hide a jolt of sudden alarm.

Katzen gave him the patented cocky smile. "Joke, man. Joke."

The colonel turned toward the door, then stopped. "Oh yeah. Before I go I have to give you your bedtime reading material." He reached two fingers into the side pocket of his suitcase and pulled out an unmarked DVD in a clear plastic case. Snapping it to Katzen, he said, "Herb Deustch, the Man, the Myth and the Pain in the Ass. That's everything we have on him. General Fuller said you'd want to look that over before we hit the warehouse. It's encrypted, but he also said you'd know the password."

CHAPTER 11

"General Fuller is always right."

Katzen hit Enter and his laptop screen filled with the list of files on the disk. *No*, he thought with a wry smile, *the phrase ought to be "General Fuller always gets his way."*

Len Fuller giving him homework after tricking or browbeating him into taking an assignment was a real blast from the past. It wasn't a blast he enjoyed, either. Still, he had to laugh at how Len could push his buttons even using a remote control in the form of Vaughn DeVries. Well, maybe not *laugh*, but there was definitely something cosmically ironic about it.

He sat back against the headboard and opened the first file. "Okay, Herbert Otto Deustch III, you rat's assed bastard, tell me about yourself."

The first thing up was Deustch's dossier. Background: rich. His only immediate family: Margaret Trevilian Deustch-Gascone, a now-elderly sister living in New York.

Schools: Ivy League — no surprises anywhere in that. Studied engineering and mathematics. Now that *was* a little surprising. Kind of unusual for an engineer to chuck it all and take up antiquities trafficking. It was more common for antiquities people to have art backgrounds — kind of like himself.

He launched the file on known associates; a long and varied list, accompanied by lots of photographs. Some of the people were apparently still on the intelligence community's radar because several of the photos looked to be current. Heading that list of both past and present surveillance photos was art dealer and gallery owner, Ludovico di Bardi, Deustch's long-time partner in business — and crime.

Deustch and di Bardi were a study in opposites both physically and temperamentally. They'd attended the same Ivy League schools and become friends there. Di Bardi was apparently instrumental in turning Deustch onto ancient art. Photos from the 70s and 80s showed Deustch, brawny, and even when wearing evening gear, looking like he wanted nothing more than to throw a punch or wrestle a bear. At his side, the flamboyant and openly gay di Bardi looked the stereotypic jet set partier. All tuxedos and flashing white teeth. It was a wonder they worked so well together — then again, maybe they worked well together *because* they were so different. Regardless, the men had shared a deep, if complex, friendship for decades.

Also figuring prominently in the past and present photos was Deustch's girlfriend, Diana Meadowes, a woman of great beauty and intelligence. The older photos showed a stunning younger woman, dressed in cutting-edge fashion, usually tucked intimately between Deustch and di Bardi. The Three Musketeers of the antiquities trade. More recent pictures showed a handsome, older woman wearing elegant, tailored clothing adorned with tasteful, artistic jewelry befitting her current position: Director of the illustrious Gant Museum in Los Angeles, California.

There had been other women in Deustch's life, but he always returned to Meadowes. For once, Katzen was in agreement with the bastard. The lady's grace and poise reminded him of the actress, Lauren Bacall — and one didn't become the director of a world-class museum like the Gant by simply being eye-candy.

Meadowes had fared better than di Bardi in the train wreck that was the aftermath of Deustch's disappearance. The art dealer had drawn prison time and had to start over with his galleries on release. The lady had managed to survive, reputation intact, but tattered, and still hold onto her position at the museum. Apparently, di Bardi didn't hold grudges. They were together in many of the recent pictures: at cocktail parties, at lunch, at the new di Bardi gallery, at the Gant. . . .

The pictures of the Gant made him smile. It was one of his favorite museums. The institution had a fantastic collection and an impressive security system to go along with it. He should know. He'd had to break into it once a long time ago when someone had hidden a microfilm in an Orthodox Russian icon. That had been a close one.

Chuckling, he closed the file on Deustch's associates and moved on to one marked Confidential: Eyes Only. It was a report on the break-in at the military complex where the plutonium was stolen along with an action report by the leader of the team sent in to recover the stolen items from the thieves. Both were so heavily redacted they were all but useless. He didn't really need to read them though, though — especially the action report. Special forces black ops team versus a gang of thieves. Yeah. Redactions or no, he had a pretty good idea how *that* went down.

The thieves weren't exactly the brightest gang, either, as was proven by the next file he opened: a transcript of the interrogation of a gang member detailing how the plutonium went missing. The upshot was that one of the gang members had worked with Deustch emptying an Etruscan tomb in Italy a few years prior to the robbery and had recommended him to appraise the loot from the lab. Why an antiquities dealer would be able to appraise high tech equipment was beyond Katzen, but apparently made sense to someone. Deustch was called in. Then the idiots left him alone with the haul. Suprise, suprise! When they came back, Deustch was missing along with several of the best items from the robbery. Soon after that, the black ops team had blown down the door.

It was right after that Deustch vanished. He was off everyone's radar for weeks until he'd reappeared at his *pied-à-terre* in Lima behaving as if nothing had happened. By that time, some of the less valuable items had found their way onto the black market, been bought and vanished from the record. The plutonium, the big ticket item, was up for auction to the highest bidder. The bidding was at its height when Deustch vanished again, this time not voluntarily.

In a last-ditch effort to recover the material, the US government had been among the bidders along with several organizations and national governments. The most aggressive had seemed to be the Soviet Union and the People's Republic of China. KGB operatives, Vasily Koulikov and Mikhail Bukharin and MSS operatives, Xu Chunwang and Hsu Shi-Ming were seen in Lima and photographed speaking with Deustch many times. The sale never actually took place, though, because Deustch went missing in the middle of negotiations.

There was a note at the bottom of the last page of the report that MSS operative Hsu Shi-Ming was known to have anger issues and had been abruptly recalled to Bejing shortly after Deustch's disappearance. Hsu Shi-Ming arrived in Beijing, then disappeared as completely as Deustch and the plutonium. It was viewed as possible evidence of Bejing's displeasure over the botched deal.

Josh reread the final line. "Possible evidence of Bejing's displeasure over the botched deal."

"Really? Ya think?" he said to no one in particular. Sometimes he wondered what world these data jockeys lived in. Then again, he'd met enough brass who had to have it spelled out with blocks. It might not be completely the fault of the analysts.

So the DSS guy whacked Deustch? Made sense. The Chinese sidearm during the 80s was the Type 77 and that certainly fit with Vic's assessment of the bullet fragments.

He rubbed his eyes, stifled a yawn, then paused. He'd been doing that a lot, hadn't he? His eyes slid to the clock on his laptop and saw a ridiculous hour. They'd be visiting the warehouse where Deustch's belongings were stored in the morning — correction — in a few hours.

Swinging his legs over the side of the bed, he groaned at how stiff they'd become from sitting in one position for so long.

He set the laptop aside and snapped off the light.

~*~

There was nothing remarkable about the warehouse complex until you noticed the guards. They were military police from both Peru and the United States.

"There's a lot of important stuff in here," DeVries said to Josh's amused headshake as the MP waved them through the checkpoint.

"Like what? The lost Ark of the Covenant?"

DeVries rolled his eyes and drove deeper into the maze of buildings, finally parking the government-tagged SUV in front of a nondescript unit with the number 86 painted beside the wide roll-up door.

"Since Deustch was a US citizen living in Peru, we've shared custody of the belongings removed from his home after his disappearance," DeVries said, punching a code into the keypad. "It's temperature controlled, but that don't mean it feels like your living room. Just means things don't freeze or melt."

Katzen stepped through into a wonderland. The dimly lit interior was packed almost to the rafters with art of all kinds. There were groups of sculpture, large and small, including one complete Inca stele. One wall was lined with racks holding paintings and engravings, tapestries, rugs and what looked to be a renaissance church triptych. Here and there were groupings of antique furniture, seemingly corresponding to the rooms they had been removed from. Trunks, boxes and suitcases were piled throughout.

Finally, he managed, "Wow! Are you *sure* the Ark of the Covenant isn't in here somewhere?"

Katzen approached a massive limestone stele that stood with a group of six other full-sized statues. Even surrounded by classical bronzes and dancing oriental demons, it dominated the room. Touching it reverently he said, "This guy is probably local."

"Local? How so."

"This is an Inca piece. Probably found right here in Peru. Whoever cut it up was good with the saw, too. A real pro."

"You approve of them stealing this thing? After your spiel about caring for the artifacts, that surprises me, Katzen."

"It shouldn't. No, I definitely don't approve the theft — but yes, I'm in awe of how they managed to cut the thing apart with such a fine cut line. Other than removing the carved faces from the core stone, there was minimal damage done to it."

DeVries came closer and squinted. "Cut apart? Looks like one big hunk of rock to me."

"Well, originally it was. Thing is, a hunk of rock this size is hard to transport in one piece. Looters go in with big saws and cut them up into smaller, more manageable pieces. Some are cut into blocks. This one was slabbed. There's probably a big, naked block of stone standing somewhere in the jungle now." He traced a line with his finger. "See? Look here. You can barely see the seam where the piece was mortared back together."

Josh turned away from the stele. "Deustch must have had a helluva place for all this stuff to fit into it."

"Yeah, it was. I never saw it, but I gather it was a pretty good sized house in one of the ritzier sections of the city."

"I believe it." He moved slowly from object to object, pausing at a bronze Chinese vessel nestling in an open box. "Beautiful *hu* — wine jar," he added at DeVries' confused look. "Looks Zhou Dynasty, but Chinese was never my strongest suit." Straightening, he said, "From where I'm standing, I see Dutch, Greek, Roman, Thai and Indian. A veritable world gallery in one slightly stuffy warehouse. I'm surprised the respective governments haven't been making all kinds of noise to get this stuff back. Especially in light of all the recent repatriation hooha."

"Oh, they have. We have petitions from a number of them. Multiples in some cases. Unfortunately, they've all been pending until our case was closed."

"You mean until the plutonium was found."

"Shhhhhhh!" He glanced back to see if anyone was near the open door. Then went over and closed it carefully. "Don't say that too loud. We're just calling it Deutsch's package. Okay?"

A slow grin spread over Katzen's face. "The brass monkeys of the DoD have never admitted the theft. That's it, isn't it?"

DeVries raised a warning finger. "Now, look. . . ."

"Pfft. Is this your first encounter with official deniability?" Josh chuckled. "This is old hat for me. I've been dealing with this kind of bureaucratic crapola since you were discovering the wonders of Pull-Ups and Underoos."

He gently touched the massive Inca stele again. "Are you seriously telling me all this stuff has been in this warehouse for all this time and no one has looked at it?"

"Well, they tried. But we didn't have anyone with a high enough clearance who was qualified to interpret it — and with Deustch in the wind, there didn't seem to be a need." He treated Katzen to a toothy grin. "Until now."

"Lucky me."

~*~

The next morning, Katzen set his laptop up on its cooling stand and plugged it into a floor outlet. Next, he unpacked his camera, assorted colored backdrop cloths, pens, pencils, pads of paper and a portable scanner onto the Chippendale dining table cleared for the purpose.

Nearby, DeVries dug through a recently delivered crate and ticked items off a checklist. "I think we got everything you had on your equipment request. Considering we're officially here as an effort to catalog and repatriate the items in the warehouse, it'll all fly with the Peruvians. The Americans might be another matter, though."

Josh looked up. "What?"

"The head honcho at the embassy is a nervous Nellie. He wants to play cover his ass. He's sending a couple of officers with the Diplomatic Security Service over to assist us."

Josh groaned.

"I think you met them before, though. They were the special agents who came out to the dig site to pick up the evidence and Doc Pale's report on the remains."

"Oh yeah. Woman named Caballero and a guy named Bramwell. Bramwell seems like a competent sort, but Caballero had her shorts in a real twist about something."

"That's them. They'll be showing up some time this afternoon. From the heads up I got from the embassy chief, shorts in a twist pretty much describes Caballero's normal attitude."

Josh turned back to plugging in cables and cords. "Beautiful."

"I think he was glad to shove her off on us for a while. Bramwell, too. Man's in spitting distance of retirement and is getting kinda picky about his assignments."

"Hmmmm. Can't say I blame him. Have they been briefed?"

"Mostly."

"Mostly?"

"Mind you, we haven't told them exactly what's in the package we're looking for. That's strictly need to know, and so far, they don't need to know it."

"Wonderfulness. Secrets on top of secrets." Katzen pressed the power button on the laptop and watched with satisfaction as all the devices lit up.

"Come on. You said yourself you've been at this game for a while. They just know that Herb Deustch made off with an item that's critical to national security. What more do they really need to know?"

Katzen made a non-committal noise, then said, "Well, there's no reason we can't get started without them. Help me get this drop cloth spread out and these lights and reflectors in place, then we'll set that Dutch altar piece up."

~*~

Katzen's decision to deal with the paintings right away was based on two things. First: given the size of the shielded container the plutonium was last known to be in, paintings, prints and drawings were easily eliminated as possible hiding places. Second: they would probably be some of the easiest pieces to send home. As a bonus, the warehouse was so crowded that freeing up the space taken up by the racks of flat pieces would be welcome.

By that logic, rugs and tapestries would also be ruled out, but those were a royal pain in the ass to photograph. Considering how DeVries was already bristling at the slow pace of lighting and shooting the paintings, it was expedient to let the textiles ride for a bit.

They'd just finished with an Italian rondo and were setting up a particularly fine Flemish portrait when DeVries' cell went off. He clawed at it like a drowning man at a life preserver.

"DeVries . . . sure! Send 'em on up." Sliding the phone into his pocket, DeVries said, "That was the MP at the entrance. Bramwell and Caballero just checked in and are headed our way. I better stand outside and flag 'em down."

Vaughn was outside and on the stoop before Katzen could reply. Suppressing a laugh, he returned to tweaking the lighting. After a few minutes, DeVries called out and Josh turned to see a bright red Jeep Wrangler, top down, with Special Agent Caballero at the wheel swing into the space beside the black SUV.

Car doors slammed and he heard murmured introductions, then Caballero saying, "Damn, DeVries! This place is a maze."

"Welcome to Aladdin's Cave: Peru Edition," Josh called out, as he stepped over to the open doorway. The two Diplomatic Security agents looked at him in surprised recognition.

DeVries said, "I believe you've already met Joshua Katzen. He's the art specialist we called in to help us identify this stuff."

Bramwell stepped in, then stopped, open-mouthed. "Damn!"

Caballero moved past her partner and turned in place to take it all in. "Holy shit," she breathed. After a moment, she looked from Katzen to DeVries in amazement. "We have to sort through *all* this? Where do we even start?"

"With the flat stuff — specifically the paintings," Josh said pointing to the staging area where the portrait sat. "I figure we'll work our way up to the big stuff. Probably save the Inca stele for our grand finale since it's the biggest piece here."

Tessa Caballero looked confused. "The Inca *who*?"

"Stele," Katzen said pointing to the towering limestone sculpture. "This guy. Looks to be some sort of storm god holding two staves. Face looks a little feline, but a lot of the pre-Columbian cultures thought cats were divine — or demonic creatures. With cats, it's sometimes a hard distinction to make."

DeVries looked smug. "See why we brought him in?"

"The art lesson is all well and good, but does he—" Bramwell began.

"—know about the package?" DeVries finished for him.

"Absolutely," said Katzen. He swept a hand at the contents of the warehouse. "Most or all of this is stolen and somewhere in here is a clue to where Deustch hid the thing he stole from our mutual uncle. To find that, we need to know what it is we're looking at and what doesn't fit. That's where I come in." He looked around at the jumble of items surrounding him and added, "We hope."

CHAPTER 12

Over the next few days, they fell into a rhythm. Caballero, Bramwell and DeVries searched boxes, suitcases and trunks while Josh assessed, analyzed and photographed artworks. Whoever was between boxes — or bored — helped him move the larger pieces he couldn't get by himself. They'd made progress this way, gaining floorspace but hadn't moved an inch toward their actual goal. The clothing donation bins of the local churches had received copious windfalls, however.

In the stuffy confines of the storage facility, formality was kaput. Jackets and uniforms were replaced by tank tops and cargo pants. The ice chest filled with water bottles stationed under an electric fan became an altar to keeping cool. Katzen was worshiping there when Tessa Caballero called out:

"Found an Indiana Jones bobblehead!"

"Oooo!" Josh said. "Dibs! It'll make Avi Rosenberg crazy."

"I'll vote for that," Vaughn DeVries called.

Tessa laughed and set the figurine aside.

DeVries broke the seal on another box and looked in. "Woo Hoo!" he said. "We have hit the mother load of underwear. Vintage Calvin Klein. Woulda been nice if the guys who boxed this up woulda marked the boxes somehow. Nothing fancy. Bedroom. Kitchen. That woulda done."

"*Aw, fuck me!*"

Everyone wheeled around to find Reid Bramwell holding his hands splayed out in front of him. They glistened.

Caballero started toward him, caught a whiff and stopped, nose wrinkled. "Goddamn, Reid. What is that?"

"A hundred years ago or so, it used to be a full bottle of shower gel with a cracked cap. Now it's glue. Smelly glue." He gingerly pulled a towel from the box and attempted to scrape the goo off. "How come we don't rate a dumpster?"

"Oh, quit whining. Just go wash it off in the back bathroom," Tessa said pulling a wooden chest over.

"Not on your life. I swear the last time I went in there, something growled at me."

"Wuss," she said cheerfully as she pulled packing out and tossed it on the floor. "Kick the door real hard before you . . . Oh my. . . ."

"What?" Reid asked, looking for a place to toss the now-gooey towel.

"This," she said holding up an open lacquerware box. It was filled with man's jewelry.

"Wow!" Vaughn said, leaving the underwear for the shinies. He came over, took the box and rooted through its contents.

"This whole chest seems to be full of jewelry boxes," Tessa said. "What are we going to do with them? The Regional Security Officer at the embassy is already bitching that we're sending too much stuff too fast for the office to process."

"Awwwww," Bramwell drawled. "Breaks my heart that the poor little desk jockeys are so overworked by the stacks of currency and bearer bonds we found behind the pictures."

Tessa rolled her eyes. "Reid. . . ."

Her partner snapped his fingers as if a thought just occurred to him. "Hey! I know! Let's swap places with them. I'll gladly count money in their air conditioned hell hole and *they* can root through all the Egyptian cotton towels marinated in vintage shower gel in stuffy, temperature-controlled splendor."

Josh pushed escaped pony tail hairs out of his face. "I'll go with you!"

"Nah," DeVries said. "You're essential personnel. You have to stay with the bath towels."

Tessa guffawed. "It's true. How else could those office wonks be able to distinguish late 20th century Bvlgari from post-modern Old Spice?"

"Bite me, Caballero," Katzen said.

DeVries lifted a diamond and ruby ring from the tangled mass of gold chains. "I bet if this stuff went to auction, it would go a ways to pay for the warehouse."

Josh took a long pull of cold water. "Maybe we should ship some of the personal items — like the jewelry — to Deustch's sister."

Caballero looked up from her growing wall of jewelry boxes. "He had a sister?"

"Yep," Josh said. "Her name is Margaret and she lives in New York City."

DeVries dropped the ring back into the lacquerware cask and nodded. "Sounds like the right thing to do — long as the stuff was legitimately bought. And as long as they ain't gonna try to RICO it. I'll check."

Bramwell looked hopeful. "If we do, can we ship the underwear and shower gel to her, too?"

~*~

Vaughn DeVries surveyed the massive, antique chest of drawers sourly. "No labels. No plan. Blocking stuff with honking big pieces of furniture . . . what sort of yahoos moved this stuff in here?"

"Probably a bunch of involuntary volunteers," Caballero said.

"Sorta like us," Vaughn agreed with a grin. "Okay folks, one, two, *threeeeee*."

The walnut behemoth resisted for a beat, then shifted a few feet to the left revealing a corner full of sealed boxes.

Vaughn dusted his hands. "Well, that's that. We can move it back when— Josh? Something wrong?"

Katzen stood silently staring at the chest. After a moment he said, "Wait a sec." Tilting his head, he ran his hands lightly over a section of the heavily carved central frieze. There was a slight click as the carving moved almost imperceptibly and the flat section between the first and second drawers popped out of flush.

Bramwell stared for a moment, then said, "Well, damn! Look at that."

"That is too cool," Tessa said. "I've heard about secret compartments, but I never really saw one before."

"Many pieces of antique furniture had hiding places built into them," he said absently as he carefully fingertipped the wooden panel out, revealing a shallow, long covered drawer. Lifting the lid revealed two passports, several stacks of money and a chamois bag.

Reid Bramwell looked at the artist with new appreciation. "You got mad thief skills, kiddo. Glad you're on *our* side," he said as he hefted the bag. "Bet I know what this is. . . . Yep."

A glittering stream of cut diamonds spilled onto the felted bottom of the drawer.

DeVries gave an appreciative whistle. "Man, oh man! Someone was sure ready to bunk on short notice."

Josh said, "We'll probably find more like this, so we better take care." He paused, then turned to DeVries. "That reminds me. I hope someone searched that house of his inside and out."

DeVries nodded. "Just short of dismantling it. We found a floor safe in the bedroom, a wall safe in his study and a hidden stash behind the commode in the bathroom. They ought to put this guy's picture in the dictionary under paranoia."

Josh chuckled. "Considering how he ended up, he had good reason."

"Oh, put those down," Bramwell said. He sounded exasperated.

Josh turned and found Tessa rolling a few of the larger diamonds around in her hand. Glaring at her partner, she said, "*Your* picture is under asshole." Brushing the stones back into the drawer, she sighed. "A girl can dream, can't she?"

Katzen laughed and scooped the glittering mound back

into the bag. "Yep. A boy can, too. Let's get these things logged and over to the embassy to add to the RSO's workload."

~*~

With the last print logged and crated, he was ready to start on something else. The man may have been a card-carrying ratsass, but no one could fault Herb Deustch's art choices. Over the preceding days, Katzen had photographed an amazing variety of work from an early Flemish altar piece to a David Hockney aquatint. He'd never let DeVries know, but he was sort of enjoying the work — environmental conditions not withstanding.

He folded his arms and looked around for the next task. Near the far end of the all but empty painting racks stood a tall shelf loaded with small artifacts and sculptures. Nothing was over a foot high with a huge range of cultures and eras represented. Perfect. He selected a pre-Columbian stone piece and headed back to his staging area.

Caballero sat close by with one of her ubiquitous sliding puzzles. She looked tired and sweaty, her dark hair escaping the silver combs in a fine mist of curls. Setting her puzzle aside, she watched him adjust the lighting to enhance the worn, intricately carved pattern on the largest side. Abruptly she said, "Thanks, by the way."

He'd been concentrating on light and shadow so her comment took him by surprise. "What?"

"Earlier. With the diamonds," she shrugged, took up the puzzle again and picked at it absently. "Reid is getting short and he's convinced I'm going to do something that will screw up his retirement."

Josh shrugged. "Hey, you weren't doing anything that I wouldn't have done. A pile of cut diamonds is an amazing sight. Kind of a natural reaction to touch them."

"Still, he overreacts sometimes. I appreciated the support."

He grinned. "Any time."

Sitting back, she frowned at the item on the stand. "What

the hell is that thing? It just looks like a sort of round rock. With a hole in it."

"It's a manopla. Think of it as an ancient set of brass knuckles. The design on this one looks Mayan. Probably worn by a ball player."

Eyes wide at the explanation, Tessa leaned forward and re-examined the artifact. "Holy shit! I'd hate to get hit with that."

"Me, too," Josh said. Pulling the catalog form up on his laptop, he started typing the description. "Actually, I'm kind of surprised Deustch held onto this. These things were selling for several thousand dollars even back in the 80s."

Caballero looked as stunned as if she'd been whacked with the manopla. "Thousands?" she asked in a small voice.

"Absolutely. There's a lot of money in the illegal antiquities market. That's why it's still going strong — and why terrorist and other criminal organizations have gotten into the act. Small items. Easily smuggled. Sell for beaucoup bucks."

She sat motionless, staring blankly at the manopla as if frozen between slices of time.

Josh noticed the silence and glanced up. "Hey. You okay?"

She straightened, and concentrated on clicking the puzzle tiles around. "Yeah sure."

Josh watched her. It was as if she had shaken free of some sort of trance and forced herself back to normal. She'd done a pretty good job, but she still seemed a little stiff. A little angry.

After a moment, she smacked the puzzle down onto the desktop and spat, "Pisses me off, though. Jerk-offs like that damned el Mago are getting *tons* of cash for these things — and me? The US government pays me shit."

There wasn't much to be said to that. Josh made a noncommittal grunt and went back to his cataloging.

~*~

He was alone in the warehouse for once and was damned glad of it. Hiding in the jumble on the shelf were a dozen Hellenistic bronze statuettes, the largest no more than nine centimeters. The three tiny, dancing ladies in the group were enough to take his breath away — and make his hands itch. Being alone gave him time to simply hold them and feel a connection with the ancient sculptor through his lint-free, archival cotton gloves. Long ago, in his own ancient history, before General Fuller had gotten hold of him, the ladies would have neatly disappeared. He had no trouble at all understanding why Herb Deustch held onto these — the plastic Statue of Liberty thermometer still had him a bit confused, though.

The outside door rolled noisily up and Tessa Caballero ducked through. She had recovered from her earlier dark mood and lifted two large take-away bags as she called, "I'm back! I brought lunch! I hit the place down the block. That joint is great, they serve a little bit of everything. I *bought* a little bit of everything, too, so help yourself."

She dropped the bags onto the desktop, then gasped as she saw what Josh had. "Ooooh! Those are such beautiful little things."

"That they are. Bronze statuettes from the Greek Hellenistic period. Look at that drapery. You can almost see it move," he said, carefully distancing the figurine from the backdrop. Her patina was dark, so he'd selected a light, neutral color to contrast her.

Tessa pursed her lips. "Valuable, too, I bet."

"Mmmmm hmmm. A piece similar to this recently sold in Tel Aviv for eight thousand through Shenhav's auction house," he said. "Very fine piece — like most of the stuff in here."

"I'm in the wrong line of work," she grumbled, plopping herself on the desk beside the paper bags. Pulling the closest one over, she unpacked it, then took out a small parcel covered with stamps. When she opened it, Josh could almost feel the happy roll off her.

He nodded toward the box. "Another care package from your sister?"

She looked blank, then brightened. "That's right. I told you about these back up at the camp. My sister just sent me a new bunch. From the way the colors look on them, I think they might be pics from when we were kids."

"That could be fun," he said. "Or embarrassing. Considering some of the pics I remember from my childhood, maybe both in equal degrees."

She smiled into her treasure trove for a few moments more, then set it aside as she remembered something. Pulling two clear plastic boxes from a deli bag, she said, "Oops! Almost forgot the most important thing. I got us some decadence. Tiramisu. Still nice and cool from the deli case. But, in order for it to be truly decadent, we have to eat it first."

"Come to Peru and get an Italian dessert," Josh laughed and turned his attention back to the tiny dancer.

"Oh come on! You deserve a treat after slogging through all this dusty stuff for days and days." She jabbed a fork into one of the desserts and held it out.

"Hey! I like this dusty stuff. It's some of the best dusty stuff I've seen in a long time."

She pushed the box toward him. "It's still cooooold," she wheedled.

Self-control crumbled and he took a forkful. Tessa was right, it *was* cold and wonderfully rich. "Why did it have to be tiramisu?" he muttered. "I could have held out against anything else — except maybe chicharrones."

"Chicharrones? Isn't that pork?"

"Yeah! Deep fried in pork fat. Second best reason not to keep kosher. It might be better for my weight if I did, though."

"Second best? What's the first?"

"Lobster."

"You sound like my sister."

"The one who sent you the puzzles?"

"That's the one. Always worrying about her weight, too."

He took another bite of the creamy dessert. "It's not as easy to take off the pounds these days."

"Oh bullshit. You look fine. Anyway, you can work it off with me later."

"Oh, now, *that* sounds suggestive."

"PFFFFTTTT. I meant you can join me on my morning run."

"Ah. No thanks. I make it a policy to only run if chased."

Tessa stifled a giggle and swatted at him. "You almost made me snort coffee out my nose." Blotting her face with a paper napkin, she said casually, "So, are you with anyone?"

He was at a loss with the abrupt change of subject, then the penny dropped. "Oh! No. No, I'm not. I'm usually in my studio, at the computer or on a dig. Not a lifestyle incredibly conducive to romance. You? You probably have them lined up."

She snerked and blotted with the napkin again. "Oh right. The life of a DSS special agent isn't too romantic, either. That is unless you get involved with someone else in the service. After the last disaster, I made a policy: never date another cop."

"I've had a similar policy for a long time."

She looked up, face alight with curiosity. "So where do *you* think it is?"

"Hmmm? Where what is?"

"Hello!" Rapping knuckles on his head, she said, "*It*. The package. The mysterious thingummy this is all about."

"Oh, *that*," he said with a laugh. "No idea."

"You're kidding. We've been sorting through all stuff all this time and you still don't have a clue to where he hid it — or even *what* it is? I mean it would help to put a name to it. I feel kind of silly calling it 'the Package' all the time."

Setting his tiramisu aside, he opened his arms wide encompassing the cavernous room. "Look at all this! Vaughn called it: it would have been helpful if the agents that seized Deutsch's house and contents had made a better record. Even if they had, though, they just tossed it in here any which way, then locked the door and left." He chuckled. "In some ways it reminds me of a friend of mine. When he moved, he put off packing until almost the last minute. Then he panicked and tossed things into whatever box was closest. When we helped him unload, there were all these boxes with no labels — nothing. We'd unpack one and it was stuff from the pantry, then the next was skulls—"

"*Skulls?*"

"Yep. He's an anthropologist."

"Still . . . *ick!*"

"Okay, I won't tell you about helping the entomologist move her office."

"That's bugs, right?"

He grinned and nodded.

"Oh, please. *Don't.*"

The door rattled again and Reid Bramwell and Vaughn DeVries came through.

"Man, I never thought I'd be happy to leave a party and come back to this place," Vaughn said.

"Ditto," said Reid. "If I had to listen to that Bejing bureaucrat drone on about Chinese history for another minute, I'd have created an international incident. It would have been known to the world as the Great Shrimp Toast Massacre."

"So," Vaughn asked coming over to the work area, "What have you guys been up to— Oh! Tiramisu!" He grabbed a spare fork and took a taste. "Man! This is good. Where'd this come from?"

"Tessa bought lunch," Josh said, laughing. "Here, you finish it."

Reid was already rooting through the bags. He nodded toward the bronzes. "What are those? They look kind of like the figures my nephew uses to play his dungeon games."

"Not quite, numbnuts," Tessa said with a wink at Josh. "Those are Hellenistic Greek bronzes. One of those sold for eight grand not too long ago."

"Yeah?" Reid said. "Okay, Ms. Encyclopedia Caballero, can you tell me where the corned beef is in this bag?"

DeVries chuckled and turned away from the kibbitzing partners. "So I gather we're back from China and on our way to Greece? At least this assignment is letting me see the world, even if it is just one embassy at a time."

Josh nodded and more collapsed than sat on the metal stool beside his photographic setup. "Y'know, sending these things back home is all real cool. It's thinning the herd and everything, but Tessa and I were just talking about how we're no closer to finding what *we're* looking for."

"Good point," Bramwell said around a mouthful of corned beef on rye that had mysteriously been buried at the bottom of a bag under a double handful of napkins. "It's been a fun treasure hunt, but we still haven't come across a single thing that's advanced the investigation."

Vaughn nodded. "Okay, now we got enough room to swing a cat in, maybe we need to refine our method. What would we be looking for? Papers? Photos?"

"Most likely, all of the above. From what I've read about Deutsch, he'll have kept records. They'll probably be cryptic, but there will be records," Josh said.

"Office-type stuff, then?" Vaughn dropped the now-empty plastic container into a trash barrel. "Well, folks, let's find us some paperwork."

CHAPTER 13

The taxi dropped Katzen at the Jorge Chávez International Airport with time to spare, but he still felt rushed. Airports always did that to him. He paid the cabbie and dove into the crush of travelers in the main terminal. For once *he* wasn't rushing to catch the flight, though, and he was damned glad of it. Much of his life had been spent in places almost indistinguishable from this, making mad dashes disguised as casual strolls, often with dangerous people hot on his heels. He mentally brushed that away. It wouldn't do to dwell on the past too much — especially those parts of it — he'd probably get depressed if he did.

Today was an altogether different circumstance, anyway. Today he was rushing to see friends heading home, a happy occasion even if the reasons they were leaving weren't good. Finding a modern murder victim in the ancient ruins had spawned a storm of problems by itself, but that hadn't been the final blow. The ultimate decision to send the students home came because of the uptick of *huaquero* activity shortly after the body was found. Katzen had been lucky that the group he interrupted were kids and armed with only a couple knives and chainsaws they didn't really know how to use. El Mago controlled the looting operations in those parts for all intents and purposes. El Mago was a violent man even by the standards of other *huaqueros*, and the members of his gang took their cue from him.

Banishing thoughts of tomb robbers, he headed for the escalators. The second floor would be the logical place to start looking for his friends since the shops and food court were up there. Not far from the head of the escalator stood a small oasis of benches. It would be a perfect location to step out of the pedestrian flow and scan for familiar faces. That wasn't completely accurate. In reality, he'd do what he usually did: look for Avi Rosenberg. If you couldn't pick Rosenberg out of a crowd, you weren't trying.

He hadn't even reached the benches when he heard: "Josh! You made it!" And found himself being bearhugged by Amelia Peters.

The girl released him, then turned back to one of the shops and called, "Hey guys, I'm taking Josh to the main group. Remember: food court twenty minutes!"

A huge, stuffed alpaca answered, "Gotcha!" A tiny Asian girl named Lin peeked around the alpaca and waved. "Hey, Josh! Glad you made it!"

He managed to wave back before Amelia pulled him into the crowd, chattering as she went. "I have no idea how she's going to get that onto the plane, but if anyone can do it, it's Lin. Robert is in the back trying on sweaters. Most everyone else is already at the food court. Folks will be real glad to see you, especially Dr. Pale. He and I are the chaperons for the group this time around since Dr. Rosenberg and Dr. Armand are staying behind to close up the camp. . . ."

Josh let the infodump wash over him and allowed himself to be towed. It was kind of nice; almost like coming home himself.

As they neared the food court, Josh spotted Avi Rosenberg and Vic Pale lounging at a table near the far wall. Rosenberg was trying to make himself inconspicuous. That never worked.

Amelia cheerfully dodged through diners carrying trays, calling out, "Look what I found!"

Avi looked up, then waved his hand dismissively. "Take it back to where you got it. It'll shed all over the furniture."

Amelia rolled her eyes. "If I didn't know you guys were

friends. . . . Well, I gotta go corral Lin and Robert, anyway. Laterz!"
and she was gone.

Vic watched her bustle away. "Man, you need to—"

"Don't start!" Rosenberg commanded.

"What?" Pale asked, oozing innocence.

Josh laughed and took in the restaurant signs. "Wow. All
the familiar places. You'd think we were already back in the
States."

"You should have heard the kids when they spotted Burger
King and Starbucks. If Manny was here, we'd be looking for a new
cook next season," Rosenberg said.

"Not to be doom and gloom, but will there *be* a next season?
El Mago and his band of goons could put a serious crimp in that,"
Katzen said quietly.

"There will be if I have anything to say about it. Not just
because of the research grants, either. We're doing good work
here and I don't want to lose the momentum we've built. It
will have to be a smaller team, fewer students and more
guards, but I plan to be here," the archaeologist said with
finality.

Katzen hummed a little and decided to change subjects. "So,
where's Harper?"

"Still in Piedras Rojas," Avi said. "She had an emergency
just before we rolled out. One of Manny's cousins found a
broken bottle the hard way. Harper stayed behind to stitch the
kid up. Her goodbyes were already said, anyway, since she's
staying on to help me shut down the camp this season."

"Yeah. Covering for me," Josh said. "Sorry to leave you in
the lurch like this. I'm sure Harper would much rather be heading
home to her son than cataloging and packing jade beads for the
Museo."

"Oh, I don't think she's all that brokenhearted," Vic said, then
smiled. "Her son is still away at school and sticking around gives
her a little more time with Diego."

"And Diego will be around quite a bit the next week or so. The kids that tripped over you are in custody, but their pals haven't been idle," Avi said.

"More *huaquero* activity?" Josh asked, suddenly concerned.

"We've been finding more and more pits in the hills surrounding the main dig. Diego is promising to keep guards at the site in the off season, but he can only do so much," Rosenberg said. "Enough about that. Talking about it won't solve anything. Tell us what you've been doing — what you can tell anyway."

Josh sat back in the flimsy plastic chair and considered. At last he said, "Truth to tell, it hasn't been all that different from what I was doing here. Just shy of thirty years ago, the authorities seized the contents of Deustch's home in Lima. Lots of art, lots of artifacts. We've been documenting it, finding out who it really belongs to and sending it home where we can. DeVries wrangled two Diplomatic Security agents, Tessa Caballero and Reid Bramwell to help us, so we're making okay progress. We're on hiatus today so Vaughn can hand-deliver some paintings and tapestries to the Italian embassy."

"Sounds non-threatening," Avi said. "I was worried that asshole was going to drag you into a firefight or something."

Josh laughed. "Nothing that exciting, I'm afraid."

"Well, regardless, I'm not going anywhere until you're free and clear, my friend," the archaeologist stated. "So if you're still cataloging when we've finished closing, I might come on over and lend a hand."

"The help — especially *your* help — would be welcome, but you have way too much to do when you get back stateside to let you waste your time with this. Vic—"

Vic raised his hand to cut him off. "Nope, don't try to get me on your side, Josh. I don't like the idea of you being down here alone, either. This might be same old, same old as far as you're concerned, but that you isn't *you* any more. You need some backup, or at the very least, moral support."

Before Josh could protest again, Avi looked past him and said, "Ahhh, looks like 'Melia is flagging me. Gevalt! That thing's almost as big as a real alpaca! How's Lin going to get that on the plane?"

Katzen watched his friend saunter away, then swung his shoulder pack around. "I thought he'd never leave. I have a going away present for you, Vic."

"Ya?" Pale asked skeptically.

Without ceremony, Josh clunked the Indiana Jones bobblehead onto the table between them. The head bobbled.

The former rocker's face lit with evil glee. "Ooooooooh! That's beautiful." The statuette disappeared into his carry-on in one swift movement. "I guarantee this a place of honor on my office shelf. Behind the desk. Where he can't reach it without going through me."

"If he sees it when I'm not there, you have to take notes."

"Deal."

"Crisis averted. Lin's passport had gotten in with her tentmate's," Rosenberg slid into his chair, then his eyes narrowed and flicked between his two friends. "Why do I feel like I've interrupted some sort of clandestine operation?"

"You, my friend, harbor a nasty, suspicious streak," Vic said casually. "I, on the other hand, harbor nothing more than the desire for a final cup of Peruvian coffee. I saw a sign for one of the local coffeehouses just around that corner. Let's grab a cup before they call for boarding."

~*~

It really wouldn't be a bad idea to bring Rosenberg into the operation, Katzen mused as he let himself into his hotel room. It wasn't just the appeal of working with an old friend, but Avi could bring invaluable expertise to the job. Convincing DeVries would be the sticking point, though. Vaughn and Avi seemed to be natural enemies.

Dropping the laptop onto the bed, he stretched and rolled his shoulders. The day had been enjoyable, but it had been busy and he was beat. Shower. Yeah. That was the ticket. Shucking his sweaty shirt next to the laptop, he'd taken two steps toward the bathroom when his mental alarms went off. Something was wrong. What?

Turning in place, he surveyed the room. Everything looked okay until he got to the tell on the closet door. It was tripped. The one on the suitcase rack was disturbed, too. Damn. Going into the bathroom, he turned the shower on full, then quietly returned to the bedroom. A more careful examination confirmed it. Someone had tossed his room. It was a thorough job, and since only the two tells hadn't been set back, most likely someone in the business. Those particular signals had tripped up quite a few searchers over the years. They were his most subtle and unconventional ones. His own brief search hadn't turned up any bugs, but he'd lay money they were there.

For the benefit of any listeners, he took a quick shower and went through the usual motions of a tourist coming back to home base. Hair still damp in case there were any watchers in the halls, he pulled a sticky note from the computer case and scribbled:

My room's been tossed by pros. Probably yours, too. Might be bugged.

Settling the case back onto his shoulder, he crossed the hall to Vaughn's room.

DeVries was on his cell and absently opened the door, motioning Katzen in. He was saying, "Sure, Tessa, we understand. The Sec State takes precedence over what we're doing.

"Uh huh. No problem. You and Reid have a job to do. We'll just pick up again when she leaves," he said, pacing and worrying his close-cropped hair. "Sure thing, Beautiful! Say, Josh just showed up, I'll catch you later, huh?"

Snapping the phone closed, he said, "Man! Talk about bad timing. The Secretary of State decided to swing by Peru on her way to god knows where, so the embassy security chief has scrambled all personnel until further notice."

"Wow. That sucks," Josh held the note up. "They'll probably have to go to a fancy party with free food and everything."

DeVries took the note and stared at it, looking stunned.

"Speaking of food, I'm starving," Katzen continued. "Let's

hit that place on the corner. I hear they have a *papa rellena* to kill for."

"Sounds good," DeVries glanced around nervously. "I was just thinking of calling room service, but this is better. Let me grab my jacket."

~*~

The cafe was small, busy and noisy, perfect for a private conversation. Perfect if DeVries could stop checking over his shoulder, anyway.

"Calm down," Josh said, as they slid into one of the few empty booths.

"That's easy for you to say. You probably been through this before."

"Lots," Katzen said lifting a menu. "Just because I know the drill doesn't mean I have to like it."

"I gotta call Len," DeVries said pulling out his cell.

Katzen shook his head and shoved a menu at him. "We're too open, too easy to overhear."

The conversation turned to nothing subjects as the server, a pretty young indio woman, approached to take their orders. As soon as the waitress disappeared through the kitchen doors, DeVries leaned over and hissed, "But we probably been compromised."

"Maybe so, maybe no. Call later. Out on the street where the phone won't be too obvious and the background noise will make it harder to listen in."

"You're right, I'm just twitchy is all. Kicking myself, too. Something didn't feel right when I got back from the embassy thing. I should have checked. Just pure laziness that I didn't."

"You might not have found anything. I didn't — well, other than my room's been searched."

The waitress bustled out of the kitchen with her arms loaded with food. Treating the Americanos to a brilliant smile, she dealt out the dishes, winked and hurried away.

Katzen returned the smile, then told DeVries, "Look, whoever did it was a pro. Most of my tells still looked pristine, but there were two that they maybe didn't recognize as tells that were disturbed."

"But, what are they looking for?"

"Same thing we're looking for?" Josh answered with a helpless shrug. "We weren't the only ones who knew what our boy nicked. We sure aren't the only ones to know his body has been found. This guy was a cosmic grade asshole. CNN even did a segment on him after his identity was confirmed."

"I hadn't thought of that. I don't know why I hadn't." DeVries paused and took a bite of his papa rellena. "That opens up a whole new realm of suspects."

Josh teased the corn husk away from a tamale with his fork. "Mmmm hmmm. Up to and including whoever iced ol' Herb in the first place — although I think the analysts nailed that. Our loose Chinese cannon was the shooter."

"I didn't need to think about *that*." Vaughn chewed a little, then brightened. "Hey, this potato stuff is great!"

"Tamales are nice, too."

"Good intel, Katzen. Have to give your CI a few extra Sols."

"Oh, I made that up. We needed to get out of the hotel to a random location. We pass this place on the way to the warehouse and it always smells *so* good. Try the shrimp with aji sauce; it's fantastic."

DeVries sat frozen in mid-chew, then he guffawed and snagged a forkful of shrimp.

CHAPTER 14

He couldn't remember the nightmares. Considering the sick, hollow feeling they left when he awoke tangled in sweaty bedsheets, he probably didn't want to. After the umpteenth trip to the bathroom to splash cold water on his face, he finally admitted sleep wasn't going to happen. He wondered what the guys listening thought about their subject waking up screaming every fifteen minutes. Maybe he was ruining their evening. He hoped so. Why should he be the only schmuck having a rotten night?

He paced, channel chased and more than once stood staring into the mini bar. That was useless, though. He knew by now that trying to drink himself to sleep was simply a waste of good scotch — or bad — depending on the mini bar. Flinging himself into an armchair, he stared unseeing at an incomprehensible program about meerkats.

He gave up, ignored the meerkat antics and tried to work out what was bugging him. Well, okay *other* than the actual listening device. No, that's what it was. Not exactly the bug. It was the whole shebang — the spy game. He'd been out and happy for once in his life. Now the Pentagon had reached out and yanked him back. Somehow, Herb Deustch triggered it, even before he knew it was Deustch. The bad nights had all but disappeared before that.

The search for the damned plutonium was another huge chunk of it. Lack of search, actually. Sure, he was glad the artworks and antiquities were going back to where they belonged — especially pleased at several Nazi-looted paintings restored to the families of the original owners. Still, the going was painfully slow. At their present pace, they might finish up by the turn of the next century. If they were lucky. Would they even find Deustch's stash by then? Who knew. One thing he did know was that the longer this thing drew out, the worse his nights got. It was only a matter of time before the daytime flashbacks returned. No. He refused to go there.

Decisively, he switched off the meerkats. If the pentagon wonks were going to nuke his retirement until he found their package, then he'd *find* their goddamned package. His way. He needed to gather all the information he could, then surround himself with it and get into the mind of Herb Deustch. That sure as hell wasn't going to happen sitting on his tochis in a hotel room.

~*~

The cabbie was reluctant to leave a lone Americano at the run-down address Katzen had given, but a few extra Sols won the argument. The taillights of the taxi shrank up the dark street and disappeared around a corner before Katzen turned and walked away in the opposite direction. The night was moonless, and without the light from the car's headlights, the area was pitch dark. That suited his purpose perfectly. No one hindered him as he walked the four remaining blocks and crested a rise to the warehouse complex. There was a part of him that was a tad disappointed. It would have felt pretty good to kick the crap out of someone right about then.

Up ahead, the warehouse complex was an oasis of light. He flattened into the scrubby growth at the perimeter as a guard cruised by on his regular rounds. The sulfur-yellow lights painted the olive drab vehicle a sickly hue and lent the unreal air of a movie set to the complex beyond the fence. As soon as the Humvee disappeared between the buildings, he slipped out of the scruffy suede jacket he'd worn for this exact purpose. Swinging the garment over the razor wire at the top of the chain link barrier, he was up, over and loping through the shadows toward building 86 in a matter of seconds.

Using the code DeVries had given him to let himself in, he was thankful that the complex was on the low end of tech. If the keypad was smart enough to actually log entries and exits, he'd have had to go a different route. That wouldn't have been hard; he'd broken into heavier security, but it would have taken time he didn't want to lose.

He made sure the metal window shades were firmly in place before he switched on the light at the desk. When the laptop booted to the home screen, he winced at the time. "Oh man," he groaned. "The rest of today is gonna suck."

"Yep, it surely will." DeVries said from behind him.

Katzen spun on him, eyes narrowed and jaw tightened. "Look, you can say what you want, but I'm going to get all the data I can onto my own systems right here, right now. I don't give a flying fuck what Washington does or doesn't want me to have."

"Cool, 'cause I don't either. You get that sucker fired up and I'll make coffee."

After a moment, Katzen relaxed, then asked, "So, did you follow me or what? You gotta be pretty damned good if you did, because I was watching for a tail."

DeVries paused, then said, "I wish I could claim that, but I have to be honest. Len warned me that finding your room under surveillance by unknown parties would probably make you go all Lone Ranger."

Katzen hid a smile by leaning over to connect the scanner. "He did, huh?" he managed at last.

"Yep, and I was lucky enough to be opening my door on an ice run when you hit the stairs. Figured you'd be headed here. Don't worry, though. I came in the back way, too. No need for any official record of what we're gonna to do." He rooted in the mini fridge next to the coffee maker. "Dammit! Any idea where Bramwell hid those pricey beans he bought? I figure if they're gonna make us do all the work, they might as well buy the coffee."

~*~

"Another passport. No cash this time," Katzen said peering into the compartment at the bottom of an 18th Century wardrobe.

"How many is that? Nine?" DeVries asked.

"Counting the ones we found earlier, yeah. Deustch was one secretive sonovabitch. Acted more like a spy than an antiquities dealer."

Shaking his head, DeVries took the booklet and placed it on the flatbed scanner. "Well, we're filling up the memory cards, but I ain't seeing anything that looks to be much use — or am I missing something?"

"Not unless we're both missing it. Given how long we've been up at this point, I wouldn't put money against that."

"Oh, do *not* bring that up. I put a sticky note over the clock on your laptop so I wouldn't have to look at it no more."

Josh laughed and scratched a line through the wardrobe on his list of large furniture items. "One 18th century wardrobe down; the early 19th century secretary is next."

"Which is? I know it ain't a really old person with a steno pad."

"It's this," Josh said, stepping over to a tall piece of furniture that resembled a buffet topped with a glass-fronted bookshelf. Lowering a hinged door at the front exposed a warren of cubbyholes and small drawers. "Sort of the precursor of the all-in-one. . . ."

As the words trailed off, Katzen crouched down to squint into the top row of cubbyholes. Fascinated, DeVries abandoned the scanner to watch the former thief's examination.

"Ah ha," Katzen said, sliding one wall of the leftmost niche out. There was a barely audible click and the top of the compartment dropped down. Reaching in, he pulled out a stack of nondescript two-ring notebooks.

"Damn! Len said you were good. Told me watching you work was better than a hundred training instructors in classrooms."

Katzen riffled through the old, well-thumbed pages, then set them aside. Reaching into the right cubbyhole, he was rewarded with another barely audible click. That compartment was full of small, dogeared binders of photographs. His smile was weary, but triumphant. "Bingo! I think we've found what we're looking for, or at least a key to what we're looking for."

"Weird," DeVries said flipping through the topmost scrapbook. "These pics are all of ruins."

"Mountain and jungle shots; probably here in Peru." Katzen nodded, then his eyes widened. "Whoa, whoa, whoa! Let me see that!"

Baffled, DeVries relinquished the booklet. Katzen carried it over to the brighter lights at the worktable, slowly paging through. Near the back, he paused, closely examining a particular group of images. Tapping one of the pictures, he said, "You want weird? This page here is what is now the Piedras Rojas dig site. That *has* to be the ceremonial platform that was collapsed on Deustch's body twenty some years ago."

"That ain't weird, that's just plain spooky."

They stood staring at the page in silence until DeVries asked hopefully. "So, you think this is it? We found everything we need to?"

Katzen puffed out a breath. "I dunno. There's only one way to find out."

DeVries turned slowly taking in the still-remaining pieces of furniture and art they had to search. After a moment, he groaned, "We're gonna need more coffee."

CHAPTER 15

"I think I'd enjoy these chiccarones more if I wasn't trying to nod out in them," Katzen said. "How's the burger?"

"It's good. Even better to not be eating leftovers from the mini fridge for the first time in. . . ." DeVries looked at his watch. "Oh, lookie! It's tomorrow."

Katzen made no response other than to spear another piece of crispy pork.

They ate in silence until DeVries asked, "Do you think we got everything?"

"You asked me that fifteen minutes ago and I still think if we didn't get everything, we got what we needed."

"Hope you're right. Damn I'm tired. Never used to get this tired."

Josh chuckled, but before he could respond, DeVries' cell phone went off.

"DeVries. . . . Hey, Tessa! Wha— Whoa! Slow down. Yeah, we can get there in a few minutes." He snapped the phone shut.

"That did not sound good. What happened?"

"We need to get over to Bramwell's place ASAP. He's been murdered."

~*~

The street outside Reid Bramwell's rented bungalow was crammed with official cars. Neighbors in their nightclothes, standing in concerned knots, looked like cardboard cutouts under the strobing light bars of a dozen different official vehicles. The normal quiet of the residential street was shattered by conversation in multiple languages and the staticky chatter of police radios. DeVries held his Pentagon ID open against the SUV's side window as they made slow progress through the barricades set up by assorted officialdom to finally park in front of the house.

The cell in Vaughn's rumpled uniform jacket went off almost as soon as the car came to a halt. He glanced at it and frowned. "It's General Fuller. I better take this."

Katzen nodded and stepped out onto the pavement. "I'll do a little recon, then."

Closing the door on the conversation, he leaned casually against the vehicle and scanned the area. He counted three separate official entities occupying the same space at the same time. Yep. Full fledged bureaucratic clusterfuck. The biggest knot of people was on the stoop of the bungalow. From the words that reached him on the windless night, it sounded like someone, probably the Diplomatic Security Service, was stonewalling the other groups. Off to one side, he was surprised to see Tessa Caballero sitting on the hood of her Jeep working one of her puzzles like she'd rather be smashing it. Her little red car sat directly in front of Bramwell's truck and was parked in by official vehicles. The positioning made sense. She'd told DeVries she'd been the first on the scene, but the fact she was outside and apart didn't.

He went over and scooted up onto the Jeep beside her. "Hey. You okay? What are you doing out here by yourself?"

She glared, then softened as she recognized him. "Hi, Josh. I guess it all boils down to the fact that the AIC is an asshole who never liked me — *and* threw me out as soon as he got here. My own goddamned partner and he throws me out."

DeVries walked up the driveway toward them, sliding his cell back into his jacket. "Well that sucks pondscum, Tessa. Who is the Agent in Charge?"

"Special Agent Arash Rastogi. We came into the embassy at about the same time, but I had more seniority with the service, so he thinks I get better details than he does."

DeVries nodded. "I know the type. Why don't you tell me what happened here, then we'll see what we can do about ruining Special Agent Rastogi's day."

She took a deep breath, blew it out, then said, "Right after we got the call that Sec State was coming, Reid started complaining that he didn't feel good." She shrugged with a wry smile. "That wasn't unusual. Bramwell hated those kind of assignments. Called diplomatic cocktail parties 'Caviar Circuses'. I think the RSO knew it was another case of the Close-To-Retirement-Go-To-Hells but didn't want to argue. Reid was supposed to be back on duty tonight after Sec State left, but he didn't show. I tried to call. . . ."

She went still, staring into the strobe of the nearest police car. Finally she said, "I never lost a partner before. I've seen plenty of dead bodies over the years, but they never got to me like this. I'm going to miss that sonovabitch."

There was an uncomfortable silence as Caballero fought for control of her emotions, then DeVries said, "I just got off the phone with my boss in D.C. and he tells me the ambassador has given us clearance to be on the scene. We're headed inside. You want to come, too?"

She shook her head. "Thanks, but I think I'm better out here. If I go inside I might have to shoot Rastogi."

Katzen gave her a brief shoulder squeeze, then slid off the Jeep. As he and DeVries turned to go, she said quietly, "They broke his neck. They trashed the place and broke his neck. Why would anyone do that?"

As they walked toward the knot of milling agents and police, DeVries said quietly, "Got some interesting info from General Fuller. Seems they sent a sweep team into our rooms while we were at the warehouse today. You were right. Bugs out the wahzoo."

"Sometimes being right sucks. They stomp on them?"

"Nope. Left them where they were."

Katzen nodded. He hated being eavesdropped on, but that was the wisest move.

"That ain't the most interesting part, though," DeVries said. "Seems the bugs were older ones, the kind the KGB used before they wasn't the KGB no more."

"Great. Possible Russian involvement, too. Well, they and the Chinese were in a hot bidding war. What else? I know Len. There's always something else."

"We're supposed to liaise with the Agent in Charge and ascertain whether this is connected to Deustch's package or just an unfortunate coincidence."

"Wonderfulness. When you said we were going in, I was afraid it was something like that."

DeVries sighed, seated his hat on his head, straightened his tie and tugged down on his rumpled jacket.

"Lost cause, man. Looks like you slept in it."

"As if I slept. Well, no help for it. Let's get this done before we're up for another twenty-four."

~*~

Katzen stepped through the open front door to a scene of brightly lit chaos. He stopped frozen in wonderment. Tessa's description of trashed didn't touch it. It was more like total destruction. Taking a step farther into the tiny foyer, a brick wall in a suit blocked his way. "Ah," he said. "Special Agent Rastogi, I presume."

Vaughn edged around Katzen, ID open at eye level for the agent. "Colonel Vaughn DeVries, U.S. Air Force, this is Joshua Katzen—"

"I know who you are, Colonel," Rastogi interrupted. "I also know the only reason you're trespassing on my crime scene is that Arlington and the Resident Security Officer gave the order for me to allow it. I do not appreciate interference no matter who that interference represents. Now, I can let you in, but it's at *my* pleasure and *my* rules, understand?"

With more aplomb than Katzen would have mustered, DeVries tried again. "Let's be reasonable, here, Rastogi. I understand you don't want your crime scene disrupted—"

"You understand nothing, Colonel," the AIC interrupted again.

"The Pentagon has no business here. *You* have no business here. This is a police matter. Special Agent Bramwell interrupted a burglar with unfortunate consequences."

Seemed Rastogi didn't do reasonable. Burying a sigh, Katzen quietly sidestepped for a clearer view of the room beyond. He'd hardly moved when Rastogi grabbed his arm and yanked him back. Before he could respond, DeVries spun the Special Agent to face him.

"No, Special Agent, that is *not* how this is going to play out," the Colonel snarled. "My orders are to do an independent assessment and report back to my bosses. Independent, Special Agent. Do you need a dictionary to see what the definition of independent is?"

The bungalow was a 1960s vintage split-level with two steps down into the living room. Taking advantage of the distraction, he descended, stepped to one side and stood where he had the best view of the chaos. His first impression was on the money. The destruction was too complete; too perfect. Tossing a room like this didn't make sense if you were looking for valuables to steal, no thief worth his or her salt would do it. Even a fight wouldn't cause this sort of mess. Fights tended to be more localized: breakage in one area while other areas stayed pristine. No, this looked deliberate. It was stage dressing — but for what?

He stepped farther into the room, noting the dangling wires from the television and stereo. A foot-high bronze statuette of a rodeo horse and rider peeked from under a slashed sofa cushion and the wreckage of a glass-top coffee table. It was a Remington reproduction and easily the most valuable item in the room. That clinched it. No thief was going to lug off a bulky TV and stereo and leave a more easily portable chunk of cash lying on the floor.

"Sir?"

The quiet call snapped him out of his thoughts. Glancing up, he saw two young men wearing T-shirts bearing the legend Crime Scene Unit. Their photo name tags read T. Taylor and F. Turkman respectively. They stood a bit back next to a collapsible gurney.

The shorter one (Taylor) shifted uncomfortably and said, "We're ready to finish collecting evidence and take him away whenever you give the word, Sir."

Damn. He'd been so preoccupied with the physical scene, he hadn't paid attention to the human element. Man. He was more tired than he thought if he was developing that sort of tunnel vision. He stepped closer, and for the first time, got a clear look at Reid Bramwell's body. It was not a pretty sight. "Oh, man."

Turkman asked, "A friend, Sir?"

"Not exactly," Katzen said, crouching beside the remains. "We were working together on a project to repatriate stolen art to the countries of origin."

Bramwell had not gone down easily. The unnatural angle of his head bore mute testimony to a broken neck and one arm was bent in the wrong place. A number of superficial cuts and slowly forming bruises on his face and hands spoke of a fierce struggle with at least one opponent. Bits of glass and cushion stuffing lay on top of the body confirming his theory that the destruction was all window dressing. He looked up at the CSUs. "So, he hasn't been moved?"

"No, Sir," Taylor said. "We understand his partner checked for signs of life, but aside from that he hasn't been touched."

Katzen nodded and stood up. "Looks like a clean break of the neck. Accident or on purpose?"

"He was in a helluva fight, that much is certain," the short CSU said. "Can't say for sure until they get him on the table, but the bruising that's forming? My guess is up close and personal."

Katzen regarded his former colleague in silence. He agreed with the CSUs. Had to have been one helluva fight.

The tall medic leaned forward. "You the spook?" he asked conspiratorially.

The question caught Katzen's sleep-deprived brain off guard. "Huh?" was all he managed.

Turkman continued with barely suppressed glee, "Rastogi told us the RSO ordered him wait for a Pentagon weenie and a spook."

Nodding to where DeVries and the AIC stood arguing by the front door, he added, "You ain't the one wearing the uniform."

Katzen barked a half laugh. "Wow. I've been called a lot of things, but that's a new one. I'm afraid what I actually do isn't all that exciting. I'm an artist and a photographer for archaeological digs."

"You seem to know an awful lot about crime scenes, man. We were watching you work through it in your head."

Katzen shrugged casually. "Well, if you get right down to it, an archaeological site isn't that much different from a crime scene, except it's older and the bodies aren't as fresh."

The CSUs exchanged a look and Turkman gave him a knowing nod. "Uh huh. We getcha."

Still shaking his head, Katzen thanked the two CSUs and headed back to the door. He gave DeVries an unobtrusive thumbs up as he passed.

Abruptly, DeVries straightened and gave the red-faced AIC a salute. "Good night, Special Agent Rastogi, the U. S. Government thanks you for your cooperation." He followed Katzen out, muttering, "That was close. Man, I was starting to think I was gonna have to slug the guy."

"Wish I'd known," Katzen said with a grim smile. "Might have been worth it."

They stopped a distance away from the now-smaller knot on the front stoop. Caballero was still sitting on the hood of her jeep, puzzle forgotten, seemingly staring at nothing. DeVries asked quietly, "Is it as bad as we thought? This is about Deustch's package?"

"Might be a little worse in some ways."

"Oh, don't tell me that."

"First off, the scene in there was staged. That room was wrecked after Bramwell was dead. Whoever did it took a lot of stuff that they thought a thief would nick. The TV, stereo and Reid's piece of shit watch are gone, but they left a sculpture that would be worth more than all those things in scrap metal alone."

DeVries stared thoughtfully back toward the house. The strobing police lights made the scrambled eggs on the bill of his service cap look alive. The knot of assorted police parted, allowing the CSUs to wheel Bramwell's zipped-up body bag through. There was silence as the men slid the collapsible gurney up and into the waiting ambulance. The thud of the rear doors closing sounded heavy and final.

At length DeVries said, "But why kill him? That don't make a helluva lot of sense, Josh."

"Not unless it was a version of Rastogi's pet scenario. Bramwell wasn't supposed to be at home. He was supposed to be at the embassy, trailing after the Secretary of State."

"Oh shit. Did they know that because of the bug in my room? I was talking to Caballero about the Sec State's visit before I knew anyone was listening."

"Hey, don't beat yourself up. Think about it: you never said Bramwell's address out loud. Whoever this is has resources."

"Yeah," DeVries said slowly. "That makes sense. I bet they also went through Tessa's place."

"That's a sure thing — and bugged the hell out of it. I'd lay money that they've been watching the warehouse, too. That would be one simple way for them to know who's been working Deustch's things." He paused, then said, "There's something else, too."

DeVries looked pained. "I'm not sure I want to hear this. Hit me."

"It may be something, it may be nothing," Katzen said uncertainly. "Someone is futzing with my cover. Rastogi told the CSUs that Arlington ordered him to wait for a Pentagon weenie and — this is a quote — a spook."

"Oooooh. That ain't good."

"To put it mildly. That kind of shit gets people killed. I have no desire to have my retirement derailed like Bramwell's."

"Shooo. This is turning into a right mess, you know that? Wait . . . That jerkoff called me a *weenie*?"

The delayed reaction made Katzen laugh in spite of everything. "Hey, Tessa's jeep is still stuck and probably will be for a while. Why don't we offer her a lift home — or wherever she wants to go?"

"Good idea. If she's got unexpected guests, we don't want her walking into it alone."

~*~

In the end, Tessa opted to stay at a hotel for the night. She wasn't exactly afraid to stay in her own apartment, but her partner's death had left her deeply shaken. Josh didn't blame her. Sometimes a neutral place is the best for purging painful emotions — or sometimes simply hiding from them.

CHAPTER 16

He'd never been to an actual wake before, but he did like the idea of celebrating someone's life rather than simply mourning the loss. From the bursts of raucous laughter, it certainly seemed that was what Reid Bramwell's friends and fellow DSS agents were doing. Not that Bramwell's mortal remains were present; they weren't, they were on their way back to his family in Wyoming. In lieu of the corpse, Reid's friends had loaded a table down with pictures, his service honors, his badge and a large silver belt buckle he'd won as a rodeo rider in his youth — which went a long way to explain the presence of the Remington sculpture in his home.

Katzen paid for his drink, then joined DeVries at the table he'd staked out near the back. As Katzen dropped into a seat, DeVries said, "Don't you find it kinda weird to be in an Irish pub in a South American city?"

"Not particularly. I've seen a lot stranger things over the years," Katzen said, raising his glass. "At least they have decent whiskey."

DeVries clinked the neck of his Kilkenny Irish Cream Ale bottle against the glass. "Damn good beer, too. I've been craving a Kilkenny since I left Washington."

An empty Corona bottle clunked onto the table between them. "Hey! Is this seat taken?"

Tessa Caballero smiled down at them. Josh pulled out a chair and Vaughn made a show of dusting it off. Tessa sat with a flourish as the server whizzed by, swapping her empty bottle for a fresh one.

"Hey," Katzen said. "I thought you'd be up there sharing Reid's shower gel incident with everyone."

She shrugged and sipped at the fresh Corona.

"You okay? You were pretty rocky last night," Josh said quietly.

Tessa shifted uncomfortably then said, "I don't think I thanked you guys for coming to my rescue."

DeVries grinned. "We're the good guys, rescuing damsels in distress is in our job description."

She seemed to relax a little and said, "The hotel was a good suggestion. I got to come to grips with Reid's death a little in a place that held no memories. I don't think I'd have done as well at home. Work managed to kick the shit out of all that, though."

"Bad memories?" DeVries asked.

"That and I work with assholes. I think I mentioned before that I'm not a real popular girl at this posting. Things were bad before, but they're worse now my partner's been killed. Some of these jerks blame me for his death." She shot an anger-filled glare at a large group beside the central table. A roar of laughter erupted at some anecdote the trio couldn't hear over the bar noise. Tessa spread her hands helplessly. "How the hell was I supposed to have helped? He was at home for God's sake!"

Josh followed her look and recognized the agent at the center of the group. Arash Rastogi. "Ah. Yes. I believe I see the asshole in question. We met him last night, didn't we?"

Tessa gave a throaty laugh. "That's right, you did. I heard about you going nose-to-nose with him, Vaughn. *Everybody* heard about it. Mr. Sore Loser didn't take it well when he realized he'd been played. Should have heard him screaming to the RSO this morning."

Josh sat back happily. "Really? Did he call DeVries a Pentagon weenie again?"

She nearly spewed her beer. Clapping a napkin to her mouth, she mumbled, "Oh yeah."

DeVries looked inordinately pleased. Lifting his ale bottle, he said, "Reid Bramwell. To departed friends." Glass and bottles clinked.

Tessa took a big pull on her beer. "Anyway, I'm looking forward to getting back to work with you guys. I never thought I'd *want* to be back in that stuffy museum, but it certainly beats the office right now."

"Not to mention the much better company," Josh said with a cocky grin.

Laughing, they toasted again. DeVries' cell went off. He looked at the screen and frowned. "It's my boss. I better take this outside."

Tessa watched him plow through the throng, then leaned closer to Josh. "He also called you a 'fucking spook'," she said.

Shit. Aloud he said, "Yeah, he told people that last night, too, but he left the F-bomb off the version I heard."

She looked at him hard. "Is it true?

"You're kidding."

She continued to stare at him. "Your Chief Ruiz wouldn't be surprised to find out you were. He's in your fan club, but he thinks there's more to you than meets the eye."

"Seriously? CIA?" He gave her an incredulous look, then raised his hand in the time-honored Boy Scout salute. "I hate to disappoint you and Diego, but I am not now, nor have I ever been a Company man." He sipped his Jameson and hoped she didn't jump on his dodge. When she didn't drop her gaze, he said, "Truth to tell, it worries me if Rastogi is saying that. Those kind of rumors get people killed."

She looked thoughtful and took another deep pull at her beer. If she was going to say anything, Josh never found out what it was because Vaughn came back, looking troubled.

"What?" Josh asked.

"We'll have to take a raincheck on getting back to the warehouse, Tessa. D.C. has pulled the plug — at least for now."

"Well, there goes another thing." Caballero spun her empty bottle on the table. Abruptly, she stood and said, "I need another beer. Maybe two."

Vaughn watched her push through the crowd toward the bar. When he finally spoke, his words were almost lost to the background chatter. "Looks like we got the homework done just in time."

~*~

Katzen let his head thump back against the adobe wall of the deserted outdoor cafe. He almost felt it. Good. He wanted to feel something. Anything to dispel that hollow, disconnected feeling. It had haunted him the whole drive back to Piedras Rojas. It had left him lost and desolate, standing in front of la Antigua Taberna, watching the SUV carry DeVries back up the road to Lima. It had lifted a little when the Conde family all but mobbed him as he stepped inside the cantina, but came back full force when he discovered he'd have to wait an hour or more for Harper to finish at the clinic. A grease-covered Luis explained that The Taberna's truck was down. It would take the rest of the afternoon to repair the brakes. That left Harper Armand and the camp's antique Mercedes bus as his best option.

He'd abandoned his suitcase and laptop in Teo's care and retreated to a table on the cantina's patio. This ennui was nothing new. It had been a familiar sensation in the days when he worked as a government agent. It usually arose at the end of a mission and was especially bad after a failed one. This bout was likely triggered by how abruptly he'd been cut loose.

Something thudded solidly against his lower leg. Looking down, he met unblinking tarnished brass eyes and an imperious mew from one of the village cats, a dilute calico that reminded of his own Boudicca back home in Chicago. Reaching down to scratch the top of her head, he genuinely smiled for the first time that day. "Hey, beautiful girl. Why the hell am I feeling this way? I didn't want this gig in the first place. I should be glad it's over."

The little calico jumped up onto the table and head-butted him.

"I bet that's your answer to everything," he laughed.

"Oh, it is, Gatito. She has been most insistent with the customers and it has earned her many handouts," Aida Conde said cheerfully from the side door of the cantina. Butt-bumping the door open, she sidled out carrying a food-laden tray. Before he could protest that he hadn't ordered anything, she shooed the cat, plopped a steaming mug of coffee onto the catless space and slid a plate heaped with chiccarones, tortillas and red onion relish next to it. "Mama made your favorite dish for you. She said you looked too thin."

"Well, thank her for me. This smells wonderful — as usual."

"I will tell her," the girl said, tucking the empty tray under her arm. "I am glad to see you, Gatito. You left in such a hurry, I was afraid I would not have the chance to say goodbye to you this year."

"It was kind of sudden," he agreed with a rueful smile.

The side door opened again. Teo leaned out, shook his head in amusement and disappeared back into the cantina.

"I think you're wanted inside," Katzen said.

"*Sí,* we are preparing for *la cena,*" she said, looking reluctantly over her shoulder. "The evening meal is our busiest time."

As soon as the girl was gone, the calico hopped back onto the table and stared pointedly at the pork, then directly into Katzen's eyes. Katzen stared back, then dissolved into laughter.

"That neon Kitty Sucker sign is over my head right now, isn't it?"

Breaking off a chunk of pork for his feline tablemate released an aroma that reminded him he'd skipped breakfast. He and the cat dug in hungrily. The savory meat lived up to the promise of its scent and then some. Before he knew it, the plate was empty. He shredded the last tortilla for the calico and sat back cradling the mug of coffee. When the cat finished her tortilla scraps, she hopped into his lap and curled up, purring contentedly.

Absently stroking the sun-warmed fur, he tried to clear his mind, but it didn't work. Time and again, his thoughts returned to the laptop case sitting behind Teo's bar and to the small wallet of memory sticks tucked into the padded back. Those cards held the mountains of data they'd collected in that last marathon session. The answer to where Deustch stashed the plutonium had to be in there. At least, he hoped so.

Sunshine and the purring animal finally worked their magic, and Katzen's racing brain slipped into neutral. Tension flowed out of his clenched muscles and he zoned out; not asleep, but not fully awake, either. He was still in this half-state when the calico gave a loud hiss and bolted from his lap. Surprised, he sat forward and twisted to see where she'd gone.

He never saw who hit him from behind.

~*~

Cold water surged into his mouth and nose, shocking him awake, jerking him back to consciousness. Blearily, he moved to wipe wet hair out of his eyes only to realize his hands were immobilized over his head and he was suspended several inches above the floor. Buzzing in his ears resolved into the sound of men laughing like someone fine-tuning a radio onto the proper station.

"Welcome back, *Señor* Katzen. I trust you slept well?" Through blurred vision, he made out a figure just at the edge of the light.

He didn't try to answer; he wasn't sure he could if he wanted to. He took the time to get his breathing under control and assess his situation. In short, it sucked. He was in a room in a warehouse. Barefoot and wearing only his jeans, he hung by a pair of handcuffs that were biting into his wrists. A rope, knotted onto the chain that linked the cuffs had been thrown over a steel support beam, wrapped several times and tied off to a wooden column in back of him. The only light came from a single incandescent bulb at the end of an orange extension hanging from a hook a few feet down the same steel beam. Just past the shadowy edges of the weak illumination, he could make out stacks of crates and boxes. The man pacing in front of him and taunting him was obviously the boss. He counted four henchmen. Two in back, beside the post and two flanking the boss. A metal bucket sat on the floor beside one of the men in front. No doubt the source of the water. He turned his attention to the pacing man. His head was clearing some and focusing seemed to help.

"What? No questions?" the man said in mock incredulity. He took a step closer. "No 'where am I'? No 'why are you doing this'? Not even a 'who are you'? I am disappointed."

As the man stepped farther into the circle of light, Katzen realized he had no need to ask the last question. That realization also went a ways to answer the previous two. This was el Mago. The knowledge didn't fill him with confidence.

El Mago stopped in front of him and said, "You have something I want, *Señor* Katzen. Where is the thing Herb Deustch stole, the . . . what ridiculous thing do you call it? Ah yes, the 'package'."

Ooookay. Not the first thing he'd have thought of to explain his present predicament, but it would certainly do. Eyes never leaving his captor, he slowly worked his fingers around the handcuff chain to support his own weight a little. It helped some; the metal cuffs weren't slicing him quite so badly.

"The package." The man repeated the phrase like the punchline to a bad joke. "Such lengths you go to, pretending you do not know what he stole."

How had these *huaqueros* found out about Deustch's last score, anyway? El Mago was far too young to have been involved in the original theft and there'd been a tight lid on it up until now. He kept his head low, hoping his confusion didn't show on his face.

"Come, now, Gatito. You can share with your old *amigo*," Mago cajoled.

Mago stepped forward to stare into Katzen's face. "The cat has still not found his tongue? Perhaps we can fix that." He snapped his fingers and the goon standing beside the bucket came forward and delivered a flurry of solid body punches. It seemed to go on forever. Just when he thought he'd slip back into unconsciousness, the blows stopped, leaving him limp and twisting helplessly on the rope. He braced for more, but it didn't come.

"We will try again. Where is the package?"

Tiny plinks from droplets of water and blood falling into the puddle below were the only sounds in the heavy silence of the room.

"Talk to me!" Mago demanded in sudden anger. "Where is the glib Gatito I hear so much about?"

Katzen shifted and brought his head up to meet el Mago's eyes. His voice was rusty as he said, "If I have something to say, you can't shut me up. Unfortunately, I don't know what you're talking about."

"Ah!" Mago applauded faintly. "He speaks!" Fury erupted and he shouted, "But he still says nothing! It is simple. You have something I want. Tell me where it is!"

The way he was suspended, Katzen couldn't have flinched if he'd wanted to. He returned the glare impassively.

Anger made the veins in the *huaquero* boss' neck throb. Suddenly, he recovered his composure and stepped away. Sitting on a crate at the edge of the light, he regarded his captive with speculation. Finally he said, "Who are you, Joshua Katzen? Who do you really work for? *¿Los Estados Unidos?* Yourself alone? I do not think you are who or what you claim to be."

Standing, he walked forward again. "I owe you, Gatito," he said softly. "Not only have you caused trouble to befall some of my men, but you did me serious harm when last we met." He lifted his arm. There was an angry scar across the top of his wrist, about the size of the edge of a wooden drawing board. "A broken wrist takes a long time recovering."

"That was you? Too bad I didn't know, I'd have sent flowers. What are you allergic to?"

Mago threw his head back and hooted. "I like you, Gatito, I will regret if I have to kill you." He looked at his watch. It was a heavy gold one. "Sadly, I must go. I will return later and resume our discussion. I encourage you to take this time to reconsider your answer."

"Don't hurry on my account."

"Do not worry, Joshua, we will give you plenty of time to think."

The men filed out the door and slammed it behind them.

He hung motionless for a few more minutes in case someone decided to return. They didn't. Biting back a grunt of pain, he followed the handcuff chains to the rope and pulled himself up by it. The cuffs had bitten into his wrists and blood ran freely down his arms. Swinging himself flat onto the steel crossbeam, he fought with the knot. His numb fingers made untying it harder than it should have been. Goddamn, goddamn, *goddamn* whatever DSS or Pentagon asshole had labeled him a spy. Even el Mago had heard about it.

Hands slippery with his own blood, he lost his hold on the beam and fell hard to the floor. Wincing and swearing under his breath, he made for a pile that he hoped was his clothing near the crate Mago had sat on. The pile was his clothes. Thank the gods for lazy bad guys. Grabbing his boots, he hoped they'd been too lazy to find his lock picks. They had been.

Free of the handcuffs, he sat to pull on the boots when there was a scraping sound just outside the door. Swearing under his breath, he dove for the shadow of a stack of crates, then levered himself for a view of the door. The door didn't move, but the lid of the topmost box did. He pushed it aside and peeked in. A face with slanted eyes and full lips curled back in a snarl stared up at him from its nest of packing peanuts. His heart stopped. It was an Olmec were-jaguar mask. Sliding his hand farther into the box, he pulled out an ornate gold crescent: a Moche nose ornament. Feeling like he was in a dream he opened more boxes. Each one held looted pre-Columbian treasures.

As he stared at a set of gold armbands that gleamed in the dull light, the door abruptly opened. He fell into a crouch, hand scrabbling for anything to use as a weapon. The newcomer walked into the circle of light and Katzen's knees turned to jelly.

He sagged against the crates. "Goddamnit, DeVries, I nearly broke an Aztec ceremonial mace on your skull."

DeVries spun toward him, then pocketed the pistol he'd held. "I came in to get you. Ruiz' people are outside and ready to raid the place."

"The police? How did. . . ?"

"We find you?" DeVries finished for him. "Your friend Aida was coming out with the coffeepot just in time to see el Mago's boys drag you into a truck. I think she has a crush on you, bubba."

"Stuff you, DeVries," he said, shakily replacing the mace in the box it came from.

Suddenly serious, DeVries rushed over to steady him. "Can you walk?"

"Walk, hell, I can run if I have to. Terror is an excellent stimulant."

"Where's the package?"

"Not here. They seemed to think I had it or knew where it was. In some ways, what they have here is worse. This place is packed to the rafters with looted antiquities. I saw stuff from all over Central and South America."

"Geez."

As soon as they were clear of the building, Chief Ruiz was at their side clucking like a mother hen. "Gatito. Once again, the cat is at the center of the disturbance."

Josh managed a grin. "Hi, *Jefe*. These guys seemed to think I could point them to a real big score. I couldn't."

"Would you if you could?"

The grin got bigger. "Probably not. My sense of self-preservation gets shaky sometimes. Oh. Better tell your guys to be careful inside. There are more antiquities in that building than they have in the *Museo de la Nacion*. I only saw four guys, but I'm sure there are more."

Ruiz sighed and patted DeVries' arm. "You had better get our Little Cat away from here, Colonel. I am afraid this is going to get ugly."

"Extra bad news, *Jefe,*" Katzen added. "El Mago left a while back. You'll get his people, but not him tonight."

Diego swore and turned to his waiting officers, motioning them forward.

DeVries didn't miss a beat, but pulled Katzen toward a waiting van. The door slid back and another set of hands reached from the dark interior to help him inside. DeVries slammed the door, dived into the driver's seat and sped them away. Josh fell heavily into a seat. The adrenaline rush was fading, leaving the shakes in its place.

"Damn, son," General Len Fuller said from the darkness. "What the hell did they beat you with?"

Katzen stared silently into the face of his mentor and former handler, then said, "Pardon me if I don't say I'm glad to see you."

"Probably about as happy as I am to be here. You certainly know how to stir it up."

"Completely innocent bystander," Katzen said. He was damned glad he was sitting down. The shakes were full upon him.

"As always," the general chuckled. "Good catch with those bugs. They raised some red flags real high. Good job parking Caballero in a hotel, too. Gave us the perfect opportunity to sweep. There were two on her. We didn't find anything in Bramwell's place, but we figure whoever planted them might have been removing them when Bramwell caught them. There's a lot of interest in this package, Joshua."

"Do tell," Josh said' massaging his wrists. They were starting to smart and discolor. By morning, they'd look like an Andes sunset. "That's what my erstwhile host was asking about, too."

Len frowned. "I was afraid of that. It was too much to hope that he grabbed you just because you're so good at pissing people off."

~*~

The farther they got from the warehouse, the more he felt his injuries. When they finally stopped, he barely registered the strong pair of hands that lifted and half-carried him inside a building. He roused as he was placed on a bed of some sort and opened his eyes to the worried faces of Avi Rosenberg and Harper Armand.

"Where am I?" he rasped, then giggled a little, realizing he'd finally asked one of el Mago's questions.

Harper looked even more concerned. "You're at the Piedras Rojas clinic . . . Avi told me those bastards had worked you over, but I wasn't expecting. . . ." She tilted his head back and shined a penlight into his eyes. "What did they do to you, Josh? It looks like someone used you for a punching bag."

"Yeah. That's close enough for jazz."

She clicked the light off and dropped it back into her pocket. "No concussion, that much is good."

"They only hit me in the head once. The rest of the time, they just strung me up and pretended I had Everlast tattooed on me."

"Hmmmm," she said, opening a drawer full of gauze sponges. "Let's get these clothes off so I can see what we're dealing with."

He sat up and tried to work the buttons, but found he couldn't lift his arms. To his surprise, the shirt was heavily spotted with blood. He blinked at it. It had been perfectly clean when he pulled it on.

"Forget that," Rosenberg said, taking a pair of scissors from the counter. "That shirt is a loss anyway. The jeans aren't in such good shape, either." Brushing Katzen's hands away, he made short work of the sodden fabric, grimaced at it as if it offended him, then dropped it into the trashcan.

In the hall, someone cleared his throat. Vaughn DeVries poked his head into the room and said, "Excuse me, Dr. Rosenberg. The police are mopping up after the raid on Mago's stash house and Chief Ruiz is on the cell asking for your help with the artifacts."

"Artifacts?" he asked. "What artifacts?"

"Oh man," Katzen said, rubbing his forehead. "Maybe they did hit me harder that I thought. I forgot all about the crates."

"Crates?"

"Yeah, it looked like Magos' guys were using the warehouse they took me to as a clearing house for their loot. There were dozens of shipping boxes full of artifacts stacked in the room I was in. I can only imagine what the rest of the place is like. None of the lids were fastened, so I looked in. I saw Moche, Aztec and Olmec pieces before DeVries showed up."

The archaeologist stared in stunned silence.

Harper gave the big man a gentle shove. "Go, Avi. Patching Josh up is my job. Yours is with the artifacts."

After a brief bout of indecision, Rosenberg brushed past the Air Force colonel, saying, "Okay, let's go."

DeVries stared after him, then spoke into his cell. "Uhhhh, yeah. We're on our way, Chief." He snapped it shut, and followed warily.

Harper made a strangled noise. Josh's head snapped around only to find the doctor trying hard to choke back laughter. She regained her composure and went back to moistening a sponge with antiseptic. "Can't say that I blame your friend for wanting to keep Avi out of striking range. What exactly did Colonel DeVries do to piss him off?"

"I don't think he had to do much of anything. It's the textbook example of oil and water."

"More like gasoline and fire." She snickered openly. "Sorry, I know I shouldn't laugh, but I've never seen Avi so angry with one individual before. Ever. Good to know he's human."

Katzen continued to stare into the now-empty hall thoughtfully. The clinic door slammed. He heard a faint "ow" that sounded remarkably like DeVries, then the door closed again more normally.

"Face front, mister. There's nothing you can do out there." Dr. Armand blotted antiseptic on another scape, causing him to flinch and suck air. Straightening, she regarded the damage and said, "I'm not finding anything broken and no serious cuts. You probably don't believe it now and tomorrow morning, you'll call me a bald-faced liar, but you were very lucky."

He shrugged, then winced. "It *is* kinda straining credulity."

She became very still, then said, "I suppose there's no good segue for this, so I'll just say it. Avi told me about you. That you used to be some kind of government agent."

He swiveled to face her, but she wasn't finished. "He also told me you'd retired and that this man, DeVries, hunted you down to force you to help with some sort of new mission."

His mind raced. Lying to protect his cover had been second nature in the past, but the residual shock dulled that reflex — especially to friends. He couldn't find anything to say.

"I'm not asking for secrets," she continued. "I just wanted to let you know that Avi told me. A little bit, anyway." Suddenly all business, she turned back to the things she'd laid out on the counter. "All right. Let's get some clean dressings on these wounds."

"Harper—"

She turned and raised a warning finger. "You may not have a concussion, but I don't have to rely on my medical degree to see you're still in shock and not thinking straight. Anything you want to tell me, we can do it later."

"Really! I—"

"I mean it, Josh. Shut up."

Recognizing defeat, he shut up.

From the doorway, Len Fuller guffawed. "By damn! That worked. I wish I'd had you around a few years back, doc."

Both looked toward the newcomer in surprise, then Katzen said, "Harper, this is—"

Harper gave him a warning look. He grinned and, still finding it hard to lift his arms, chicken-winged for the gauze she was wrapping around his chest.

Stepping into the room, the general took a closer look at Katzen's blooming bruises. He whistled softly, then glanced over at the doctor. "Don't let me interrupt, Dr. Armand. As Joshua started to say, I'm General Leonard Fuller. I was this incorrigible young fella's handler back in the day."

"Handler?" Harper asked, confused.

"Think of it as a commanding officer," he said taking up a post beside the doorway. He shucked out of his jacket and tossed it over a chair back. "I have to beg your pardon, I wasn't trying to eavesdrop, but I did overhear what Dr. Rosenberg told you. That was right on the money. Josh was *supposed* to be retired. New name, new life — a reward for a job well done many times over. Damned well done in my book, but some people just don't understand what a promise is."

Harper stopped wrapping gauze around her patient and looked from one man to the other, eyebrows raised. Finally she said, "Why do I think you aren't referring to anyone here in this room, General?"

"Please, call me Len. Down here, I'm not Air Force, I'm just Josh's uncle Len — although, to use your words, son, Chief Ruiz's credulity is being strained at present."

Katzen was zoning out again. He startled a little when Dr. Armand closed the supply cabinet. "Okay, all finished — and before you ask, no, you won't have to keep *all* the dressings in place after tonight. I just want to keep something sterile between those oozing scrapes and *señor* Tovar's good linens."

"Good," he said, fingering the tape on his right side that was beginning to itch.

"Don't pick at that," she ordered. "Josh, I'm going to ask you to stay quiet for a few days. Mind you, I'm *asking*, not ordering because I know that orders put your rebellion glands into overdrive."

"You do know him pretty well, doc," General Fuller said. "There were a bunch of folks at the Pentagon that never quite figured that out. Caused no end of trouble."

Katzen glared at him, then slid off the gurney, secretly pleased that his legs didn't buckle when he did.

"Come on, son," Fuller said, reaching for his jacket. "Let's get you over to the hotel and bedded down. You'll be sharing digs with Dr. Rosenberg for a while, but something tells me all that stuff from the raid is going to keep him busy for a bit. Someone's gotta keep an eye on you, so I'll sit with you until Rosenberg comes back."

CHAPTER 17

"Son, you took a helluva beating last night, you need more than coffee."

Katzen regarded Len Fuller over the rim of his coffee cup, then reached over the table and took the folded newspaper out of his hands. After examining the headline, he handed it back. "Nope. I didn't do a time-slip. Must be the painkillers giving me flashbacks."

Setting the paper aside, Fuller said, "Now, Josh, you know I fought against this. I never wanted you to be dropped back into the shit."

"The problem, *Uncle Len*, is that it isn't just me dropped into it. A DSS agent is dead, a bunch of college students had their field trip cut short because thieves were invading the dig site — and look around. It's seven a.m., we're sitting at breakfast in Avi Rosenberg's hotel room. Where's Avi? That's right, he never got back to his room because he's helping the local police clean up a *huaquero* hide-out!"

"Look, I know you're pissed, but don't blame me for this cock-up *or* my cockamamie cover ID." The general sat back and shook his head in half-amusement. "The cover story was Vaughn's fault. Kid doesn't think well on his feet. The rest of this? Herb Deustch. Going on twenty-five years dead and still stirring up trouble."

Katzen made a noise of grudging assent deep in his throat and freshened his coffee. "I wish *I'd* shot the sonuvabitch."

Fuller looked up in surprise. "What? Why?"

"I'd have tossed his ass into a volcano. No body. Future problem solved." He snapped his fingers and dusted his hands.

Fuller laughed out loud, then he said, "Well *part* of the future problem solved. We still don't know where he stashed *it*."

"Ah, yeah," Katzen sighed. "You had to bring that up."

Fuller laughed again, smeared a toasted bagel with cream cheese and tossed it onto the plate in front of Katzen. "Eat."

A key scratched in the lock and Avi Rosenberg let himself in. His face was haggard and he was covered in enough dust to double for Charles Schulz' Pig-pen. He looked blearily around the room and spotted the set table. "Ah! Food," he called over his shoulder.

Vaughn DeVries, looking just as rumpled, entered behind him.

Katzen offered up the bagel. DeVries made for it. "Breakfast! I'd almost forgotten what it looked like." The bagel didn't last long.

Rosenberg sat and helped himself to a slice of toast. "Man, Josh. You have no idea what was in that warehouse. The things you saw were just the tip of the proverbial iceberg. Worse, there was way too much stuff there for this to just be a local operation."

DeVries heaped eggs and sausage on a clean plate. "Avi's right. Seems el Mago has become involved with something far larger than we expected. It'll be sorta interesting to see where this leads. Diego Ruiz was talking like the *Federales* would probably be poking their noses into this, too."

General Fuller asked, "Any line on Mago himself?"

"None," DeVries said around a mouthful of scrambled eggs. "The men we questioned said he had a meeting with someone he referred to as *la putona,* but he never came back afterwards."

"The big bitch. That's nice and respectful," Katzen observed. "Could he have got wind that his place was busted?"

"Who knows? All we know is that he didn't show his face while we were there. We got the guys who jumped you, if that helps."

DeVries shrugged and spooned more eggs onto his plate. "Is there any ketchup?"

Katzen shrugged, then regretted it. He turned his attention back to his coffee.

"Ah, that reminds me," Fuller said. "Vaughn, you got that thing I asked you for?"

DeVries nodded and pulled a cell phone from his inner pocket. He plopped it on the table in front of Katzen. "Burner. Yours."

"I want you to keep that with you at all times for as long as you're still in Peru," Fuller said. "I don't want you getting caught flat-footed again."

Katzen slid the device back toward the general. "We're in the mountains, Len. Lousy coverage."

"And you hate for anyone to be able to keep tabs on you," Fuller added. "Tough. Piedras Rojas is a good-sized town. There's a tower not far from here. You ought to know that, you heard my phone ringing all night. That proves DeVries' phone works fine, too."

As if for additional proof, the device in question went off. DeVries looked sheepish and stepped away from the table to answer it. After a murmured conversation, he was back, looking serious. "That was the *Jefe*. They just found el Mago. Looks like he caught one through the head."

~*~

The body on the stainless steel tray seemed shrunken. Josh Katzen stared down at the flaccid face of Alberto Vargas for several beats before he said, "Yep. That's the guy who kidnapped me and strung me up from a rafter."

"And it is the man I knew when I was younger, the man responsible for the deaths of my brother and wife," Diego Ruiz agreed, dropping the sheet back over el Mago's face. "Strange. For many years, I have looked forward to this day. I thought I would feel triumph or vindication, but I feel only sadness."

"I hear you, *Jefe*. Death is rarely a good solution," Katzen said, stepping away from the gurney. "At least we don't need Vic to explain this one. A single gunshot to the head at close range kinda draws its own diagrams. Seems like *la putona* didn't respect our boy any more than he did her."

"She was careful, too," said DeVries. "The meet was on a side street where the businesses were shuttered for the night. No witnesses to the shooting. Nary a shell casing to be found, neither."

"Better and better."

DeVries said, "You ain't heard the best yet. Nobody ever saw the lady, so we don't even have a physical description. Might not even have been her. Mago was so afraid someone might go into business for himself, no one ever met any of the customers or contacts."

"Mago had no second in command, either," Ruiz said heavily. "The warring has already begun. As I was waiting for you to arrive to confirm the identity, Lt. Quijano was called to the aftermath of a gun battle to the north of town."

"Any innocent bystanders?" Katzen asked.

"No, this was strictly *huaquero* on *huaquero* violence. It was bloody, but no innocents were involved."

"This time," Katzen said with undisguised hostility. "Too bad they won't keep killing each other and thin the herd a bit."

"¡Gatito! Such an evil thought," Ruiz said in mock severity.

"Sorry, *Jefe*," he said. "I guess I'm feeling a little cranky today."

Ruiz preceded them out the morgue's door and into the early morning sunlight. "Colonel DeVries, Joshua tells me you and his uncle will be returning to Lima this afternoon. I will be sad to have you go. Your help in organizing the stolen goods from the warehouse was beyond value."

"No problem, *Jefe*," DeVries said. "Glad to help. Organization comes second nature to a Pentagon desk pilot. About time it was useful"

~*~

The view from the Posada de Piedras Rojas' window was the same this time as on the other dozen or so times that his pacing orbit brought him to part the curtains. The street was still deserted, dusty and bright in the midday sun. And boring. Very boring.

If Diego and Avi hadn't been so pig-headed, he could at least have been helping clear the warehouse. Truthfully, it wasn't just Rosenberg and the *Jefe*. Since the beating, everyone had been treating him like he was made of glass. Okay, he still hurt and he was damned stiff but he'd had far worse. If he couldn't do something more than pace soon, they'd have to move him to a new room. A white one. With nice, padded walls. He sighed and looked out at the surrounding hills with longing.

Why not? What would it hurt if he went out sketching? All Harper said was that he needed to rest and drawing always relaxed him. He knew just the place, too. There was an old Spanish wall within easy walking distance; the ruin of an old homestead. The place was crumbling and being reclaimed by nature. Last time he'd passed it, an amazing number of plants were taking hold on it, including several indigenous orchids.

It took no time at all to gather his drawing equipment and even less to leave a note for Rosenberg on the dresser. He cut the hotel registration desk a wide berth so no one would be tempted to be "helpful" and stop him. He hurried westward, into the foothills, enjoying the sunshine and the fresh scent of the air. He was almost halfway to his destination before his abused muscles told him it might have been a good idea to drive. Too late.

He pushed on in spite of the discomfort and was glad he did. Several of the orchids were in full bloom, making clouds of color against sharp green foliage and the dusty earth tones of the crumbling adobe. Several good photographs later, he unfolded his chair and easel and broke out the pencils.

~*~

The drawing was taking shape under his hands. This was the part he liked best, when the areas of color took on definition and the composition in his head happened on the illustration board. Even his bruised ribs felt better. Smiling to himself, he leaned over and rooted in the pencil box for the right shade to deepen the shadows of the foliage. Suddenly, something smacked into the ground a foot to his left. Dirt and gravel sprayed into the air and pattered onto the drawing. Before he could make sense of it, a spot on the Spanish wall powdered.

He was being shot at! Goddammit!

Before that thought completed, instinct launched him forward and he rolled behind the ancient wall for cover. Another bullet impacted close by. From the cover of the ruin, he crouched low, peering through a crevice between the adobe blocks. Just at the top of the hill opposite, he could make out two figures crouching in the undergrowth. They were too far away to make out any detail, but one held something that looked to be a rifle. As if for proof, the man raised the object and the ground beside his easel exploded in another spray of dust.

"Joshua Katzen, that was a warning," a man shouted.

Well, duuuuh. Of course it was a warning. Nobody was that bad a shot. Given their location and how preoccupied he'd been, if they'd wanted him dead, he'd be dead. Who the hell were they? El Mago's people? No. The shouter didn't sound Latin, he sounded . . . Middle European? Baltic? Russian. Great. That's where the bugs were from. Were these the people who planted the bugs? Maybe the ones who killed Bramwell? How in hell did anyone even know where he was — unless they were following him. And he wasn't paying attention. Wonderfulness.

"Where is it, Katzen? Tell us and we will let you live."

Yeah. Deustch again. Somehow he knew that was going to be it. If he'd known what trouble that asshole was going to cause, he'd have dynamited the platform to microdust before they got the chance to dig the creep out.

Another shot. Another wide miss. "Second chance, Joshua. Deustch hid the plutonium. You know where it is. Give us the location and we will let you live."

We. Were there more than the two guys on the hill? Were they all in the same spot or scattered around? So far, no one had come up behind him. "I don't know what you're talking about,"

Josh called out at last. Several more shots smacked into the wall. He ducked lower, pressing against the mossy stone cobbles of the old homestead floor and crept a few feet to his right behind a higher section of ruin.

"Now look!" he shouted again. "This is getting real old real fast. I've been kidnapped, beaten and now shot at all because someone seems to think I know something I don't. I have no idea where Herb Deustch hid the plutonium or whatever the hell it was he stole from whoever the hell he stole it from. I never even met the man!"

In answer, the sniper fired a short burst that sent a rain of adobe, leaves and orchids over on top of him.

"Wrong answer, Katzen."

Cursing and swearing under his breath, he commando crawled along the ancient foundation. At the end, the ground dropped off into a vine-choked trench that was deep but dry at this time of year. If he remembered its path correctly, it would give him a perfect covered route around the snipers' rise and under the road to the other side in back of them. He had no idea what he'd do when he got there, but he was willing to play that part by ear. Without a second thought, he slid in and crouch-ran along the ditch. About the time he reached where it crossed the road under a small concrete bridge, he heard a car engine rev. A speeding Land Rover nearly hit him as he pulled himself up onto the roadway.

Knowing he wouldn't find anything, he pelted up the rise to where the two men had been. He was right. Nothing but scuffed soil and crushed undergrowth. Not even a brass shaving. The view from the hill confirmed his earlier theory. If the shooter had wanted him dead, he'd be sprawled over his brain-spattered drawing board, not grousing that they'd policed their brass before they left.

He sat down with a groan. The adrenaline that had propelled him behind the wall and through the gully shut off like someone had flipped a switch. Dead might feel better. He became aware of an unfamiliar weight in his pocket. The cell that Len had made him take in case he got into trouble. Yeah. Right.

It actually had a signal. Amazing.

Punching in the number he'd memorized, he laid flat on the ground and waited.

"DeVries."

"Hi. I have a new entry for the list of shit you dragged me into. Someone just shot at me."

"Shot . . . !" DeVries seemed to have turned away from the phone, because the next words were slightly muffled, "Josh says someone just tried to kill him."

Fuller took the phone. "What happened? Who tried to kill you?"

Katzen sat up and stifled a groan. The trek back to the hotel wasn't going to be anywhere near as pleasant as the walk out. "I didn't say tried to kill me. I said shot at me."

"Okay . . . Tell me what happened."

"I hiked out to an old ruin to draw a little. Someone — only two guys, I think — must have followed me. They tried to rattle me by using me for an Annie Oakley recreation and demanded I tell them where that . . . ummm . . . thing is."

He could almost hear Len's brain clicking. "Were they Mago's people?"

"No. They sounded Slavic or something."

"That is not good Josh."

Anger rose, wiping away the lethargy. "No shit, Len!"

"Now, Josh," Fuller said. "I want you—"

"No, Len," Katzen spat. "I don't *care* what you want."

"Josh. . . . Don't smash that phone."

"Len? Fuck. Off." He hit the End button. Almost immediately, the cell began to ring. He pulled the battery, snapped the SIM card, then threw the device as hard as he could against the concrete abutment of the bridge.

~*~

Anger carried him most of the hike back to town but drained away almost as soon as the main street was in sight. He stood, indecisive, at the corner debating whether to go directly to the

Posada de Piedras Rojas or drop into La Antigua Taberna. He could certainly use a drink. A good, stiff double. A glimpse of himself in a plate glass shop window made his mind up. If he went into the Taberna looking like that, they'd probably run for the shaman again. Posada it was. In spite of everything that happened at the ruin, he hadn't been gone all that long. With luck, he'd get back before Avi. If he could get into the room, clean up and nuke the note, nobody had to know anything happened.

As he resettled his art gear on his shoulder, another thought struck him: he'd also have a chance to search for bugs. He'd lay money the guys taking potshots at him were the same ones messing with his room in Lima. He hoped so, anyway. If there was more than one group out there tracking him, he didn't want to know about it. They were following him, that meant they knew where he was staying and they certainly weren't shy about sharing their little electronic pals.

His luck held — in the sense that it stayed bad. As soon as he opened the door, he saw Avi's backpack tossed onto the dresser right beside the wadded up note. Damn. Taking a deep breath, he stepped in and sang out, "Hey! You beat me back. Did you make it through a few crates before you knocked off?"

Rosenberg emerged from the bathroom drying his hands on a towel. He didn't look happy. "About damned time you got ba— what the hell happened to you?"

"Don't get excited," he said. "It looks worse than it is."

Rosenberg shoved him into a chair and grabbed a damp washcloth from the basin. He dropped it into Katzen's hand, saying, "It *looks* pretty damned bad."

"It's all cosmetic," he lied. "I went out to sketch at that old Spanish homestead; the orchids are blooming along that wall. Guess I shouldn't have trusted my balance yet. Slipped and went down the hill on my ass."

"I'm calling Harper."

"No, don't. All I need is a shower and a change of clothes."

Rosenberg didn't look convinced. After a brief silence, he said, "I can't believe you went out by yourself. After everything that's happened?"

"El Mago is dead, Avi. We saw what was left of him at the morgue this morning."

"Maybe so, but his henchmen aren't, and even though you didn't pull the trigger, I doubt they're very happy with you right now."

"Tell them to take a number." Katzen rooted through his suitcase, tossing toiletries and clean clothes onto the bed. His hand closed on his old, well-traveled shaving kit and he went still inside.

Rosenberg sat down on his own bed and scrubbed at his face with his palms. "I'm sorry, Josh. I know you've been through a lot these last few days — we all have, but you got the dirtiest end of the stick. Look, I only came back to grab some food and a fresh notepad. I have to head back over. We still got a shitload of crates to catalog."

Josh brought himself back to the conversation with a barely perceptible bump. "You going to need me?"

"No, the *Museo* sent a couple of their guys down early this morning. Diego and I are just briefing them so they can take up where we leave off. Once they're on the right page, I'm outta here. You, too." He stood and jabbed a finger into Josh's chest. "But until then? *Rest*. No more walkabout, got it?"

"Okay. I have a few things I need to do here, too."

As the door closed behind his friend, the stillness returned. Part of him knew what had to be done, the other part didn't want to go there.

The battered green plaid toiletry bag was still in his hand. He stared at it. He should have tossed the damned thing a long time ago. Maybe if he had ditched it, made a clean break with the past, things would have been different, Maybe they never would have called him back and he'd still be sitting in the War Room sweating happily as he finished copying the last mural. Maybe — oh, to hell with it. Magical thinking never won him anything but trouble and he was in enough hot water now to supply an ancient Roman caldarium.

Opening the kit out flat, he worked the backing off. Inside were sealed packets of contact lenses, two passports and several ID cards. He pulled a thin stack of US bills from under the bottom section and counted it. Not a lot, but more than enough to get him to Lima and to buy the items he'd need. There were several more caches he'd left in place once he was back in the US. Paranoia was a difficult disease to rid oneself of and he hadn't been able to make himself let all the safety nets go.

An hour or so later, he had showered, disassembled the passport (Matthew Knight, Louisville, KY), copied the entry stamp from his own passport and reassembled Matt's to reflect a one week stay in Peru. Replacing the money, ID and passport in the shaving kit, he sealed it and tossed the megillah into a duffel with a few clean clothes. Next stop: Trujillo, where Josh Katzen would go into the case and Matt Knight could come out to play for a while.

Now, how to get to Trujillo? Good question. He went out the side door, the one closest to the cantina and spotted Manny and his son, Luis, getting the Taberna's truck ready for a journey. Was it to go into the city to pick up supplies for Teodoro and the inn? Mentally, he crossed his fingers and called out,"Hey! Manny! Headed into Trujillo?"

"*Sí*, Gatito! I thought you would be with Dr. Rosenberg at the *huaquero* warehouse."

"Nah, my bit's done and I'm headed out. Mind if I cadge a ride?"

"Of course! We would be happy to have you along," Manny said.

"Great! Give me a minute to let Avi know where I went and we'll be good to go!"

CHAPTER 18

The antique truck and the even more antique Peruvian roads did nothing good for Katzen's abused muscles, but Manny and Luis were excellent company. The two hour trip into Trujillo passed quickly. It seemed like they'd just left Piedras Rojas when Manny pulled the van up to the Hotel Libertador Trujillo. Josh buried a wince as he waved goodbye to his friends from under the hotel's ornate main doorway. As soon as they were out of sight, he headed for the shopping district.

Several hours later, he stood in front of a cloudy mirror in a motel that would have had to work hard to be more different from the Hotel Libertador Trujillo. He hadn't even bothered to remember the name of the place. It wasn't important, he wasn't going to be there long. It had what he needed, though: privacy and a working bathroom.

The dark rinse was almost dry. He switched off the blow dryer and finger-combed the hair back from his face. Good thing he was finished, the cheap dryer smelled like it was about to burst into flame. Leaning closer to the mirror, he slid a pair of contacts in, instantly changing dark blue to deep brown. A pair of stone washed jeans, hiking boots and a t-shirt reading "I went to Machu Picchu and all I got was this lousy t-shirt" completed the *tourista* ensemble. His wrists presented a different problem. The cuts were healing nicely, but the surrounding flesh was purpling up like a bad tattoo job. Way too memorable. A wide leather watch band and a couple woven friend bracelets hid them to satisfaction, though.

Tightly banding his long hair high on his head, he pinned it and snugged a University of Kentucky ball cap that, against all logic, he'd found in the Trujillo market over it.

Voilà! Exit Joshua Katzen, enter Matt Knight.

He backed toward the door, wiping the room down as he went. Fingerprints probably wouldn't be a problem — unless someone had managed to follow him to Trujillo. If they had, he was sunk, anyway. Thinking back, he hadn't touched much inside the room. Long years of training were hard to shake and it was frightening how easy it was to slip back into the old ways. Well, he'd spent more than twenty years in that life and far fewer out. Maybe not so surprising after all.

~*~

It was nice to sit still for a while. He fiddled with his drink and relaxed into the padded seat near the back of the coffee shop. His table gave him a clear view of the door and the other patrons; there had been no familiar faces cycling through and no one else had lingered. Looked like he could breathe a little easier — for a while, at least. The shop also had free Wi-Fi and he'd been able to book a late evening straight through flight out of la Aeropuerto Internacional Capitán FAP Carlos Martínez de Pinillos. Quite a mouthful, but that's what it said on the map. He'd be eight to nine hours in the air and dead on his feet by the time he hit Miami, but it was workable. The real downside was all the time he had to kill until boarding.

There was one thing he'd been putting off, though. He needed to check in with Rosenberg. Pulling out one of the two burner phones he'd bought at the market, he punched in the number for la Posada de Piedras Rojas. He didn't recognize the girl who answered the phone. More importantly, she didn't recognize his voice and simply connected him to Avi's room with with a polite, "*¡Sí, Señor! Momentito.*"

The phone was picked up after one ring. "Rosenberg."

"Hey! Finally got a chance to light and check in."

"Josh!"

In the background, he heard Harper Armand exclaim, "Is he okay? Hi, Josh!"

Katzen laughed. "Hey, Harper. Yes, I'm fine. Did you guys get the message I left at the desk?"

"Yeah, Eduardo hailed me as soon as I hit the door, and before you ask, yes, we changed our rooms right after."

"Good," he said, hoping his extreme relief didn't color his voice. "I couldn't say much in the note. Still can't. But trust me, it's better. It still might be good to watch what you say in the hotel."

There was a stunned pause, then Rosenberg said, "What's going on, man? Why did you take off again?"

Good, Avi was playing it cool. He didn't think it would take a man of Rosenberg's intelligence very long to add two and two. Katzen said, "Sorry about the repeat vanishing act, but when we were arguing—"

"Discussing. We were having a *discussion*."

"Uh huh." He wondered if Avi could hear the smile. "While we were *discussing* my going walkabout this morning, it occurred to me that going missing might be the best way to keep the rest of you safe. The shit shower seems to be following me. I hope Manny and his kid don't get sprayed, but it was an impromptu move. . . ."

"They're fine. They got back a little while ago. They said they dropped you off at the *Hotel Libertador Trujillo*."

"Yep."

"Why do I think that you never even saw the lobby?"

The laugh burst out before he knew it was coming. Finally he said, "Because I'm rubbing off on you. Look, I'll be out of touch for a while, but it's cool. I just need to drop off the grid. I'll reemerge when things either settle down or I work out what to do about them. Oops. Better go. I need to grab some food before moving out again."

"Can you at least tell me where you're headed? Harper and I—"

"Nope. Not yet. Take care!" He ended the call, then very quietly disassembled the phone, removing the battery and destroying the SIM card. He'd ditch the pieces on the way to the airport.

CHAPTER 19

The tiny Cuban bistro's *tostada* wasn't anything to write home about but the *café con leche* was very good. Even better was the establishment's location: directly across the street from the small, but exclusive bank where his cache was. Stifling a yawn, he turned to the coffee like a lifeline. Even if the flight into Miami hadn't been turbulent, he'd been too keyed up to sleep on the plane. It was catching up to him now. At least he didn't look as tired as he actually was. The facilities at Miami International weren't five-star, but they were good enough to wash the travel dust off him. His dress was a little more casual than he liked, but that couldn't be helped. He'd ditched his Machu Picchu t-shirt in favor of a tank top with a button-down shirt over it and picked up a pair of aviator sunglasses. He retained the ball cap, though. Pulled low, the bill would help slow ID if anyone ever cared to look at security footage. The bank had opened twenty minutes before. In fifteen, he'd go in and soon after, if all went well, he'd be set to catch his noon puddle jumper to Chicago.

He forced himself to go slow on the espresso, then paid his bill and leisurely strolled across the street to the old-fashioned looking bank where he identified himself as Gulliermo Méndez.

Ten minutes and one signature later he was alone in a small room with a flat metal box on a table in front of him. The lid flipped back easily and quietly on well-maintained hinges revealing a hodge-podge of cash from several countries, wallets of IDs rubber banded to matching passports and a Ruger 9mm semi-automatic handgun. Shoving the handgun and identity packs aside, he gathered the US currency and snapped the lid back in place. He stood for a while, with his hand resting against the cool metal, wondering again if it was laziness or remaining paranoia that he hadn't let his caches go. It didn't really matter in the long run. They were there, and at present, he needed them to get back home to Chicago. What he'd do once he got there was still up in the air. The quick list included checking on his three cats, then finding a place to go to ground for a while so he could study the data he'd gotten in Deustch's notebooks. He needed to find the plutonium. No one was going to give him any peace as long as that damned stuff was in the wind. He exited the bank, mentally consigning Herbert Otto Deustch III to a particularly nasty circle of hell for setting this mess into motion. Why couldn't the greedy bastard have stayed happy with antiquities?

~*~

The grip on his shoulder brought him up out of his seat. In one fluid move, he had the hand's owner flipped and pinned, only to find himself staring into the terrified eyes of a flight attendant. Behind the frightened woman, the second attendant stood stunned into immobility. At the end of the aisle, the pilot and copilot were halfway out of the cockpit. Abruptly, he released his hold and helped the woman to her feet, stammering apologies.

"I am *so* sorry, ma'am. Are you all right? I screwed up. I know better than to fall asleep in an unfamiliar place. I really do."

The fear on the woman's face faded to deep concern and he noticed for the first time that both women wore American flag lapel pins embedded in loops of red, white and blue ribbon. Her companion stepped closer with an identical expression.

"It's Post Traumatic Stress, isn't it?" she asked in a concerned tone. "My brother came home with that."

The first woman's eyes widened. "Are you a veteran, Mr. Knight?"

The pilot said, "Iraq or Afghanistan?"

That's right, he was Matt Knight of Louisville, Kentucky. His brain was still foggy. He heard himself saying, "Afraid so, Ma'am. Iraq, Afghanistan . . . all over that territory, Sir."

He felt a little guilty for the instinctive lie, but it really wasn't all that far from the truth. He was a veteran, just not of the war they were thinking of. It was the other war. The one most people rarely got a glimpse of.

To his absolute amazement, the copilot snapped a salute.

A few minutes later, he stepped out of the disembarkation chute into the concourse, having been sent on his way with handshakes and hugs. They'd actually *thanked* him for his service. That was the first time that had ever happened — then again, few knew that Joshua Katzen had ever served in the military and Major Daniel Durand, USAF, certainly never wanted it known that he was a spy who was sent into trouble zones. Well . . . spy, thief — whatever the hell he was. Still, it was kind of nice.

Bemused, he reshouldered his computer case, popped up the handle on his one suitcase and headed for the nearest coffee shop. Preferably one that served espresso. He had a couple hours before he could call for a ride home and he needed to stay awake until he was on safe ground. He'd screwed up badly by dozing off on the flight. He was grateful his wakeup had been as benign as it was. It could have been far worse. As it was, the short nap had left him groggy and his body whining for more. Later. There would be more sleep later. For now there would be coffee.

~*~

"Okay, Vic, I'm the guy in the UK cap approaching from your left. Gonna be right up beside you . . . right about now. . . ." He said, opening the rear passenger door of the silver SUV and swinging his cases in onto the floor of the vehicle.

"Wow," Vic said, lowering his cell phone. "Good thing you were talking to me when you came up. Otherwise, I'd have wondered who the hell was getting in the car."

Josh grinned. "Just a sec." Casually, he destroyed the phone he'd been using. Part of it went into the storm grating behind the car, part went into a trash barrel and the remaining pieces disappeared into a pair of planter shrubs.

Sliding into the passenger seat, he pulled the door solidly closed and said, "Okay! Good to go!"

Vic fired the ignition and shook his head. "Damn. If I ever had any doubt about the story you and Avi told about your life as a spy, that little bit of business just went a long way to knock that doubt in the head."

Josh sighed. "Yeah. Old habits and all that jazz."

~*~

Victor Pale didn't look up from chopping onions. "No. Absolutely not. That rattletrap Mazda stays in my garage and *you* stay in my house until you've eaten and gotten some sleep."

"Vic—" Katzen began.

"We've been through this," Vic interrupted, scraping onions into the hot skillet. They sizzled, adding their aroma to the spicy scent of the sauteing meat mixture. "I know you. If you go home now, you'll spend the rest of the day unpacking — and I know my daughter, too. There won't be a scrap of food worth eating in the whole house."

That elicited a smile from Katzen. "I still can't get used to you talking about 'my daughter'."

"You think it's weird for *you*?" Pale said with a laugh. "I didn't even know Victoria existed until she was eighteen."

"She's a great kid, Vic. I can't tell you how much I appreciate her house and cat sitting for me."

"Well, we may be father and daughter, but we're still in the getting to know each other phase. House sitting for you gave us some needed distance," he said, then gestured at Katzen with the spatula. "— but you're changing the subject. It won't hurt you to crash here for a few more hours. Vicki isn't expecting you back for two more weeks — none of us were."

"*I* wasn't expecting me home yet," Josh said, then sat back, suddenly tired. "It's crazy, Vic. Everything was cool, then Herb Deustch's body turns up and WHAM! Everything went to hell. Do not pass go. Do not wait for handbasket." The wide watchband was chafing. Impatiently, he peeled it off and massaged the inflamed skin beneath it.

"Holy shit!" Pale said, crossing the kitchen in two long strides. Seizing Katzen's arm, he examined the red, weeping wounds. "Looks worse than it is, I think, but I bet it hurts like hell. Is this some of what Mago's people did?"

"Yeah, but these are just samples. The real show is on my back and ribs."

"Right. Let me get some supplies and I'll clean this up. Shuck out of that jacket and shirt."

Josh complied with a wry laugh. "I'm not sure how I feel about getting first aid from a medical examiner."

"We get medical training, too," Vic said, rummaging in a drawer. "Anyway, you need that looked at immediately. I've had cadavers on the table that looked better than you do right now. What happened, anyway? Avi was light on details other than el Mago kidnapped you, worked you over and you got away from him."

Vic's cell buzzed and bounced around on the counter. He looked at the screen, swore a little, then hit Ignore.

"That's got to be the fifth or sixth time your phone's gone off," Josh said. "Maybe you ought to answer it. It's probably more important than hearing me tell about getting the crap beat out of me."

"Nope." His friend shook his head, scooped up an impressive amount of gauze, tape and ointments and headed back to the table. "It's just the lawyer I have working on some remaining music business contracts out in California. David Durand is a damned good lawyer, but, as a person, he's a prick. I pay him enough. He can wait. I'm more interested in working out a way to keep you in one piece — more than you are, it seems."

Josh went quiet so suddenly, Victor looked up in surprise. After a moment, Josh asked, "David Durand? In San Francisco?"

"Yeah. You know him or something?"

Katzen went even more still. Finally he said, "Can you make an appointment with Durand for me?"

"Sure," Vic said in confusion. "When do you want it?"

"I dunno." The familiar cocky grin was back. "How long does it take to drive from Chicago to San Francisco?"

"Drive?" A look of horror crossed Victor's face and he pointed in the general direction of the garage. "Not in *that* thing?"

"Hey! 'That thing' is a vintage 1980 Mazda RX-7!"

"That hasn't seen a mechanic in the five years that I've known you. No, if you insist on driving, you'll take one of my cars."

"Vic. . . ."

"Nope. Not budging on this. I know my cars will make the trip — which is more than anyone can say about that Mazda From Hell. Besides, they might know your car, they probably won't know mine."

"C'mon, Vic," Josh said with a broad grin. "Sounds like you think someone's trying to kill me or something."

Vic sighed and sat back. "I wish you wouldn't make jokes about everything, Josh. It makes me nervous."

~*~

Three days later, Katzen sat in a tastefully decorated, wood paneled waiting room, leafing through a glossy architectural magazine under the skeptical glare of the law firm's receptionist. He didn't blame her. He'd been on the road four hours already that morning, and even though he'd showered before checking out of the last motel, still looked pretty travel-worn. He was early, but that was on purpose. David used to arrive at the office thirty to forty minutes before his first appointment. He kept one eye on the the door, pretty confident old habits would still be in force. He was not disappointed. At half-past, the door opened and David Durand stepped into the reception area, calling a greeting to the receptionist. Katzen let the lawyer get several steps into the room, then stood, so that the man would have to turn and put his back toward the woman at the desk.

"Good morning, Mr. Durand," Josh said, with his hand extended. "I'm Joshua Katzen."

The lawyer turned and automatically took the extended hand, then his face went slack with surprise.

"I'm a little bit early, but I have an appointment," Josh said, not giving the taller man time to react. "Well, I hope I do. It was sort of last minute, but Vic Pale made it for me. . . ."

Durand's face darkened with anger, but you'd never know it from his steady response. "Yes. I was aware Dr. Pale made an appointment for a friend this morning. We'd better go into my office. Julie, hold all calls until I finish with . . . Mr. Katzen."

As soon as the door closed, David Durand swung on his visitor. "You jackass. We thought you were dead."

"Sorry to disappoint." Josh grinned ruefully. "How are Mom and Dad?"

"Do you care?"

"I asked."

David loomed, trying to intimidate with superior height. That hadn't worked even when they were kids. "They're fine considering their youngest son has been missing without a trace for five years."

Unfazed, Josh snorted. "Give me a break, David. The only thing that could worry Mom and Dad would be that I might show back up."

"Well, you have, haven't you?"

The blond man frowned at the far wall, then said quietly, "No."

"Goddammit, Danny, you can't just disappear for better than five years then waltz into—"

"Josh." At his brother's glare, he added, "Please?"

"What the hell do you want, anyway — and what's with the Jim Morrison look?" Smacking at the long, wind-blown hair curling around his brother's shoulders, he stormed past and flung himself into the chair behind the desk.

"Wow, this is going well," Katzen said, absently smoothing the strands back. He sank into the visitor's seat, frown deepening. "What I want is your help." He raised a hand to forestall the tirade he saw building. "But first let me tell you a story.

"Once upon a time there was an Air Force pilot who realized his access to military aircraft gave him wonderful latitude to ferry things across borders. Sometimes those items were slightly warm to the touch—"

"I knew it!" David smacked the desk. "I always knew you were mixed up in something crooked. Stealing art, weren't you?"

The cocky grin returned. "Forgery, too. I'm very good."

"And overconfident. Using the U.S. military for cover. Asshole. Surprised you didn't get nailed but good."

"Oh, I *did* get nailed — sort of."

"How do you 'sort of' get nailed? Wait! Are you telling me you've been in jail for the last few years?"

"No." A shadow crossed the younger man's face. "You'd have to say I've been *out* of jail for the last few years. For the previous twenty or so, I've been under virtual house arrest."

"WHAAAAAT?"

"Well . . . remember the TV show *It Takes a Thief* when we were kids?"

"Yeah. Where the thief cuts a deal with the government instead of going to prison. I loved that show."

"So did General Leonard Fuller, and he tells me I'm lucky he did. You're a lawyer. I don't have to tell you what sort of charges they'd have had me on."

"General Leonard Fuller. . . ? Wait. Wasn't he the Air Force guy who came to tell Mom and Dad you were missing in action?"

"Yeah. Len's been my handler since I made the deal."

David stared.

Josh continued, "So, for the last twenty years give or take, I've been a good little soldier for Uncle Sam. I didn't mind. For the most part, what they asked me to do has been for the good of my country. Then, several years ago, they offered me the keys to my cage in exchange for one last big job. I did it. It almost killed me, but I did it. I got a new name and a new life out of it." The grin widened. "Meet Joshua Aaron Katzen, archaeological photographer and artist." He waited, braced for an outburst of disbelief or angry accusations of lying. It never came.

After a long silence, David remarked quietly, "Five years. The timing is telling . . . I don't suppose. . . ?"

Josh shook his head. "Sorry. Classified — although considering they broke their part of the deal, I shouldn't be such a stickler. But I am."

"What did they do?"

"They reneged. They called me back."

"They can't *do* that."

Josh chuckled. "You sounded remarkably like Avi Rosenberg just then."

"Rosenberg? The archaeologist?"

"And good friend. I've been working with him since I got my new life."

Durand sat back and went silent. Katzen followed suit, recognizing his brother's deep thought mode. At last, the lawyer blew out an amazed breath. "Do you want to sue them? Offhand, I'd say the chances aren't good."

"Snowball in hell, viewing recent history. From where I sit, it looks like all anyone got out of a lawsuit was a lot of unwanted publicity, a pat on the head and a fifty gallon drum of Vaseline." He paused. "Do I sound bitter?"

"You sound like you're taking it better than I would." He shook his head as if to clear it. "Whew. All this time and I had no idea."

"That was kinda the way it was supposed to work." Katzen shrugged. "What good is a secret agent who prints it on his business cards?"

David gave in to a laugh, but sobered quickly. "Still it seems like you're on the run again. Or at least in trouble."

"I'm actually not sure. I need a place to lay low until I figure out what *is* going on. Someplace no one would think to look for me. You still have that house on the beach?"

Durand fished in his pocket and tossed a set of keys that Katzen scooped out of the air.

"Internet access?"

"Cable."

"Awesome!"

"I don't know how to phrase this." David looked uncomfortable. "The people looking for you. Are they . . . ours?"

"I seriously doubt it. Besides, coming to you wouldn't throw Len Fuller off — at least not for long. On top of that, our guys want me to do something for them and killing me would sort of screw that particular pooch." He mulled it over. "No. The guys who were taking potshots at me in Peru sounded European—"

David sat forward so suddenly, his chair skidded backwards. "People shot at you?"

Josh waved him down. "Whoa! They weren't actually trying to hit me or I wouldn't be sitting here talking to you." He sighed at his brother's skeptical look. "Geez. You and Vic. He's convinced there's an assassin behind every tree waiting for a clear shot at me."

"Vic. Victor Pale made this appointment for you and you've been working with Dr. Avi Rosenberg. You've got some high-powered friends these days."

"I've been very fortunate."

"That's putting it mildly." Durand glanced at the clock. "Dammit. I'm nowhere finished talking to you, but I have to be in court today and I need to prepare. Why don't you head over to the beach house and I'll come by later?"

"Works for me," Josh said as he stood up. "I've been on the road for several days. It'll be a relief to sit down somewhere that isn't moving."

His hand had just brushed the doorknob when, from behind him, his brother asked, "So how have *you* been?"

Katzen paused, then turned with a genuine smile. "Good. Happy. These last years have been the happiest of my life. It's gonna hurt to lose that."

"Are you sure it's lost?"

The smile vanished. "Yes. No. I . . . I suppose I'll find out."

~*~

The Crockpot was just where he remembered. In the bottom cabinet, way at the back. David never did like cooking for himself. Josh crouched and pulled the pot out, awakening fresh protests from his bruised and abused back. The shooters may have been Europeans, but the people with the fists of iron were home-grown Peruvians. He stood and leaned against the counter until the spasms stopped. Damn good thing David wasn't there. He hadn't dealt well with the shooting part. Who knew what he'd do if he found out about the kidnapping and beating.

There'd be plenty of time to worry about that later, after a nice long shower and some food. He plugged the cooker in and busied himself with the stew makings he'd picked up on the way to the house. He'd even found a decent Cabernet in the grocery store's wine section.

~*~

He emerged from the bathroom in a cloud of steam, roughing up his hair as he went. The shower had helped, but when he pulled his ratty kimono on, the scrapes across his shoulders stung like the soft cotton was lined with sandpaper. Grimacing, he dropped the kimono back into the open suitcase on the bed and snagged a pair of jeans. Hell, it was a sunny afternoon in California. Like he was going to get chilled. He regarded himself in the full length mirror and winced at his reflection. Good news, bad news. The bruises were going Technicolor. That meant they were healing, but looked even worse than the day after it happened.

The rich scent of stew filled the kitchen as he padded barefoot across the cool ceramic tiles. It would be a couple more hours before it would be ready, though. There was a half bottle of Cabernet left and he rummaged through the cabinets for wine glasses. There were none. Looked like David was still on the wagon. Good. Kudos. He'd be sure to get rid of the wine well before his brother showed up.

Taking a juice glass, he poured a generous splash, grabbed a handful of carrots and a slice of bread, then went over to the table where he'd set up the laptop and wallet of memory cards. He stiffly lowered himself into the chair as the machine powered up. He hadn't gotten much actual rest on the drive west and the beds in the cheap motels he'd stopped at hadn't helped much. At that moment, he was feeling every mile as if he'd walked it. The only positive thing he could say about the places he'd stayed was that the harsh complimentary shampoo had removed the brown wash from his hair in record time. Taking a sip of Cabernet, he set the glass down and rubbed his face, stifling a yawn. The wine might have been a bad idea.

Shaking it off, he leaned forward and opened Photoshop.

CHAPTER 20

The thunk of a ceramic mug right by his ear and the strong scent of coffee woke him. He sat back to find his brother looking down at him, face filled with concern.

Josh groaned and pointed at the cup. "Is that spoken for?"

Wordlessly, David pushed it to him and he took a grateful drink, then looked around, noticing the sun was much lower in the sky. "What time is it?"

"About seven pm. Now it's my turn. What happened to you? You're covered with bruises, your wrists are cut to hell and your shoulders look like hamburger."

Josh stretched and winced. "Man I knew the wine was a mistake — wine. . . ." He looked around in sudden panic, then at his brother. "Geez, David. I'm sorry. I was going to have it put away before you got here."

"I recorked the bottle and put your glass in the fridge. I'm a recovering alcoholic, but wine was never a big temptation to me. You deflected my question. What happened to you?"

His brain still wasn't engaging. Instead of trying to answer, he sat back and sipped at the coffee.

That was too much for David. "Daniel! Don't fuck with me. You show up after being presumed dead for years, tell me people have been shooting at you and ask to stay in my house. You owe me an answer. You look like you've been beaten."

"That's because I was. A gang of Peruvian toughs thought I knew where something was. When I didn't, they figured they'd just beat me until I did." He held the warm cup against his temple. Damn he was tired. "And please, my name is Josh now. Really. It's all legal and everything."

He looked up into his brother's face, which hovered somewhere between horror and amazement. Josh set the cup down and stood. "I'm sorry. I shouldn't have come. I don't know what I was thinking. Maybe I just *wasn't* thinking. Gimme fifteen and I'm gone."

"No."

Katzen turned in surprise.

"You're not going anywhere. I'd like to think you came here because you trust me. True, we've never gotten along all that well, but you're still my brother no matter what your passport and driver's license say."

A slight smile played around the corners of Josh's mouth. "You checked my ID?"

"Damn straight I did. If you don't want me to look through your stuff, don't leave your suitcase open on my bed. I Googled you, too. J. A. Katzen has some nice artwork up for sale. Got a problem with that?"

They squared off for a few beats, then David strode away in disgust. "Oh sit down before you fall down. I'll get a couple bowls of that stew and we'll talk as we eat." Sounds of clinking crockery came from the kitchen. "Leave it to you to make a gourmet meal as soon as you land."

Josh followed. "It's just stew."

David laughed. "Your idea of 'just stew' and everyone else's isn't the same. Sort of like that car out there. Pretty fancy. Archaeological art must pay well."

"The silver BMW? It's Vic's." He cut the bread into thick slices. "I don't know if he was more worried about assassins or that my rattle-trap RX-7 wouldn't last the drive out."

David laughed and Josh continued. "He had a valid point with the Mazda. That car and I have a love-hate relationship. It would have probably blown a rotor in Arizona just for spite."

~*~

He enlarged the text on the archived news article and leaned in to read it. The movement caused a cascade of printouts and hand-written notes onto the floor. Katzen sighed and resisted the urge to sweep the rest of the stacks after it. Coffee. He needed more coffee. No. What he really needed was a break.

Retrieving the scattered papers, he shuffled them back into a semblance of order, then dropped the stack onto the table. Who was he kidding? What he *really* needed was a new approach; the one he was using sure as hell wasn't working. He'd been studying Deustch's notes, photos and records for more than a week and the only thing he'd gotten was eyestrain — and headaches. Lots of headaches. He scrubbed the heels of his hands into his eyes and wandered toward the open sliding glass doors that looked out over the beach. The salty breeze and stretch of sand beyond the redwood deck were inviting, but he knew better than to give in. All that netted him in the past was a few hours of aimless wandering and a growing collection of cool shells.

Turning his back on the ocean, he made for the kitchen. In truth, coffee was probably the last thing he needed. He was pretty wired already. In the kitchen, he veered off and rooted in the fridge for one of David's Maine Root Ginger Brews. The sugar wouldn't do his coffee buzz much good, but at least it wouldn't drop another load of caffeine on top of it. Twisting the cap off he took a pull at the bottle. It was ice cold and burned a little going down, but it helped.

Returning to the paper-strewn table, he paused once again in front of the picture wall. A mini shrine to his brother's life. When he'd first looked at the array, he'd been amazed to find photos of himself among the pictures of the kids, ex-wives, sailboats and trophy shots of David with celebrities and political figures. He smiled down at the long table filled with stand-up frames. Right next to the studio portrait of himself in his newly-minted major's uniform was one of David's eldest, his daughter Dee Dee, in *her* Air Force dress uniform.

He smiled and lifted the picture. He suspected the positioning of the portraits had a lot more to do with Dee Dee than with her father. She and her uncle had always had a special bond that annoyed both of her parents to no end. They even shared such a strong resemblance, people frequently mistook them for father and daughter rather than uncle and niece. There was no end of bother when she'd up and joined the Air Force just like her uncle Danny. That was where the resemblance ended, though. She was a damned smart kid; he'd never have to worry that she'd make the same boneheaded mistakes he had.

An image of what his own picture wall might look like flitted across his mind: a bank of mostly empty frames with the word "REDACTED" stamped across them. He chuckled, then frowned. But did it have to be that way? Could things have gone differently?

Shut up! he ordered. *You played the system, dumbass, and you lost.*

But did he really lose? All in all, he'd had a pretty good life. Sure, there'd never been time for long-term relationships, and in his profession, relationships could be dangerous for all involved. Would he have been happy in a so-called normal life, anyway? Was David any happier? Successful lawyer. Alcoholic. Married three times. Divorced three times. Granted, there were three pretty good kids to show for it, but still. . . .

Dammit! No! More magical thinking. What the hell was wrong with him? Even after all this time, he still got caught up in the what ifs. He put Dee Dee's picture down and said quietly, "Take care of yourself, Darlin'. Uncle Josh has work to do to get himself out of yet another jam."

~*~

The ocean breeze lifted his hair, billowed his Hawaiian shirt and danced lightly over his skin. A promise of evening cool lurked within the warm flow even though the sun was still well above the horizon. It felt great. Just standing still, leaning on the deck railing he felt free. The sensation couldn't have been more opposite from fifteen minutes earlier when he'd had to peel himself off of the leather chair to stand up.

The medium-hair gray tabby cat from down the beach hopped onto the weathered railing, head-butted him and purred.

"Hey, Merlin," Katzen said, scratching his visitor under the chin. "Doing the evening rounds, huh? Well, everything at Beach Base Alpha is good to go and the jet is Fried Monkey Chicken. The stick actuator is bored as hell and in a permanent state of Alpha Foxtrot Uniform, but still relatively functional."

There was a laugh from behind him and the screen door slid open. David Durand stepped onto the redwood planking holding two ice-covered bottles. "I take it that was pseudo Militaryese for you're still chasing your tail."

"Hey! I didn't even hear you come in — and yeah, chasing my tail pretty much nails it."

"Not surprised. Before your furry pal arrived, you looked like something had seriously pissed you off somewhere near the horizon. I won't mention the fact that the Brian Setzer Orchestra on the music system could have drowned out a herd of dancing hippos." He popped the caps off the bottles and handed one to Josh. "Also, either somebody's been shopping or Maine Root Ginger Brew is more magical than I thought. Yesterday, there was one carton, now there are four."

Josh grinned sheepishly. "Yeah. I kind of decimated your supply. Thanks for the new addiction, Bro."

"What's family for?" They clinked bottle necks and David settled back into one of the lounge chairs. Merlin hopped from the railing onto the lawyer's stomach. David OOOFed, then dumped the cat onto the floor. "Damn! *And* I see cats still follow you around. Some things never change."

Katzen picked the cat up and put him on the railing. "This is Merlin. He lives two doors down that way, but he likes your sun deck better than his own."

David took a sip at the ginger and jerked his thumb back toward the house. "That's a helluva lot of paperwork on the table.

Looks like my desk when I'm doing homework for a big case. Who's Herbert Deustch III and why does his name sound so familiar?"

Katzen wheeled, mouth open to protest, then stopped. "Right. Right. If I don't want you looking at things. . . ."

". . .don't leave 'em out. Bingo," Durand said with a shark-grin. "It's beside the point, anyway. Why is that name familiar?"

The younger man turned to watch the surf and absently pet the cat. "Probably heard it on the news. He got a lot of coverage a few weeks back. High profile antiquities dealer found dead in a Peruvian ruin?"

"Oh yeah! I remember now. Rich guy who got into some pretty shady things . . . there was something else, too, though . . . something before that. . . . shit storm of court cases right after he disappeared?" He closed his eyes and Josh could almost hear drawers in the mental file cabinets opening and closing. At length David snapped his fingers and said, "Yeah! Some high-powered international stuff. Stolen art — antiquities?"

"That would be it. I'm impressed you remember all that. Art has always been more my purview than yours."

"It wasn't the art that got my attention. It was the law. Some of that got beautifully complicated." He sipped ginger beer thoughtfully. "Weren't there two partners in particular that got caught up? One was tried abroad . . . Italy if I remember."

Josh rooted through the stacks of paper beside the laptop, returned with two photographs and put them on the deck table. "Right again — mostly. One partner, Ludovico di Bardi, and one girlfriend, Diana Meadowes."

"Yeah. Meadowes was some mucky-muck with some big museum."

"Still is. She's the director of the Gant down in LA."

David nodded. "She's the one that got dragged through the Italian courts. It went on forever, but didn't go anywhere in the end. If I recall, the evidence against her was all circumstantial."

"Yep. She was acquitted of all charges."

The lawyer huffed a laugh. "She was damned lucky in my book. Sometimes lack of evidence doesn't mean squat in the Italian system if they've decided you're guilty. The other guy, di Bardi, was more straightforward. Not much interesting there. Wasn't he implicated in looting when they found a gold crown hidden in Deustch's home?"

"Gold laurel wreath, actually. Macedonian. Roughly from the time of Philip II. They were usually awarded to the winner of an athletic competition."

"Showoff."

Josh laughed. "Only a little. I especially remember that one because you don't usually hear of a Macedonian victor's wreath being found in a bathroom."

"In a *bathroom*?"

"Yep. Behind a false wall. Friend Deustch had a long-standing habit of hiding things like some gigantic, paranoid squirrel."

"That sounds like the voice of experience." David laughed, then stopped suddenly. "Wait. This is what it's about, isn't it?"

"What?"

David waved his hands to encompass his brother, the laptop and the paper-strewn table. "This whole thing. The beatings, getting shot at, fleeing Peru . . . Oh my god, Danny, tell me *you* weren't involved with this asshole, too."

"It's *Josh* and why does everyone jump to the conclusion that I had some connection with this ratsass?"

David raised an eyebrow. "If the shoe fits. . . ?"

"*No!* I did *not* know Herb Deustch. We never met. Ever. He's been dead almost longer than I've been in the business. Trust me, I'm not that good with a Ouija board."

"Okay! I get it. Complete strangers. Then what in the hell is this all about? —And don't give me that need to know shit."

Josh turned back toward the ocean, weighing words internally.

Finally, Katzen turned to his brother and said, "Deustch was a notorious tomb robber, but that was only one facet. He was a wheeler dealer who wasn't above making off with anything that

wasn't nailed down and flogging it to the highest bidder on the
black market. The problem arose when he stole something
very nasty from some mercenaries who stole it from Uncle
Sam. From the look of things, it got him killed. The thing he
stole hasn't been seen since, and I, for one, would be very happy
if it remained that way — or better — if the good guys found
it first." He paused and looked his brother in the eyes. "Does that
work? It's about as close as I can come without stepping into
redacted-all-to-hell-hope-you-like-prison-food territory."

David sat back. "Wow. The implications are. . . well . . . nasty.
Is there anything I can do to help? Gather information or something? I have a lot of connections."

"I'm not sure, but the farther away you are from this mess, the
better I'd feel about it."

David laughed. "I'm already in the middle of it, Moron. You're
staying at my house remember?"

Josh looked nonplussed, then grinned. "Yeah. Guess so. Sorry
about that."

A Siamese cat chose that moment to saunter up the stairs and
stretch out on the decking. Durand shook his head. "Another one.
I could never figure out what it was with you and cats."

His brother dropped onto a lounge and leaned down to stroke
the newcomer's creamy fur. "Me neither, but that's okay. I like
them, too."

"So, since you're in San Francisco again, are you going to
look Maxine up?"

The hand stroking the cat faltered. "Uh, no. I think that would
be a bad idea. Besides, I heard she got married."

"Oh yeah. That lasted about five minutes." Durand let the
silence stretch, then said, "She took your disappearance pretty
hard."

"I don't know why. We were quits long before that."

David made a non-committal noise deep in his throat.

"No, no, no! Any contact with the glamorous, high-profile CEO
of Alexco would be asking for trouble for someone trying not to

be seen. You know as well as I do that where Maxine Alexander goes, so goes the paparazzi."

"Good point."

The younger man looked away toward the encroaching tide again. Finally, he said, "Look, David, if this gig works out, Danny Durand is dead and will *stay* that way. I'll vanish back into the woodwork. Scout's honor."

"I'm not sure how I feel about that. Y'know, it's weird. In the past, the two of us were usually at each other's throats within minutes of being in the same place. What the hell changed?"

Shrugging, Katzen offered, "Perception?"

It was David's turn to look nonplussed. "Well . . . yeah. I guess. I was pretty damned convinced that my little brother was a criminal. I'm still wrapping my head around what you really did."

Josh guffawed. "We're back to perception again. I can think of several countries that still have me down as a criminal — under almost as many names. A few probably still have warrants out for my arrest."

David joined the laugh. "Call me if you need a lawyer."

They sat in silence for a while, watching the sun dip closer to the horizon. After a while, David said, "You're right about perception. Take my first thoughts when I saw that mess of papers inside."

"Yeah?"

"The first thing through my head was 'Oh my God. He's writing one of those tell-all books.'"

His brother laughed again and drained his soft drink.

Silence descended between them again — until, "All right, I can't stand it any longer: what the hell is Fried Monkey Chicken?"

~*~

Storm clouds boiled and the wind whipped up a chop that scattered reflected moonlight like a handful of glitter across the waves. He snapped the lid to the laptop down and swiveled to watch the growing storm outside. Looked like it was brewing up a good one.

This is what he'd always thought retirement would be like: relaxing in a comfortable chair and watching the world rage by from a distance. Okay, what he'd *hoped* retirement would be like. In his line of work, retirement frequently came in a wooden box and a very small allotment of land — in Arlington if you were lucky. In an anonymous foreign place if you weren't. It could still go that way. Lightning flashed and danced across the water.

Back in Chicago, he'd been flip with Vic, his ingrained form of self-defense kicking in. It wasn't that he didn't take the threats against him seriously. He'd be an idiot not to recognize that things were hotting up. It was simply that it did no good to get himself tied into knots over it. In truth, that could actually kill him. Just because the guys with the rifle didn't put one through his head in Peru, didn't mean they'd be so considerate the next time they crossed paths.

He swiveled back to the laden table. His equipment and papers had seemingly taken on a life of their own, like some semi-sentient paper-creature in a B science fiction movie. Oh, how he wished he could take a flamethrower to the lot. He yawned and stretched, then stopped in surprise realizing he wasn't stiff any more. His injuries were healing and the bruises were almost gone. Now, if he could just make some progress with the Deustch puzzle.

Better get back to the slog. He needed to find something of value pretty soon. It was taking so long, he was halfway expecting Fuller or DeVries to show up on the doorstep. The thought triggered a chuckle. David would have a real cow if they did. Might be almost worth it.

Raising the laptop lid, he woke it up and Deustch's dossier appeared on the screen. He sighed and closed the program down. Why look at it again? The damned thing seemed to be etched into his memory. He needed a new approach. Yeah. Right.

Idly entering the man's name into a search engine brought up all the things he'd seen a hundred times before. There were the first flurry of articles sparked by the discovery of the remains.

There were countless links to archived articles. Many of those were hard-to-read scans of pre-digital newspaper pieces; it gave him a headache, but he could read enough to tell him that his memory of the man's reputation for a violent temper was accurate.

There were a few new entries. Looked like some buzz about a recent expose of the illegal antiquities trade. . . hmmmmmmm. Could be an interesting read.

Wait. What had David said earlier about him writing a book?

CHAPTER 21

He'd actually made the time window he was shooting for. Considering that the five and a half hour drive from San Francisco had actually taken closer to seven, it was beyond amazing — still, it dangerously tightened the schedule. Patrons at the bank wouldn't simply vanish at the stroke of the hour, but they would thin out. That would play hob with him getting in and out without sticking too much in anyone's memory. The LA bank was considerably larger than the one he used in Miami's Little Havana. Helpful, but he still needed to get a move on.

Now for the truly hard part: getting out of the car. He slid out of the low-slung BMW and straightened with a barely suppressed groan. Rolling his shoulders eased the tightness some, but he was bone-tired from hours spent on the congested roads. Nothing would really help but a hot shower and a good night's sleep, and that couldn't happen until he knew who he was this time. There was something just plain silly about that, but it couldn't be helped. He crossed the busy street and, ignoring protesting muscles, strode casually into the bank lobby, smiled pleasantly at the matronly lady at the safe deposit desk and presented his key.

~*~

Inside the bank's private room, he stared thoughtfully at the pistol nestled amid the papers in the safe deposit box. It seemed to stare back.

If the guys who shot at him in Piedras Rojas came at him again, it would probably be from a distance. He'd never know what hit him. A pistol wouldn't do him a helluva lot of good in that case. No, the only reason he'd need the Ruger would be if he wasted too much time standing there debating whether he needed a gun or not. If this box had been flagged by anyone, or if this long-idle account suddenly going live raised an alarm, dithering could prove disastrous. It could be worse if the Miami account was also flagged.

Shoving the weapon aside, he lifted the stack of IDs. Most were far enough out of date, he didn't want to mess with them. Three were fresh enough to work.

He examined the first: Matthew Knight. Noooo. Too hot. Matty boy just came through customs.

Next.

Stanley Lieber. Bingo! The best part about Stan was that he didn't require any makeup. Sometimes the Man of a Thousand Faces bit was a pure pain in the ass.

Pocketing the Lieber ID packet and most of the US currency, he tossed the rejects back in on top of the pistol and snapped the lid closed.

As he left the private room and handed the box back to the attendant, he couldn't shake that crawly feeling that he'd done something wrong; that someone was a few steps behind him. It was probably nerves. Probably. It didn't pay to stick around and find out.

Exiting the bank through a side door, he turned away from where he'd parked the car and strolled casually for several blocks, window shopping and watching for tails. Satisfied he walked alone, he doubled back and bought a cappuccino at a shop that provided a good view of the parking lot across the street. As he slipped into a booth, his mistake hit him like a sucker punch. The little silver BMW with its Illinois tags seemed to glow like a beacon. Idiot. Why the hell hadn't he left the thing at San Francisco International and driven a rental to LA? Damn.

Next stop LAX and the long-term parking lot.

~*~

With the BMW safely buried in the hodge-podge of long-term airport parking, he joined the throng of travelers making for the car rental kiosks. On reflection, he realized the situation could work to his advantage. Stan Leiber was now leaving a trail that began at LAX just like anyone else who'd flown into the city on business. That didn't make the mistake any less stupid, though. Dumbass moves like that could get him killed.

Another frustrating hour of navigating paperwork and dealing with bored, overworked clerks and he was finally on his way. For all the frustration, he was pleased with the rental: a five-year-old white Hyundai that had seen better days. It was exactly the type of vehicle a freelance writer on a tight budget would wind up with. He tossed his bags into it and went in search of a mid-range motel near the airport.

By the time he found one with vacancies, he didn't have to feign being tired and rumpled. It had been a long, tiring day and even the wonderfully high-pressure shower in his room didn't help much. Hair still damp, he set his tells and fell across the bed. Tomorrow he'd buy a new burner phone and Stan Lieber, boy reporter, would start setting up interviews.

~*~

He pulled the battered rental into the parking space, switched off the ignition and resisted the urge to bash his head against the steering wheel.

He snatched the laptop case from the passenger seat and stepped out onto the sun-warmed pavement, thinking, *Kaka. Not even* good *kaka. Spread this stuff on a garden and it might* kill *the tomatoes.*

Truthfully, he was more surprised than anything else. He'd spent hours sifting through and researching names from the dossier Fuller had given him. First, he'd eliminated everyone who didn't live within driving distance — which had unfortunately eliminated Deustch's remaining family. Next, since his Ouija skills were weak, he scratched off all the deceased. He then eliminated everyone currently in prison. His ID documents were good, but he didn't see any reason to push his luck. The final list had looked promising.

It lied. He'd wasted the better part of a day exploring places in Los Angeles that he hoped never to see again, tracking down people who didn't want to talk to him or had little of value to say — and wanted cash on the barrelhead to do it. An alarming number were scratched off because they'd vanished as completely as Deustch himself. It didn't really matter, though. This next interview was the one he'd been looking forward to as much for the venue as for the woman he'd be talking to: Diana Meadowes, director of the Gant Museum and on-again-off-again lover of Herb Deustch.

Pausing at the base of the museum's gleaming marble staircase, he scanned the colorful banners flanking them. Cool! An exhibit on ancient glass and glassmaking was in the Garden Gallery right across from the Terrazza Cafe where he was to meet Ms. Meadowes. If the interview went sour, he could at least take in the exhibit.

Maybe even if it went well. It sounded interesting.

The Gant's open air cafe was all but deserted save for a few patrons lingering over coffee and staff clearing and wiping down tables. Pausing just inside, he looked around and let the peaceful atmosphere wash over him. Sunlight streamed past the soaring stone columns, painting puddles of warmth against the rough flagstone floor. Stepping through the tall bronze double doors always felt more like he was entering some sacred precinct rather than a museum's restaurant. He ordered a cappuccino from the hostess who greeted him, then took advantage of the near-deserted state to claim his favorite table alongside the stone balustrade. The seat provided a magnificent view of the museum's sprawling gardens. The warm breeze that brought the mingled scent of exotic flowers up to him came close to erasing the day's frustrations. Sadly, it didn't entirely work. Sighing, he powered up his laptop. If he was going to be frustrated anyway, he might as well be productive and frustrated.

He was deleting yet another empty interview file from his hard drive when someone said, "You *must* be the writer working on Herbert Deustch's biography. Only Herb could cause that fierce a frown."

The voice was deep and smoky. He stood and turned, extending his hand to its owner: the tall, elegant woman whose photos had been peppering his research files. Age had changed, but not erased her beauty. "And you can only be Diana Meadowes. Stan Leiber. I'm honored that you could meet with me."

He pulled a chair out for her. She treated him to a warm smile and sat, silver jewelry chiming as she folded her arms onto the tabletop. "So, is this your first visit to the Gant, Mr. Leiber?"

"Absolutely not! The Gant is one of my favorite places in LA. I try to make time to spend a day here whenever I make it to the city. It kind of clears my head."

She looked pleased. "Mmmmmm. Flattery *will* get you somewhere." She signaled for a cup of coffee from the hostess, then said, "So you wanted to talk about Herb Deustch? Even with the rather dramatic discovery of his . . . remains, I'd think he was old news by now."

"The discovery of his remains *was* pretty intriguing. Murdered, then buried in a collapsed ancient ruin? It kind of brought him back to the headlines."

"I suppose so. It was somewhat fitting, too — he'd have loved it — well, other than the murdered part." She laughed, a sound almost as slivery as her jewelry. Sobering, she said, "Still, I can think of at least three books and countless articles that have already been done. Surely there isn't much to add."

"I disagree, Ms. Meadowes. I've read them and they're mostly dry facts. I'd hoped you might be able to give me some insight on the man himself. I . . . uh . . . understand you and Mr. Deustch were close?"

She threw back her head and laughed again. A genuine, hearty guffaw. "So polite! Don't sugarcoat it, dear. Herb and I were lovers."

Her laugh was infectious and he found himself smiling in response. "Okay, then. Gloves off. How did you first meet Herb Deustch?"

"Oh! It was right here at the Gant."

"Really?"

"Yes, in the Italian wing. I was just starting out as a conservator, fresh from art school. Part of my job was to check the humidity levels in the Florentine Gallery. I'd just finished my rounds when I noticed this man with his nose all but touching Botticelli's *Portrait of a Young Woman*."

Katzen/Lieber chuckled in spite of himself.

She raised an eyebrow. "What?"

"Oh, nothing, really," he said. "I just sympathize with him. There are some artworks that seem to invite you closer in spite of the velvet ropes."

She looked a little surprised, then smiled. "There *are*. It's like an enchantment." She became thoughtful, then said, "Herb was the same way. One thing those books and articles have never really gotten right was his charm. I suppose that's a hard quality to put into words, though — I know I can't. He was incredibly charismatic." She paused and seemed far away for a few beats. "I can't even tell you how it happened, but one moment we were standing in front of the Botticelli, the next we were having an intimate lunch in an exclusive restaurant that I'd only read about in magazines."

She grew silent again, staring into the distance. He watched her expression morph from soft remembrance back to elegant cynicism. Finally she said, "I'm not a fool, Mr. Lieber. I never believed I was the one and only." After a moment, she added, "We'd fight, then split, but we kept coming back to each other. There *did* seem to be something a little special there — then again, what girlfriend doesn't think that?"

He hesitated before asking the next question, feeling more than a little voyeuristic. "The next question is a bit delicate, too—"

She didn't wait for him. "The looted artifacts," she supplied matter-of-factly.

"Ummmm. Yeah."

She suddenly looked tired. "I know. I've asked myself the same thing over and over: 'Twenty years and you *really* had no idea?'"

"Any answers?"

"I'd be lying if I said I never wondered, but the provenances he and Ludovico — that's Ludovico di Bardi, his business partner — were so good. . . . I just never looked at them too hard." She paused and her face went wry. "Paid for that one in spades. Even after all these years, my reputation — and the Gant's — has never fully recovered. I guess I owe the bastard for that one, too."

"Why didn't you you leave? I'm sure there were museums and galleries all over Europe who would have snapped you up in an instant."

The steel came back. "I don't run, Mr. Lieber. I'm not made that way."

"Please. Call me Stan and I'm not sure *I* wouldn't have ducked for cover a little. Maybe hightailed it to that villa in Crete. Somewhere they would have had to reach a little to smear me, anyway."

She smiled again. "Only if you call me Diana." Another thoughtful pause, then she said, "I admit, it was damned tempting, but the villa wasn't mine at that time. If Herb had come back, I would have had to share it with him and I was so mad, I probably would have killed him with my bare hands. It wasn't until his family had him declared officially dead and his will was read that I ended up with the Cretan estate."

She fell silent again, lost in thought. He sipped at his cappuccino and waited.

At last she said, "That family. They didn't waste any time. Seven years to the *day* that he was officially reported missing. They must have timed it with a stopwatch." She shrugged. "But then again, I might have done the same thing in their place. He wasn't very nice to them. Most of them weren't at all happy about the villa, either. I still haven't decided what to do with it. I love it, but there are some memories I'd rather not revisit." She fixed him with a sharp look. "And, no. I won't tell you what those memories are."

He laughed. "I wouldn't dream of asking. I will ask if he sent love letters, though."

Another hearty guffaw. "Love letters? Herb Deustch never did anything so prosaic."

"He never wrote? Not even a post card?"

"Oh he wrote. Reams — although revisiting them is a lot more work than I care to do."

"Ooookay. Can I ask why?"

"Have you ever heard of a book code? Soon after we started seeing each other, Herb had to go abroad. He gave me a first edition of Elizabeth Barrett Browning's collection, *An Essay on Mind, with Other Poems*, as a parting gift. I thought it was such a romantic gesture — until I got his first letter. It was in code. *Three pages* of code using the Browning volume as the key."

"Code?" he asked in amazement. "In a love letter?"

"My reaction exactly. Now, it was quite steamy once I'd decoded it, but the decoding part did reduce the effect a bit. That was Herb right down to the ground, though. The man simply loved being mysterious. Thrived on it."

"So, how did you feel when they discovered his body in Peru?"

"I felt exactly the same after as I had before. The same way I do to this day: I'm furious with the sonovabitch."

He was taken aback and she laughed at his expression. "Surprised? Don't be. The man was infuriating. He often simply vanished. He'd be gone for months only to show up on my doorstep in the middle of the night with a lavish gift or at the Gant with a new find for acquisition, acting as if we'd talked yesterday. I was always angry with him, but I always took him back. More fool I." Her expression changed then, becoming troubled.

"The last time was different, though. He called. He rarely did that. Hated the telephone. He was excited about something and even more mysterious than usual. He said he had something big in the works — bigger than anything before. He even said that, when it was over, he and Ludovico might open that gallery and auction house they always talked about. It alarmed me. I begged him to be careful, but he didn't listen. He never did.

"Then, he went silent again.

"When the silence went from months to years, I knew he was dead. Considering some of the people he'd been hanging around with toward the end, it was probably inevitable."

Katzen grew silent, too. He knew who Deustch's associates had been in those final months. Diana had been right to worry. Finally he said, "They were a rough crowd, then?"

"Heavens, rough doesn't even come close. Herb had always loved hanging out on the fringes. He was a thrill-seeker — probably some hold-over of the rich boy playing with fire, but these people. . . ? They weren't the usual shady companions. They were into much more serious things. That's when the legal problems really started."

"There'd been questions before, though, right?"

"Questions, yes, but he and Ludovico had always been careful. Suspicions could be brushed off. When Herb took up with this bunch, he got . . . I don't know . . . sloppy. Overconfident."

Oh yeah. That'll bite you in the ass every time. Aloud he asked, "Why do you think that was?"

"Truthfully? I'm not sure. I can tell you that a couple of them made my flesh crawl. You'd have to ask Ludovico about that, since he had more direct contact with them than I did. It's a shame he's out of the country. I'd suggest that computer video thing, but Ludovico is abysmal with computer *anything*." She thought for a bit, then said, "Margaret! Have you spoken to her yet?"

"His sister?" He shook his head. "Not yet. I'm working out of San Francisco at the moment, so I wanted to talk to folks on this coast first."

"But Maggie's here! Well, over in Beverly Hills, anyway. She's a sweetheart. The only member of the Deustch family who didn't hate me."

He was floored. Margaret Trevilian Deustch-Gascone was in California? It wasn't often that Len's information was wrong, but this time it was. With bells on. It would be fun to rub his nose in it later. Aloud he said, "Wow. I didn't realize my information was so far off. I have her down as living in the family home in New York with her son, Andrew Gascone."

"She was until that last nasty winter they had. She took a fall on an icy sidewalk and that was all she wrote. Packed up and moved into Herb's place in Beverly. Left the New York house in the hands of that vulture son of hers." She chuckled. "Her words, not mine."

A nervous young man fidgeted in the Terrazza's doorway for a moment before hurrying across to their table. He bent low and murmured into Diana's ear. "Ms. Meadowes, sorry to interrupt, but Dr. Fitzgerald needs to speak with you about the new Greek acquisition."

Diana rolled her eyes. "Again? That man is driving me insane." She turned back to Josh and said, "Our new metal conservator. The idiot is absolutely convinced that any purchase I've made in the last fifteen years will bring some angry government down on his head. I swear, he's jumpier than that Flores man."

Before he could stop himself, Josh said, "Flores? *Morty* Flores?"

It was her turn to be taken aback. "Yes. He worked for us last year. Briefly. Dr. Flores isn't a friend of yours is he?"

He'd already stepped in it up to the hip. He decided to go for as honest an answer as he could. "Mmmmmm. No. Suffice it to say I am not now, nor ever will be on Morty Flores' holiday card list."

She threw back her head and guffawed again. "Oh good. I didn't think I'd misjudged you *that* badly."

Before he could respond, she leaned forward, touched his arm and said, "Walk with me, Stan. I'm enjoying our conversation and you might enjoy seeing some of the Gant's lesser known treasures in their natural habitat."

It was too good an offer to turn down. Before he knew it,

Diana was leading him through the back areas of the museum not usually open to the public. Along the way, she kept up a running commentary on the art and artifacts they passed. He was in heaven. These were the areas he liked best, the unadorned places where the art wasn't so much displayed — it just *was*.

They were standing beside a Roman marble copy of a Greek bronze when he noticed she'd gone silent. He glanced over to find her staring at him with a strange smile playing around the corners of her mouth.

"You remind me of him," she said.

"Uhh . . . pardon?"

"Of him. Herb"

Oh shit. Not again. Why did everyone keep linking him to Deustch?

She enjoyed his discomfort a moment, then said, "Now, don't take that the wrong way. I don't think you're going to knock the place over. I meant that in a good way, actually." She became serious and treated him to a searching look. "I think it's your reverence for the art. You look at the pieces . . . lovingly. Yes. That's the best word. Herb looked at them the same way."

He had nothing to say to that, but it didn't matter, because she turned and moved over to a battered wooden door with a brass "Staff Only" sign affixed to it. Pausing with one hand on the latch, she asked, "Are you an artist as well as a writer?"

Still processing the latest comparison to Deustch, he stammered, "Uhhhh, yes, I am. . . ."

"I thought as much. Most creative people are creative in more than one way. Come on, then. You're going to love this part."

They stepped through into a large, but cluttered conservation studio and he froze in his tracks, almost afraid to breathe. A mosaic depicting the abduction of Persephone in still-vivid blue, black, white and gold dominated the floor a few yards in front of them. The scene showed Pluto in his chariot being guided into the underworld by Hermes. He could almost feel the pair of white horses straining against their harnesses and the wind whipping

Persephone's hair as she struggled against the grip of the lord of the underworld. It was one of the most magnificent mosaics he'd ever seen seen. A young woman in a white bunny suit lay prone on a low scaffold, carefully cleaning the tesserae forming Persephone's flowing hair with a cotton swab.

Diana's amused chuckle beside him brought him back to the cluttered workroom. "Told you so," she said. "You stay here and appreciate. I'll get Fitzgerald sorted out, then we can continue our conversation in my office — and I'll call Maggie to get an interview set up for you. If you really want to know who Herb Deustch was, she's the one you need to talk with."

~*~

It was a good thing Diana Meadowes had called ahead. Without that additional credential, he doubted the faceless drill-sergeant manning the gate controls would have even listened to him, let alone buzzed him through. Security was tight at the Deustch-Gascone homestead. Considering the sprawling mansion that hove into sight in the waning afternoon sunlight as he followed the driveway up, it probably had to be. Likely more so since its previous owner was back in the news in circumstances as notorious as those he'd lived under.

It would be great if the interview proved worth his time. In spite of all the facts, figures and photos he'd been given, he still had a limited grasp of the man whose mind he was supposed to be getting into. It felt like there was some key, some vital piece that was just out of his reach. He hated that feeling and this case had been one frustration after another since the Pentagon brass monkeys had so thoughtfully dropped it in his lap. His knee-jerk reaction was that interviewing Margaret would be a time-waster, too. After all, if Deustch hadn't shared the shadow part of his life with his lover, why would he share it with his sister? The temptation to blow it all off and return to San Francisco with what he had was strong. He couldn't do that, though. If nothing else, he had to maintain his cover. What real reporter would turn down an exclusive?

Ahead, someone waited beside the open front door — not the owner of the intercom voice unless the young Latina in the severe black dress had a nasty head-cold. After he'd parked the rented rattletrap where she indicated, she smiled and said, "Please come in. Mrs. Deustch-Gascone will be with you shortly."

Nope. Not a sign of a head-cold.

The young woman led him into a cavernous foyer that was lit from above by a crystal chandelier the size of a small asteroid. Just below, stood a life-sized bronze statue on a marble pedestal. In spite of the overhead crystal opulence, the sculpture dominated the room. Almost without conscious thought, he stepped closer. The bronze depicted a nude youth holding aloft a lantern and the pedestal it stood upon looked to be the barrel of an ancient column.

The statue was thought to have been cast in Greece and imported by a wealthy Roman citizen sometime before Mount Vesuvius blew and buried a large chunk of the ancient Roman version of the Hamptons. It had probably graced an elegant triclinium. The figure of the youth was amazingly pristine, but the lantern had been replaced in more modern times. Italian authorities suspected it had been illegally excavated from the Pompeii/Herculaneum area sometime in the mid-1970s. That's when it first appeared on the antiquities scene, anyway. Like its late owner, the bronze was immersed in controversy. Its provenance had come into question during Herb Deustch's lifetime and had been at the center of a political firestorm for decades. The saga had fascinated the younger Katzen.

"Ah! Mr. Lieber! Diana told me the Lamp Bearer would catch your attention."

A tiny, elderly woman smiled at him from the doorway to his left. She looked like a work of art herself with white hair caught into a perfect upswept style and strands of creamy pearls gleaming against her floor-length indigo gown. He didn't notice the ebony walking stick until she stepped into the foyer. The hand she extended, though blue-veined and fragile-looking, did not shake in the slightest. "Good evening, Mr. Lieber. I'm Margaret Deustch-Gascone."

He took her hand and was mildly surprised at the firmness of her grip. "You'll have to excuse me for gawking. I've been reading about this piece since I was in high school, but I never thought I'd actually see it, let alone stand in touching distance of it. The photographs didn't do it justice — then again, photography can only go so far."

She smiled up at the bronze. "He is beautiful, isn't he. He was one of my brother's favorites." Her gaze slid from the bronze to her guest. "Please, join me in the library. I've had Consuela set out coffee and sandwiches there."

~*~

She'd called the room "the library" and, to be fair, it did have bookshelves lining three walls. It also had one of the finest collections of Italian renaissance art he'd seen outside of a museum. A Cellini bronze had been moved off a table that was probably an antique when the Spanish colonized California, to make way for an elaborate silver service and a three tiered serving tray laden with crustless sandwiches.

She poured coffee into a translucent porcelain cup that looked too delicate to hold the liquid. "Black with no sugar, I'll wager."

The way the statement was phrased puzzled him a little. He took the offered cup with a lop-sided smile. "You got me pegged."

"I thought so. When Diana told me how like Herbert you were, I doubted her. After all this time, you'd think I'd know better."

"I'm still not sure how to take that."

"As a compliment," she said filling her own cup. "A very definite compliment. Actually, that's the only reason I'm talking to you. Diana said you were asking sensible questions, not like some of the sensational nonsense that's been out there so far." She fixed him with a stern look. "Why are your questions so different from all the other reporters who've called, Mr. Lieber? What is it you're trying to do?"

He paused with the cup halfway to his lips. The best lie was not a lie, but part of the truth. "I'm not a regular reporter, Mrs. Deustch-Gascone. I'm a completely different sort of animal. Freelance. The sensational stuff doesn't interest me. I can find that anywhere. What I'm trying to do is to get inside the head of Herbert Deustch. I want to know who he was and how he thought. Not so much what he did, but *why* he did it."

For a second, he was afraid that had been the wrong answer. The stern schoolteacher look remained, but dissolved in an instant to be replaced by a smile of pure pleasure. "Oh, I'm so glad to hear that! My brother was such an interesting man and the news people are being so unkind about him."

He pulled a micro recorder from his pocket and held it up. "In that case, may I?"

"Of course! I appreciate someone who finally wants to get it right."

Then she started to reminisce. Stories of growing up in that "Have" society, of summers spent at Martha's Vineyard and winter vacations in the south of France. Some of it was amusing, but not useful. He found himself on autopilot, only half-listening until she mentioned entering university.

He set his empty cup down and she filled it without asking. She really did have him pegged. "He studied engineering, didn't he?"

"Oh yes! We both did."

The response surprised him. It must have shown, because she gave him a coquettish smile. "I saw that look. I saw it often enough while I was at school, too."

"It must have been unusual for a woman to be in that field, especially at that time."

"Unusual for a *woman* to be at *university*, don't you mean? The Deustch family didn't follow conventions. When I said I wanted to be an engineer, too, our Daddy made sure it happened," she said with pride, then took a delicate sip at her coffee. "Of course, I was never as good at it as Herbert. He had more of a knack for figures than I. He could work out equations in his head in half the time I could with pencil and paper."

"That's where he switched fields, wasn't it? That's one thing I've never understood: if he was so good at it, why did your brother leave engineering to pursue a career in ancient art?"

"He fell in love."

"Love? Who with?"

"With the art, of course."

He must have registered blank again because she laughed out loud this time. "Oh, you know *exactly* what I mean. I saw how you looked at the Lamp Bearer and the other pieces of art we passed. Diana saw it, too."

She had him again, and seemed to enjoy his uncomfortable silence. Diana Meadowes did the same thing. It was no wonder the two women were friends. After a moment, though, her face clouded. "I blame myself for the change in Herbie. It came about the year we were supposed to get together for a skiing holiday, but I canceled at the last minute because I had a new boyfriend." She gave him a wry smile. "Turns out the bastard wasn't worth it and Herbie was introduced to Ludovico di Bardi at some college New Year's party. Disaster all 'round."

She shrugged and said, "Don't misunderstand, I have nothing against Ludovico. He's a lovely, charming man, but when Herbert spent the next summer break at the di Bardi family home in Italy . . . well, he wasn't the same once he returned. There'd been some sort of excavation on the estate, a Roman villa, I believe. He and Ludovico helped with the digging. I never understood how something so mundane as scraping around in the dirt could change someone so deeply."

Katzen, on the other hand, understood all too well. Seeing a piece of ancient beauty emerging into the light after thousands of years entombed in darkness was magical and holding a solid piece of history in your hands was a powerful thing.

She'd fallen silent. When he looked up, he found her stoically holding back tears, dabbing at her eyes with a lacy scrap of a handkerchief.

"Just look at me," she said. "Going all maudlin. It's not like he died way back then. He simply changed his focus."

There was nothing to say, so he gave her a respectful space. After a moment, she sniffed, regained control and tucked her hankie away.

"He hadn't changed all that much, really. He was still the same Herbie — and he didn't exactly leave engineering so much as he turned it to new uses."

"New uses? How so?"

"The co-ordinates and formulas used in engineering. He used them to send coded messages and I'd have to crack them to figure out what it was about." She lifted an ornate silver box from a table beside her and slid one side back and the other forward, then smiled at him as the lid sprang open, saying, "It's a puzzle box."

"A gift from your brother?"

"Of course. Everything was a puzzle for Herbie," she said with a chuckle. She pulled out a sheaf of yellowed hand-written letters. Selecting one, she held it out to him. "See this?"

Josh took the heavy, creased paper and stared at the lines of what appeared to be random sequences of numbers and letters. A few sections looked hauntingly familiar. A little niggling feeling in the back of his brain pinged. "I see it, but I don't. . . ."

"Took me three days to crack that one. It turned out to be an invitation to lunch at the Algonquin on the same day I'd solved it." She took the paper back and laughed happily. The years seemed to fall away from her and he got a glimpse of what she must have been like in her youth. Vivacious. Fun-loving. "Of course, when I arrived, I never let on that I had only solved the code forty minutes before I was supposed to be there."

"So he was a big one for games and puzzles?"

"Absolutely sotted with the damned things. Jigsaws, word puzzles — the more difficult and obscure, the better. One of his favorite games was to send his friends on treasure hunts. He'd hide something like a case of champagne, then give us cryptic clue sheets as long as your arm with all sorts of strange coordinates on them."

The ping became a jackpot buzzer. It took all the control he could muster to say, "Coordinates? Like latitude and longitude?"

"Heavens no! That would have been too easy! Our friends and I learned more about obscure location systems than we ever wanted to. He used . . . let me think . . . I remember two in particular: Earth Centered, Earth Fixed — that name always made me laugh — and the Universal Transverse Mercator one."

It was a wonder he wasn't hyper-ventilating. "Wow. I have enough trouble with the Rand McNally Road Atlas. I never even heard of those."

"Well, most of our crowd hadn't either. That's what made it so much fun."

"And made the prize worth it, too?"

"Oh, absolutely! That champagne wouldn't have tasted half so good if we hadn't worked so hard to get it. Herbert was always a bit wild, but fun. We had such good times when we were young." She stared into the distance for a while, watching her memories play in her head like a feature film. From the expressions flickering across her face, the majority of the memories were pleasant, but suddenly her demeanor darkened and her eyes snapped back to sharp focus. "All that changed when he and Ludovico got into business with that European antiquities crowd. Well. I'm sure you know about that. Otherwise, you wouldn't be here."

"I'm afraid that is what he's best known for."

Sadness replaced her previous joy and he was afraid she was going to break down again. Instead, she sighed. "As far as I'm concerned, the best thing that came out of that part of his life was Diana."

"I understand you two are still friends."

"Diana is a good friend to have. She's there when no one else is — including family. I kept hoping Herb would settle down with her, but that could never have happened. Not really.

He loved his jungles and exotic climes too much for that.

"Mind you, he still kept in touch. Right up to the end, I think." She rummaged in the casket again, pulling out a letter written on heavy linen stationery. "Here it is. This is the last letter I had from him. From the date, I suspect this was sent about the same time he made that final call to Diana. When nothing else came, I knew in my heart he was gone." She looked up with a sad smile. "Silence was one thing Herbert could never be accused of."

~*~

Dawn tinted the sky as he pulled the BMW up to the beach house. Ignoring exhaustion and stiff muscles, he charged up the front stairs two at a time. All tells were still in place. It looked like no one, including David, had been there since he'd left. Dumping his laptop case onto the table, he made for the tiny laundry area. Unscrewing the light switch plate, he carefully pulled up the bag holding the memory cards. Before he'd left Los Angeles, Margaret Deustch-Gascone had spread the contents of her silver puzzle box out on the tabletop and let him take pictures of it all. The image of the coded invitation to the Algonquin hummed promise at him from inside the camera. Some of the lines of numbers and letters on that message looked very similar to the ones in Deustch's notebook. If he was lucky, those lines referred to the physical location of the Algonquin hotel and could be the key to deciphering the locations of looted sites and caches. If he was even luckier, it might point him to where Deustch stashed the plutonium — or as General Fuller would have it — the package.

Oddly enough, the time in LA had also given him a new and unexpected perspective. He wasn't seeing Deustch as simply the guy in the black hat; instead an image of a flesh-and-blood person was taking shape. That was good. Anything that gave an edge to understanding the man's thought processes would be worth it.

He did feel a little guilty, though — especially in regard to Margaret. Her loneliness, half-sensed throughout the interview, cut through the self-assurance of her society armor as she'd said goodbye to him, a tiny lady outside a huge mansion. The story she hoped would be told could never be written — not by him, anyway. There wasn't a lot to be done about that.

Three hours later, he knew he'd struck gold. The co-ordinate system took him to a place where satellite photos showed ruins that roughly matched a set of Deustch's Polaroids. He sat back with a sense of accomplishment for the first time since he'd begun working the case. He wasn't home free by any means. The only way to be 100% sure was to go back to Peru and check on the ground.

CHAPTER 22

Travelers hurried through San Francisco International, intent on their destinations. Some of them paused just long enough to give the four uniformed men arguing in the middle of the concourse a dirty look. Most just ignored them.

"I'm telling you boys," Vaughn DeVries said, "the only thing you're gonna accomplish by detaining Katzen is to make the pooch more raw than she already is."

"Sorry, Colonel DeVries, we have our orders—" the burliest of the Security Force trio repeated for what seemed like the millionth time.

"So do I, Chief Master Sergeant Hunt. I also have rank on you. I suggest you check back in—"

"Sir! I have already called in and—" Hunt's phone went off with a snatch of a pop tune. He glared at it, then moved a short distance away to answer it.

The other two SFs closed rank against DeVries to keep him from moving closer. It wasn't necessary. It was easy enough to see that the conversation wasn't going the way the Chief Master Sergeant wanted. After a bit, Hunt returned and told his companions, "We been pulled. Let's get back to base."

From his vantage point in the coffee shop, Katzen watched DeVries watch the SFs stomp off. The colonel remained straight-backed and resolute until the trio were well gone, then he sagged, stepped out of the flow of pedestrians and scrabbled at his own phone.

Ditching his mostly empty cup, Josh pocketed his sunglasses, brushed his tousled hair away from his face and walked up behind DeVries.

"No, sir, I don't know where he is. The SF guys probably spooked him. They surely gave *me* a turn—"

"Man, I thought they'd never leave. Some people just have no manners."

DeVries paused, glanced behind him and said, "Yes, sir, that was. We'll be on our way in a tick."

The tall man slid his cell back into his pocket and said, "Now, before you start in, those fellas were not our idea. Apparently, some brasshole still has his shorts in a twist about you dropping off the grid. I've been arguing with them forever. Len's been pulling strings and just got their orders changed."

"Yep. I gathered that, but can we get more out of sight? All this is making me a little twitchy."

DeVries nodded and led him to an unmarked door that opened with the swipe of a magnetic card. They hurried through anonymous back corridors to a jet waiting on the tarmac.

Once in the craft, DeVries raised the gangway and said, "The general is back there. You better get strapped in 'cause we're outta here as soon as we can get a runway."

Suddenly very tired, Josh went aft and flopped into the seat across from his former handler.

Len Fuller looked up from the open folder in his hands. "Other than the fact you look like you've been dragged by a truck right now, I'd say the beach did you some good."

"If you're trying to tell me you knew where I was, don't bother. I wasn't trying to drop off *your* radar."

"It was an unexpected choice of bolt hole." Len chuckled and set the folder aside. "I'll admit it took me a week or so before it occurred to me to look there. How's your brother?"

"Fine — but you know that, too. One thing you didn't know, though, was that Margaret Deustch-Gascone moved to Los Angeles a couple years back. Took over her brother's house.

Sloppy. Your researchers need a good swift boot in the ass. Now, can we get to why you dragged me straight to the airport as soon as I called? The last few days have been intense and I'm fighting against auguring in."

The jet started its taxi to the runway and Fuller gestured to Josh's seatbelt. "I can tell. Put that on so you don't slide out of the seat." He waited until Katzen complied before he said, "I think you have a pretty good idea to the answer of your question."

"The SFs at the terminal."

Fuller nodded. "It seems someone pretty high up doesn't want you to succeed. We traced the spook leak back to the Pentagon, but couldn't get any closer."

"That sounds awfully familiar, Len. The last time this happened, my cover was blown sky high and I almost wound up dead."

"All the more reason to get back to Peru ASAP. The sooner we find Deustch's package, the better." Fuller paused. "And I was worried about you. You've had some close calls lately."

"Tell me about it."

"It might have been unexpected, but going to the beach house was a pretty risky move considering Major Daniel Durand is officially presumed dead."

For a moment, everything inside Katzen flatlined, then anger erupted. He jerked forward against the seat restraint. "Risky? Did you actually mention risk to me? Never mind that someone high up seems to want me dead for real, but how risky was sending a desk jockey to buttonhole me in a cantina that half of Piedras Rojas frequents? Or to follow me to the dig site? Y'know? Those places no one had ever even heard of Major Daniel Durand?

"Oh! And how about hauling me off to a government-owned warehouse—"

"Josh. . . ."

"Oh no! *That* stood zero chance of screwing the hell out of my new identity. I nearly died for this Len. They *owe* me this."

"*Enough, Major!*"

That worked. Katzen went silent and sulked back against the seat.

After a beat, Fuller said, "Every point you make is justified. Justified and an echo of what I've been saying to the people in charge of this op from the beginning. I don't know how many more times I can apologize for sending Vaughn in cold like that. He's not a field agent and what happened proved it with bells on, but he was the one man I knew I could trust. He's been spoken to about the mistakes. He's a fast learner, so it won't happen again, but that can't repair any harm done."

There was a heavy silence between them, then Fuller asked, "How much harm *was* done?"

"I have no idea. I guess I'll have to wait and see. Avi and Vic already knew. Harper Armand took it in stride. Seems like Diego Ruiz already had a pretty good idea I wasn't what I said I was."

That elicited a chuckle. "You don't need to worry about Chief Ruiz. You have a real friend there."

Katzen merely stared out the window. They'd achieved altitude and leveled off. The sun turned the clouds into a blanket of snow beneath them.

"Look, if it goes bad, we can start over. New name, new background. . . ."

"I don't want to start over, Len," Katzen said almost to himself. "I was happy the way it was. For the first time in my life, I was truly happy."

"Then we'll do our damnedest to make sure it stays that way."

The only response was a half-grunt as the younger man continued to gaze out the window.

"Now, tell me about Deustch's code."

Katzen roused himself and said, "For starters, it wasn't so much a code as a co-ordinate system. I actually realized that early on. It was the only thing that made sense with what we had. I could tell that each entry in the notebook corresponded to a photo in the album, but without knowing the physical location of the ruins in the pic, that didn't help much. That's where Margaret Deustch-Gascone came in."

"The clue you almost missed."

"Yep. Incomplete intel will screw you every time. I've learned that the hard way on more than one occasion. Anyway, even after Deustch left the engineering field, he took bits and pieces of it with him. His sister told me that he used to send friends on treasure hunts using unusual co-ordinate systems. Universal Transverse Mercator co-ordinates was one of his favorites."

"UTM? That's pretty damned obscure."

"Apparently the more obscure, the better Herb liked it. Margaret showed me a coded invite he sent her for lunch at the Algonquin. The hotel's location was in UTM. That was the key that unlocked the whole megillah."

Fuller beamed. "That's my boy! I knew I could trust you to do your homework."

Josh rolled his eyes. "Thanks, Pop. May I be excused, now?"

"Go. Sleep. We can talk more when we land in Lima."

~*~

It was emptier than the first time he'd seen it and the air was slightly less stuffy, but there was an odd sense of homecoming as Josh Katzen entered Unit 86 of the Lima military warehouse compound. Even the cat-faced storm god on the towering stele in the center of the room seemed to welcome him back.

"C'mon, Josh," DeVries said breaking the mood. "You seen it all before. You gonna share what you found out or you gonna gawk all day?"

"Sorry. It's just a funky sensation coming back after being gone for so long." He turned to Fuller. "Are we absolutely sure this place is secure? After what happened at the hotel. . . ."

"And the DSS agents' homes. That was a wake-up call," Fuller agreed. The general motioned for DeVries to close the door and flip on the overheads before he continued. "We've been sweeping this facility ever since. It's secure — for now, anyway."

A layer of dust had settled over the Chippendale dining table and the still-uncatalogued artifacts littering its surface. Katzen wiped it off, set his laptop up and rooted in the case for Deustch's battered notebook and picture album. When he pulled it out, the little black binder was festooned with brightly colored markers made from torn sticky notes

The silence grew tense as the computer booted up and Katzen logged into the satellite feeds. After what seemed like an eternity, he entered a set of co-ordinates and zoomed the focus down onto a site surrounded by jungle. "See that? That's an extensive ruin in Costa Rica. Probably the remains of a town." Pulling a photo from the album, he held it alongside the screen. "And *this* is a snap of that temple right here."

Fuller and DeVries leaned in for a closer look until DeVries straightened and said, "Oh! I see! This here's the temple and these two lumps are those structures in the background of the picture!"

Josh laughed. "Give the boy a kewpie doll! You're pretty good at this. I wish I'd had you at the beach house. I gave myself some serious headaches trying to figure out what photo went where."

Pulling out another picture, he said, "It helped to have a couple known locations to use as starting points, though."

Fuller took the photograph and smiled. "Ahhhh. Piedras Rojas."

"Yep. That and the Algonquin were my two test cases to verify Deustch was using UTM — then there's this little doohickey," he said pointing to an inked square on one of the notebook's yellowed pages.

DeVries leaned in and squinted at the figure. "Which is?"

"I don't know for sure."

"Goddammit, Katzen!"

"Hey! I said for sure."

General Fuller picked up the book and regarded it thoughtfully. "What do you *suspect* it is, son?"

"It might indicate a cache. Here's why I think that. . . ," he leafed back to another torn paper marker, then unfolded a print-out map and pointed to an entry mid-way down the page. It had the rough-drawn square at the end of the string of numbers. "This UTM co-ordinate corresponds to the previous location of a small family-owned private bank. They've moved now, but—"

"You found a twenty-year-old map of Lima?" DeVries said.

"Fifteen, but who's counting? The Internet is a scary wonderful thing, Colonel. Anyway, according to the intel files, a safe deposit box registered to one of Deustch's aliases was seized by our guys shortly after he was declared legally dead. Aside from the usual emergency identity papers and such, the box was filled with cash, gold and jewels. Some of the gold and jewels were in the form of antiquities." Flipping forward, he pointed to another entry. "And there's this. Piedras Rojas. The co-ordinates on the square icon correspond to the ceremonial platform we found Deustch's remains under."

"I think I see what you're saying," DeVries said. "When you guys dug him out, he had a bunch of goodies that seemed to come from all over the place, didn't he?"

"A cache," Fuller said nodding. "I think that's a reasonable assumption. How do you plan to test it?"

~*~

DeVries slapped at his neck, glared at the palm of his hand, then wiped it against his khakis. "Dammit, Katzen. Yesterday you tried to dry roast me, today you're making me a blood sacrifice to the mosquito gods."

"I'm not any happier about the back-to-back hikes than you are, but we need to prove or disprove my theory on the symbols in the notebook. If the squares next to the locations really indicate Deustch's cache sites, then we can concentrate our searches on the entries made around the time the stuff went missing."

DeVries slapped again. "You're not making my day. There's an awful lot of itty bitty squares in that book."

"Quit kvetching. We're lucky these two sites were so close to the city, otherwise we'd be looking at a major excursion."

DeVries groaned.

"It won't be that bad. We know that Deustch didn't travel too far afield between the time the stuff went missing and the time he died. Any caches he used then should be pretty localized."

"Good to know." He swatted again. "Are we there yet?"

Katzen checked the GPS. "Pretty close. It ought to be over this way."

He veered off through the undergrowth. DeVries hurried to keep him in sight. They emerged amid the ruins of a group of ancient houses.

"Cool!" Katzen said. "This was likely a settlement or outlier community to a larger city."

DeVries nodded and looked around. "Okay, this is your show. Where do we start looking?"

"The cache won't be here. These ruins are too obvious — too big a target for *huaqueros*. Deustch's co-ordinates point farther ahead. Somewhere around that rock outcropping, I think."

The closer they came to the outcropping, the quieter Katzen got. His pace slowed, too, until he came to a full stop a short distance from the rockface and stood squinting up at it. Frowning slightly, he moved to one side, crouched, stared up again. He repeated the moves until, at last, he smiled and pointed to a spot two thirds of the way up. "There it is."

Climbing up took some time, but their triumph at the mouth of the opening was dashed once they shined their lights into the recess. The passage was blocked with fallen stones.

DeVries sighed in disappointment. "Damn. Looks like a false alarm."

Katzen regarded the blockage, then said, "I'm not so sure. This could be part of the camouflage." Reaching in, he tugged experimentally at one of the rocks near the top. It came free with little resistance. He removed another and peered in again. "Looks like an open space behind the rocks. Help me clear it."

The cleared passage was short, but narrow; more a crawlspace than anything else. DeVries shined the light in again. It didn't reveal much. "Yep. Opens up to some kinda space all right. Don't you get tired of being right all the time?"

"That's why they wanted me for this job, remember? I'm your so-called expert."

"Man! That's a tight squeeze and dark as all get out. What now, O, Expert?"

"We check it out. I hate this kind of thing. You want to wait outside?"

"Don't mind if I do — but be careful. Lord knows what mighta set up housekeeping since Deustch got hisself killed."

"Hmmm. Thanks for the comforting thought."

The passage wasn't long, but by the time Katzen emerged into the chamber at the end, he was covered in a sheen of sweat. What air there was inside was hot and stagnant. As he turned, he bumped against a wooden crate just beside the tunnel mouth.

"Josh? You okay in there?" DeVries' voice from outside sounded distant and hollow.

"Yeah, just trying to catch my breath. Looks to be a natural cavity. There's almost enough room for me to turn around. Deustch was a good-sized guy. This must've been hell for him."

"Yeah? He was also a ratsassed bastard, so I wouldn't waste much sympathy on him. Anything in there?"

"Four boxes." He shined his light into them. "Three empties. One has a jade figurine and a couple pieces of pottery. Dusty, but they look genuine."

Seeing how Herb Deustch had indeed been a ratsassed bastard — and a devious one at that — Katzen turned his attention to a thorough search of the chamber. Once he'd satisfied himself that the handful of artifacts in the crate weren't simply camouflage for the real stash, he headed out, pushing the lone occupied box ahead of him.

DeVries was surprised. "You brought the stuff with you?"

Katzen gulped fresh air and wiped sweat from his face before he said, "Absolutely. If we leave it here, it'll either sit there until the rock crumbles or it's found by *huaqueros* and winds up on the black market. This way, we can at least catalog it with the other things Deustch stole and send it home where it belongs." He stood and stretched. "Moses, that was tight. Makes the Mercury capsule look like a Presidential suite."

"Okay, then! The squares in the notebook mark Deustch's cache sites."

"Looks like it — well, I hope they do anyway. . . ."

"Come on, man! The site we checked yesterday didn't have a square and didn't have a cache. This one has a square and we just found us a cache, so it looks pretty good."

"Yeah, but the last site was too flat to have anyplace to hide anything."

DeVries guffawed and handed Katzen a water bottle from the pack. "Here. Drink this. I think you cooked your brains in there. Even if it ain't perfect, we got something to go on now. Let's get this stuff back to home base and work out where to try next."

~*~

The chunk of ice clinked into the bottom of the glass. Katzen stared at it, then at the still-sealed bottle of single malt Len had given him as a "Good Boy" reward. Shades of old times: alone in an anonymous hotel room while Len was off hacking a path through red tape. He was more than happy to leave the reports and red tape to Len, though. Especially considering there was someone among the people his former handler was dealing with who couldn't be trusted. Someone high up who wanted him dead. Not a comforting thought.

It was good scotch. A well-aged Glenlivet that was probably going into the casks about the time he was running his first official mission. Still, considering his mood and his family history — alcoholic father, brother in AA and a nephew who seemed to be treading that same path — drinking alone in a rented room was probably not the best idea. He dumped the ice back into the bucket and clapped the lid onto it. Maybe he'd just binge-watch something on one of the streaming services until he unwound enough to fall asleep. Yeah. Sleep. Like that was gonna happen.

A light tap sounded at the hall door. Katzen frowned. He wasn't expecting anyone. General Fuller would be tied up for heaven only knew how long and DeVries wasn't slated to be back in Lima until after the weekend. The tap came again as he crossed to answer it. A quick glance through the peephole lens revealed Tessa Caballero looking uncomfortable in a dressy black pantsuit and fidgeting with a silver-trimmed handbag.

He opened the door wide, saying, "Saved from drinking alone! I was just about to open a fresh bottle of scotch. Would you like to join me?"

"Yeah, sure," she said. She seemed nervous as she entered and sat in the chair he offered, still fidgeting with the handbag.

He busied himself cutting the seal on the bottle, glancing at her in the dresser's big mirror. "You look great, Tessa. Headed for an evening out somewhere?"

"No . . . well, *here*. I never got to see you after that jerk el Mago kidnapped you. I heard he really beat the hell out of you. I just wanted to see if you were okay."

He shrugged. "Oh, that was all superficial. Healed up just fine and hardly left a mark. Rocks, splash or straight up?"

"Ice, please."

Dropping in a couple cubes, Katzen handed her the glass, then lifted his own in a brief salute and sipped. The scotch lived up to its promise. He savored it a moment, then perched on the edge of the dresser and said, "I'm flattered you were worried about me. How'd you know I was back?"

"Actually, Rastogi told me when I went in for my paycheck this afternoon."

"He did? I didn't know I was on the DSS radar."

"Well, officially, you aren't."

"Sounds like there's a 'but' there."

She laughed and was suddenly much more her normal self. "But Rastogi really, really hates you."

Katzen shook his head in silent amusement.

"Seriously," Caballero said. "As soon as he saw me come in,

he yelled 'hey did you know your spook boyfriend was back?' across the room."

"Subtle. But still way off the mark."

"That's Rastogi. The man doesn't just hold grudges. He makes mad love to them — and he hasn't forgotten that you made him look bad at Reid's apartment. Probably never will."

"Speaking of Reid, how you doing with that?"

She blew out a thoughtful breath. "Honestly? I'm not sure. Considering I wound up decking Rastogi and pulled an indefinite administrative suspension with pay, I think not real well."

Katzen nearly snorted scotch through his nose. "Whaaat? You decked Ratasstogi? What for? — uh — not that I doubt it was deserved. . . ."

Her restlessness came back, she stood and started pacing. "You want a reason? Pick one. First Reid got killed and somehow that became my fault. After that, the special assignment got canceled and the asshole had all these jabs about lowering myself to associate with the 'regular agents'. Things really got rough right after you were kidnapped, then you up and vanished. Got the spook stuff started again — that was my fault, too, somehow — *then* DeVries and the general went back to the states . . . I told you I was an outsider here . . . dammit—" Suddenly, she plunked her glass down and stepped into him, planting a kiss as passionate as it was unexpected.

His surprise lasted only a moment before he wrapped his arms around her and returned the kiss with interest. A few heartbeats later, they toppled onto the king-sized bed.

CHAPTER 23

Dawn filtered gray shafts of light onto the piles of their discarded clothing through the gap in the ill-fitting hotel drapes. Josh awoke to find Tessa curled against him in the rumpled bed, snoring softly in deep, unfeigned sleep. He stroked her hair and kissed the partially open lips. She moaned petulantly and rolled over with her back to him. Josh grinned, rose and stepped gently away so as not to wake her, then padded quietly over to the pile of her things. Opening the silver-trimmed purse, he searched the contents, flicking frequent glances toward the sleeper; she didn't stir. He found nothing. He would have been surprised if he had.

Shrugging, he left everything the way he'd found it and headed for the shower.

Thirty minutes later, with hair still damp, he kissed her awake. "Hey, you were dead to the world. Good thing I'm an honorable guy, or I could have taken all kinds of advantage."

"I never liked honorable guys. They're boring."

"I'll bear that in mind," he said as he pulled on his boots. "I don't know about you, but I'm starving. I'm going to head down to check out the breakfast buffet."

She sat up and yawned. "Mmmmm. Sounds great, but I want to freshen up first. Meet you down there?"

"You got it," he said. "Don't take too long, though. My self-control only lasts so long in the presence of bacon."

The door closed on her laughter and he strode down the hall

toward the elevators knowing she'd be up and searching his room in no time. She wouldn't find anything, either.

~*~

The hotel's upscale mirror and chrome dining area was between waves of customers, meaning it was almost empty. Katzen knew that wouldn't last long, though. During the time he'd waited, the sporadic influx of one or two sleepy patrons wandering past the hostess station had increased to a steady flow — but no Tessa Caballero. The waitress was topping off his coffee for the third time when the lady finally appeared. She must have done an exhaustive search of the room; she'd had enough time to take up the carpets.

He caught her attention and rose, pulling a chair out for her. As she neared, he said, "I was beginning to wonder if you'd had second thoughts about last night."

Dropping her purse into the chair, she wrapped her arms around his shoulders and said, "You don't get off that easily, Mr. Katzen. Bear in mind that I expect a repeat performance real soon."

The kiss that followed drew amused glances from the staff and other patrons.

Grinning, Josh said, "Well, not that I was organizing a search party or anything, but my willpower was about to give out. You see, they just restocked the buffet and the waftaroms from the fresh bacon nearly lifted me and dragged me across the room."

She gave him a good-natured shove toward the food. "Don't let me stand in your way. Have at it!"

They had the steam tables to themselves and foraged in silence until Tessa suddenly leaned across the scrambled egg tray and whispered, "You're back because you know where it is. That's it, isn't it?"

The abrupt turn confused him. Tongs hovered over the beckoning mound of pork. "What?"

"It," she scoffed. "The *package*. You know where it is, don't you? Why else would you be back here?"

"Are you serious? There are a lot of reasons to come back. I like Peru and Lima is a great city, for starters."

She shrugged. "Okay, have it your way."

They were sliding in behind loaded plates at their table when she said, "So if you haven't located the package, is the repatriation project starting up again?"

"Why? You bored or something?"

She rolled her eyes. "Out. Of. My. Gourd! I hate time off and I don't even know how long this suspension will last."

"Ooooo. They made it open-ended? Not good. What the hell happened? All you told me last night was that you and Ratsasstogi got into it."

An odd look crossed Tessa's face.

Suddenly concerned, he leaned forward. "What? Did I say something wrong?"

"N-no. It's just. . . ." She laughed and was suddenly herself again. "It's just that's what Reid always called him, too."

"If the shoe fits. . . ," he said lightly. "So what happened? It must've been a doozy."

She made a growling noise deep in her throat. "I better not discuss it — at least not in public. It tends to make me homicidal. Especially since I still don't get why *I'm* the one who got suspended and nothing at all happened to Rastogi." Making a dismissive gesture, she turned her attention back to her plate. "Anyway, I need something to do really bad and we weren't finished, were we? I mean sending the art stuff back home?"

"Wait. . . are you actually telling me that with time off in a city like Lima and a country as wonderful as Peru, you can't think of anything to do?"

Tessa didn't reply other than to viciously stab a lump of scrambled egg.

"Okay. . . well . . . it's suspension, not a total goodbye. How long do they usually last?"

She looked thoughtful. "Hmmmmm. The worst I know of was a little over two weeks — not me or Reid — another agent."

"That's not too bad."

"Maybe not, but the reason I never take vacations is I get bored quick. About three days is my max. I spend the rest of the time going nuts with nothing to do."

He treated her to a wicked grin. "Well, then. We'll just have to find something to do, won't we?"

~*~

"You are evil!" Caballero declared, dumping her armload of shopping bags onto her living room couch.

"Yeah?" Katzen kicked the front door to her bungalow closed. "How so?"

"Because going to the market was *not* what I thought you meant at breakfast."

"Really? What did you think I meant?'

"You *know* what I thought."

"Nope. I have no clue," he said with an air of exaggerated innocence. "Where's the kitchen? I'm about to lose my grip on the groceries."

"Right through there. I'm afraid I don't use it much," she said, nodding toward an arched doorway to one side of a brass and glass curio cabinet. The shelves were filled with ceramic pieces spanning a wide range of cultures. At the center stood one lovely jade piece in a wooden display box. "I mostly do takeaways and microwave stuff," she added a little apologetically.

"Do tell," Katzen muttered, shoving aside a stack of takeaway containers to make room for the bags. Once they were situated, he stepped back through into the living room and pointed at the cabinet. "May I?"

She chuckled. "I should have known you'd zero in on the art. Knock yourself out."

He studied the objects for several silent minutes, then gently lifted a stirrup pot with an incised geometric design and turned it in his hands. "Chavin. Well, it's *supposed* to be Chavin. It's a fake — they all are. Damned good ones, but still fakes."

Tessa made a noise somewhere between amusement and disgust, then turned to unpack the shopping bags. "That could be a description of the guy who gave them to me, too."

"Generous guy."

"He could be when he wasn't being an asshole. Most of them were his idea of make-up presents. We'd have a fight or something and he'd show up a few days later with some sort of gift."

"Yeah?" Josh leaned in to re-examine the jade piece. It was a delicately carved pendant, about three inches long, depicting four frogs of graduated size standing nose to rump totem pole style. "This one must have involved grievous bodily harm, then. At least a broken bone or three."

She laughed. "Yeah. Something like that. Hey, didn't you say you were going to cook lunch? Hope you weren't lying about that, too. I'm dying of hunger over here."

"Lie?" Josh said, drawing himself up in mock outrage. "I beg to differ. I did not lie. I knew perfectly well what I meant. It's not my fault if you misunderstood my intent." She made to lob a box of tissues at him, but he ducked back into the kitchen and started filling the counter with the groceries. "Besides, I needed time to prepare my evil plan. I intend to backward engineer Manny Conde's lomo saltado and you will be my guinea pig."

"Manny. . . ? Is that the cook out at the camp?"

"One and the same."

"Can you backward engineer those aguas frescas, too?"

He fished a fresh melon from one of the bags and held it aloft like a trophy. "Ta da! Did that a while back. How about you make it?"

A short time later, Tessa poured a splash of the cold melon drink into a glass and sipped at it. After a moment she grinned. "Hey! That tastes great!"

"You sound so surprised."

"Well, I made it after all." She prodded the pile of takeaway containers, now bagged up, ready for the dumpster. "I told you this was the extent of my cooking expertise, remember?"

"C'mon. That was easy. Almost doesn't count as real cooking."

"Uh huh." She watched him sprinkle a spice mixture into the skillet of sizzling beef. Sniffing appreciatively, she said, "Wow. It smells even better now. I didn't think that was possible. Where did you learn to do all this?"

"What? Cook?" At her nod, he shrugged. "From my grandmother, mostly. We had a sort of extended family and my grandmother's house was the center of it all. I grew up helping her cook for the hordes."

She chuckled. "Sounds like you're talking about masses of barbarians on shaggy ponies."

He looked up in surprise. "You've met my family?"

The chuckle blossomed into full, throaty laughter. It was a nice sound. Finally, she took another pull at her drink, then said, "Josh, I think you might be the most interesting man I've ever known."

"More interesting in general, or more interesting than the guy who gave you jade jewelry for letting you beat him up? I'm not sure how I feel about that."

"Oh, come on! My relationship with Beto wasn't anything like that."

Josh didn't look up from the onion he was mincing. "Uh huh," he said dubiously.

Her glass of melon aqua fresca thunked against the tabletop and she wheeled toward him, face dark with anger.

He put the knife down, went over and took her into his arms. "Hey, easy, now. I'm just teasing."

She relaxed against him and said, "I know. Sorry. I don't take teasing well. . . ."

"I understand." He grinned and brushed her cheek with a light kiss. "Considering some of your workmates, there's a pretty good reason for that."

She returned the kiss and they remained locked in the embrace until the beef in the skillet popped.

"Oops!" Josh snatched the spatula and turned the sizzling meat over. "Ah, good. Not scorched or anything. Hey, how about you slice the potatoes? I think I have my hands full here for a bit."

They fell into a quiet rhythm, chopping, slicing, stirring, chatting about the day at the market. . . . It was comfortable and Katzen found himself enjoying her company. Ingrained cynicism didn't allow him to believe for one second she was as interested as she pretended, but he was having a good time. She seemed to be, too. Nothing wrong with that.

Behind him, Tessa gave a sudden yelp. He turned to find her holding one hand clutched tightly in the other. Blood dripped onto the tabletop and the potato slices on the cutting board.

"Whoa! I said slice the potatoes, not yourself. Where's your first aid stuff?"

The cut was long, but not very deep. He slathered it with antibiotic ointment and bandaged it with supplies from her kit.

"See. I told you I was lousy with kitchen stuff," she said as he snugged the gauze wrapping down with medical tape.

"I never doubted you for a minute," he said, then rooted in a shopping bag and pulled out a net pouch tied with ribbon. "Here, mess with the puzzles we got at the *mercado*. Nary a sharp edge in the lot."

She flipped him the bird with her mummiform hand, but happily ripped the ribbon off the bag and emptied the contents in a heap in front of her.

He returned to his cooking, adding the unbloodied potatoes, putting the lid onto the skillet and sliding it into the oven. Comfortable conversation reigned again and they talked of nothing in particular until he checked the clock and announced, "It's bound to be done now."

"Good. I'm starving," she said. Suddenly, she set the slide puzzle aside. "You really do know where it is, don't you?"

He turned from the stove in confusion. "Where what is?"

"The package, dummy. Whatever it was that guy Deustch hid."

"Oh, that." He shrugged dismissively and turned back to spooning the fragrant beef mixture onto plates. "Why does everyone think I know where the damned thing is?"

"Maybe because you never say no."

He slid the filled plates onto the table. "Uh uh. I keep saying no, but no one ever believes me." He picked up the puzzle. "Hey, you finished it already!"

She snatched the plastic square out of his hands. "Give me that, you'll mess it up!" Checking to make sure all squares were where they were supposed to be, she added, "I finished the whole bag. No challenge."

He slid into his chair. "We'll just have to find you something a little harder to crack, then."

She leered at him. "Well, that won't be you. You're a pushover. It's a wonder el Mago didn't get you to spill everything you knew and then some."

"Sure, sure." He forked some beef from her plate and popped it into her mouth. "Eat. You'll need your strength for tomorrow."

"Mmmmmm," she said, giving him a sultry sidelong look. "And why is that?"

"Because I booked us on the Machu Picchu tour."

She stopped in mid-chew. "What?"

"Well, you said you'd never been there before. Mazeltov! Today you are a tourist! Our bus leaves at six."

~*~

"I thought you were bullshitting me about this place, but now I see what you were talking about," Tessa Caballero said in a hushed voice, as they left the modern gates and ticket booths behind and entered Machu Picchu. "It's magic here."

Katzen chuckled, but the lady was right. Their tour bus driver had timed their arrival perfectly. The sun was at the optimal angle in the sky and the ancient ruins glowed in the morning light. Their bus had been the first transport of the day and they almost had the site to themselves. The air was thin and sharp, but Josh felt energized. The place always had that effect on him. He felt as if the barrier of time and space was especially fragile here and past and present could collide at any second.

Shaking off the mood, he pulled a camera from his shoulder bag and handed it to Tessa. "Here, let's get going before we lose this light."

She gave the device a dubious stare.

He elbow-nudged her and said, "Come on! You said you wanted to try your hand at photography. I can't think of a better time or place to start."

She took the camera a little doubtfully, then sighed. "Okay. It's digital, so it's not like I'll be wasting film or anything." Breaking into a schoolgirl laugh, she snapped a shot of him and hurried away. "Come on, Slowpoke, let's get to the ultra-famous Sunstone before everyone else does."

Four hours and two memory chips later, they stopped to rest in the relative shade at the foot of a long staircase leading up into an area that was still mostly wild. Tessa leaned on Josh's shoulder as he swiped through the last group of pictures he'd taken.

"Ooooh!" she said, jabbing a finger at the screen, "I like that one a lot."

"Yeah, it worked pretty well. Let's see some of yours."

"Nope." She swung the camera out of his reach. "Not yet. The ones on here right now are awful."

"Maybe I can help."

"I'm not going to let you laugh at them."

"I won't laugh, but if you're going to turn your nose up at some free photography lessons. . . ."

Cradling the camera, she leaned back against him, snuggling comfortably. They sat that way for several minutes before she said, "You know, you've still never told me why you're in Peru. If they shut down the repatriation thing, there doesn't seem to be a lot of reason to come back. . . ," she moved closer and whispered in his ear, ". . . unless you really *do* know where the package is."

"Back to that again. Aren't *you* reason enough to return?"

"Uh huh. You're clairvoyant. You knew I was going to come to your hotel room as soon as you landed." She pulled away and gave him a swat. "Liar."

"Hey! You'd be amazed what my Magic Eightball tells me."

"Magic screwball is more like it." She stood and dusted off the seat of her jeans. "Anyway, *my* crystal ball says there's a trip to the ladies' room in my future."

He started to rise, but she shook her head. "You don't need to come with me. I'm a big girl, I can go potty all by myself. You take more pretty pictures and I'll catch up in a few minutes." Brush-kissing his cheek, she turned and strode away.

"It's not a crystal ball!" he called after her. "It's a Magic Eightball! Whole different scrying method."

Without turning, she flipped an obscene gesture over her shoulder.

He laughed and watched until she melded into the growing crowd of tourists. There were an awful lot of them now. Yet another bus load must have arrived. Well, he and Tessa would be headed back to their bed and breakfast soon. He'd be more than ready to go. The increasing population was making him a bit twitchy.

Experiencing Tessa's first time at the site had been fun — sort of seeing it with new eyes — but one of the things he enjoyed most about Machu Picchu was the sense of solitude. Eleventy million buses packed with eleventy million tourists sort of spoiled that. He eyed the area at the top of the stairs. Far fewer people up there and it might be a good place to get more photos. Unless the guards had gotten a lot more unreasonable than in the past, they often allowed photographers to stray off the prescribed paths. He mounted the steps and scanned the jungle-like growth. There was a flash of brilliant color amid the otherwise unrelenting green up ahead. Bromeliad? Orchid? Couldn't tell from where he was. He pulled out his camera and headed for the bored guard at the top.

~*~

The guard hadn't been exaggerating when he'd said there were more plants in bloom than usual for this time of year. Katzen had already taken several good shots. He was sure most of them would translate into fantastic drawings, as well. That included the one he was currently setting up. Crouching, he zoomed in tight on the fully open *sobralia dichotoma* orchid framing it against a seam in the ancient wall it grew upon, turning it into abstracted shapes of vivid magenta and spikes of green against the weathered surface of the stone block.

"Cats and orchids. I only have to look for one to stand a good chance of finding you — both, and it's a sure thing," Tessa said from somewhere to his left.

He made a show of looking around. "I see no cats here."

"Nope. Only a Gatito and a bunch of orchids. Good thing I found the guard who let you through or I'd have been searching forever." She stopped and regarded the surroundings. "Seriously, though, I can see why you want to shoot here. We're only a few steps from the regular path, but it's like another world."

"That it is. It doesn't take a genius to see why the high-muck-a-muck chose this site to build his getaway." Over her shoulder and through the lush foliage, he spotted another tourist. A tall, thin man, dressed all in tan and brown stood on the stone stairway. The man had his back to them, but Josh had the distinct impression he'd been looking their way just moments before.

Tessa pulled his attention back, saying, "Anyway, I give up. I'm tired of snapping crappy pics. Can you show me how to do it?"

"Ah. Looking for those free photography lessons after all?"

"Well...," she said playing with a pocket on his photographer's vest. "Maybe they don't need to be completely free. I'm sure we can work out an acceptable payment plan."

"I can certainly take that under advisement," he said with a smile. The area behind her was now empty. The man in beige had vanished completely. Tamping down the surge of paranoia, he took her camera and thumbed through the photos. "Okay, let's see what you have . . . yeah. You have lots of potentially good shots, you just have to focus closer in. Like this. . . ." He tweaked the image on the screen, zooming in on part of it. His voice trailed off because the photo was of himself climbing a stairway. The beige man was right behind him.

Not noticing his silence, Tessa said, "Oh! I see what you mean. That's way better. Maybe they all aren't crap, then."

He paged back through more shots. Mr. Beige was in a number of them. Usually in close proximity to Katzen. Resetting the camera, he handed it back to her. "Absolutely not crap. I can do some judicious cropping when we're back at the B&B this evening."

"Would you? That would be awesome!"

~*~

Their cottage was small, but cozy. He'd have to give the clerk at his hotel back in Lima an extra tip for setting up the reservations. Sure, she'd said it was her cousin's bed and breakfast inn, but he knew from painful experience that could mean anything from high-priced palace to omigawd roach motel. This was a case of the Goldilocks Zone: it was just right. Katzen propped himself against the cushioned headboard of the king-sized bed and stretched his legs out in front of him. After a full day of hard stone and dusty ground at the ancient site, it felt good to be on a surface that gave a little. He savored the cool fabric against his bare back for a moment before he pulled his laptop onto his knees and powered it up. In the bathroom behind him, the water cut off and he heard the splishy sounds of Tessa stepping into the whirlpool tub. Then there came a low moan.

He called out, "Was that ecstasy or did you keel over in there?"

She groaned again. "I think I'm dying. It's insane. My legs felt fine until after the ride home on the bus."

"Well, you did an awful lot of hills and stairs today." He slotted Tessa's first SD card into the laptop and opened his graphics program.

"So did you. Why aren't you sharing my agony?"

The screen filled with images of their day at Machu Picchu. "Lots of hills and such at Piedras Rojas, too. I'm used to it."

"I hate you. Have I mentioned that lately?"

He guffawed.

"Go ahead and laugh. I intend to take over this bathroom for the duration of our stay. See how you like *that*."

The first photo was the blurry close-up of himself that Tessa had snapped at the entrance. There wasn't much hope for that one beyond vague amusement value. He closed it and moved on. The next half dozen or so were fairly standard tourist shots. Not exciting, although they'd work pretty well with a little cropping and color balance, but then . . . . Yep. There he was. The tall guy dressed in muted colors carrying an expensive German-made camera on a wide strap around his neck. Normally, the muted colors the man wore would have been great to remain unobtrusive. This time it backfired. Surrounded by a crowd of brightly dressed tourists, the man stood out like a turkey in a flock of peacocks.

He paged through more pictures and found Mr. Beige in a slew of them. Oddly enough, he only appeared in Tessa's pics, but not in a single one of his own. Had the guy been staying in back of Katzen and ignoring Caballero? Another backfire if he was. Tessa caught almost as many pics of Mr. Beige as she had of the ruins. Coincidence? Maybe, but he didn't much care for coincidences.

He was busy cropping and adjusting Tessa's photos when she finally emerged from the bathroom, swathed in towels, accompanied by a cloud of spicy-scented steam. Sliding onto the bed, she snuggled against him so she could see the computer screen.

"Hey! You're fixing my pictures!" she exclaimed happily.

"Yep. Just like I said I would," he said, giving her a quick nuzzle. "Mmmm. You smell great."

"It's a special soap I found. Goat's milk with frankincense and myrrh."

"Ah!" he said with a wicked grin. "Traditional middle eastern funerary spices. Well, you *did* claim to be dying."

She pulled back with a frown. "Ha ha, Mr. Smartass. They also make very nice soap."

"I never said they didn't. One of the reasons frankincense and myrrh were used was because they smelled good," he responded as he hit a final sequence of keystrokes. Closing the laptop he said, "There! First SD card adjusted and sent to your cloud drive."

"Well, then," she said, taking the laptop and setting it aside, "I guess it's time for the first installment on that payment plan."

"Good idea. We wouldn't want to accrue any penalties." Her towels hit the floor and he pulled her into a tight embrace.

Her exploring hands came to a stop over the knife scar. She ran gentle fingers along it. "I've been meaning to ask you what happened here?"

He glanced down and shrugged. "Ah. That. Constant reminder of a moment of stupidity."

"Looks like some serious stupidity. Car wreck?"

"You know how it is. One moment everything is going along fine, then next it's all gone to hell." He shrugged again. "Anyway, I survived and it was a long time ago." *Almost in another lifetime*, he added to himself.

Her caressing lips traced a path down to the old injury. A moment later, his jeans joined her towels on the floor.

~*~

There were two of them now.

Mr. Beige had apparently followed them to Machu Picchu and back to Lima again. Here in the *mercado*, he'd been joined by a shorter, stockier man who Katzen had dubbed Lumpy. At that particular moment, Lumpy was directly behind Tessa and himself and apparently intensely interested in embroidered ladies' handbags. Beige was nowhere to be seen. Standard tag team technique. Switch off so the mark doesn't realize he or she is being followed. That might have worked pretty well if Beige hadn't screwed up so that Josh made him at Machu Picchu.

"Oooooo! Look at this one," Tessa said, lifting a turquoise and silver choker into his field of vision.

He pulled his attention away from the jewelry store's mirror and onto the necklace. It was a gorgeous piece: handmade silver tube beads linking traditional Incan hummingbirds with tiny cabochons of turquoise for eyes. A cluster of miniature silver jingle bells hung from the centermost bird like a tinkling waterfall.

"Beautiful," he answered truthfully, then looked at the price tag. "Ah, it seems you share my talent of zeroing in on the most expensive item in any shop."

She held the necklace to her throat and regarded her reflection for a moment before she said, "I don't care. I want it."

Amused, he stood back and watched the purchase, noting Tessa's almost sensual pleasure as she lightly stroked the silver birds while the shop owner fastened the piece around her neck. It kind of reminded him of him — and that wasn't necessarily a good thing. Then again, there was that bit about glass houses and chucking stones. Almost unconsciously, his eyes slid back to the mirror and its view of the street. Lumpy had moved out of sight.

Lumpy's vanishing act surprised him and it took every scrap of self-discipline he had not to look around. All became clear, though, when they left the store and Beige picked them up. Ah. A hand-off. More standard tag team procedure. He didn't have time to think about it, because Tessa touched his arm and pointed to a small pushcart down the street.

"That guy is selling fresh mangoes with chili," she said with a look of rapture. She pulled Josh closer to watch the man deftly skewer a mango on a stick, peel it, slice it until it looked like a lacy flower, sprinkle it with chili powder and hand it to a waiting child. "Watching someone who knows how to do that is like watching a magic trick. My grandmother used to make those for us when we were kids," she added.

It did look good, but seeing food also made him realize how late it was. He said, "Man, it's way after lunchtime. Why don't we head back to my hotel and—"

He didn't get to finish the thought because her cell rang.

She pulled the phone out and her brow furrowed as she looked at the screen. "It's my boss. I better take this."

She moved a short distance away to the relative privacy of a small cafe and he watched the conversation unfold by her body language. When she first answered, she was tense, ready for a fight, but she slowly relaxed as the call progressed. By the time she pocketed her phone, she looked fairly upbeat, smiling slightly as she returned to where he stood near the fruit vendor.

"I'm no longer on suspension," she announced with a little surprise. "I'm to report back to duty . . . ." she paused looking at her watch. "Wow. In three hours."

"That doesn't give you much time," he said. "Well, congratulations! I know you've been champing at the bit to get back to work."

"Well, sort of," she said a little doubtfully. "It's funny, but a part of me wishes I didn't have to go." She laughed, and continued, "I surprised myself by actually having *fun*. I didn't know time off could be so enjoyable."

Josh pulled a small, velvet gift bag from his pocket and put it into her hands. "Here. Maybe this will help work be a little more fun, too — the downtimes, at least."

She peeked in the pouch and squeaked, then drew the object out. "A new puzzle? Such *tiny* squares, too." She paused, then glared at him. "Wait a minute. Where did you get this, you sneak? I haven't seen anything like it in any of the markets we visited."

He treated her to the patented cocky grin. "That's because it's not Peruvian. A friend in Mexico City found it and shipped it down." Tapping one of the tiles containing a glyph depicting a flint knife with sharp, pointy teeth, he said, "See? That's the date One Flint. This is the Aztec calendar stone — or Sun Stone — depending who you ask. Different culture, but it's still a good one."

"Thank you! I'm betting I'll have a lot of need for distraction today. Unless something has changed in the last ten days, this puts me on the same rotation as Rastogi again. I gotta run." She shoved the puzzle into its bag and gave him a quick peck, then hurried off. A few yards away, she slowed and called back, "I'll thank you properly later!"

He stood looking after her long after she'd disappeared from view. He probably looked the part of Wistful Lover — he hoped so, anyway. He was actually watching to see if she sprouted a tail. It looked like she'd made a solo exit, though. Beige was still on him and Lumpy was nowhere to be seen. Maybe Lumpy had doubled back and picked her up down the street? Possible. He fingered his phone and considered giving her a heads up that she might be being followed, but decided against it.

There was something else he could do now that he was on his own, however. A couple things, really. One that Len Fuller would approve of and another that he'd have a shit-fit about. Katzen pulled out his phone and put it to his ear, as if making a call, snapping a couple full face pics of Mr. Beige in the process.

Lowering the cell, he looked at it in disgust, then glanced toward the cafe Tessa had used earlier as if seeing it for the first time. Pocketing the phone, he went in. It was a tiny place, but it had several high-sided booths along the sides that were perfect for his purposes. He ordered a mango *aguas frescas* at the counter, then took it to a table in one of the alcoves. If he'd played it right, he should have abruptly disappeared from Beige's radar. That ought to put his shorts in a pretty good twist. He grinned to himself, placed the cell on the table and sampled his drink. It was delicious. Some of the best cover he'd ever tasted.

He didn't have to wait long. He'd only taken a few sips when Lumpy strolled in and moved casually to the counter. Josh lifted the phone to his ear again and snapped several photos of the big guy while having a one-sided conversation with a non-existent friend.

Unless there were more than the two he'd already seen, they hadn't put a tail on Tessa. Not smart. Not smart at all — but maybe a little worrisome.

Katzen let the man settle at a table and begin dropping sugar into his glass of tea before he rose and slid into the seat opposite him.

"Tea looks good. Nice and dark. You should try the mango next time, though. It's got a great flavor," he said in Spanish.

Lumpy, hand poised half-way between glass and sugar packets, goggled at him and swore in unmistakable Russian.

"Ah!" Katzen said, switching languages. "No problem. My Russian is pretty fluent, too."

Lumpy still stared in amazed silence. Through the shop door and across the street, Mr. Beige stood facing the cafe, looking as if a bee had just gone up his trousers.

Katzen treated Lumpy to a sympathetic smile and continued in Russian, "I've caught you at a bad time, haven't I? Don't worry. I just wanted to let you and your friend know I was headed back to the hotel now. You know. Take some of the guesswork out of the surveillance?"

Beige was in motion. He'd entered the cafe and was almost to them as Katzen looked up. "Greetings, Comrade — or do you guys say that any more?"

"Is there a problem?" Beige asked in English.

The arrival of his partner seemed to jump-start Lumpy's brain. He said, "I do not know. This gentleman is under the mistaken impression I am following him."

"Nonsense," Katzen said with a laugh. "I'm under the impression you're *both* following me."

Mr. Beige said, "I'm sorry, but you *are* mistaken. My friend and I are simply tourists in this lovely city."

Katzen turned to Lumpy. "Speaking of tourism, I'd be pretty pissed if I were you. Your pal goes off to one of the greatest ancient sites on the face of the planet and *you* have to stay back in Lima?" He shook his head. "Nope. Unfair division of labor if you ask me."

Before either man could respond, Josh stood and said, "Anyway, as I was telling your pal here, I wanted to give you guys a heads up that I'm going back to the hotel now. Shower. Stream a few shows. Maybe crash early. I tell you, it's been a crazy day!"

They were still staring at him wordlessly as he exited the shop and re-entered the stream of pedestrians outside.

~*~

By the time he got back to the hotel, the penny — or perhaps the *kopek* — dropped. Although neither man had said much, there was something familiar in their words and syntax. He'd lay good money that Lumpy and Mr. Beige were the guys who'd shot at him before he bunked for the states. Then there was the fact that the techies had identified the listening devices discovered in the various hotel rooms at various times as the sort favored by Eastern Bloc operatives. Couldn't get much more Eastern Bloc than those two. They were most likely former KGB. He'd ship the photos off to DeVries ASAP. If they were KGB, they'd probably show up in one of the databases.

He let himself into his room and froze.

In the dresser mirror, he saw something on the bed, but then laughed out loud as he recognized the object as a brown and white Moche-style stirrup pot in the shape of a crouching cat. The cat held a folded piece of paper between its incised shell teeth. Coming around, he took the paper. It was a note from Tessa.

Thanks for the last few days. They were fun and wonderful. I thought my Little Cat might like this little cat.

XXOO

He lifted the pot, enchanted by the expertise of the piece as well as the subject matter. The little ceramic feline crouched with its tail wrapped around its body, head lifted to gaze at the viewer with wide eyes. The mouthful of shell teeth gave the animal a whimsical Cheshire Cat feel. It was a fake, but a good one. It was the same quality as the confiscated ceramics Ruiz had showed him back in the Piedras Rojas cook tent. Damn. That seemed like a lifetime ago.

CHAPTER 24

"I was kind of surprised to hear from you," Katzen said as he slid into the passenger seat of the Land Rover. "I mean, nothing, nothing, nothing, lots more nothing, then hey choose a site, we're going to start searching today."

Vaughn DeVries laughed and put the Rover into gear. "You oughta be used to that by now. Hurry up and wait is the unofficial military intel motto, ain't it? Besides, I thought you were busy with Miss Diplomatic Security Service."

"She got called back to active duty yesterday. How many strings did Len have to pull to get her out of the way?"

DeVries grinned. "Not many. Losing Reid then Caballero left them real short handed. They was ready to bring her in out of the cold anyways."

"Any word on the photos I sent yesterday?"

"Not a peep, but that ain't too surprising. Facial recognition software is amazing stuff, but it still ain't magic. Only seems like it sometimes. You said these guys was following you and Caballero?"

"Yeah. For several days since I became aware of the tail in Machu Picchu. Probably for longer, but I wasn't paying attention."

DeVries' grin became wider. "That's not like you. You musta been *real* distracted."

Katzen ignored the remark. "It seemed they were mostly following me, though. Unless there are more I didn't see, no one followed Tessa when she left the *mercado* yesterday."

DeVries' grin faded. "Now, that ain't good. You think she might be working with them?"

Katzen was quiet for a moment. "No," he said at last, "I don't think so."

"You sound pretty sure."

"I am. For one thing, if she was working with them, there'd be no reason to expend resources by putting an extra tail on me. Especially not a tag team of two or more. Secondly, the guys following me were Russian. The big guy swore in idiomatic Russian when I sat down at his table in the *mercado* cafe. The other guy spoke English, but it was accented. Both Russian. I'd bet on it."

DeVries abruptly pulled the Rover out of traffic. "You were being followed by two Russian agents and you sat down and *talked* with 'em? Did you buy them coffee, too?"

"Don't get so excited! It wasn't all that big a deal."

"Listen to him. 'It wasn't all that big a deal.' General Fuller is gonna have a cow."

"Seriously. It wasn't. They were either being clumsy or they let me see them on purpose. Personally, I think it was clumsy, but I still wanted to let them know I saw them."

DeVries just stared at him.

"Can we get back on the road? There are four sites on today's list and I'd like to hit at least two of them before nightfall."

Wordlessly, DeVries guided the Rover back into traffic. After a while, he said, "Might be they didn't think you'd be able to spot them. The average Joe don't know that much about surveillance techniques."

"Maybe," Katzen said thoughtfully, "or maybe not. There's more, but I want to be sure you aren't going to wreck us if I tell you."

"Oh, man. Hit me."

"When I was talking to them, I recognized their syntax on a couple phrases. I'm pretty sure those are the guys who took potshots at me before I went stateside."

DeVries gave him a wild look, then turned his attention back to the road. "General Fuller ain't gonna have a cow. He's gonna have a whole herd."

~*~

The scene was utter devastation. *Huaquero* holes dotted the hillsides and ancient walls lay in tumbled heaps. The only thing left standing was a raw stone pillar that jutted up from the rubble like an obscene skeletal finger. The jungle was reclaiming the ruin. Roots and vines entwined fallen stone. Saplings sprouted from gaping holes left by looters. Ferns obscured the base of the naked pillar while tall stands of Heliconia draped panicles of vivid red and yellow flowers across its top and sides.

Katzen hovered at the edge of the clearing, held back by something indefinable.

"Are we waiting for something?" DeVries asked.

"I don't know," Katzen said. "There's just something familiar about this place."

"Of course it's familiar. You only been looking at pictures of it for weeks on end."

"It's more than that." Stepping carefully to avoid looters' pits, Katzen picked his way over to the pillar and ran his hands across the sides. "Yeah. It's been slabbed by Deustch's crew. I'd have to take measurements to be sure, but visually, the dimensions match the stele at the warehouse." He examined the saw-marks closely. "Really great work — destructive, but precision destruction."

"Now, that's your thief side talking. 'Precision destruction.' Ain't no such thing. . . ."

"Oh, but there is, Colonel DeVries."

The voice came from in back of them. Katzen knew who he'd see before he turned. Yep. Lumpy and Mr. Beige. Lumpy held a pistol. "I wasn't followed — I'm sure of it."

Beige laughed. "Of course not. You are a pain in the backside to keep track of." He pointed at DeVries. "We planted a tracker on his Rover."

"Oh, maaaan," DeVries moaned. "If they don't kill me, the general will."

"Relax, Colonel, we only want to talk," Beige said soothingly. "We are after the same thing. Let's be friends, yes?"

"Kinda hard to do when you're holding a pistol on someone," Katzen said.

Beige considered this. "He has a point, Vassi."

"I do not trust them, Misha. Especially that one." The big man waved the Makarov in Katzen's direction. "He is trouble."

"Vasily also has a point, Gatito. You *are* trouble," Beige said with a broad grin and broader shrug.

"Moses." Katzen rolled his eyes and sat down on a heap of rubble beside the pillar. "Something tells me this is going to take a while."

"Get up," Vasily ordered.

"Bite me, Lumpy," Katzen said, making no move to stand.

The pistol locked onto Katzen, but Misha quickly put his hand on the weapon.

"Not yet, Vasi," the tall man hissed. "We do not yet have what we want."

DeVries spoke up. "Pardon me if I'm denser than a box of bricks, but I'm just not seeing *what* you folks want."

"Then I will say it in simple words, Colonel DeVries: we want Deustch's plutonium," Misha said. DeVries started to say something else, but the tall man held up his hand. "Please. Don't protest that you have no idea what I'm talking about. It is only a waste of our time. You know because it was stolen from your government and *we* know because we were Herbert Deustch's KGB contacts."

DeVries said, "Whaaat?"

"Are you saying that Herb Deustch was KGB?" Katzen asked.

It was the tall Russian's turn to roll his eyes. "Don't be ridiculous! The man was a mercenary. Nothing more."

"We were part of what you might call a procurement team for the U.S.S.R.," Vasily added. "Deustch was one of our providers.

Not the best, but solid. We tried to buy the plutonium, but he was playing coy."

Katzen nodded. "He was talking to other potential buyers."

"Yes. It turns out he was," Misha said.

Almost as an aside, Vasily said, "He should never have been talking to the Chinese. Their head of station at that time was noted for being . . . unstable."

Katzen winced. "Ooooo, yeah. I heard about that guy. An agent with anger management issues. Not good."

Misha was getting impatient. "Enough history, Joshua Katzen — or whoever you are — we want to know where the plutonium is."

Katzen sighed. "You and half the people in Peru. But why? Something tells me you aren't in it for Mother Russia any more."

"Very perceptive, Gatito," Vasily said with a nasty grin. "We are in it because the KGB have no 401K."

Katzen was silent for a beat, then said, "So, you two are freelancing this?"

"That is a good way to phrase it. Yes," the tall man agreed. His burly companion nodded.

"Okay." In one swift move, Katzen lobbed a baseball-sized chunk of debris then rolled sideways off the rubble pile and behind the pillar. The stone hit Vasily in the chest about the same time a bullet pinged off the ruined stele.

Katzen shouted, "Get Beige! I got Lumpy!"

DeVries was already in the air. He tackled Misha, knocking him down. They tumbled backward, bouncing and rolling down the rubble-strewn hillside and abruptly vanished from sight.

Katzen couldn't worry about them, though, because the big Russian bellowed like an enraged bull and charged. Limestone powdered and sprayed as Vasily emptied his weapon into the obelisk. Katzen tossed another chunk of rock, then ducked around out of the larger man's reach. The man bellowed again and lunged, his hand grabbing at empty air, because Katzen had dropped to the ground and placed both feet against the rough-sided monolith. He shoved for all he was worth. With a crack like a pistol shot and the rattle of a mini-landslide, the abused stone gave way and toppled over. Vasily's bellow changed to a scream of pain, followed by a string of curses in Russian.

Katzen came up to find his opponent sprawled on the ground, pinned in place by the shattered stele lying across his legs. The Russian launched another stream of invective and scrabbled for the pistol that lay several feet away. Katzen dived on it, but the slide was back showing an empty chamber. He tossed the useless weapon into the brush with a few choice swear words of his own and pelted toward where he'd last seen DeVries and the other Russian.

He found them at the bottom of a small ravine fighting over a blocky black and yellow weapon. A stun gun. He watched for a beat, but they were too evenly matched. Neither combatant was making any headway. He needed to tip the odds in DeVries' favor.

Launching himself into the gully, he slid to a halt a short distance from the grappling pair. He hammered a double-fisted blow to the side of the tall Russian's head, making him loosen his grip on the gun. DeVries seized the weapon, crab-crawled backward and pulled the trigger. There was a loud pop, then fast-paced ticking and the slight smell of burnt hair as the former KGB agent spasmed, then went limp.

DeVries tried to scramble to his feet, but his leg folded under him. "Dammit, my knee won't hold."

Without another word, Katzen helped him up and they traveled as quickly as they could for their Rover.

Loading DeVries into the passenger seat, Katzen turned the vehicle toward town and floored it. A short distance down the road, however, he slowed and stopped.

"What's wrong," DeVries asked.

"Nothing," Katzen said. "I think I see their truck."

DeVries struggled up to look. "Gotta be. It's not like this is a hot tourist destination."

Throwing the Rover into park, Katzen jumped out and opened the hood of the Russians' truck. Grabbing a handful of wires, he yanked hard and threw everything that came loose into the undergrowth.

"Good move," DeVries said, as Katzen slid behind the wheel again and started them back toward town. "The big guy really had it in for you. I take it he was your lunch date from the other day?"

"Yep. That was Lumpy."

"Didn't the other guy call him Vasily?"

"Yeah . . . I dunno. He'll always be Lumpy to me."

~*~

"I know it's mean-spirited, but I'm glad it wasn't me on that gurney this time. It usually is," Katzen said as they entered Fuller's suite.

"I'm sure it seems that way, but it isn't always true," Fuller said.

"You sure about that? I seem to remember coming home with a very flashy souvenir sticking out of me. Leaked all over the medivac chopper, too."

"Your memory does not fail you. That particular souvenir currently resides in a snazzy glass case in my office. It would be quite a conversation piece if I could actually talk about it." Fuller motioned Katzen to a chair, then went over to a bar built into the wall and pulled out two glasses. "Scotch?"

"Wow, you get a bar? All my room has is one of those little fridge-like things you have to pay to open the door."

"The perks of having stars on your shoulders, son." He splashed a generous amount of scotch over ice and handed the glass to Katzen. "Actually, we're damned lucky the only casualty was Vaughn's knee. It could have been much worse. Why in hell didn't you tell me about the incident in the *mercado* cafe right after it happened?"

Katzen sipped scotch. "I sent the photos right away."

"Yes. Yes, you did." The general paused. "How did you take those, anyway? Some of those were a little more off-kilter than I've come to expect from you."

"Ah!" Josh said, pulling out his cell and holding it to his ear. "The old pretend you're talking on the phone trick."

"Good work," Fuller said with a laugh. "Still, you really should have reported actual contact with an enemy agent."

"How did I know it was going to be time-sensitive? Anyway, when I got back to the hotel, it was late and there was a gift from Tessa that kind of put it out of my head."

Fuller raised an eyebrow.

"No. Nothing like that. She didn't tie a bow around herself or anything. She left a replica stirrup pot in my room. Reminded me of the stuff el Mago was putting on the market toward the end. I think it might be from the same workshop."

"Really? Any idea how she came into possession of it?"

"I haven't asked, but I do know she has a shitload of equally good fakes at her house. She says she got them when she was in a relationship with someone she calls Beto. Apparently every time they got into a fight, he'd give her a lovely consolation prize."

"Well, that's interesting."

"Isn't it, though? My favorite was a little jade pendant of three frogs. Beautiful piece. It *looked* Costa Rican."

"But it wasn't?"

"My money's on it being purely Peruvian homegrown."

Fuller swirled his drink thoughtfully. "Beto. That's a diminutive of Alberto, isn't it?"

"Yep. I believe it is."

"Joshua, I know how you hate when I ask about your private affairs, but how serious is this relationship between you and Special Agent Caballero?"

Josh shrugged. "There's not much to it, really. She's bored. I'm available. That simple."

Len gave him searching look over the edge of his glass.

"What? I can't have a little fun while you and Uncle Sam are ruining my life?"

"All right, then. I've known you too long to start mistrusting your judgment now." The general drained his drink, then set the empty aside. "So who else is involved in this Deustch deal? Have you seen any sign of the Chinese? Intel suggests they were the high bidders at the time Deustch disappeared."

Katzen shook his head. "Nope. No sign of the Chinese anywhere. Either they're better at surveillance than the Russians, or they aren't in the mix. Then again, Lumpy and Mr. B. aren't exactly here officially, either. They admitted they were going into business for themselves — oh — we have names now."

Fuller looked interested. "We do? What are they?"

"Okay. We sorta have names. Lumpy called Mr. Beige Misha and he called Lumpy Vasily."

"Michail and Vasily. Not exactly unusual names, but the extra parameter might speed up the ID process."

"This might help, too. Providing we can trust anything they said to us. They claim they were also part of an acquisitions section of the KGB. They'd dealt with Deustch before."

"They had? According to our information, Deustch was new to that particular branch of the black market."

"Would that be the same intelligence that neglected to mention Herb Deustch's sister was no longer in New York City?"

"It would, indeed."

"Uuuuuh huh. Well, at least they got one thing right. According to the Dynamic KGB Duo, the Chinese agent with the bad temper was responsible for Deustch's death. Apparently, he got pissed off when he discovered there were other bidders."

"I'll refrain from mentioning blind squirrels."

Katzen grinned and finished his scotch.

~*~

In spite of the drink Len Fuller had given him, delayed shock was setting in by the time he arrived at his hotel. Reaching for the elevator buttons, his hand shook. He swore softly and massaged it as the brushed aluminum doors slid closed. He needed to relax, center himself — and maybe more scotch.

Yes. Definitely more scotch.

At the door to his room, he pulled out his keycard, but froze with it hovered over the slot. A shadow moved across the bar of daylight bleeding under the door. Someone was inside.

Cautiously, he swiped the card and fingertipped the door open. As it swung back, Tessa Caballero poked her towel-swathed head around the corner.

"Oh there you are! I wondered when you'd get back." She disappeared from whence she'd come and he caught the scent of her frankincense and myrrh soap. She called, "I hope you haven't had dinner yet because I'm ravenous."

Nonplussed, he stepped in and pushed the door closed. "Um, no, I haven't eaten."

She'd dropped the towels when she reappeared and her damp hair curled around bare shoulders. "Great! It's been a helluva day." She kissed him, then ran her tongue over her lips. "Mmmmm. Scotch. Getting started without me?"

He kissed back and said, "Not exactly. I had a drink with General Fuller. Vaughn DeVries had an accident today and we were just back from the hospital."

Her smile vanished. "Oh, no! Poor Vaughn! Is it serious?"

He was rapidly regaining his footing and brushed past her to pull the half-full bottle of Glenlivet from the dresser drawer. He sat it down next to the grinning Moche cat. Unwrapping two hotel glasses, he said, "No, not too serious. He took a fall today and banged his knee up pretty good, though."

She hooked a terry-cloth robe from the back of the bathroom door and shrugged into it. "Even if it's not serious, it sounds painful."

"Oh yeah. You would have thought he was mortally wounded when the ER docs started poking at it." He pulled the ice bucket toward him. It had a half-inch of water in it. He poured the whisky neat and handed her one of the glasses. "Who needs ice, anyway?

You *did* say you'd had a helluva day. What happened in your neck of the woods?"

She sipped, then said, "Well, compared to Vaughn's day, mine wasn't so bad. Even if it did include being temporarily partnered with Arash Rastogi."

"That sounds like a whole lot of no fun."

"It was a diplomatic escort for a conference, so we spent a lot of time cooling our heels, but there was one up side." She went to the pile of clothes beside the bed, rummaged through them and held something aloft. "Ta DAAA! I finished your puzzle."

He reached for it. "Cool! Let's see it."

She snatched it back, but held it out for him to look. "Nope. You can't touch it. Only admire from afar."

"So, it wasn't as hard as it looked, huh?"

"Oh no! It was horrible! Your ears should be scorched because I've been cursing you all day. I'd still be working it if I hadn't had so much down time and . . . well . . . ."

"Rastogi?"

"Yeah." She was quiet for a beat, then dropped the puzzle onto the bed and snatched up her clothes. "Go get freshened up. I'm thinking steak. Thick, rare and juicy. Something I can jab a knife into."

CHAPTER 25

Tessa snuggled deeper into Josh's arms and hummed contentment. "Thank you for a wonderful evening. It went a long way to make up for an utterly craptastic day."

"I can't take any credit. You made the suggestions, I merely ran with it."

"Whatever," she laughed. "It was great."

He smiled into her hair. "I was just glad when the wine took effect. The way you were going after that meat with the knife was making me nervous. I kept expecting to hear 'die, Ratsass! DIE!'"

She pulled away and sat bolt upright, jamming her fingertips against her temples. "No! No! You will NOT make me think of Rastogi. I am too happy right now."

"Okay. We'll talk about something else, then. What will we talk about?"

"We'll talk about how happy the cat is on your dresser," she said pointing to the stirrup pot sitting in pride of place across the room.

"I'm pretty happy with it on my dresser, too. I meant to thank you for it earlier, but we got sidetracked talking about DeVries."

"I'm glad you like it. I thought of you as soon as I saw it. I think it was that cocky smile."

"Thanks — I think. It really is a great piece. Seriously, where did you find it? Whoever made it is a true artist."

"I'll never tell. A girl's got to have a few secrets."

"Yeah?" He pulled her down onto the mattress and leaned close in. "How about I try a few interrogation techniques? See how many secrets you have then."

One of the cell phones on the bedside table chirped. She buried her face in a pillow. Her voice was muffled as she said, "Is that you or me?"

His cell chirped and vibrated. The screen read Uncle Len. "Me . . . Hey, Len. What's up?"

"Is Caballero with you?"

"I suspect you know she is. Why?"

"Don't get your shorts in a twist. It looks like Vaughn is going to be out of commission for a while. We'll need to recruit help if we want to keep on schedule."

"Oh. Okay."

"Can you both be at the warehouse in an hour?"

"Ummmm. Sure. See you then." He thumbed the End button and regarded the phone thoughtfully.

Tessa had come out from under the pillow, listening to his side of the conversation. "You were talking about me, weren't you?"

"Yeah, we were. That was General Leonard Fuller. I think he's about to offer you a job."

~*~

The military warehouse facility security detail must have been watching for Tessa's Jeep because the barrier rose even before they'd cleared the driveway. The MP in the booth simply waved them through. The door to Unit 86 stood open, silhouetting Vaughn DeVries leaning on a crutch against the back lighting. An inflatable cast added bulk to his right leg.

"Evening, folks," DeVries called. "I apologize in advance that my clumsy butt has inconvenienced everyone."

Tessa gasped, swatted Josh and pointed to the crutch and cast. "Liar! You said it wasn't serious. That looks pretty serious to me."

"Don't go getting mad at Josh," the colonel said — although he seemed to be enjoying the display. "It really looks worse than it is. I just gotta keep weight off this knee for a few days. Go on in. General Fuller is waiting for you."

Fuller sat behind a massive antique desk he had commandeered from Deustch's belongings. An art deco lamp shed light across the paper-littered surface.

"Looking very authoritative, General," Josh said. "Almost makes me want to salute."

"Oh, don't do that," Fuller laughed. "My heart might not stand it."

Tessa slid amused eyes toward Josh. "I can see he knows you very well."

"That's for damn sure," DeVries muttered as he flopped into a chair. A groan and a muffled curse escaped him as he hoisted his injured leg onto an embroidered ottoman.

Rising, Fuller reached across the desk and extended a hand to the DSS agent, "Good to finally meet you, Special Agent Caballero. I've been hearing good things about you." He gestured around. "Pull up some chairs and we'll get started. There's quite a selection to choose from." He sat back down and ran an appraising hand along the smooth expanse of oak. "Actually, I really like this thing," he said almost to himself. "Might check into what the people in charge are planning to do with it and see I can get a bid in."

"Cool! I'll have to show you the secret compartments later," Katzen said, straddling a chair.

The general turned his attention to Caballero. "I'm sure you're aware we've been searching for something that Herb Deustch stole from the American government shortly before he died."

"Yes, sir," Tessa said. "I was part of the team who searched the pieces in this warehouse earlier in the year."

"That search has been on hold for a while, but recently, Josh, here, managed to decipher some of Deustch's notes. That enabled us to locate caches where he hid items of value until they could be moved on to a buyer." He pulled a map to the front of the workspace. It was covered in handwritten notations. "We've been investigating the sites within a reasonable radius of Lima. That's what Vaughn was doing when he was injured."

Josh stopped listening and studied a carved detail on the arm of his chair. He could already tell that Tessa wasn't going to get the full story. He wasn't sure how he felt about that, but he understood — sort of. As the general's words spun on, he checked off the omissions. Nothing about the listening devices. Nothing about them having been followed to Machu Picchu and back. Nothing about the former KGB agents at all — not even how DeVries actually got hurt. Nothing about what the package really was. Well, it wasn't absolutely necessary to tell her the package they kept talking about contained plutonium, but omitting the former KGB agents was asking for trouble. Out of the corner of his eye, he caught DeVries watching him. The other man frowned and quickly looked away. Didn't look like the colonel was too happy about the retconned history, either. Katzen leaned heavily against the back of his seat and kept quiet because that's what a good little spy does when his handler is dishing out bullshit.

He tuned back in as Fuller said, "So we need someone with official connections to continue investigating the cache locations until Colonel DeVries can rejoin the operation. As a Diplomatic Security Service officer, you fit that bill admirably. Would you be willing to sign on?"

"I don't even have to think about that," Tessa said. "When do I start?"

"Right now. Vaughn, will you bring Special Agent Caballero up to speed? There are a few more things I need to discuss with Joshua."

The Chippendale dining table was still being used as a computer station, but it had been moved to the far side of the room in one of the areas that had formerly been crowded with statuary. As DeVries and Tessa headed for it, Josh said, "What? You want me to show you the secret compartments already? You don't even own it yet."

"Nothing quite so entertaining, I'm afraid. We have an ID on your Russian friends."

A manila folder slid across the desktop. Katzen caught it and measured the thickness. "Oooo. Lumpy and Mr. B have been busy boys."

"You are looking at Vasily Yurikovich Koulikov and Mikhail Sergeiovich Bukharin. They were, indeed, contacts for various black market suppliers in addition to other duties up to and including the odd assassination."

Katzen leafed through the pages. "Mmmmm hmmm. I knew no one could be that bad a shot."

"Most definitely not," Fuller said. "Take that with you. I think you'll find it interesting reading."

"No doubt," Josh said, closing the folder and glancing back toward the pair at the computer station.

"You don't agree with my redacted version of our mission, do you?" Fuller asked abruptly.

For a moment Katzen said nothing, then he lifted the folder. "I have no problem omitting what's in the box, but this?"

"Think of it as a judgment call on my part to be amended if and when the need arises."

"I hate need to know shit."

"I'm painfully aware of that, but *you're* aware of what information in the wrong hands can do. You should be anyway." Fuller paused and fingered the edge of the desk. "I wish I could slide another folder across to you and tell you we found exactly who leaked about you being a former intelligence agent. But I can't. We keep hitting dead ends and stone walls wherever we look."

"Wow. So much has happened since then, I'd almost forgotten about it."

"I haven't," Len said. "I'm still pissed as hell. Someone

obviously has it in for you, son. It's been tracked back to the Pentagon, but *dammit*, I still can't get any farther. That has me convinced it's someone pretty high up, but we'd suspected that for a while, too. We're also dealing with someone very good at covering their tracks."

"Someone within the intelligence community, then."

"It would have to be, wouldn't it?"

Silence stretched between them, and Fuller stared at the empty blotter until Katzen said, "There's more, isn't there?"

Fuller sighed. "I'm afraid so. Everything I've been able to uncover points to the fact that this is the same individual who leaked your identity to the extremist terror cell you were investigating on your last mission."

"The same person who blew my cover and nearly got me killed."

Fuller nodded. "Whoever they are, they are now aware Major Durand isn't dead."

"And won't give up until I am."

"I hope that's a worst case scenario, but it's something to bear in mind."

~*~

Katzen edged farther into the rock chamber and lifted his solar lantern higher to illuminate more of the floor. There wasn't much to see.

From outside, Tessa called, "Tell me there's something in this one. Please."

He blew out a breath he hadn't realized he was holding. Sweat rolled down his neck and into his collar. He wasn't sure if it was hotter inside the cave or outside on the ledge.

For the first three days, Tessa had enjoyed the search. That slowly changed as they found more and more dry holes. Not completely dry in some cases. They'd recovered a few artifacts here and there, but nothing remarkable, and no sign of Deustch's package.

"Joooosh," she called again. "Is there something in this cache?"

"Well, there is . . . sorta," he said.

"Really?" She sounded hopeful. "What is it?"

He prodded the remains. "Looks like it might have been a rat . . . or something. . . ."

There was silence. "You're joking, aren't you?"

"Ummmm. No, there are several gnawed up wooden boxes and a skeletonized rodenty-sorta-kinda-thing."

More silence.

"I'm coming out."

"Okay."

The hot breeze that swirled the dust of the ledge actually felt cool as he emerged from the tunnel. He found Tessa sitting with her back against the rockface, her arms on her knees and her head on her arms.

"Hey! You all right? Do you need some water?"

"No — on both."

He propped himself against the cliff, wet a handkerchief and applied it to his face. It felt like heaven. The only sound for a while was the distant squawk of tropical birds and the trilling of tree frogs until Tessa finally said, "You really *don't* know where it is, do you?"

Katzen threw his hands wide and looked heavenward. "Finally! Someone believes me!"

She looked up, exasperation on her face. "You don't have to be so melodramatic. You could have just said 'No, Tessa, I really don't'."

"Okay. No, Tessa, I really don't." He laughed and put his hand down to help her up. "Come on. Let's go back to town, get cleaned up and go kill something for dinner."

"You're on," she said, dusting off her backside. "As long as I get to decide who to kill."

"Just for the record: You can't kill Herb Deustch. He's already dead."

"Party pooper."

~*~

The slog to the jeep took even longer than the hike out to the cache site. At least it seemed that way. It didn't help that Tessa remained silent the whole way back. He'd attempted to start conversations, but after the first few tries died miserably, gave it up. They were almost to where they'd parked when a voice called out from ahead of them: "Joshua! I must say I approve of your upgrade in partners."

Katzen froze mid-step, closed his eyes and swore under his breath. Sliding a sidelong glance at Tessa, he said, "Do you have your sidearm? This could get bad."

He slowed as Caballero reached under her jacket to unsnap the holster at her back and to flip the safety off her Beretta. Satisfied, he picked up his pace and she fell in behind him without a word.

It was as bad as he'd thought. In the clearing, Katzen discovered Michail Bukharin seated comfortably on the hood of Tessa's Jeep. Vasily Koulikov, sporting a full plaster leg cast and leaning on crutches, stood a short distance away, resting his weight against a tree trunk. They both had pistols pointed at him this time.

"Good afternoon!" Bukharin called amiably, motioning him forward with the Makarov. "Since poor Vasily was badly injured in our last encounter and unable to make the climb, we decided to wait for you here. You are empty-handed. I am assuming there was nothing of worth at this cache site, either. Such a pity."

Tessa entered the clearing, glancing between Josh and the Russians. "Josh? Who are these guys?"

"Tessa, meet Lumpy and Mr. B." Katzen eyed Koulikov. He looked pretty out of it. Considering the meds they'd put DeVries on for a simple sprain, Lumpy was probably loaded to the eyeballs.

Kulikov gave an inarticulate growl, but Bukharin spoke over it. "Ah, the lovely Miss Caballero joins us. You must forgive Gatito for his bad manners. Having dropped a large piece of rock on my partner, I am sure he did not expect to see us again so soon. I am Mikhail Sergeiovich Bukharin and this is my associate, Vasily Yurikovich Koulikov." He sketched a theatrical bow.

"Yeah?" Caballero's face darkened. She took a couple paces closer and jabbed a finger toward the ground. "Well, I don't care if you're the Grand Dutchess Anastasia. You're scratching up my paint job. Get off the Jeep."

Bukharin looked past her toward Katzen. "You are really disappointing us, Joshua. All this time and effort and you still produce nothing. Are you trying to convince us you actually *don't* know where Deustch hid the plutonium?"

"Plu—? What's he talking about?" Tessa demanded.

"Oh! You haven't told the lovely lady what you're really looking for?" Bukharin turned his attention to Caballero. "What did he tell you it was, my dear? Coins? Jewels?"

Katzen saw Tessa's anger mounting. A good deal of it was aimed at him, but another big whack was pointed right at Bukharin. "Look, guys," he said. "We can definitely talk about this, but it wouldn't hurt you to be polite. The lady asked you to get off her car."

"That's right, Lumpy, I did," she said.

"Uhhhh, he's Mr. B," Katzen said. He pointed to Koulikov. "*That's* Lumpy."

Koulikov pushed away from the tree and took an unsteady step toward Katzen. The Makarov's barrel wavered dangerously. "Stop calling me that!"

"Would you rather I called you Clarence?" Katzen asked, dripping innocence. Lumpy was getting pretty fired up, too.

"I don't care what you call him," Caballero said, taking yet another step closer. "By the time I get through with him, he's going to be lumpy *and* black and blue. Move your ass, Mister. *Now.*"

"Please, Miss Caballero. Our business is with Joshua." Again he looked past the angry DSS agent and addressed Katzen. "As I said, Vasily and I owe you for our last encounter—"

"That would be *Special Agent* Caballero to you, asshole."

"May I remind you who holds the pistol?" Bukharin began. He didn't finish because Tessa stepped in past the pistol, jerked the former KGB officer's arm up and out. Before he could so much as yelp, she punched into the extended shoulder. The joint dislocated with an audible pop.

As soon as Tessa moved, Katzen had dropped and rolled, coming up right in front of Koulikov. The big Russian fired wild as Josh yanked his crutch away and gave him a good shove.

Koulikov went one way and his Makarov the other. Katzen turned back toward Tessa in time to see her smacking Bukharin in the side of the head with his own weapon.

Tossing the pistol onto the front seat, she slid in, fired up the engine and shouted, "Get in!"

Josh barely had time to comply before she slammed into reverse and floored it, dumping her former opponent unceremoniously onto the rutted ground. Then, she surged forward, missing Bukharin by a hair, tore down the path to the road and turned the Jeep toward Lima.

The struggling, angry men dwindled in the distance and were hidden by a curve. Katzen turned forward in his seat. "Man! That was intense. I'm glad they didn't decide to pay us back *exactly* for the other day."

"Why?" Caballero asked through gritted teeth.

"Because I sort of yanked a bunch of wires out of their engine compartment and lobbed them into the jungle."

There was a moment of silence before Tessa spoke again. Enunciating each word carefully she said, "I think you should maybe tell me exactly what happened. NOW. And it better be the truth this time."

The story took most of the journey to Lima. Tessa was, if anything, angrier when he finished.

"Do you mean to tell me you and Vaughn ran into these guys before? They pulled weapons on you and *you didn't tell me*?"

"I wanted to, but General Fuller said—"

"I don't care what General Full-of-Shit said. *You* should have told me anyway."

"You're right. I'm sorry—"

"And about Machu Picchu and about . . . ." Seeming to run out of steam, she sat back, blew a breath out slowly and loosened her death-grip on the steering wheel. "Oh, never mind. I know what it's like to be ordered around."

In Lima, Tessa dropped him off in front of the warehouse complex's guard house and roared away.

CHAPTER 26

The MPs from the guard shack, who had seen his near-forcible ejection, expressed sympathy tinged with something a little akin to admiration. He was uncertain if it was for him or Tessa. One of them gave him a lift back to Unit 86. As before, Vaughn DeVries stood just inside the open door. This time he was sans crutch, the inflatable splint having disappeared the day before.

"General's in the back waiting for your sitrep," he said.

"Hey! You lost the stick!" Katzen said, as he entered the relative cool of the warehouse.

"Yep," DeVries said. "Things are going just like the doc said they would. I wouldn't have credited it the first day, bad as I felt, but I'm down to an elastic bandage already. Long as I don't do anything stupider than usual, I'm good." He looked out at the conspicuously empty parking spaces. "Where's Caballero?"

"Yeah. About that."

"Oh man. Is that as bad as it sounds?"

"Probably worse. Let's do that sitrep."

Silence weighed heavily after Katzen finished his account. General Fuller drummed fingertips on the arm of his chair and stared at a spot on the concrete floor. At last, he said, "You both said the same thing about not reading Caballero in on the Russian involvement. I should have listened." He looked over at the two men sitting in front of him. "You have my apologies, both of you. Especially you, Josh."

Josh nodded, then shifted in his seat. "That isn't what's bugging me the most, though. Yeah, what happened with Tessa was bad, but all the way back to Lima, I kept thinking one thing: Bukharin was right."

DeVries looked over in confusion. "You mean you *do* know where it is?"

"No," he said, "but *that's* the point. We've been expending all this time and energy and we're still no closer to finding the damned plutonium than when Deustch's remains were first identified."

"Now, Josh," Fuller said. "I wouldn't go that far."

"I would." Katzen abruptly stood and paced. He ticked off items on his fingers. "What do we have so far? We found a lot of gold, gems and cash in the items from this warehouse. We figured out Deustch liked to play games. We deciphered a code and have since found a lot of empty hidey holes, some mediocre quality artifacts and a few dead critters. Nothing else."

"Son—" Fuller began.

"No," Katzen said, waving his hand impatiently. "Seriously, that's the sum and total of our results to date. The frustrating thing is that we have everything we need. There's something I'm missing."

"Son," Fuller said more firmly. "Sit down."

He waited until Katzen actually sat, then said, "No, we haven't found what we're looking for yet, but we've come a lot farther than it feels from your point of view. You won't like it, but we need to push through this."

"You mean keep doing what we've been doing?"

"Yes. Exactly."

"You do know what the definition of insanity is?"

That elicited a laugh from the older man. "Yes. I do. Still, it's all we have. Until you find this key you keep talking about, we need to keep hammering at the lock." The general paused, then said, "Do you think you can iron this out with Tessa Caballero? We'll need her help if we're going to continue."

"I don't know. I was going to give her tonight to cool off and take some breakfast over to her place in the morning. The thing with Koulikov and Bukharin really pissed her off, though."

"I can't help you find whatever it is you feel you're not seeing, but I believe I can solve the Russian problem." The general was actually smiling.

DeVries looked interested. "Sir?"

Katzen looked puzzled. "How do we do that?"

"We toss their asses in jail. They've given us the perfect charge to do it with, too: they assaulted a United States citizen — a federal agent, no less."

Katzen couldn't help himself. He laughed.

~*~

He shifted the aromatic bundle to his other hand and knocked harder. "Tessa! Breakfast is getting cold."

The door remained closed and he heard nothing from inside. He knew better, though. He could almost feel her on the other side of the barrier. Pressing the doorbell, he held it for a ten count. "Come on! Open up or I'll give the neighbors something to talk about."

The door opened violently inward and Tessa, clad in a kimono-style silk robe, blocked the way. "What the hell do you want, Katzen?"

"To apologize again," he said, lifting his parcel and looking hopeful. "I brought food offerings."

"Did you bring your Russian friends, too?"

"Nnnnooo. I wouldn't waste my croissants on them — besides, they're having breakfast courtesy of the Lima City Jail this morning."

She stared at him. He waved the grease-spotted sack again. Relenting, she stood aside and allowed him to pass. She said, "You're joking, right?"

"Nope, this bag is chockablock with croissants, bagels, cream cheese and all kinds of good breakfasty stuff." The kitchen table was covered by a thick layer of slick-paper shopping catalogs. He cleared a space and began filling it with warm rolls and tubs of spreadable cheeses.

"I meant about those KGB guys being in jail."

"Absolutely serious. They were arrested last night for assaulting a U.S. federal agent. I understand the ambassador was quite upset about the incident."

"As—*what*?"

He popped lids off the tubs and rooted in her kitchen drawers for utensils. "Yeah. The local authorities were more than happy to assist. U.S./Peru relations and all that sort of thing. I believe they caught up with them at an emergency clinic. It seems neither will be trying out for the Russian state soccer team this year. Sad."

He put a loaded bagel into her hand and she munched absently, eyeing him with the same fascination as a rabbit watching a snake.

Smearing a thick layer of cheese on another bagel, he continued, "Now, as long as no one figures out the federal agent assaulted them worse than they assaulted her, we're cool." He sucked cream cheese off his thumb and searched through the now-empty bag. "Damn. I forgot to get any bacon."

Later, as they sat on her couch and sipped coffee, he asked, "So, can we count on you?"

"Look, I'm glad those two creeps are out of the mix, but I'm still not sure I want to come back."

"Why not? Don't you think finding something like what Deustch stole is important?"

"Well, yeah, but . . . I guess I thought this was about something else."

"Like what?"

"I don't know. Something valuable and exotic, I guess."

"I'd think the actual package fits that bill."

She gave him an exasperated look. "You *still* won't say the actual word. Why not? Will General Fuller spank if you say plutonium out loud?"

He started to reply, then stopped and thought for a moment.

"I don't know," he said at last. "I guess I'm so used to not saying it, I just don't."

She got up and stalked into the kitchen to top off her mug. "I hate this hush-hush-need-to-know-bullshit."

"Trust me, I know how you feel. Still, we need your help. Will you come back? It won't be immediate. It'll take a day or so to do a new assessment of the cache locations."

She stared into her mug in angry silence — although she wasn't as angry as before. Josh took this as encouragement.

"Or would you rather spend more quality time with Special Agent Arash Rastogi?"

"Oh my god." She set the mug down hard. "I'm in!"

~*~

"You sure you don't want me to spell you?" Katzen said, as they bounced along what passed for a road.

"Nope." Tessa said, as she deftly steered the little vehicle around a sapling sprouting in the middle of the track. "Nobody drives my Jeep but me. Besides, the GPS says we're almost there."

He looked up at the sheer cliff face that rose to their left, then down at the gully to the right. It wasn't a sheer drop on that side, but some places could more be called ravine than ditch. None of it looked inviting. "That might or might not mean we're within reasonable walking distance of it. Remember that last one wound up being fifty feet straight up from the last GPS reading."

"Yeah. All that for three mano-whatevers and a jade pendant."

"The word is manopla but stone knuckles works fine. At least we're finding stuff in these last caches. It's not anything exciting, but they haven't been cleaned out. This one has some extra pencil marks beside it in the book, too. I'm not sure what they mean."

"Let's hope they mean there's something worth the trip here." She frowned. "When is Vaughn coming back in? He seems to be getting around pretty well."

Katzen shrugged and eyed the too-close ravine again. "No idea. Pretty soon, I think. He and General Fuller seem to be working on something. Also, they said the doc wants him to stay out of rough terrain for a while longer."

"Rough terrain." She barked a half-laugh. "Like there's anything else out here."

They whipped around a bend. Tessa yelped and braked hard to avoid a rockslide that had taken out part of the path and covered the rest of it with debris. "Dammit," she said, when they'd finally skidded to a stop. "It looks like this is as far as the road will take us. You grab the packs and I'll backtrack to that last wide spot and turn this thing around, okay? I'd rather be facing the way I want to go when we get back to the car."

"Wide spot. Riiiight."

The rest of the trek to the cave marked on Deutsch's map was steep, but not unmanageable. Just what someone bringing heavy items to the top by themselves would want. The entrance to the cache was well hidden, though, and it took several minutes searching before they found it.

Solar lantern held aloft, Katzen cautiously navigated the entryway. It was a little snug but high ceilinged. "Hey, I can actually stand upright in—"

"Josh?" Tessa called. "Are you okay? You didn't find a pit the hard way or anything?"

"Uhhhh, no. I just feel a little like Howard Carter," he answered slowly. "You need to see this."

The cavern was like the entry: long, narrow and high ceilinged. Crates, stacked three and four high, lined the whole of the chamber's longest wall. Almost every box was full of antiquities. Every place they shined their lights, they saw gold, silver and other precious and semi-precious things. There was nothing for it but to start opening boxes.

Closing the last crate, Josh straightened and sighed. "Well crapola. *Still* no plutonium." He turned and grinned at her. "See? I said it out loud this time."

Tessa didn't reply for a moment. She was bent over, digging into a mass of packing peanuts. Airy pink, white and green objects drifted around her feet. "Who cares?" she said. "This is WAY better than plutonium." She held a piece of gold jewelry up to her lantern. "How much do you think this is worth?"

"No idea. It's hard to put a dollar value on things like these. The authorities will probably invent a monetary equivalent for the papers when they announce the find, though."

She acted as though she didn't hear him and moved from box to box like a kid in a candy store. "Look at this," she said, fingering a jade mask with coral and onyx inlay. She leaned in closer. "Listen! I think this guy's talking to me. Yep. He's saying 'new house'."

"Come on, Tessa," Josh said. "Stop joking around. We need to get back to the Jeep and let Fuller know what we found."

She regarded him over the carved jade. He didn't like her expression. He liked her next words even less. "Who's joking? We've been busting our asses for absolutely nothing so far. Now we have this. We could be out of here and all the way to Rio before General Full-of-Shit even realizes we're not coming back."

Stepping over, he took the mask, replaced it and closed the crate. "No. It goes back to the people it was stolen from."

"What people? They're all dead, Josh. They have no use for it anymore. We do."

"No."

"I was afraid you were going to be a bastard about this." Tessa's hand crept around to her back.

"Looking for this?" Josh grinned and pulled her Baretta from his jacket pocket. "I snagged it when I closed that last box. Got the jeep keys, too."

"You picked my pockets!" Shock and anger flowed across her face as she patted down her pockets and empty holster, then she straightened. "You won't shoot. You artsy types don't have the balls."

"Really? I'm glad one of us is certain."

She snapped a kick at him. He dodged and fired in the same move. The shot hit her in the side and she fell to the rocky floor more from surprise than anything else. Pulling herself up slowly against the crates, she stared incredulously at the blood on her fingers. "You shot me! You *asshole*!"

He shrugged apologetically. "Maybe I'm not the artsy type, after all. Does that mean I have to give my pencils back?"

Tessa gave a very unladylike and injudicious guffaw. The sudden pain doubled her over. Clutching the wound, she gasped, "Chief Ruiz suspected you used to be a thief. Looks like he was right."

"That's one spin to put on it. Just depends on your point of view."

"Point of view." She slid down onto the nearest crate, hand pressed to her side. "Now what, Obi Wan? Other than letting me bleed to death."

He shook his head. "The wound's not that bad and we're not that far from the Jeep and the first aid kit. Just what the hell were you trying to achieve here, anyway?"

"Oh really." She rolled her eyes. "Good question coming from *you*. Money. What else is there? Truth, justice and the American way were all non-starters. This . . ." she swept her non-bloodied hand around to include the crates, ". . . is way better than any plutonium. Sure, that stuff might be worth a bundle to some people. But the same people who'd buy it would be the same people who'd use it to blow the hell out of the world I want to live it up in."

She winced and he could see mental wheels turning. Reaching a decision, she said, "Look, Josh, we can make a deal. Before I knew what we were really looking for, I was going to split the find with el Mago, but he couldn't get you to talk. Now he's dead and his men are busted, so I'll share with you. There's plenty here for both of us."

"You sicced el Mago on me."

"Don't get pissy about it. It was strictly business."

"Naturally."

She looked at him closely in the glare of the solar lantern. "You don't really act surprised."

"I'm not," he said. "I'd hoped I was wrong, but I suspected you and el Mago — or should I say Beto? — were working together for a while."

"You did not!"

"See, something bugged me about the way Mago knew when and where to find me when I got back to Piedras Rojas. Then, when he questioned me, he kept calling what we were looking for the 'package'. Nothing else. Just 'the package'. The way I saw it, there were only four people who knew those things: DeVries, Bramwell, you and me. I know I didn't tell him. DeVries was vouched for by someone I trust implicitly and someone snapped Bramwell's neck. He was dead before I even went back. That was the Russians, by the way, but they called it exactly what it was: plutonium. That left you. Sorry."

The trip back to the Jeep was full of slips, slides and whimpers from Tessa. At last, at the bottom of the trail, Josh bundled her into the passenger side and bound her to the car door with plastic holdtights taken from her DSS equipment case. Next, he dug a handful of gauze pads from the first aid kit and slid them under her shirt onto the wound.

"It's just a graze, but if you keep pressure on it against the armrest, it'll slow the bleeding," he said as he slid behind the wheel and turned the key.

"Josh, I'm sorry. I really did like you. You should have accepted my offer. We'd have had a lot of fun together."

He turned to find her free of the plastic restraints.

"Good thing you weren't on the other side of the law, Josh You're lousy with those plastic ties." She punched him solidly in the side of the head. Stars showered and he felt himself being pushed up and out of the now-moving vehicle.

Adrenaline and the hard jolt of hitting the road's narrow shoulder roused him enough to grab at some scrubby bushes as he slid over the side. It slowed his fall, but pulling himself up was another problem entirely. Above him, the Jeep's engine revved. Spinning tires sent gravel and small rocks bouncing down the wall he clung to as Tessa floored it. A few seconds later, the roar of the engine was joined by a woman's scream that was almost immediately drowned out by the shriek of tortured metal.

Then there was silence.

He hung from his scraggly lifeline for a few more minutes, catching his breath, before he thought to look down. The bank below him wasn't a gentle incline, but it wasn't a sheer cliff, either.

Moving carefully, he made his way to the bottom of the ravine sliding on loose scree from shrub to shrub to sapling. Everything seemed to hurt all at once, although nothing appeared to actually be broken. The final, short drop to the dry creek bed at the bottom of the gully ripped a yelp from him and made him freeze in a crouch against the uneven surface until the pain subsided. Rising at last, he staggered along, following the stream's path until he found the mass of twisted metal that had once been Tessa's pride and joy. It took him a couple more minutes to find Tessa.

She had been thrown free of the vehicle and landed atop a group of boulders. She sprawled with a rag doll limpness that told him checking for a pulse would be futile. He tried anyway.

His boot clicked against something that skittered across the ground and ponked off the remains of the jeep. It was a small square of plastic. He had no idea how long he stared at it before his shocky brain identified it. It was the Calendar Stone puzzle. It must have spilled from her purse in the impact. He picked it up, feeling hollow. Not all that long ago, she'd been happy, whooping to the sky that she'd solved it and cursing him because it had been so hard to work.

He'd never allowed himself to believe she felt anything genuine for him — certainly not love, anyway. He'd tried to avoid that emotional trap himself. He'd mostly succeeded. Still, he liked her and an unwelcome prickle stung the corners of his eyes.

He looked at the puzzle again. One row of tiles had slipped, putting the edge of the image out of whack. Tessa would have a fit. He absently clicked them back with his thumb, then froze.

Someone behind him said, "Aw, shit."

Katzen wheeled, fist tightening on the puzzle, and was amazed to see Avi Rosenberg sliding down the incline. Vaughn DeVries stood on the road at the top.

Katzen rubbed his eyes and looked again. The vision hadn't changed. Avi Rosenberg still bulled his way across the boulder-strewn ravine.

"Josh?" Rosenberg stopped short when he saw his friend's dazed look. "Are you okay? You're pretty banged up. . . ."

"Hey, Avi!" Katzen swayed and held up the puzzle. "I know. I know where it is."

Still a little uncertain, the archaeologist called, "He's okay. I think. Still standing, but I don't know for how long." He looked to the side, swore softly and added. "Caballero didn't make it."

CHAPTER 27

They hadn't been back in the warehouse long when DeVries' cell went off. He moved a short distance away, speaking softly for several minutes. When he returned, he said, "That was my contact at the Embassy. The Diplomatic Security Service has secured the wreck site. They're recovering Tessa Caballero's remains right now."

"They don't know it was anything but an accident, right?" Katzen asked.

DeVries was a little taken aback by the urgency in the question. "No. So far, only we know what really happened."

"Good," Katzen said. "No one outside of here needs to know she died any other way but in the line of duty."

"Josh, the woman was going to kill you — or at least try to," DeVries said. "Everything points to the fact she *did* kill el Mago."

"I know. I'd rather her family remembered her as a good guy, though. Also, there's a part of me that knows I might have once done the same things she did."

Avi Rosenberg grunted slightly and said, "I'd tend to disagree with that assessment, but I admire what you want for her family. They're innocents and it won't hurt to let them keep good memories."

Josh looked over at his friend. "I still can't get my head wrapped around the fact you're here."

"Dr. Rosenberg contacted us a while back about returning to

Peru to help with the operation," General Fuller said. "We accepted the offer hoping a second team would streamline things."

"We wanted to surprise you. That's why Colonel DeVries and I were headed out to the cache site," Rosenberg added.

"Well, it was a surprise all right. When I saw you on the mountain, I thought Tessa's head thump had shaken something loose," Katzen said.

Fuller gave him a critical once over. "You still look like you've been through the mixer, son. Are you sure you want to tackle Deustch's last hiding place right this minute?"

"Hell yes! I want to get this over with." Katzen opened a canvas bag and pulled out a sculptor's mallet and chisel. He held them up, saying, "If it works like I think it will, these probably won't be needed — but just in case. We'll need a ladder, too."

"Okay," Rosenberg said. "*That* I'm not letting you do. You can hardly stand, let alone climb a ladder. I'll climb it instead. Where are we going?"

Josh turned and pointed with the chisel. "Right over there. To the storm god stele."

A ladder was found and put in place. Rosenberg climbed.

"Try moving the top plate. Like one of those puzzle boxes," Katzen said, miming the move with his hands.

DeVries chuckled. "You mean we ain't going to need a chain saw artist?"

Rosenberg regarded the stele thoughtfully. "No, that might be bad." Spreading his huge hands across the top slab, he pushed. The piece slid back from the carved front with the rasp of stone on stone. Underneath was a gleaming aluminum plate.

"I'll be damned," said DeVries.

"You did say it was important that the man liked games and puzzles," Fuller commented.

"Tessa's Calendar Stone slide puzzle dropped the penny. When I picked it up today, some of the tiles were out of place. As soon as I slid them back, I remembered the puzzle box Deustch had given his sister; the one she kept his letters in."

The top was fully exposed now and Rosenberg probed the aluminum mechanism beneath it. "Looks like this side might be next," he said tapping the left slab. "It probably slides in the same direction as the top."

It did. It didn't go back as far, but left just enough room for the face stone with its grimacing cat-demon to slide aside.

Rosenberg dismounted the ladder and folded it away. Turning to Katzen, he said, "All yours, my friend. You've earned this."

Josh stepped forward with a grin. "Thanks. It'll be nice to finish this myself. It's between me and that bastard Deustch now."

He pushed at the front plate. At first it resisted, then a gap appeared and a flood of pink, green and white cascaded out.

Fuller prodded the objects with his foot, then picked up a handful. "Packing peanuts?"

With another shove, the snarling feline slid all the way back, revealing an aluminum framework inside. The stone slabs were fastened to upright supports and, when the top slab was moved from the lock position, they slid along channels in the inner structure. The interior had been converted into a set of shelves spaced roughly a foot apart. Each shelf bled packing peanuts from around wooden boxes crammed into the spaces.

On the bottommost shelf was a cylindrical mass of bubble-wrap. Radiation symbols and the official seal of the United States were just visible through the plastic.

~*~

The plutonium, accompanied by General Fuller, went back from whence it came almost as soon as it was recovered. No fanfare accompanied its departure outside of a farewell drink shared among friends.

By contrast, the artifacts from the mountain cache became a major news item. World famous archaeologist, Dr. Avi Rosenberg, and the antiquities division of the *Policia Nacional*, acting on an anonymous tip, had discovered a trove of looted treasures. It took a week to properly record and remove the items. The hand-off to the *Museo Nacional* was almost as big a story as the discovery.

Very few people paid more than passing attention to the small item detailing the tragic death of a Diplomatic Security Service agent who died in the line of duty when the car she was driving plunged off a mountain.

The wake for Tessa Caballero was hard, but Katzen and DeVries attended it anyway. The glowing remembrances of her colleagues — including Arash Rastogi — left them undecided if they should cringe or laugh. In the end, they merely joined in a few toasts. No one noticed when they stepped out for some fresh air and didn't return.

Shortly after the wake, Colonel DeVries returned to his duties at the Pentagon.

Joshua Katzen and Avi Rosenberg boarded a plane bound for home soon after.

~*~

The sun was low in the sky by the time Josh and Avi collected their baggage, reclaimed Rosenberg's car (a second cousin to the battered Mercedes camp van), escaped the airport and made it to Katzen's house on the outskirts of Chicago. It was good to see the place again. He hadn't even swung by when he'd come back to the states to go to ground. There was something out of place, though. Brow furrowed, he looked again.

"Wait. Why is the RX-7 sitting in the driveway? It should be in storage over at Vic's," Katzen said, suddenly rousing from the travel-induced brain-fog.

"Because Vic had it brought here when his mechanic finished working on it," Rosenberg answered. He didn't even try not to grin. "He said, — and I quote 'It runs great now. So there.'"

Before Katzen could muster a response, the house's mudroom door opened and Victoria Pale pelted down the driveway. She threw her arms around them, saying, "Josh! Avi! Welcome back! I've been watching the news stories about those artifacts. That sounded exciting."

"Mostly it was just dusty, Vicki," Rosenberg said, returning her hug. "Are you ready to go? I told your dad I'd give you a lift home."

She nodded. "Yeah. All packed. I have to admit I'm torn about going back to Dad's. It was sort of nice having a place all to myself — even if the cats *were* demons from time to time."

Josh laughed. "Only from time to time?"

Vicki's belongings seemed to have increased exponentially since she'd first arrived. It took almost a half-hour for the three of them to stuff it all into Avi's car. When they finally left, Josh waved them off from the end of the driveway. For a long while after they'd disappeared over the hill, he simply stood; enjoying the familiar scents of the flower beds, the neighbors' charcoal grills and the tang of the woods across the street. Perhaps to others, all this wouldn't seem like much. To Katzen, it was worth more than gold.

He'd been pleased to learn that none of the students had found anything odd in the explanation given for his sudden disappearance from the dig. That had come as a relief, but relief faded in the face of what Len Fuller had told him. Whoever had blown his cover, and almost gotten him killed on his last official mission, now knew the attempt had failed. Worse, he still had no idea who that was. Whoever it was had his new identity, though, and with that, it would be cake to locate him and finish the job. Somehow that knowledge only served to make the life he had now all the more precious.

He turned to look at the house. There were cat faces in the windows, mouths open in unheard meows. Inside, he was mobbed by what seemed to be thirty cats, although he could have sworn he only had three.

After a few minutes of wild purring, Boudicca, the apricot and smoke calico, remembered she'd been abandoned for months, and stalked away. Soon after that, Flash, the Turkish angora, noticed the luggage and left to rub his face all over it, claiming it as his own. Whozits, the gray and white Maine Coon, didn't give a damn and alternately tried to become one with Katzen's shoulder or to dislocate his neck with head butts.

Leaving the luggage to Flash's ministrations, he dropped into the wing-back chair in front of the wood stove and enjoyed his welcome for a while. Whozits' frantic purrs had slowed by the time Katzen stood, saying, "I missed you, too, guys, but I better unpack before I crash and burn right here. Sleeping in this chair after interminable hours of airline seats would probably put me in traction."

Deciding the laptop and art stuff could wait until morning, he wheeled his suitcase toward the stairs. Partway there, the liquor cabinet beckoned. Knowing it would probably put him to sleep, but not particularly caring, he snagged a bottle of scotch and a glass in one hand, the handle of his suitcase in the other and headed up to the bedroom.

Upstairs, he tossed his suitcase onto the bed and splashed a generous amount of whisky into the glass. He sipped and savored it before unzipping the bag and flipping it open. From its recesses, the little Moche cat stared up at him all wide eyes and goofy grin. He'd forgotten about it. He didn't know how he could, but he had. Lifting it from the cushioning cocoon of clothing, he held it for a moment, feeling its weight, enjoying the texture of the rough clay and smooth glaze. There seemed to be a faint scent of frankincense and myrrh about it, but that was doubtless his imagination. After a moment, he cleared a spot on the bookshelf beside the bed and placed the grinning cat in it.

"Rest in peace, Theresa Margaretta Caballero," he whispered, raising his glass. "May you find what you're looking for in that land to the west."

www.ingramcontent.com/pod-product-compliance
Lightning Source LLC
Chambersburg PA
CBHW060900250626
47159CB00008B/2818